HUN
& Vanessa

C000051146

"Believable and exciting"

**Bill Donnelly
Manchester**

"An adrenalin fuelled, fast paced roller-coaster ride that elevates Steve Cage into the Premier League of writers"

**Kelly Ball
Cheshire**

"Hunter stands to become another iconic hero"

**Sally Lay
Phoenix AZ**

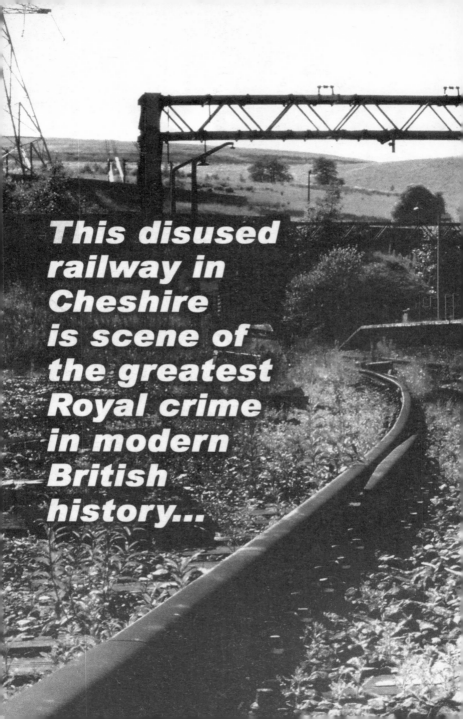

This disused railway in Cheshire is scene of the greatest Royal crime in modern British history...

Hunter and Vanessa are back

"Fast American style with a British setting"

Nathaniel Banks
Bolton

NAME: Craig Connors
NATIONALITY: American
OCCUPATION: Mercenary
MISSION: Take out the
British Queen...

www.twitter.com: @stevecageauthor
www.facebook: steve cage

Steve worked in film, TV, and advertising for nearly thirty years. During that time he created sci-fi hardware and SFX models for movies and TV shows, ran his own visual FX studio, and worked on hundreds of ad campaigns for top British companies.

Using assumed names he's published fiction and non-fiction books—serialising two for BBC radio—and been a newspaper leader-page columnist. Married since 1991 with a son, he is also an award-winning movie producer, writer, and director.

www.stevecage.com

STEVE CAGE

TO KILL THE QUEEN

MAGNUM

TO KILL THE QUEEN

First published in 2015 by
Magnum Publishing Ltd
99 Wallis Road, London, E9 5LN

CIP catalogue available at the British Library

ISBN 978-0-9565914-4-9
eISBN 978-0-9565914-5-6

Typesetting by Hot Metal Retro
Hunter photo figure © Blacksheep, London
Extra special thanks to everybody at Amtrak

Printed and bound in Great Britain
by Clays Ltd, St Ives plc

For my amazing wife Julie,
who makes it possible

Part ONE

1

Craig Connors stuck his foot on the brake but it was too late. As he shot from the mountain tunnel the road went AWOL to his left while he carried straight on.

To counter it he spun the steering wheel hard but hit a serious skid then heard rubber burn and saw double yellows snake crazying under him. Still the car wouldn't tango and slewed across the hairpin, screeching blue smoke, towards a cliff.

No chance of correcting now. He smashed through a metal guardrail and headed out to where birds flew. Bits of shit cracked his windshield. Stuff *pinged* and *peeowed* as a mile-deep canyon yawned under him.

Car nosedived and Connors saw pines come from nowhere. Ripping through them, he slammed into solid rock. Felt his legs trash as the car crumpled and slid down ass first, breaking up. Engine popped from under its flapping hood. Glass shattered. Fire rolled in. He was being totalled. Stunk himself hamburger-sizzling in his own fat as the fireball ploughed through branches, taking half the Austrian cliff with it. Last thing he saw was a king-size boulder, meteorite-spinning at him CG fast before a mega whiteout topped him.

Or should have topped him, he thought smugly. Neat trick with the cliff the computer had rendered nanoquick. But even while he was being splattered he eyed the dash, where his pulse kept a steady 78—same as when he'd climbed in the simulator. That would piss off the doc. Sweet Thai pixie assistant Chan would be impressed, as she had been by his six-pack when she stuck electrodes to his chest to measure his HB.

Lights came on and the sim whined slickly as it reset, ready for next punishment sucker. Fans blew away toxin-free smoke clogging the cabin. Numerous tiny air jets and skin stimulators that made it feel as if everything hit him and fire had fried him shut down.

Connors shot his harness and slid open the door. Not only had he pushed himself to the edge.

He'd taken off from it.

'Seventy-eight,' he shouted, waving a fist at the guys. 'On the button.'

'Impossible,' Doc Hartman's tinny voice said over lab speakers. 'Not with settings so critical.'

'Nothing's impossible for the US of A's finest,' he threw back. Standing up from the sim he gave the bony Brit a straight middle finger salute.

Control booth door slid open and Hartman emerged, yellow-smocked, shaking his head with disbelief. Alex Freeman was in tow. Steel browed. Steel faced. Shiny steel-suited. Always seeming like he needed to be some place else. Chan tagged with an expectant look daubed on her pretty oriental face. Tall Freeman ducked under the jamb as the doc yakked his stuff.

'The conscious mind knows it's not real but the sub-conscious doesn't. It's like an optical illusion. No matter how determined we think we are, our senses can't shut off. And with virtual reality sims being this sophistica-ted, most folk should black out with settings so danger-ous. For it not to faze him indicates an iron will. I'd say this beefy jumped up yank is your man.'

'So would I, you over-educated pompous English shit,' Connors said, hearing Hartman's quip while he clumped down blue Expamet steps.

'Physical stresses don't come much tougher,' Hart-man confessed. 'And I went to a mixed comprehensive you big Arizona tosser,' he added, punchlining a wise-crack he'd left dangling earlier.

Connors got the joke, showing his teeth while he lost his T-shirt and let Chan unpluck the electrodes. The Doc had a sense of humour. Ice-cold Freeman didn't. 'You're not perspiring, Mr Connors,' Chan said, looking up with smiley silver-shadowy eyes. She took time at his bronze chest, tugging at clear-rubber suckers.

'OK you've made your point, Craig,' Freeman butted in. Tiring of macho tough-speak, he stuck a plastic cup in the water cooler and made it boogie.

To Connors, deadpan English toffs like Freeman always seemed uneasy confronting grunt stuff. This particular lanky streak used to be a bent casino banker before switching to crooked high politics. Conscious of Hartman and the petite broad, he reached for the full cup. Gave it to the American brick shit-house who eclipsed his height and was twice his width if not three times his weight, then filled cup number two.

'Let's talk, shall we?'

They headed out to a rooftop garden baking in midday sun. Vapour trails raking blue sky pointed accusingly at Heathrow. After aircon, greenhouse heat of hottest Brit summer since '76 got Freeman puffing cheeks. Connors knew heat and strode through it to a glass balcony, sticking on wrapmirror shades, knocking back ice water. Freeman stuck on retro Raybans like specs Oscar Goldman wore when he briefed Steve Austin. He set his laptop on the ledge. Grass everywhere had morphed to straw. Giant steel letters did K-Tech's logo backwards from their elevated POV. Toy cars parked near admin shimmered through a heat haze.

'You wanted the job, didn't you?' Freeman told him, firing the kit, loosening his necktie.

'I wanted to show I'm your guy,' Connors said. 'Under the circumstances you don't have a choice. I mean to make the hit. Not to hire me for two million bucks.'

'I think we can take it that you're our man. Delegating an assignment that strikes at the heart of the British constitution to a kick-ass foreigner with, uh-hum, biceps excites the powers-that-be. But they still feel dirty because of the daringness of the plan.'

'Glad to know they got feelings.' Connors sipped his water. 'I feel like an A-lister, flown in to bring US box office to one of your subsidized little social issue movies about which nobody gives a shit.'

Definitely no sense of humour he decided, as Freeman wrecked his neat silk cuff eyeing his Rolex.

'Dangers of this mission are—how would you put it?—"awesome",' he said, failing to match the observation with enough voice cool. 'There hasn't been a serious plot to take out a reigning British Monarch since Francis Walsingham in 1586. It'll bring the country to its knees, plunging us into a crisis of the first order.'

Connors was amused. For eighteen years governments had hired him to do dirty work, ostensibly for political gain but really so they could stockpile financial booty. Nothing wrong with that. Modern politics was really a kind of upmarket crime. At least guys like Freeman stuck within parameters set by "democracy". Alternative was abiding by laws of the jungle, which nobody wanted. Guys like Connors provided a service exploiting swift boaters at the top who, come election times, vied to dupe the unsuspecting masses.

He explained his philosophy to Freeman while they watched a Virgin helijet drop towards Heathrow, hot-spotting sun. 'Only thing in your way,' he added, draining his cup, 'is stubborn media guys who'll do all they can to expose your crap-doing.'

'Speaking of which, or rather whom,' Freeman said, turning the laptop screen away from the sun.

Up popped two face-grabs.

Good-looking guy, early 30s, thick dark hair, and an older sexy silver-blonde. Freeman zoomed her out to show she'd a decent chest.

'Don't be fooled by their looks. You'll need to give them a wide berth.'

'Hunter. Ain't he the TV guy?'

'Yes he is.' Touching keys he made stuff pile about the broad down her side of screen. 'Hunter and Vanessa are shooting a Royal TV doc, unaware that, uh-hum—how would you put it?—"big time shit" is headed their way again. As award-winning TV producers they've been granted special access to travel with Her Majesty aboard Amtrak's new Royal Train. They had to wait three years for the privilege because Royals do their homework before they let anybody breathe the same air.'

'How come two TV guys are dangerous?'

'It's not so much them being dangerous as you needing to ensure the hijack happens before they get to the Queen. They're not due aboard the train till it gets to Manchester but are shooting trackside flypast stuff first, to supplement their onboard filming.'

'Choo choo going past camera?'

'Correct. Meaning we've a narrow window to make the Bermuda Triangle thing happen, on the West Coast main line north of Crewe.'

'So I got the job?'

'My dear chap,' he said, slipping back into Brit toff speak. 'There was never any doubt you'd be our man. Meanwhile, you've these to contend with.' Two good-looking young Asian guys popped on screen. 'Others plotting to make life difficult for Her Majesty when she takes the train.'

'Reece told me about this. Shades of 9-11, huh?'

'Something like that,' he said, fastidiously smoothing his cuff. 'If only they were brainwashed simpletons, holed up in a grubby northern backstreet. But they're not. They're clever well-bred types festering within.'

'Go figure,' Connors said.

'Yes,' Freeman agreed, this time with enough voice cool when he slipped into US lingo. 'Go effing figure.'

MONday

2

Randeep pulled over when he saw Nahid scrimming up through heather at the side of the road.

Midnight in high summer meant daylight still plied the horizon, where South Yorkshire moors rolled up like tundra to kiss it. Verge fell steeply to the massive Dunford Bridge Freightliner rail terminal, its lights blazing in the valley bottom where it looked as out of place as a McDonald's on the moon.

It was a bleak outpost, built in the middle of nowhere because of cheap land. Chunky sci-fi container cranes straddled floodlit sidings outside three-mile Woodhead tunnel on the reopened Manchester-Sheffield railway. Randeep knew the line had shut controversially in 1981. Eurorail rebuilt it in 2011, to ease congestion on Trans-Pennine motorways. Concrete-lined tunnel was only one in the UK built to Continental standards. Ironically, tax breaks urged road hauliers to piggyback their rigs through it by train.

Nahid was puffing when he got in the Range Rover. 'It's arrived,' he said. 'Use the farm track. He's knocked out infrared sensors along the fence.'

As Randeep set off it struck him that since Oxford ten years ago, thanks to his smart, rich, second generation dad, he seemed to have been picking Nahid up late at night in flashy 4x4s.

Hitting the track he kept company with twin electric security fence, bumping ruts till Gate 5 where they got out and crunched limestone gravel. Triple pointed aluminium palisade they arrived at meant business. Five-metres high. Sizzling with 240,000 volts of lethal live juice, according to pics of a guy getting fried.

Half a mile away a train was being loaded at the hub, meaning it was a good time to sneak into the huge compound. Heavy switchgear oscillated across the hot night as rigs were shoved about like they were on a robo-production line at a factory. Trashed ship containers were stacked five or six high. Partying hazards bounced off every shiny surface.

They spotted an approaching stocky figure, farting unselfconsciously, hawking and spitting as it waddled across. Torchlight flared in their faces when the guy's feet stopped making noise.

A gruff Middle Eastern voice struggled with English. 'You got here, huh?'

He had a lecherous look in his dark piggy eyes when he typed at the gateframe and *fdunked* it open, ushering Randeep and Nahid over to a reefer-trailered rig with its twin vari axles slung off ground. Fancy vinyl self-stick and loud candy stripes cramming the trailer sides hid its black market long-task. A fat Arab paced tarmac in front of it, cigarette-glow waving, gut wobbling. He was more amenable, nodding uncertainly before he shot bolts in the trailer's nearside door and pulled out some Expamet steps. Randeep followed him up, Nahid and the bone-head tagging.

Inside, a faecal stink of filthy humanity met them. Walk-through clear vinyl door strips split main storage area from bulkhead refrigerator. They squeezed down the side into a compartment where everything had been stripped out to make a secret bunny hole. Humid as a hot-house, air stunk so godawful ammonia-bad Randeep could taste it.

It was like landing in a pigsty.

Maybe a dozen exhausted, unshaven young Indian and Pakistani guys slobbed against the bulkhead. Bone-head swore at them and stuck the boot in.

'Stand up you bastards,' he said. 'Hey, come on. Get the hell up.'

As they shuffled to their feet, Bonehead dragged them roughly into line.

Randeep paced before the sweaty submissive faces. He might be related to the poor bastards back down his bloodline but he felt nothing. No more than slaves, they were lambs for the bloodiest slaughter. 'I'll take him, him, and him,' he said, and turned to leave.

'You like good-looking guys with beards, huh?' Bonehead said, seedily.

He smacked Randeep up his backside, squeezing it suggestively before they headed back through to main part of the trailer.

'Bet you like them nice and hairy too,' he added, showing rotten buck teeth to goad his handsome young Pakistani guest.

When they were back on terra firma Randeep pulled a fat envelope from his tracker vest pocket and threw it at Bonehead. 'Three thousand sterling.'

Nahid escorted the three bought guys through the gate. The loitering fat Arab struggled up into the rig's cab and banged shut his door. Revving her, he stuck her in gear and got hauling, pronto.

'I thought we said four thousand,' Bonehead shouted as the rig wiped behind him.

It was a wind-up but Randeep stayed cool. Being educated and English meant you didn't take it personally if common crap dissed you.

He tailed Nahid through the gate across to the RR. The three guys dived in the back, ransacking the fridge and popping Red Bulls.

Bonehead checked the cash then tough-guyed over to lock up. 'Hey,' he said, whacking across a chunky bolt. 'What you gonna do with those bastards, huh? Train them to kill the Queen of England?'

A bomb might have gone off.

Randeep took a few secs to digest what Bonehead had said. In the background another train noisily arrived at the terminal.

Soon as waiting rigs entered holding area they were shunted sideways onto flatbed loaders. Safety clamps sprang up and locked behind wheels, *fdunking* falling dominoes fashion along the line. Cool stuff backed up by some serious kit.

Gracefully big.

Energetically clunky.

Like movie SFX happening for real.

Randeep turned to Nahid.

'Kill him,' he said.

'He was joking for God's sake.' An unlit cigarette bobbed at his mouth.

'It doesn't matter. The thought's in his head. Kill him.' Saying no more he got in the RR and sent down his window because of the stinking guys.

He watched Nahid walk gravel back to the gate, calling to Bonehead for a light.

At the terminal the loco got ready to haul. Gave a loud throaty roar and shot fumes like a whale spurting through its blowhole.

From that distance noise made by overhead cranes sounded like a construction site. It soaked up the gun's slick silencered *phut* but stood no chance when a fat bastard's head went pop.

3

It was 2.03am when Bill Martin eased the brand-new Class 68 loco over a maze of tracks into Wolverton railworks. Taking her past the Royal Train prep sheds into a siding, he brought her nearly to the bufferstop, shut her down, and reached for his snapbag.

Unlike the old Class 66 the Class 68 was a joy to drive. Air conditioned. Practical console layout, with a computer that did what the tin said. Bill had been driving for thirty-five years, switching latterly to freight because pay was better and Health and Safety less of a bind. In his time he'd seen kit go from clockwork to microchip. He'd also seen British railways go from Beeching's leftovers to a few mainline routes. Too many crooks both sides of the Commons had vested interests in the road industries. As they had since black-and-white telly days, when an allegedly Conservative Government installed a rail-hating Minister of Transport who owned a motorway building company.

Shaking his head at the memory, Bill climbed down backwards from the cab, bag slung at a shoulder, thanking God he was near retirement and would soon be out of it. Puffing at the sultry night when he hit the ground, he crossed oily tracks.

Wolverton was a hive of activity at such a godforsaken hour because trains needed maintaining 24-7. Southern England was lucky. It had kept some semblance of a railway because of white-collar voting power.

When he reached the Timekeeping Office, Pete Robbins was there with his teenage son who was researching a 6th form college project.

As the lad stood in hi-viz safety togs he'd been given to wear on site, self-consciousness worked his hot spotty face. He was a good kid. Brought up in a typical suburban semi, with Hornby trains in the loft and respect for Britain's glorious industrial past, but computer savvy and headed for a life in IT.

His rotund stepdad spent too many nights propping up Wolverton Railwaymen's Sports and Social Club bar. Wiping his red face he puffed at the stifling heat, nodding for Bill to stick his card in the Payclock.

'I hear it's your big day tomorrow, Bill.'

'My last time,' he said, slotting in his card. 'I'm out of it in September.'

'Off somewhere good?'

'Tuscany. Pauline's over there with the brother-in-law and his wife. I couldn't let the old girl down. Not with it being my last call.' He took his card. 'Only told me on Friday. An hour from us getting a cab to the station.'

Pete laughed at mention of the "old girl" and told his son, 'Bill's one of a select few who get to drive the Royal Train.'

'Somebody has to do it,' Bill said, turning to the door. A loco rumbled past outside, wheels hissing-binding. 'Trouble is, they don't let you know till a few days before. Security I guess.'

'How cool is that?' the lad said, taking a step back in his dayglow waistcoat.

'Tell him about the six-inch thing,' Pete said, sticking his card in the Payclock.

Bill told the lad.

'To be her driver, you've got to be able to stop within six inches of a mark so Her Majesty ends up smack bang in front of posh nobs waiting on the station platform.' He winked his near eye. 'Only she knows I can make it closer to an inch.'

'How cool is that,' the lad said again, seeming unsure if he was butt-end of a joke.

'Actually'—another eye wink—'I do get a bit of help. Somebody stands at the front of the train and holds up a yellow flag. It's how they've done it since Queen Victoria's time. If I end up in line with the flag, I know I've stopped in the right place.'

'Nay,' Pete said. 'You're spoiling it.'

As Bill shouldered through the door out to the car park, Micra keycard in hand, he swiped away a moth and caught a look on the lad's face. If kids didn't sneer at mention of Royalty there was hope for Her Majesty's sinking ship.

Bill wondered if he'd get chance to tell her, with it being his last trip.

4

'Jesus Christ. Slow down Kath,' Conrad Reece said. Ignoring him, she trod the gas pedal and drove straight into the night, sending the digi-speedo ballistic.

Guys in the back were hidden by a steel partition. They swore as the Transit lurched round a bend, snagging branches. Mean killer Kath—hardnosed, shit crazy, daughter-of-a-bitch Kath—was wearing a black Cody combat vest and fingerless black leather gloves. Flame tattoos raked her muscly arms. When Reece despaired at her mad driving she shunted everybody, making them swear again as she screeched out of a hairpin.

Van headlights shovelled darkness, scattering moths and finding passing hedges and trees. Two miles north of Wolverton, they were nearly at the place where they'd ambush Bill Martin on his way home. Fake cops a mile in each direction would keep away unwelcome spectators. Guys at south end, at Ouse Valley Park entrance, would let only the target Micra through. If real cops showed, North Bucks boys-in-blue might have some real cop deaths to keep them busy.

They skidded to a stop round next bend. Two phoney cop cars were waiting, plastered with hi-viz Battenberg square stuff. Before the Transit's tyres stopped screeching, Reece jumped out and banged the van side, OKing it for the guys to chop chop.

Back doors flew open and half a dozen bogus, Kevlar-togged cops piled out, like a SWAT team going into action. Unloading traffic cones, plastic barriers, and tripod spots, they started setting up a roadblock. Trained eye would know fine detail wasn't kosher. Anybody else would get spooked if they hit a corner in the early hours and got caught unawares.

Sweltering night was oppressive. Reece lived dangerously and could take tropical heat when it was chucked at him. A week ago he'd been machinegunning Columbian drugs runners. His tough pockmarked face was scarred from being Northern Ireland's top dog hero-for-hire, hired by Rambo Connors to take out Her Majesty's fave choo choo driver. Sweating cobs in Robocop bodykit in flat Middle English scenery was a climbdown. But the money was good and bumping off Royalty carried prestige value.

Kath lobbed him an Uzi before climbing in the back of the van to get changed.

Wondering what gave at the railworks, he bootclumped over to the verge. Dinosaur-like roar of a nearby London express split the night. They'd had to fine-cut their timing. Daylight would also happen soon, meaning they'd be exposed convoying back to base. Reece was Blutoothed ready.

'Talk to me Mitch,' he said, swiping moths beelining for roadblock spots.

'He's just leaving,' Mitch said, from the Hummer.

'Long or short haul?'

'Too soon to tell.'

'Tell me he's taken a left.'

'Whatever you say, boss.'

'Stop taking the piss you asshole or I'll rip your balls off and feed them to my dogs.'

Getting the message, Mitch OK'd, affirming the Micra had driven out from the railworks and done a left on the main road toward town. Other guys patched via open frequency piped up as the Micra joined dots of its home run. Somebody wondered if the driver was using his phone when he bumped a mini roundabout near Tesco's then went *nah*, must have been mistaken.

They'd watched Bill Martin (BM) for two weeks, sussing his routine getting to and from work. He lived at Castlethorpe village just north of Wolverton. Sometimes he went home the long way, via the A5 and Northampton Road. They'd banked on him going this way tonight 'cause he'd done it three times on the trot, after being on lates. BM's fifteen minutes had come. Less than twelve hours till the Royal Train hit.

If he bunked off home wrong ways they'd have to nail him at his smart chalet bungalow with a FOR SALE board stuck out front. Neighbourhood Watch meant a home blag could be messy.

Reece pulled a stick of Big Red gum when Mitch sang at his ear, in DJ Klub Kool, 'Showtime. I'm seeing his tails fade to a night-time place where foxes and badgers strut their funky stuff.'

Meaning BM was being a good choo choo driver and taking the Haversham road away from town. Over his headset Reece heard Ouse Valley guys fire their fake cop 4x4, ready to block the road when BM passed and took a corner.

'ETA your end: middle of next week,' Mitch added, sounding pissed. 'He's one of those annoying folk who do 20mph in a 30mph zone.'

'Lose yourself,' Reece told him, not convinced about the slow speed thing.

'Sure thing, boss.'

Reece was detail conscious. It helped keep him alive. On previous home runs BM broke speed limits like anybody else. One of the guys wondering if he'd pulled his phone near Tesco's had also got Reece feeling jumpy.

Time to rock-and-roll anyway.

Coolly chewing, he stood in the road facing muggy darkness. Arnie gun slung across Kevlar'd chest. Big pseudo-Goth platform booted feet nicely spread. Temp lightbars stuck to cop car roofs would party for thirty seconds max, either side of the hit. Sixty secs, tops, is all it would take to smash a good guy's life.

5

Hunter was stuck in never-never land. Dreaming he was in bed with Vanessa in the old weaver's cottage they were renting near Haworth.

After passionate lovemaking, they'd fallen asleep quickly. In his dream they were at it again. They'd been at it fairly constantly since she moved in with him a few weeks ago. She had an amazing sexual appetite, meaning he didn't have to work too hard at her pleasure before indulging in his own.

Suddenly a loud bell hit off. His phone. Must have forgotten to switch it off when they went to bed. Last time he had his kids for the weekend Jenny changed the ringtone to old-style noisy analogue. As he came round, another sound filled the bedroom on a stifling summer night. Vanessa lying on top of him, saying she wanted him. It was happening more. They'd go to sleep but wake themselves up making love. Reaching out for each other even while they slept. He rolled her onto her back to take her. She beat him to it, complaining at the phone for breaking her concentration.

When it was over he flopped away, chucking off the quilt to get some air to their hot bodies.

'Christ,' he said, and puffed his cheeks.

'Likewise,' she said, meaning it.

They lay panting, getting it together.

There was nothing else Hunter could say except how much he loved her. He kept saying it like an excited teen on his first love trip.

She switched on the lamp and got out of bed to clean herself up in the en-suite. He remembered hearing his phone. Sensing it had flipped to voicemail, he reached for it on the bedside cupboard.

Bill Martin on screen.

Wondering *what the hell* Hunter hit 1-2-3, waiting while 02 girl said he'd a message.

'Who was it?' asked Vanessa from the loo.

'Bill Martin,' he said, still groggy, not quite getting the brief message when it had done. 'Says he left the rail-works to go home and thought he was being tailed by a Hummer. Then sounds relieved and says false alarm, the Hummer turned off.'

They were interviewing Bill for the Royal Train TV gig but wouldn't board the train till Tuesday because they had to shoot trackside flypast stuff first. Establishing shots of Amtrak's ace new train, tonning it through a green and pleasant land. Killer commission. Destined to pull mega ratings, it would catapult indie producers Hunter and Vanessa to TV stardom.

Hunter reckoned Bill would have just finished a night shift. Yawning, he gave Vanessa the phone when she got back into bed, so she could listen. 'He said he gets jittery when he's due to drive Royals,' he told her, leaning over to cup and kiss her nearest boob.

'Call him back,' she said, pushing him away, passing back the phone.

Reece saw Micra lights flare across the fields but turned as Kath flung open the Transit's back doors. She stepped out transformed into her insane take on a girly traffic cop, jackboot-zipping to a wolf-whistle chorus.

Black leather blouson.

Matching mini.

Shiny, sheer black tights.

She danced a little jig then turned and lifted her mini to show off her nice tight bum. The guys applauded. Reece felt something trigger downstairs. Since popping his red cherry at 16, doggying a fit Naughty Nurse kissogram on a pile of coats at a party, he'd had a soft spot for tough birds in uniforms.

Red-and-blue lightshow began as headlights found them and the Micra arrived, slowed, stopped. Reece high-fived Kath and let her steal the show.

Silencered gun in hand, she waltzed over and stooped to the little car. Said to its worried driver, cranking it when glass lost itself before his 60-something moon face, 'Can you get out of your car please, sir?'

'What's up, love?'

'Get out now please.'

Sucker obeying law did as asked, taken in by the tall tough bitch who made him stand hands spread on the

Micra, like she was gonna frisk him. Instead, she stood back, aimed at the back of his head, and fired.

Shooting people was no big deal for Reece.

It was why he'd let Kath score.

Watching her amazing bum, he'd other stuff on his mind when the grey-haired guy slumped to blacktop, almost in slow-mo. Coins jingle-jangled as they rolled from his trouser pocket.

While the guys cleared up, Reece lit a cheroot and got back in the van. Kath was back at the wheel, an *uh-oh* look on her face. She held up BM's phone.

'Trouble.'

Reece took it, eyeing the screen. 'Hunter?' he said, amazed. 'Why the hell's he ringing?'

Phone buzzed with a message.

Reece was all ears. Hitting voicemail he wedged a size 12 booted foot up at the dash.

'Hi Bill. Got your message. Point taken about you being on edge but I wouldn't worry too much about the Hummer. I'm sure it wasn't tailing you. Feel free if you want to call back. I'll try your home number. Otherwise we'll see you at the interview tomorrow.'

'Shit,' Reece said, cutting off 02 girl in her prime.

'What?' Kath asked him.

'BM must have called Hunter when he left the railworks. I knew something was up when the guys said he was driving funny. He must have seen Mitch.'

'Does it matter?' She popped a Red Bull.

'Sure it does.'

Pulling his phone, he found Connors's sunspecced ugly mug. Hit call and waited.

Stuff banged behind them as it got chucked in the van. Daylight was happening fast, in that British high summer way. Flat fields stretched to low horizons bathed in eerie silver mist. Sun would be up soon. Gonna be another hot one.

Connors swore. 'This had better be good, Reece. I like my beauty sleep before I party.'

'This TV guy, Hunter.'

'What about him?'

'He just called Bill Martin.'

'You woke me up to tell me that?'

'I'm serious, Craig. Martin must have seen the Hummer and got spooked. Hunter's on the case.'

'BM was always gonna be observant 'cause he drives trains. Worst scenario means not spotting stuff on the line at 140mph, at night. But him clocking the Hummer is no big deal. You made the hit—I assume you made the hit?'—Reece went *yeah yeah*—'OK, you made the hit and now Bill Martin's history. Move on.'

'What if Hunter called the cops? They might be heading over to BM's place.'

'I'll call Freeman. He's not UK plc's Internal Security chief for nothing. He's one of those corrupt, utterly depraved bastards, lacking an essential streak of humanitarian DNA, who've screwed your crappy old fleabitten Britannia to the wall. But he pays good, and it's not our job to poop in front of party guests. He eats crap like Hunter and the broad with the chest for breakfast. If cops are kicking down BM's front door right now, Freeman will take care of it.' He got Reece's drift. 'You're doing good, son. It's why you're my number two. We're nearly there. Ross, Thinnes, and the guys are snoozing on a bus at the hijack site. Pover is tucked up nice and cosy in a motel near Crewe Gateway. Get back to base and get some kip.'

Reece OK'd and said he'd catch up later. He kept forgetting just how "fixed" modern UK plc was. Smart talking bad guys at the top, mostly skunk politicians in City banker palms, controlled nearly everything. Funny how they still needed grunts like Kath and Reece to do tough stuff and get sweaty.

Speaking of Kath and grunting, banging behind them had stopped. Job done, cop cars faded through fumes, taking the guys with them.

Young guy tasked with taking BM's Micra back to base thumbed-up, car kangarooing as he set off, swearing through his open window at stuff being wrong Jap ways round when he tried to drive.

Sunshine had started.

Blue sky was happening.

Way off on the road, some small brown animal shuft-ied across.

'Looks like it's you and me, Kath,' Reece said slyly. 'No cop stuff. Just a plain white van parked on a quiet country road.'

'Guess so,' she agreed, getting his drift.

Still kitted as high-powered Ms Lady Cop, she shifted in her seat, creaking leather.

Her mini had ridden up showing her fantastic thighs. She drained her Red Bull and crushed the can. Bollocks to kipping Reece decided. They got out, banged doors, and went to the back of the van.

7

8.00am on the dot.

Grotty industrial backstreet in a dump of a place cal-led Brightside, Sheffield.

Not far from the M1.

Uneven cobbles. Sunken flagstone pavements missing most slabs, thieved by scum to fund pathetic drugs-fuel-led non-lives. Halfway along the street, remnants of a big steel mill. Victorian philanthropist's name embossed in stone above a central arch. Ducting. Pipes. Messed cables. Sci-fi techadence bolted with chunks of salvaged machine scrap across every wall.

Another scorching day to piss off Randeep as Nahid turned the Range Rover under the arch and pulled up on an old iron weighbridge, framed by greasy cobbles other end. Randeep sent away glass but didn't lose the wrapmirror shades.

It had been a long hot night.

'We're here to buy some hardware.'

Target of his words: big black guy, rolling a cigarette in an upside down shipping container with blow-torched holes for windows. Passing for a security booth in this stinking back of the northern bloody beyond.

'Names?'

'They're expecting us.'

'Names?'

'Our names are irrelevant. We've shown punctually. Tell them their two VIP guests have arrived. It's all they need to know.'

Black guy finished making his cigarette, took time to set fire to it, and puffed twice.

Wedging it in a gob corner, he squeezed sideways through a rusty homemade door opening to get outside. His massive shoulders meant he'd have got stuck if he'd gone in a straight line.

He gangsta ponced over to the RR in pleated Puff-daddy pants with a baggy low-flying arse. His bull neck was broader than his Bluto small head, which seemingly was supported by thick diagonal muscles like roots of a tree. Fine plaits ploughed his short hair in neat straight lines. Elaborate tattoos, lost against his skin, covered his bodybuilt, vein-embossed arms bulging from his string combat vest.

Emphasizing his height, he made a thing of stooping to Randeep's window. Made a bigger thing of pointing across the crappy sunlit mill yard, getting Randeep to follow his fat, gold-ringed forefinger.

'See that red door over there?' Door was blue, hence a knowing glint in the bastard's beady eye as his cigarette bobbed with his squeaky voice. 'Drive across and somebody will come to fetch you.' He sucked his cigarette and blew smoke in Randeep's face. 'Meantime, I'll let them know two nameless tossers just arrived.'

Randeep coughed and made a thing of looking at the blue door. Made a bigger thing of looking at black guy, adding casually, 'Colourblind as well as stupid,' then nodded for Nahid to set off.

'Jesus,' Nahid said, treading gas, one-hand-spinning the powered wheel. 'These guys are glorified animals. You'll get us slapped.'

They were met by a shaven-headed, tattoo-covered midget who introduced himself as the Tall Man. He ushered them through a musty warehouse crammed with blue-shrinked washing machines and kitchen appliance stuff, piled up to mucky cobwebbed skylights.

In a hot, sunlit office at the back they shook sticky hands with an obscenely huge fat guy who called himself Slim. Randeep found it tough to believe anything so disgustingly obese could function as a human.

He jelly wobbled when he moved. Jabba the Hut in a cream silk suit with a scabby-spotty shaved head and a wide downturned mouth. Smelt like he needed a change of underpants too. No prizes for guessing why. So much fat hung at his chin it impaired his larynx, making him talk girly.

Rounding off the freak show were two sunglassed, combat vested Yorkshire beefcakes—obligatory minders: absurd Hollywood *Expendables* clones—Uzis parked on big hairy shoulders, to show who was boss.

'This deal should have been done and dusted two weeks ago,' Randeep noted, pissed off.

'It takes time to source this stuff,' Slim said, sounding like a grotesque, androgynous creature who'd gorged helium. 'First it went to South America, before coming all the way back here, just for you.'

With so much BO loading the cramped office, he switched on a small wall-mounted electric fan. Humming this way and that, it made a wire mesh safety cover sing each time it did a turn.

Dumped on a steel table was a monster Sheuze minigun. Double barrelled. Twin drainpipe tubes panpipe-bolted. Cast in plastic alloy called codimum. Tough as titanium yet light as polymer. Finished in stylish anodized silver and black satin, it was serious kit, straight from a *Terminator* movie.

It was gimbal mounted to an iso-elastic chest frame, which worked like a steadicam harness. Slim nodded for the beefcakes to give Randeep a hand. They hooked the harness over his head while Slim supported the gun-sled. Memory foam took on Randeep's body shape as Beefcake # 1 snapped together the chestplate and locked it. Beefcake # 2 steadied the gun on its gimbal. Over at the wall, the fan kept going and coming, wafting a foul BO cocktail spiked with poop.

Slim flicked a panel on the gun and pressed something. Servos whined.

Chips kicked in.

The thing jumped to attention, diode-igniting to life when its onboard computer took over.

With a spooky mind of its own, the gun danced a sort of stop-motion electric boogaloo before parking in a default, pre-fire position.

Randeep took hold of her confidently and swung her to and fro, getting off on the feel of such a mean piece of kit. He imagined Royal Trains and Queens and shocked news headlines. You kinda held her side-on and used a sweeping motion, making her real easy to aim. Cops had such kit bolted to gunships.

Japs knew their big weapons stuff.

Showstoppers were a virtual keypad and gunsight, hologramming in front of him.

Slim said, 'I saw a TV thing about Sheuze. Guy fronting it was news last Christmas. Some noise about bent cops in Manchester.'

'Hunter,' Randeep said, boogying with the gun.

'Yeah that's right. Wears a trademark long leather coat. Cool kinda guy. You know him?'

'I know he's gonna be news again.'

'How come?'

'Just a hunch.'

Taking his cue, Nahid put a brand-new silver texalium attaché case on the table, spun the three-digit combi code to shoot the latches, and stood back.

Beefcake # 2 lifted the lid.

$3m in used US banknotes.

Neatly bundled.

'It's legit,' Nahid said, heading off Slim's discreet nod to the midget. 'We're not stupid.'

Nevertheless, the midget set up a small scanner on the table and spot-tested banknotes.

Pulling random bundles, he pulled random hundred dollar bills and stuck them flat on the scanner bed. Shut the lid and waited while intense UV light fussed back and forth.

Slim said, 'Coming minutes are critical. If notes are dud, we shall hurt you both.'

'Ahead of a potentially fraught situation turning nasty,' Randeep said philosophically, cosying up to his lethal new kit like a kid with a new toy, 'an intelligent mind considers the outcome before deciding on a course of action, particularly if it might lead to violence. A ball-brain opens its stupid big gob and blunders in.'

Muzzle-ends of two Uzis got shoved up Randeep's nostrils as made no difference.

'Easy,' Slim said. 'The boy has a sense of humour.'

Uzis parked back at hairy shoulders.

Fan came and went, along with the poop niff.

After some more minutes of the banknote stuff, the midget was happy, said, 'Legit,' then shut the case and switched off the scanner.

8

Hunter, sitting in bed, was on the phone to Wolverton CID. Vanessa was in the shower. Sarah and the guys had just arrived and were down in the kitchen, making coffee. 8.23am on another glorious summer day.

After picking up Bill's message last night Hunter tried his home number a few times and also the cops. No reply. He finally got through to the cops ten minutes ago. Guy on the phone moaned about cuts and Anti-Winsor stuff. Wolverton crime room shut between 11.00pm and 8.00am. A central Hotline took "emergency calls", suggesting some crimes were more worthy of fighting than others. Archetypal syntax chewing Pythonesque plod, he used big words when small ones would have done.

'Why did he phone you, Mr Hunter, if he was so concerned about his safety?'

'He must have realized I was turned on.'

'I beg your pardon?'

Netwerk Connex told you if phone numbers in your address book were switched on, like Facebook said if Chat friends were online. Panicking when he saw the Hummer, wondering who to call, Bill must have checked his address book and realized Hunter's phone was still switched on at 2.20am.

Cop got Hunter's drift but tried to downplay the call's seriousness. 'And you'd like some officers to go check if Mr Martin's car is parked outside his house.'

Jesus, Hunter thought. Flinging back the quilt, he saw himself reflected from three places in clunky mirror-covered bedroom furniture. 'He's been on nights and finished at two this morning,' he said, getting up when a breeze came through the open window. 'He was off home to get some sleep before going to Milton Keynes this afternoon, after a union reg twelve hours off, to take over driving the Royal Train.'

Speaking of which, on a mute flatscreen TV on the wall, *BBC News* ran live aerial stuff of the sleek silver-blue bullet train tonning it through Bucks checkerboard summer country.

Hotspotting sun, flashing under bridges and out, it was on its way to London to fetch the Queen. Intercut were shots of it emerging, spanking new, from Wolverton prep shed first thing that morning.

Vanessa emerged nude from the en-suite, rubbing her wet hair with a towel. Being a natural platinum blonde her face was out of focus without make-up.

Hunter puffed his cheeks at the cop being hard work. Vanessa sat at the dressing table to plug in her hair dryer but waited for Hunter to quit his call before switching on.

Cop keypad picked, whacking slowly with a finger. 'Address please.'

'I don't know his home address.'

Pause from other end. Long slow pull from first on-duty cuppa. 'Mr Hunter. We need to know where to go to investigate something.'

'We've dealt with him by phone. All I know is he lives in a village near Wolverton. If I can find an address on 192.com, haven't you got something just a little bit more sophisticated?'

'We're a bit behind out in the sticks,' cop said, typing very slowly now.

'Clearly,' Hunter agreed. When he made the end of the call he swore and chucked his phone on the bed. 'I bloody well give up.'

On TV, the Beeb's freckle-faced Royal Correspondent stood outside Buckingham Palace. Rush hour traffic surged behind him.

Discussion seemed to be about the Royal Train's route north. Hunter told Vanessa to kill her hair dryer while he brought up TV sound. Palace guy thought it odd the train was going from Euston. Usually it went to York-shire from King's Cross via the East Coast mainline. To-day it was using the West Coast mainline from Euston, diverting to Sheffield north of Crewe.

'Do you know why?' studio black guy asked.

'"Manoeuvres",' palace guy quoted. 'Probably code-speak for a potential security risk.'

'Sounds worrying,' studio guy said.

Too right, Hunter thought, alarm bells kicking off when he rewound to Bill telling him same thing when they booked his interview.

'The palace will be keen to downplay talk of a security issue,' palace guy added.

'Who'll have authorised the route change?'

'Decision making at this level is cloaked in secrecy. Captain Tom Packard, Director of Royal Travel, will be involved, as will Royal security chief, Sir John Massey. But Head of National Security, Alex Freeman, will have given it the greenlight.'

Up flashed Freeman's mug. They discussed his meteoric rise from investment banker to political bumlicker to national security chief.

Hunter sent away TV sound and picked up a clean bath towel. 'Bill flagged up the route change,' he told Vanessa. 'Something's up.'

Crossing to the en-suite, he looked out the window at stunning sunlit moors and thought *hello world*. First day of a mega dream job. Bad vibing, he sensed it was gonna fall apart before it had begun.

Dazzling unlight became a blurred, barred, sunny frosty window.

Though everything was black, he managed to feed his hands between liquid darkness, found an ebony split, and climbed up to the other side.

As he focused, he realized the bright unlight wasn't unlight but halogens embedded in a ceiling overhead. He could smell hot plastic and fresh coffee and seemed weightless, floating. Voices babbled through a stud wall. A door opened and a young guy swept in, white smocked like a hospital doc and carrying something chucking light. Probably an iPad.

'Ah good. They said you were coming round. How do you feel this morning?'

'Where am I?' he croaked, rolling onto his back. His eyes wouldn't work. His head fizzed. His neck ached. He felt like death. Although his body pressed down on the bed, he drifted up, in, out, all at once.

'Safe, Mr Martin. Quite safe.'

'I thought the girl in the short skirt had killed me.'

51

'Yes, I doubt if you're the first person who's been shot by a Sheuze tranquillizer gun, thinking they'd been shot for real.' He seemed amused. 'It would have been Kathryn whom you encountered, showing off because it's how she is. Like most guys getting their hands dirty for us she lives dangerously and thrives on adrenalin. But she was only doing her job and meant you no harm. As grunts go she's intelligent and quite pretty. Looked like a cat that had licked up a full saucer of cream when she got back this morning. She's in the gym. I'll get her to come and apologize when she's showered.'

'Where am I? he demanded, disliking the guy's middle classness already.

'All in good time, Mr Martin.'

'I should be driving the Royal Train.'

'And so you still shall, Mr Martin.'

Bill tried to take in what the guy said but dived back through a curtain of blackness, fighting the dazzling unlight. Events leading up to cops snatching him flew back like a movie.

Turning out from the railworks.

Seeing a Hummer parked in Foster Street.

Ridiculous big black American thing. Back in there now, key detail is black tinted windows, meaning Bill can't tell if anybody's inside. He takes it slow. Railworks curtain wall wipes left. Houses right. Night sky looms over deserted Wolverton town.

Hummer pulls out behind him but stays tiny in his rearview. He gets edgy when he's due to drive Royals. Heart in mouth he gets past Tesco's and pulls his phone.

Bingo. Hunter's number flashes but fades as Bill floats up but lands on the bed and somebody else in the room crashes in saying, 'How is he, doc?'

Despite the cool suffix, new guy sounds posh, like a toff, and seems heavily built. Outside, a ballsy American swears at somebody then doors bang shut and a big engine fires. Bill senses the Hummer growl past the frosty window, making shifty shadows work the room.

'He's still groggy but otherwise OK,' doc guy tells toff guy, looming over the bed.

'I can't see properly,' Bill tells them, blinking hard. Back in the movie, like he's outside himself looking in. Weird dazzly lights as the roadblock hits. Sexy girl tells him to get out of his car but he can't move.

Doc guy gets out one of those pen torch things used for checking a patient's eyes. Stooping to Bill, he clicks it on. 'Look up,' he says.

Bill tries but light flares like a Roman Candle. He can't take his eyes off the girl's amazing legs.

Then hard road shoots up fast.

'His pupils are badly dilated,' doc guy says to toff guy clicking off the pen thing. 'The drug relaxes the eyes like atropine. Imagine a camera aperture locked wide open at F2.8, meaning you can't focus on anything. Everything blurred with no depth of field beyond a few centimetres.'

'How long?' toff guy asks him.

'A couple of hours. As with conventional anaesthetics, how long it takes for this stuff to wear off depends on an individual's metabolism.'

'Where am I?' Bill insists.

Blurred toff guy relents.

'My name is Philip Poulson. This is Mark Hartman. He manages the operation. He isn't a qualified doctor but that doesn't matter. Where you are doesn't matter either because this place could be anywhere.'

Before Poulson can add anything, a young Scottish girl pokes in her head. 'Craig and Reece have just left. Traffic's slow on the M42 so they set off sooner.'

'How's Reynolds?'

'Fine and dandy.'

'We're winning?'

'Scary to see.'

'And Pover?'

'Brushing his teeth, I should think. Guess it's make or break time for our hairy Welsh tech geek. How's our Royal Train driver?'

'Still delirious,' Poulson tells her. 'Kath says she felt like a rotten bully.' Still looming over the bed, he tells Bill a tad condescendingly, 'I know it's a lot for you take in but please don't worry for your safety. We're not going to harm you. When it's all over you'll be released. Actually, you'll be found. You can sell your story to the papers and make some money for your retirement because by then we'll be long gone.'

'When what's over?' Bill manages.

'All in good time, Mr Martin,' Poulson says, dittoing what Hartman said when he came in, fishing for his phone, turning to leave.

10

After messing about for an hour, naffing off Randeep even more, they'd got the stuff outside. Big gun was aboard the Range Rover.

Nearly time to go.

Beefcakes finished loading ammo from a metal trolley. Nahid dragged a blanket over everything to hide it. Banged down the RR's back hatch when he'd done. On went his mirror shades. Out came his Marlboros. When he waved the pack, heads shook all round, except for Beefcake # 2. Making a cocky point he pulled two fags and wedged them behind a jewel studded ear, shades showing clear sky when he turned.

Randeep despaired at the pathetic creatures populating this vile underworld he'd to move through to get what he needed. Slim looked absurd, wrapmirrorshaded, hinges bodged with sticky tape. Rounding off, Slim nodded at the RR, telling Randeep, 'Enough octane to start a small war.' Holding out a sausage fingered free hand he steadied himself with a stick because his knees were shot. 'I won't ask you what it's for.'

'Good,' Randeep said, dismissing the proffered hand as if beturded. 'If I told you I'd have to kill you.' Deal done, he'd mentally moved on, phone ready to check e-mail when they hit the road.

Slim appealed to his goons.

Slim turned nasty.

Slim's shades filled with sky, hotspotting sun, when his fat head turned riding multiple chins.

'Is this boy serious?'

Midget chomped a king-size cigar, sending it from one gob side to the other. Weird squeaky voice came out with, 'Serious, boss.'

Distracted by a nearby passing freight train, Randeep coolly stuck on shades and opened the RR's nearside door. Something hit the back of his head, hard. RR door opening's top edge flew up, smashing in his front teeth. KO'd he fell. Second face collision and he kissed greasy cobbles and feet. Serious face damage. Bunny teeth wagging soon as his tongue got to work.

'You've an attitude problem boy,' Slim said. His walking stick found Randeep's chin. 'Most folk who get in people's faces end up getting slapped.' Girly voice made old school malevolence seem bizarre.

'You did some tooth damage, boss,' the midget said. He bent over and blew smoke in Randeep's face, making him cough blood.

'Ahead of a potentially fraught situation *not* having got nasty,' Slim said sarkily, 'a ballbrain does the honourable thing and concludes a deal amicably. Self-centred middle-class idiots, who should know better, open their stupid gobs, failing to comprehend the world of brute strength they actually live in.'

The Midget's stumpy sausage hands came at Randeep and felt in his bloody mouth. 'You did the boy good and hard, boss.' Grinning, he pulled Randeep's buck teeth and held them up, one in each podgy hand.

'Put them in his top pocket,' Slim said. 'His posh dentist can glue them back in.'

Showing unsightly gaps where some of his own rotten front teeth once hung out, the Midget did as Slim asked and smoothed the velcro flap. Slim chucked out an immense fat arm, so he could check a Rolex nesting under his mucky cuff.

Beefcakes, treading bloody bootprints, hauled up delirious Randeep, dumped him in the RR, and belted him in. Still reeling, he heard Slim tell Nahid, 'We have work to do young man. Have a safe journey.'

When they were on the M1, shooting south across Tinsley Viaduct's top deck, Randeep sucked air to cancel excruciating pain. Tracker vest bibbed blood red, he looked back over Sheffield's sprawling Don Valley.

Filling foreground: Meadowhall shopping centre with its big fancy greenhouse glass dome.

Vast car parks empty, with it being early. Brightside, where they'd turned up at a freak show and bought a big gun, was hidden by full summer trees. Randeep pulled his phone and got a number. Turned to look where he'd been looking, coolly hitting the button. A gigantic explosion erupted in the distance, weirdly muted from so far off. They hardly heard it over the RR's slick engine. Like a mini Hiroshima, the fireball rolled skyward, a massive thing pushing a vast mushroom cloud. Traffic showing in wingmirrors braked when drivers opposite got spooked by the mini nuke blast.

Fire and smoke still found sky when a big steelworks came in at carriageway right, blocking the view. Some of Sheffield had done the Atlantis thing and departed from maps. Media were gonna have a field day. Steel case containing US $3m had been a bomb. Fangled new plastic explosive, with a Jap name Randeep couldn't remember, packed in every tiny inner space. Embedded in the lid: phone gubbins hardwired to the jelly. Twenty times nastier than Semtex. When the phone got called, a connection got made and Jap stuff obliged.

Boom.

Slim and his cronies would have become history anyway. Unfortunate that Randeep had ended up getting his mouth busted first. Pain killers he'd gorged while they drove back to the M1 kicked in. He stuck his phone away and laid back his head. They'd been up all night.

God was he tired.

'That's us done for a while,' he said. 'Let's get some shut eye and recharge our batteries before we make hell break loose this afternoon.'

Nahid OK'd and stuck down his foot. 'Still seems like a waste of three million bucks,' he said.

'It was only money,' Randeep reminded him.

He worked his tongue across a swollen mush of ruptured gums. Vapourized fat bastard who smashed his mouth never knew the simple pleasure not of saying it was only money but meaning it.

11

Connors and Reece hit the M6 Toll.

Reece at the wheel. Connors tipping bottled ice water. On dash TV, *BBC News* kept them up to speed on Royal Train stuff as they headed north. But now something was BREAKING NEWS, screen scrolling like crazy.

Beeb boys and girls in a tizzy.

Big bang in Sheffield.

Big-time hole in Mother Earth.

'What the hell's this?' Connors said, smacking shut the bottle.

Live helicopter stuff of bang site. More like a meteorite hit. Colossal crater in the ground. Millions of tons blown away. Flames raged, waving almost slow-mo like fire seen from distance does. Black smoke went up, as if a bunch of oil wells had ignited.

Top edge of picture, a railroad blown in half. Lines bent up like wire. Black studio news guy, who'd been talking to some guy stood outside Buckingham Palace, said, 'Early reports say the explosion centred on a domestic appliance wholesaler. Numerous other businesses have been wiped out in the blast.

'Fortunately it happened at 9.00am, when many firms would have just opened. We're hoping fatalities are minimal.' He touched his earpiece when his director got him to cue live scene. 'What's happening, Jess? Any news on casualties?'

Connors got out his phone while TV cut to the blast site. Pretty young black girl, whom studio guy said had raced there from BBC Sheffield, ducked and dived as firefighters and cops went crazy behind her and sirens *weeooo weeoooed* from all sides.

'It's unbelievable, Mark. I hope you can judge the scale of the blast from the helicopter. Seeing it down here takes the breath away. It's like a war zone.'

'Are emergency services citing a cause?'

'No. But speculation is rife that it could be a huge gas explosion. Let me stress this is unconfirmed.'

Connors said, 'That's no gas bang. Jesus Christ. Railroad's same route the Royal Train would have taken. It was never gonna get that far, only somebody who might have caused that shit doesn't know it.'

'Coincidence?' Reece said, checking his rearview as he overtook a chrome-rammed, roaring Yankee rig.

Connors swore and hit a number, watching the rig get tiny in his wingmirror, yearning for home. M6 Toll was a ghost road. Paying for them was never gonna catch on in tightfisted, smalltown UK.

Phone did some fancy beeps.

Phone got answered.

'Alex Freeman.'

'You seeing this stuff on TV, Alex?'

'They just told me.'

'What do you reckon?'

'They've said it's gas.'

'Crap. Serious explosive does that.' Freeman wonder-ed about new Jap stuff but said surely not. 'Has to be,' Connors told him. 'Somebody's making noise.'

'What kind of noise?'

'Warning noise.'

'From whom?'

'Jesus Alex. How the hell do I know? You're intelli-gence guys with your noses to the ground.'

'There's nothing on the wire.'

'Then listen harder. I'm nervous.'

'Don't be Craig.'

'Most of my bounty's on delivery of Her Majesty. I did the gig with assurances of full ground support.'

'You've got it, Craig.'

Connors calmed.

Reece powered past another big green rig. Some guy called Stobart, whose rigs were everywhere.

On *BBC News*, Connors heard first tentative mention of the blast being a terrorist bomb. They superimposed a Google Earth grab over bombsite epicentre. Domestic appliance wholesaler's had disappeared off maps, along with everything for maybe a quarter of a mile round. Like the comet which hit Siberia early last century. Live helicopter showed a freight train arriving from the north heading for Sheffield. Dead stopping when it found no more railway.

Serious speculation now, from a la-dee-da university bod, pooh-poohing talk of a gas explosion. One of those ass-faced liberal experts on bad people, which TV sucked up to, insisting the blast *must* have been maliciously man made.

'They're talking party poopers, Alex. Such a bang gets spotlight. Railroad which took a hit was gonna carry the Royal Train, had it got that far. Somebody might be trying to gatecrash.'

'I'll increase surveillance,' Freeman assured him.

'What about these two Asian guys?'

'They've left the picture.'

'You ain't mentioned them since we clinched the gig.'

'Nothing more to say.'

'Big timers?'

'Small fish.'

Connors stuck on shades to give his head time to go to work. Thought back to when he'd showed off to Freeman in the crash sim when they first hooked up. How he'd big mouthed about his pulse rate not gaining a tick. Funny how shit smelt like shit when the stink was real and not CG.

'What about the Queen? If the run north gets knocked on the head, serious penalty clauses kick in on the finance front. Even though there ain't any.'

'The Royal Train still runs.'

'Assurances Alex 'cause I don't buy. TV's seeing what I'm seeing. Adding two to two. Speculating about why this stretch of track got KO'd. Her Majesty keeps clued up on what goes on. If she pulls out you'll make footprints in your own crap.'

'Don't worry, Craig. TV can speculate all it likes. The Queen's advisors listen to me. Cause of the explosion is a duff gas main. Other rail routes go to Yorkshire. The Royal Train will still go via Crewe, as planned. I'll make sure the right stuff gets thought and said.'

After they'd chow chowed Connors lifted his bottle water and knocked it back.

They tossed coins at the toll plaza and soon hit the M6. Traffic surged in left, clogging lanes. Overhead stuff freaked about congestion.

Reece swore and slowed the Hummer. Bags of time to make the hit site. But Connors needed to be at the wheel treading gas, going full throttle. Smashing crap outta shiny Brit cars bugging him like hell up front.

12

'Jesus,' Hunter said. 'Let me see that.'

Vanessa passed him the Nexus. She was front passenger in the Volvo. American Sarah was driving. Putting her foot down as they came off Barton Bridge on the M60 and tonned it past the Trafford Centre.

Shopping complex was so big it was more like a Mancunian suburb. Soundman Harry, cameraguy Gordon, and two runners chased in Harry's Royal-blue Qashqai. High summer. Pale skies. Too many cars travelling too close too fast. Hot. Hot. Hot. Hottest summer since 1976. *Thank God for aircon* was last proper thought Hunter had before the Nexus piped up with news of a massive explosion in Sheffield, got worried about Royal Trains, and stuck the knife in his day.

He was e-mailing his kids holidaying with his ex-wife Vicky in France, when ITV got excited. Vanessa had news channels minimized on the Nexus. Keeping up on Royal Train happenings as they headed to Macclesfield Station to shoot flypast stuff from central platform.

Hunter saw raging fire and boiling black smoke. Distance shots showed it blotting Sheffield's skyline. From the air, toy fire engines looked to be spraying salt, not water. Part of inner-city Sheffield had been wiped out. Epic scale of the destruction tough to take. It ranked with 9-11, not because of its audacity, size, impact, but body count, which was stacking up. He'd had a premonition of disaster since the phone stuff last night with Bill, whom he'd still not spoken to.

But why Sheffield?

Apart from smashing a railway which the Royal Train would have used, there was no reason to blow that part of town. Assuming it was terrorism, which it sure as hell must be. Creepy Alex Freeman came on live from Westminster, downplaying talk of it being work of nutty extremists.

'This affects us,' Hunter said, and swore. 'They'll divert the train. Or pull the plug.'

Losing the Royal gig hardly mattered because they'd get another shot. What mattered was the cruel loss of human life. Shots of bloodied, distraught faces. Bulging black zip bags all lined up, ramming home the horror of what had happened.

'Will they tell us if it's off?' Sarah wondered.

Vanessa said, 'We've got security clearance to turn up at the station tomorrow to go aboard the train. We're not exactly a priority now.'

'Today at Macclesfield is flypast,' Hunter said. 'Train won't stop. If it gets that far.'

As he said this, ITV studio guy Thom Bailey, whom Hunter knew from way back, cued uber snob and general high society bottom fondler, Harry Goddard, ITV's greasy Royal Correspondent. He was outside Buckingham Palace, p'd off by noisy traffic stacked behind, tosser horns goading him while he got excited about Royal Train latest.

'Apparently it will still run,' he said. 'Still going via the West Coast mainline. But rather than cutting across to Sheffield it'll go through Wilmslow near Manchester, divert at Stockport to Ashton-under-Lyne, and use the Trans-Pennine route via Huddersfield to Leeds.'

'Meaning it'll not do Macclesfield,' Hunter said. 'Shit.' He got a local railmap on the Nexus. 'Divert to Wilmslow Sarah. Past the airport on the M56.'

On TV, Thom Bailey said to Harry Goddard, 'The Queen could fly, Harry. Why is she still going by train, after the carnage in Sheffield?'

'I'm assured security will be water tight, Thom. But the Queen will want to send out the right signals, letting it be known that she won't allow her plans to be disrupted, if the explosion is sinister. She'll also want to show strong leadership. In today's tenuous economic climate, anything which makes the markets jittery needs to be quickly knocked on the head. But the Palace must stay sensitive to this morning's terrible events. I understand that Her Majesty may visit the blast site when the Royal Train returns to London on Wednesday.'

'That'll involve us,' Hunter said. They were shooting fly-on-the-wall on the train back to London.

Everybody in the car was thinking Sheffield would be an ace added bonus for the film. Nobody was saying it because it would be inappropriate.

They loved shooting TV documentaries because of how spontaneous stuff happened.

What Hunter hated was filmmakers exploiting suffering. Horrific scenes on the Nexus made him feel like a voyeur when he imagined them cut into his film. Such thoughts lurked at the back of any honest documentary producer's mind.

13

Bill felt much better. Kath, the leggy girl who'd done the roadblock dirty, had just been in to apologize and left him a full English breakfast.

Rough as they came, with a smoker's hoarse drag queen drawl, she had stacked black hair and looked a bit like Sandra Bullock. Wearing a white combat vest because of the hot weather, her supple muscly body made her look like an Olympic athlete. Fire tattoos cramming her arms and silver studs loading her bottom lip added to a general scariness.

She said the guys nicknamed her "Mean killer Kath" but she'd never killed anybody and doubted she could. Some of the guys had killed but she made it clear to Bill they'd taken out bad folk only. She was sorry for what she'd done but assured him she was doing "it" as paid work for her little boy, Toby, who needed an operation which the NHS wouldn't fund. What "it" was she refused to say. Bill assumed it was to do with an attempt on the Queen's life. This had bothered him then terrified him the clearer his head got as the drug wore off.

Although he quite liked Kath, and sympathised with her kid sob story, he didn't like Poulson, who'd made it clear Bill wouldn't be harmed. Those surrounding him hardly seemed like the sort to want to bump off Royalty. He was being kept under lock and key. The room's frosted window was barred. But he didn't feel intimidated, or in danger, and couldn't put his finger on why.

Poulson came in as Bill finished his coffee and stood up from the desk under the window, where he'd eaten his breakfast. Now his eyes were working, he could see that bald Poulson was about his age but taller and heavier. From a very privileged background, judging by his upper-class accent. His cold grey eyes gave no indication of what he was thinking.

'How are you feeling?'

'OK,' Bill said, sliding his chair back under the desk. 'You're treating me well but I don't know why I'm here. I should be driving the Royal Train. I should be phoning my wife in Italy because now's the time'—just gone 11.00am—'when I'd be putting on my uniform, getting ready to drive to Milton Keynes Station.'

'I'm aware of your schedule,' Poulson said.

'You must be up to something dodgy with the Royal Train, otherwise why kidnap me and be bothered if I'm OK? But you must understand I'm loyal to the Crown. I'm about to retire. I don't want any trouble. I won't go through with it, whatever "it" is.'

'Admirable,' Poulson said, massaging his chin, weighing something up. 'Actually, you've done your bit for us, Mr Martin.' Playing on Bill's defiance, he sounded as if he'd decided to let a cat from a bag. 'It's why we drugged you, to ensure your co-operation.'

'You're talking in riddles, Mr Poulson, as you have been all morning.'

Hartman appeared at the door. Blond, maybe 40, very public school posh, he said, 'Nearly time, Phil,' flinging out an arm to show Poulson his watch under his crisp white smock cuff.

Poulson turned to Hartman. Vehicles swished to and fro from a nearby main road. Louder since Kath unlocked a window to let in some fresh air, after Bill complained the stuffy room stunk of hot plastic.

'I think we should reveal all to Mr Martin. I feel obliged morally, if nothing else.'

'Is it wise?' Hartman said.

'I'm in charge. I take full responsibility.'

Poulson took Bill along a passage next to the office and through a metal door into a small former warehouse or one-level factory.

Corrugated plastic skylights had turned amber from the sun which poured in, giving the space an agreeable ambience. An open rollershutter let in a fine summer morning. Nearby Bill sensed one of those long straight main roads in open country, with big pubs and cafs every five or ten miles. Place was set back from the road behind trees. Yard outside was all ribbed concrete tufted with weeds. Parked cars, a couple of flashy motorbikes, a white Transit, and a bogus cop 4x4 gleamed in hot sun in front of a dilapidated outbuilding.

A dozen men and women of varying ages, in T-shirts and shorts, cleared mixing bowls and kitchen-looking paraphernalia from an 8x8 wooden table. To one side, exhibition screens framed a makeshift booth where a tripod-mounted spotlight shone at something which was going on. Bill had seen same spotlight at the roadblock last night. A hot food smell came from where they must have fried up his eggs and bacon.

Everybody smiled or nodded at Bill when Poulson ushered him through. They arrived at the makeshift booth. A smart Latin-looking woman, small and white-smocked, maybe 50, long black hair swept back in a tail, leant across somebody who was lying on what looked like a dentist's chair. A portable electric fan blew cool air across her and whoever lolled under her.

As Poulson and Bill arrived she stood aside, holding a paint brush. No, Bill realized, a make-up brush used for puffing on foundation. He'd been married long enough to know girly face-paint tackle when he saw it.

Then it hit him.

Like a head-on smash.

Years ago, new to driving trains, he'd taken an old HS 125 north from King's Cross. Shooting along, eyes on job, he was thinking how much he loved doing what he loved doing when another train came at him on same track. Or so he'd thought. Trick perspective where distant lines bent round in a sunny autumn haze. During that scary moment he went to a hellish place all train drivers feared.

Head-on collision.

Similar feeling now.

Everything shoved mentally sideways when he least expected it. Holding up a mirror as he smashed head-on into himself. Guy in dentist's chair looked back at him. Bill thought *Oh my God* then said it when he saw reference pics on a laptop next to sponges, jars loaded with brushes, stuff for doing faces.

Poulson wanted to "reveal all" to Bill because he wanted to show off. 'I'd like you to meet yourself, Mr Martin,' he said proudly.

Bill saw himself looking back from the dentist's chair. Exact double. A doppelganger. Likeness was terrifying. Down to his thick wiry grey hair and small mole on his left cheek. He thought he'd smelt hot plastic in his room. Wrong. It was rubber being mixed. Cooked. Baked. He was in a movie make-up shop, where actors' faces were changed into something they weren't.

14

Deep shocked, Bill tried to get a grip.

Poulson said, 'Everybody you can see used to be a make-up artist in film and TV. The best in the business.

Carmen here worked on some of Hollywood's biggest films. Sadly, the relentless onset of CGI means skilled special effects and make-up people have become obsolete. Actors once spent hours in make-up before filming. Now their faces are scanned on a computer and changed effortlessly in the "digital domain".'

'I don't care,' Bill said, trying to take himself in. 'This is totally bloody obscene.'

'Not obscene,' Poulson said, hardness in his voice, 'but supremely clever. We need you to take over driving the Royal Train today. You'd not have gone along with it so we had to make it happen another way.' He looked at the guy in the chair. 'Say hello, Mike.'

The guy sat up and stuck out a hand.

Bill could see it belonged to somebody much younger than his fake 64 year old face.

'Mike Reynolds. Pleased to meet you.'

Bill automatically extended his hand but quickly pulled it back when he realized the impostor didn't speak southern working-class but posh middle class. Hearing him talk wrong was scarier than seeing himself gawping back in tight grungy T-shirt, trendy barbed-wire tattoos helixing his muscly upper arms. When Bill declined the handshake Reynolds shrugged indifferently and slumped back, steepling his big hands across his solid belly. The woman carried on working at his eyes.

Poulson stood next to some fancy lab looking thing bolted to a wheeled metal frame outside the booth. Carrying on the dental analogy, it looked like sit-down kit used for X-raying a patient's head.

'We had to knock you out because we needed you to keep dead still. While you were unconscious we applied a skullcap and scanned your head three-hundred-and-sixty degrees with this.'

He patted the kit.

'We transferred the scan to a 3D laser-printer which cut an exact copy of your head in solid acrylic. The scan happened at 3.15am this morning, soon after you were delivered to us from the kidnap site. It took another two hours to finish your solid dupe head. Around six this morning, moulds were taken of host Mike's head. These were combined with casts of your dupe head. Prosthetic appliances were attached to Mike's face. Several more hours of painstaking artwork and wig applying by highly skilled technicians, and here we are. It's exactly how they did it in the movies.

'Mike's a bit taller than you but nobody will notice. You're superstitious and never speak to anybody on the day you drive Royalty till you're safely in the loco cab. That helps us enormously, meaning Mike won't have to talk to anybody at the station. He's also been learning how to drive the right train.'

'Why are you doing this?' Bill demanded, panic setting in. 'I've a right to bloody well know.'

'Because we've no choice, Mr Martin.'

'Yes you do. You can stop it now.'

'Not possible I'm afraid.'

'And just what *are* you doing? Planning some idiot plot to kill the Queen?'

Poulson didn't bite back, which said it all.

Bill was out of his depth, confronted by posh types who were arrogant and confident, who had no commitment to their country. All he could do was rustle up some honest patriotism and lob it at them.

'The Queen is old and revered by most,' he said. 'Folk like you screw this country for every last lousy penny. Have you no conscience? You're bent as nine bob notes the damned lot of you. Exploiting me for your selfish, no doubt money-grubbing ends, with no consideration for how it'll destroy my life.'

Oppressed by his silver surfer age, he wished he was as fit as he once was. He'd have taken them on, sodding consequences.

The young Scottish girl appeared who'd poked her head in Bill's room when he came round. Breaking his diatribe she gave Poulson a live iPad.

'She's just leaving, Phil.'

Bill saw *BBC News*.

Helicopter shot of the Royal motorcade leaving Buckingham Palace. On its way to Euston Station. Overwhelmed, he felt like he was part of bad things happening even though he wasn't.

'Where's Glyn?' Poulson asked her.

'Nearly at the signalbox.'

Poulson fished for his phone. Two young guys were sitting at table's near end. 'Take Mr Martin back to his room and lock the door. One of you stay outside till I come through.'

The guys OK'd and got up. Bill had no choice but to let them frogmarch him back along the corridor. He was too old to fight. Too tired. Desperate to be with Pauline and his grandkids. Desperate to rewind time and make it happen some other way.

15

Crewe Gateway signalbox was brand new. A seriously big chunk of award-winning Modernist Revival architecture straight from *Thunderbirds*.

All brute concrete wrapped in yellow slab plastic, it controlled the West Coast mainline and central England's feeder routes. Rumour had it the dinky horizontal comb-shaped Watchman radar, spinning red then white then red then white, was for effect.

As bearded 36 year-old, Welsh and damned proud of it, Glyn Pover arrived in his bogus Railteckh van, he half expected the radar to sense danger and sink the building, earth defence style, below ground.

Two guys on the gate couldn't be arsed with clearance. Pover pulled up, sent away glass, and held out his fake ID, end of a gorilla-hairy offside arm. Guys were arguing over something in the younger guy's *Sport*. Older guy took time off from sarkily paper poking to prod the barrier button. Not obliging contractually with what he'd signed his life away to do, he shot Pover a look and waved him through. Oh dear, Pover thought. Somebody's gonna get strung up by his testis.

Parking near box steps, Pover sure felt the gunmetal-grey, US of A coveralled part, banging van doors and treading pink herringbone setts. Laptop-handed one side, to do some dirty. Toolbox other side, for effect. Bogus Railteckh logo slapped across his back.

CCTVs spied from high on grey slab walls when he squeezed his key fob to cue van alarm with some fancy *pips*. Baffled transport cops would take apart HD footage, scratching piggy heads at such audacity. Pover could see frame blow-ups of himself in the *Mail*, appealing for readers to help nail those nasty HRH choo choo knobblers.

Up Expamet steps he went to a service entrance on top deck. Now it got serious. Out came a swipe card, loaded with more fake ID. Red entry panel went green. Kit went *fdunk* as a slab door *Star Trek* thingied away to a slick pneumatic hiss. Inner sanctum first, rehearsed virtually on Freeman's piss crazy sim. Hand slapped on backlit perspex, like they did in sci-fi movies back in the 70s. Not so cheesy after all.

ID card into ATM slot.

Crunch time.

Tight space. Green light hit him and shiny stainless-steel while his face boogie woogied, house kit got suckered, *pinged,* and said he was good.

'ID confirmed,' said sexy husky lady.

Cool. Clever beardyman was in.

Pover had time for sexy husky ladies. A tattooed leggy husky lady back at base had got everybody going. Her ex had dumped her and left her with a cute kid who needed a major op. Connors had secretly organized a whip round. Guys earning serious dough meant cute kid was gonna get his life saved, Stateside. Poulson said he'd make up any difference. An upper-class twit but a swellish guy under the stiff top lip.

More door faffing then Pover was in Mission Control. Big 3D railmap an impressive centrepiece, hanging in midair. Seemingly suspended from nothing. Held up by empty space. Letterbox-shape motion graphics slab, solid but see through, like thick glass with a silvery tint. It showcased every UK rail route to a dozen guys sitting at keypadded starship consoles. Guys zoomed in if they needed to check a train's progress. Signal centre lighting was subdued nightclub blue so the map could show off. Tiny halogens, embedded in the ceiling, cosied with coffers getting up to some fancy design stuff where slab outer walls angled in hard, at forty-five.

Pover needed to access the Computer Bay. Console guys glanced across but hardly saw him because house ID kit had let him delude it. He waved a hand. Hoodwinked, a few waved back, joining the bearded Sikh-in-charge's nodding turbaned head.

Pover went through some more ID stuff at door panel to the UPS area. In the nerve centre now. Ready to cause aggro. Room hummed with live kit, stuffed with computer banks lined up in rows.

He knew where to go and what to do. Down went the toolbox, lid open, trays popped, looking the part if anybody came in to offer him a brew. He set his laptop on a pull tray.

Easy bloody peasy.

Mission Control's railmap zipped up on screen, ready to isolate the required section of track and kick off tomorrow's shocked news headlines.

Time to cue Ross and Thinnes, twenty miles north. He pulled his phone and hit a number. It got answered but all he heard was running water, birds tweeting, and somebody swearing.

Some rustling then Cockney Ross said, 'Glyn, you arsehole. We've just parked and I was having a pee. Last time you rang me I was on the bog. You gotta bloody lavatorial fetish or what?'

16

Hunter and Vanessa stood at south end of Wilmslow Station's island platform. Midday sun blazed down. Hunter bet he could crack eggs and fry them on the ribbed concrete coping.

Nearly two hours till the Royal Train came through. Not taking chances with busy motorways they'd arrived early and lunched at GBK. Time would fly because they were gearing up to shoot some link stuff to set the Royal scene. Gordon was sitting on a platform seat, checking the camera gear. Elderly soundman Harry disliked hot weather and was in the Waiting Room, writing up his sound sheets. The two runners were sitting about a lot, as runners tended to do.

They'd have one chance when the train flew past. To supplement main camera, Vanessa would shoot trendily handheld with a baby HDcam. Footage would probably end up being graded like grainy pop-video-looky stuff they routinely did for *Crime in Britain*. Bit edgy for a Royal TV doc. Presumably the Queen knew about it from their original proposal and was happy for Real Life Pictures to shove the envelope.

To be sure they covered the train well on its inaugural run they'd hired six camera crews for the day, dotted up the West Coast mainline. They'd grab establishing shots in rural and urban English landscapes. Some close, some from a long way off, to cut with scenes Hunter and the guys would shoot aboard the train.

Budget hadn't run to aerial shots. Vanessa had given a keen girl film student a break whom she'd met after a media school talk. Usually it was girls who stayed back, abstaining from the exodus to café and smoking areas. They were part of 0.05% of 32,000 kids expunged each year from uni media courses who'd be lucky to get work in an industry which employed 48,000 tops.

Vanessa walked Hunter through where she wanted him for her opening shot. Because of the hot weather, he wasn't wearing his trademark long leather coat. Two- or three-piece suits, routinely worn by stuffy TV presenters, also were no-go for him.

Instead, he was in grey chinos, royal blue scoop-neck tight muscle T-shirt, and heeled brown suede Gringos. He worked out with Vanessa and was looking good. Impressive chest muscle complemented his strong bronze arms. Unshaven he looked suitably anti-nerdish and *CSI* posy cool to front a major TV doc which had one foot in British tradition—the Royal Family for God's sake—and the other in modern hi-octane telly.

As Sarah dabbed stuff on his face, to take away the shine, his phone kicked off from his back pocket. It was the plod he'd spoken to at Wolverton CID, wondering if he'd managed to get in touch with Bill Martin.

'No,' Hunter said. 'But after you and I spoke this morning I remembered how he doesn't talk to anybody on the day he drives the Royal Train till he's aboard. Some superstition thing he has going, which explains him being tough to get hold of.'

'Well,' cop said, 'I thought you might like to know he's reported for duty at Milton Keynes. There's a media and police presence at the station. An officer informed us that Mr Martin had just arrived.'

As he said this, Vanessa maxed *BBC News* on the Nexus. With Milton Keynes being stop-off for the journey north, and driver changeover hotspot, TV crews had descended. Sarah had booked a couple of guys to be there for the film. Hunter saw Bill in jerky telephoto, crossing Station Square carrying a black case.

'Thank God,' he said, relieved. 'And thanks for letting us know.'

'Thank you too sir,' cop said, sounding grateful. 'Not many people bother to thank us.'

Gordon and Harry arrived, ready to shoot. As he killed call Hunter felt a weight lift. Feeling good now that he knew Bill was OK, not getting carried away out of respect for those who'd died in Sheffield, he said, 'Let's do it.' On went his shades. Squaring his broad shoulders he assumed first position.

Vanessa lifted her shades and ran through everything a final time. Tanned Sarah was barelegged, in a corker red mini dress that had drawn wolf-whistles when they walked back from GBK.

She got her phone ready to shoot Hunter from a *Batman* Dutch angle. Wouldn't be the first time they'd used grungy low-res hand-held phone vid to break up shots. Better to have it than not.

Harry, who'd recently turned 73, said he was turning. Anticipating, he watched digi markers bounce on kit slung at his rotund waist. 'And I'm at speed.'

'Action,' said Vanessa.

17

Big moment for Reynolds when Milton Keynes Central's entrance doors got excited and split, cueing those pesky CCTVs to get sniping from the ceiling.

Supremely confident, he looked 100% Bill Martin. Smart blue uniform. Right navy-blue tie diagonally gold striped with a Royal Train crest. Not BM's actual tie because that was at his house and the guys had thought it too risky to fetch it. Instead, something got rustled up via the web and printed off as an iron-on transfer. Not perfect. Not millimetre exact. But easy good enough.

Crossing the entrance hall dodging bored Robocops and commuters, nearly treading on a pooch, Reynolds got the buzz he craved strutting his public stuff.

He was an actor but a very different kind of mercenary, specializing in bogus face jobs and high-end impersonations. He'd done drama school. Like many who pursued the acting dream, he struggled for a few years doing provincial theatre, TV bit parts, corporate vids, and no-budget indie movies. But like most in the same boat, dreaming of a break that was never gonna happen in an industry skewed in favour of a chosen few (but more especially their bastard agents), he'd drifted into other stuff, trying to make ends meet.

One night he got drunk with some mates and ended up bedding a smart older woman he met in a Soho bar. She was a naughty lawyer who needed somebody to impersonate somebody to stitch up a bent boardroom exec. Reynolds said *Hey I can do that*, got some film school guys involved who could do make-up and hair, and one thing led to another.

Buzz had been incredible. More than that, the money rocked. OK there was a gangster underworld to go at. But a corporate underworld also existed, which most folk new nothing about. He'd touted himself to it as a special kind of actor, which was still his thing. One in the rotten eye for those luvvy-duvvy tossers, chucking each other "awards" from their fashionable exclusion zone (when they weren't picking pubic hairs from each other's drinks at sordid shag parties). It was how he'd come to Poulson's attention and landed arguably the greatest theatre job of all.

Hitting a walk how BM jived he got his actor buzz. A 34 year old guy pulling off somebody who'd hit the last-lap age Beatles opined about.

Nod to rail blokes at barriers, who put heads together when they saw BM getting close, giving him the all-clear to access platforms.

More flag wavers, Roboplods, and TV guys on boiling Platform 1. Barriers cordoned off north end where a guy in dayglow, looking hot and bothered, held a yellow flag which had obviously been pressed. Reynolds exchanged nods with him, slipped between barriers, and found a seat.

Case next to him.

Latches shot.

Mail out.

Case back to shut position.

Latches re-clicked.

BM aborted his trusty snapbag, switching to a *Joe 90* attaché case when he did Royal runs.

Quick glance up and down, to check all OK. Paper open, revealing insipid gossip about dodgy Irish priests, the RC Church, and women's undies nicked from washing lines. Fine and dandy.

Quick fiddle with correct red iPhone parked on seat, patched to *ITV News* keeping up on Royal Train prog. Heli shot of it snaking through Greater London suburbia. As it went under the M25, north of Watford, Royal crest CG stuff spun-fed next bunch of ads to an overblown synth hullabaloo.

Reynolds got ready and felt a surge of anticipation brought on by the majestic sight of his approaching destiny. Two-three minutes till HRH. Two-two minutes till big driver switch.

18

Randeep and Nahid were back on the job.

Platform 1 at Wilmslow Station.

Randeep sitting on a seat with his laptop on his knee. Shades on. Clean togs on. Ponging of cologne in scorching sun. Nahid stood nearby, using his phone to video Hunter and his guys shooting TV links on the island platform. Its long brick building was original. Canopied with a fretted wooden edge. When Hunter fluffed a take under it, the yank bird called reset. Randeep waved at Nahid not to overdo it with the phone. Getting the message he moseyed on back and parked his bum.

Lucky they knew Hunter and his gang were there. They were supposed to shoot at Macclesfield Station but Tweeted the gig change after the Sheffield bomb rerouted HRH. Vibe coming over from the film crew was that Nahid must be a starstruck bystander. But Randeep sensed beady eyes. Vanessa's especially 'cause he knew she was a ball of fire. Hair stacked, she was dressed all summery yellow. Yellow skinny jeans. Yellow peep-toe wedges. Floppy pale-yellow blouse. You could tell she was top dog 'cause of how she walked up and down, calling shots.

It was like tightening a steel wrench. The nerve of it. The audacity of two guys who blew away some of Sheffield being under Hunter's nose.

Nahid e-mailed what he'd shot. Randeep opened it on the laptop and got to work. His puffy face was settling but he lisped words because of his missing front teeth. His dentist wanted him to go in right away. Not possible Randeep had said. Small job to do. Suit yourself dentist said and talked Neurofen Maxi. Holes would still be there on the morrow.

A local train came and went. When its rear white lamp got small in the direction of Styal, Nahid puffed at the heat and popped bottle water. 'Hunter's screwing her, isn't he?' he said, meaning Vanessa.

'Yep,' Randeep said, hitting Return.

'She looks older than him.'

'Nine or ten years.'

'Sounds like the Joe Lampton thing.'

'You've lost me there, my friend.'

'Sometimes I feel obliged to remember I did English Lit.' He knocked back water, smacked shut the nozzle, and slouched back on the seat, bringing a Niked foot to a knee. 'Vanessa's surname is kinda *Room at the Top.* Alice Aisgill is the older bird Joe Lampton shafts. I reckon Aisgill's a Yorkshire place name, like Aysgarth is for sexy Vanessa.'

Randeep wasn't interested. He plopped Nahid's stuff on the timeline, hit Play Movie and turned the laptop so they could watch phone video of Hunter with his kids and ex-wife at Heathrow airport. Shot secretly by Nahid a couple of weeks ago. Crappy handheld quality gave it a cool pop video energy. Hunter crouched for two sweet little girls who ran across shouting, 'Daddy, Daddy,' in pink Lelli Kelly trainers. Ex-wife came off an escalator, looking tired as her make-up. Tall, dark, Sloaney, with good legs, you could see she'd crapped on Hunter by her guilty body language. Hunter had an eye for posh birds with pins.

Next up some TV award bash.

Vanessa and Hunter got up from a table going OMG. VO went on about how some cop thing of theirs caught a nation's heart. Jump to Hunter and Vanessa joint-nursing a gong on stage, towering over a gobby comedienne whose jokes fell flat as spent farts.

Vanessa looked like a million bucks. Long powder-blue leather jacket Mandarin cut. Matching skirt so short she needn't have bothered.

As if sensing Randeep's thoughts, Vanessa shouted 'Cut' from across the tracks.

While the guys reset, she eyed Randeep and stood hands on hips, doing bored kick stuff with her feet. A kid helper passed her some bottle water from a carry cooler. She sat down to pop it and crossed her legs, watching Randeep while she drank, wagging her suspended peep-toe foot speculatively.

Randeep couldn't outstare the bitch, even from behind his shades. 'Time for another call,' he said coolly, and pulled his phone. Hunter got ready for a new take, traipsing with his guys to platform's south end. 'I want you to zoom in and shoot his reaction.'

Nahid waited till Hunter was ready to go again then got up and held out his phone. Hunter looked across from behind his shades. Like Vanessa, seemed like he was getting bad vibes about boys on Platform 1.

Another OTT swirly coloured commuter train ambled through, heading north, far side of the island, feeding off overhead wires messing blue sky.

Brit summer's sweaty glory. Pissing off folk like Randeep. Punch-drunking most. When a signal flicked back red, back came a sombre sparrows-tweeting echoey sad English station sound.

Vanessa told Hunter to go for it in his own time.

Nahid got to it with his phone cam.

Randeep, his phone ready, hit a number.

The number.

19

Connors and Reece had left the M6 and were nearly at the hijack site when news channels got excited about a second massive explosion.

Connors wondered if he'd heard the bang as Reece trod gas and Twemlow Green became bit-bigger Twemlow. One of those timeless English villages which gobsmacked Americans. Big square grass patch framed by black-and-white houses basking in hot summer sun. Old folks treading old bike pedals. Screwable middle-class broads in jackboots and tight horsy pants. And dogs. Always that funny Brit thing for dogs. Worlds from World War 3 hitting dash TV but not far as birds flapped wings. Hence Connors sussing he mighta heard opening bang.

North Dean Oil Terminal, south of some place called Stockport. Lottsa silver *Quatermass* domes and pipe towers no more. Explosion so big it had taken out the Stoke-on-Trent leg of the West Coast mainline.

An outrageously big-haired Indian Beeb girl yakked away. Sheffield was still an item. Now media went OTT with another meteorite hit on the Chattanoonga melodrama front.

TV made do with phone vid from Joe Pub. Connors saw raging fire and smaller explosions pumping debris and sheet flame which kinda dissolved. Home movie feel made it seem ethereal, like aliens had invaded and this stuff was coming from front line. Everything jumped sideways when soundwave soundsmash arrived, shoving fiery *pings* and *peeows*, causing spooked phone-cam waver to run for it. Excited voices made it sound like a crazy rock gig. Connors hated that.

Getting Freeman on the blower, he cut crap and got to what the hell had bugged him since Sheffield boomed.

'These two young guys, Alex.'

'What about them?'

'This shit's gotta be them. You said honcho boy has cash behind him plus a history of brokering small time arms deals?'

'Mostly overseas,' Freeman said. 'Randeep Parveer. Fancies himself as an international playboy. Likes big guns and likes picking up two girls in casinos in Monte Carlo and indulging in threesomes. Has a seriously evil streak but for him it's about winning. He doesn't need the money, which isn't the same as saying he doesn't want it. Super arrogant, making him dangerous and unpredictable.'

'Oxbridge?'

'Oxford, ten years ago. Walked it to a First. Rich banking family. Christian not Muslim. Money screwed him. In another life he might have channelled his brainpower and served a purpose. He craves excitement.'

'Sounds like the kinda bored, cash rich individual who'd like to get drunk at a Royal bash.'

'Or gatecrash and cause a riot,' Reece butted in, nodding at the dash.

First heli shot. More quasi end-of-world stuff. Hole punched in blazing earth. Rail carriages chucked like toys across fields.

Reece slowed, taking a leafy lane. Nearly there. Freeman's roadblock cops did thumb-ups as the Hummer passed. Mottled sun wiped its windshield. Long brick rail viaduct arched in right, striding flat fields. Jodrell Bank's giant dish loomed, mid left.

Connors popped fresh ice water and dragged back of empty bottle hand across his mouth. 'What's the story this time, Alex?'

'Oil explosion,' Freeman said, sounding like he had it all worked out. 'Newsrooms will get a press release saying North Dean management ignored staff warnings of a potential safety hazard.'

Connors laughed.

'Yeah and the bang takes out another stretcha railroad close to where HRH is gonna run.'

'Don't worry, Craig. The Queen's in session aboard the train. She won't know about Stockport. People close to her will make sure of that. On my orders.'

'Two mini nukes in one day when HRH is on a train and you tell me not to worry? Jesus. And what about the train? Two bangs might become three.'

'Train was finetooth-combed before it left the depot this morning and again before it departed from Euston. The Queen's an hour from you. I'll organize a hardware escort some of the way but that's all. I need to justify my obscene public pay. Trust me when I say the job's still on.' After some more reassurances he broke call.

Connors swore and killed TV, needing quiet.

An overgrown railroad came alongside in a cutting. Rusting girder support poles had been stripped of overhead power lines. Up ahead, on a road bridge across the line, a derelict village station had covered stairs running to an island platform, two miles from Twemlow which gave it a name. Windows steel blanked. Roof tiles looted, exposing structural timbers. Wildflowers pulled bees and butterflies along rusted tracks. Connors connected with why abandoned English railways seemed evocative, especially in summer.

Plan was for the Royal Train to get diverted off the main line and run over this one parta the way, to a small reception committee.

Connors should have been buzzing ahead of making it happen. But if two rich boys were as bright or as dangerous as Freeman said, odds on they were game playing. Building to something mega.

Train Officer Chris Hendry was at his workstation in the Royal Train's rear power car.

Looking good, feeling great, in neat grey slacks, white shirt, and navy Royal Train tie. Amtrak's nifty climate control meant he could have worn his black blazer on such a scary hot day and not suffered on the BO front. But he had an OCD thing about creased jackets. He'd left his hanging up till Milton Keynes, where he'd pose for excited flag wavers and make sure everything was Hunky D after driver changeover.

Forty minutes out of London and making good time. Live aerial shot on a TV embedded in his console showed them going under a bridge and out.

Chopper feeding ITV its shots buzzed the train then was up and away for another pass while some ads happened. ITV milked it. Theirs was final media chopper granted Royal Train airspace. When it left Milton Keynes, sky ten miles either side would be no-fly till Greater Manchester. Alex Freeman's diktat after Sheffield blew, and now poor Stockport. Security was mega tight. Roadblocks had been imposed where cars could get near the West Coast mainline.

BBC News showed more aerial stuff of North Dean oil carnage. Chris had all news channels running at his console, sound mute. Amtrak had done a fantastic job on the tech front, in partnership with Apple.

Last Royal Train had been more Ikea than gilt and plush House of Windsor indulgence. His new workstation was like a space shuttle cockpit. Centrepiece a very comfy, two-tone grey padded contour seat. From it he managed the Royal Train crew, including Train Foreman, Traction Inspector, Amtrak's Tech Rider (in case of loco glitches), three tech staff, a Network Rail inspector, Chief Steward, Royal Chef and three caterers, plus obligatory beefy transport cops, hiked from six to twelve after Sheffield. Chris was surprised the Queen had risked it by train. But Freeman had assured HM's worry team that security was in hand.

When Chris switched his attention to *Sky News,* something spooked him. Chopper flying low over the train.

He assumed ITV's then realized not. Its thudding Chinooky turbines were too ballsy. Heading purposefully north it came so close he felt double-glazing shake when he got his face to his window.

Before he'd finished taking in a large chopper another thundered overhead blotting sky.

Police gunships. Halfway between Bell Hueys and big CG choppers in *Avatar*. Buzzing the train. Hanging insect heavy like serious US made chopper hardware, angling round motion-control heavy.

When Chris felt the train slowing he grabbed his interphone to call the driver. 'What's up, Bryan?'

'Looks like a gunship escort.'

'Are we stopping?'

'Not sure yet. Signal's going from green to amber. Speed limiter's kicking in. Something's funny, Chris. Has been since we set off.'

'How do you mean?'

'Just a feeling. Signals changing too soon or too late. Like butterfingers new to the job is typing the wrong keys. Checkpoints have gone west an' all.' Checkpoints were trackside markers Royal drivers watched for, to make sure their timing stayed bang on. 'Not sure if we should be carrying the old girl.'

'Freeman gave us the all-clear.'

'Freeman is a devious bastard. Absolute twat on legs. Wouldn't trust him as far as I could chuck him.'

'Wonder what Bill thinks. Rumour has it she might invite him into her carriage for a farewell cuppa and a toasted currant teacake.'

'Get away.'

'I didn't say anything Bryan.'

'Not a word did I hear, young sir.'

Grinning, Chris hung up and stuck his face back to his window. Console GPS showed them go under the B488 at Church End. Wild flowers smothered the cutting's chalky sides.

Up ahead, the gunships banked over trees near Pitstone. Hazards flashing. Missiles slung. Monster Arnies gimballed at cop-manned open side doors.

21

Sir John Massey, Royal security chief, was sitting with the Queen in her saloon carriage going over filming before the TV crew boarded tomorrow.

The Queen always briefed herself. Today's meeting was last minute for a Royal journey given diary space last year. Because of a state visit to Canada, she hadn't been able to get together with Massey till now. He finger pinch-and-wiped his iPad and passed it across. On screen were Hunter's face and that of his attractive co-producer, Vanessa Aysgarth.

'Today ma'am,' he said, 'they're shooting the train while it's in motion. They have one- and two-man teams dotted along the route. These exterior views will cut into the film and give a sense of the passing journey.'

'Establishing shots, ma'am.'

This was Carole Kelly, the Queen's vivacious PA, arguably closest to her outside Buckingham Palace, and slowly sinking with her into a deep, Royal-blue leather sofa. Assertive and impeccably middle class, like Massey she'd recently pipped half a century and like him was salt-and-pepper grey. She was attractive and had good legs, which compensated for her prominent nose and small boobs.

But like lots of women Massey encountered in Royal circles, she was too aloof and emotionally cold for an Enfield council-estate-boy-done-good, and one-time Sweeney. The Queen, if you got to know her, wasn't aloof because she'd spent her life dealing with folk from all walks. Massey got on with her like he got on with his elderly mum.

'And they work for the BBC?' the Queen asked him, watching him over her glasses.

'Not any more,' he said. 'The film is for the BBC, but under independent commission.'

The Queen, always people focused, was more interested in weighing up the filmmakers.

'She's striking,' she said, touch-screening Vanessa bigger, with help from Carole's long thin fingers. 'And the young man is quite ruggedly handsome. He has sincere eyes but there's hurt in them. I wonder if he might have come through a bad patch.' Checking herself, she added quickly, 'Did you say they're married?'

'Not married,' Massey said, unapologetically.

Carole nudged nearer the Queen, adding with mild disapproval, 'They co-habitate ma'am,' primly asserting what she thought while putting recently-divorced Massey in his place with a knowing schoolma'amy nod.

'I see,' the Queen said, understanding Carole, crediting Massey with a sympathy smile. 'And we're happy for there to be an association, John?'

'As you know ma'am, we made them wait nearly three years for this opportunity. During that time we subjected them to rigorous scrutiny. They're not grubby documentary filmmakers with chips on their shoulders but mature grown-ups with no history of insurgence or anti-Establishment activity. I wouldn't go so far as to say they're staunch Royalists or gung-ho reactionaries. But they're not raging dissidents either.'

Phone buzzed at the table.

Massey had been expecting it.

They were running slow.

Gunships had recently flown over, deadened by the train's amazing sound insulation. Feeling encumbered in his grey silk suit, despite aircon, he struggled to keep his eyes off Carole's bronze ultra-sheer-stockinged legs. He caved in, indulging himself when the legs unfolded and she reached for the phone.

'Thanks Chris,' she told it, and passed it to Massey. 'For you John.' Creaking couch leather, she adjusted her skirt with an exquisite womany body wriggle.

'Hello Chris,' he said.

'Sorry to bother you, Sir John, but you might have noticed things happening outside the train. Alex Freeman has been on. He didn't call you because he knew you were in session. He's ordered a brief unscheduled stop at Leighton Buzzard. Unprecedented because it'll delay us slightly. But nothing to worry about. After another potentially dodgy explosion at Stockport, he wants the train checked underneath yet again.'

'Understood,' Massey said.

He hung up and brought the ladies up to speed. Carole hadn't enough room to fit her long legs between the sofa and a blue-tinted glass slab dumped in front of it, which Amtrak wittily called a coffee table.

They'd made a very good job of the new Royal Train, which was stopping so smoothly you couldn't tell. From outside all Royal blue, chrome, and anodized steel, for Massey it had the magic of a 1960s Blue Pullman. No British HST had managed it since.

But blow-moulded everything inside, and a fussy use of padded leather and stretch spandex plush, made it feel too sci-fi for a staunch traditionalist whose ideas on décor matched his taste in women.

22

Hunter was still getting over North Dean.

Scary, talking to camera when a minor nuclear explosion happened not far from the station. Blinded by the flash, he'd sworn and ducked as the platform literally shook under him. Quick-thinking director Vanessa had got cameraman Gordon to swing round and keep shooting, so soon after the blast that debris and a mushroom cloud were still going up.

In the heat of the moment the two smart young Asian guys, who'd watched them for ages from opposite platform, scarpered. Odd how they'd hung around at a rail station but hadn't got a train. Everybody agreed they'd seemed unusually interested in run-of-the-mill filming. Nothing wrong with that. Film crews, even tiny ones, got an audience. Sarah wondered if the guys had been screwballs, ogling her and Vanessa.

Big question was if the Royal Train would reach Wilmslow. TV insisted it would but Hunter wasn't so sure. Funny how, after two massive explosions, Alex Freeman got wheeled on live from Westminster after each saying no need to worry about the Royal Train. He'd reassured the media and the country. But his smooth flap-jowling came across like crypto codespeak, getting Hunter wondering where his game was at.

Vanessa's phone rang. Guys at Milton Keynes, saying the train was nearly there but running seven minutes late. Hunter knew Royal Trains ran on time. Other camera crews had called from Bushey and Kings Langley, saying they'd shot their stuff. Train had been punctual going past each. Meaning the delay happened between Kings Langley and Milton Keynes. Kings Langley guys said two gunships had taken off after the train. Something was going on. Hunter knew it.

He brought up *BBC News* on the Nexus. Sure enough the train was approaching Milton Keynes. Station kitted in Royal bunting, little pics of HRH hanging still, due to lack of breeze.

Security stuff was happening. Cops on the platform ushered back a large crowd. Studio black guy explained how security had been tightened with North Dean going up so soon after Sheffield. Nobody would be allowed near the train while it was at the station. He cued a bubbly young blonde live on Platform 1.

'What's happening, Sue?'

Cut to cute popsicle, foam-nipple lolly mike nearly as big as her rosy face. She turned to give viewers a look-see as cops drove back teeming multitudes. Cut to car park exterior as everybody got squeezed outside.

'After changing drivers the train will depart quickly to make up for some lost time,' she said over exterior shot. Back to her on Platform 1. 'Royal driver change-overs happen because they're restricted to a three-hour shift. Current driver took the train from Wolverton to London this morning. He'll be replaced by soon-to-retire local driver Bill Martin'—up came pink retro Swatch for a time check—'in about a minute.'

Reynolds watched the Beeb news report on his phone and heard the blonde big up BM. She needed shagging to shut her up. She cued BM's mugshot, saying he was known to the Queen who preferred to surround herself with familiar faces.

That made Reynolds go *ha*.

He stood up as the train thundered into the station, its shiny nose hotspotting sun.

Moving across, he got near yellow flag guy. On dinged the station announcer but Reynolds didn't really hear 'cause suddenly he got emotional. Trains did that. Feeling weirdly patriotic, he was pulled two ways. Committing the ultimate crime but deep down quite liking Her cocky little shit-heap of a country.

Platform trembled when the loco arrived, pristine, spoilt only by insect splats covering her bullet nose. She hardly had cab windows. Just cool looking angled slits. Growling in his face, she gave off a funny pong 'cause of her revolutionary bio fuel. Reynolds was spooked by the overwhelming size and power of the beast, now she was in front of him. Practise runs and sim tests had led to this. Scary last minute jitters most actors got before they walked on stage. His time had come.

Cab door popped and slid sideways, like it had decompressed. Out came a rough-as-hell short-arse, fifty-ish with a squashed up boxer's mug, incongruously togged Royal like Reynolds but doing Elvis hair.

'Awright Bill,' he said. 'We stopped off at Leighton Buzzard. Another security check after all these bombs. Internal phones are up the spout 'cause they've knackered summat they can't fix till Manchester. Keep your mobile switched on, in case Chris needs you.'

Reynolds hadn't got BM's phone, which was switched off. Excuses could be made about why BM wasn't contactable. Freeman had also fixed phones aboard the train so driver wouldn't have to speak to Train Officer (TO). Real reason for Leighton Buzzard stop. Reynolds was a cool BM double but talked nothing like. TO was at the back. Never went through the Queen's carriages, except in emergencies. Between Reynolds and the Queen were the kitchen car and catering staff.

Nobody would come near.

He climbed aboard and hit the door button, making it slide-and-pop in reverse, sealing him in with a cool hiss. In terms of design, to a guy of Reynolds's generation the cab was like a cross between some outrageous gaming console and the cockpit from the spaceship Altares. Snap-together blow-moulded modular this and that. All rounded corners and groovy split lines.

Recessed computer screens side bunked, flashing red, green, or blue across anything shiny. Central, a padded grey-and-black leather pilot seat enclosed him memory-foam snug.

He did safety harness buckle stuff. Signal up ahead did amber-to-green. Driving Amtraks was about computers as much as it was about lever cranking and button pushing. If he'd programmed the kit he'd have made every driver have a unique password. They hadn't done it that way. All he had to do was stick real BM's driver ID card in an ATM slot. In it went.

Kit beeped. Loco seemed to relax around him. Taking hold of her twin joysticks, he eased them back. Just like a jet fighter. Away she went. Buzz Reynolds got helming such a monster was out of this world. If this was the future, boy was he up for it.

Soon as he was up to speed he pulled his phone and hit the boss's number.

'We're on,' he said, after Poulson hello'd.

When Poulson heaped praise, Reynolds heard a rousing full-house HQ cheer.

23

Pover had finished at Crewe Gateway, distancing himself to park in Lockitt Street, across main tracks. North of Crewe Station, it was a no-man's land of weeds and shiny steel palisade zinging sun. He'd expected cops and trainspotters 'cause of the grandstand POV. Not so. He was on his tod.

Through fence up front was the station throat. Crewe Gateway opposite, where three lines diverged, gave the signalbox a name. Left and straight ahead went to Chester, North Wales, Liverpool. Right—the Royal Train's route—went to Manchester. Signalbox overlooked the triple split. Part of it carried on the *Thunderbirds* thing, reaching across massed tracks.

On the next seat sat his open laptop, Crewe Gateway's track diagram up on screen. It showed the Royal Train had just left Milton Keynes. An hour till it showed and Pover lobbed a serious spanner in the works. Game on. Meanwhile, out came a double BLT and a Coke courtesy of Tesco Express. He popped the can, pulled the sarnie vacpack, sniffed, and got munching.

It was gonna happen like this.

When the Royal Train hit Crewe Station and took the Manchester line, Pover would control schematics right to the junction where disused tracks broke off to Twemlow, twenty-one miles north.

Guys at Crewe Gateway would see the train doing Manchester on the box's cool 3D track dio. They'd still see it doing Manchester when it had done a bunk. Pover would tell the box computer one thing while stuff happening did another. Everybody would see HRH heading north when she wasn't. He'd also control tracks so he could switch junction points. By time shit hit the fan it would be too late. Royal Train would have stopped at overgrown twee Twemlow Station, where Connors and some brick shit-houses would bundle HRH away.

Pover had promised himself to make sure he switched back points. If he didn't, the express following HRH would crash when it hit wrongways tracks at 140mph, when Crewe Gateway said they were clear. Only thing left to do was for Ross to hook up track circuit breakers near Twemlow Junction.

Pover finished sarnie one, knocked back Coke, belched, and got to it with sarnie two. Halfway through, he heard approaching wheels. Nearside wingmirror showed a white Range Rover, chucking dust where Lockitt Street's lumpy blacktop ended and ruts and baked clay began. Making an entrance, banging big music, the RR swept round and pulled up, maybe twenty metres from Pover. It finished close to razorwired ten-foot steel fence keeping the railway strictly out of bounds.

Driver door opened. Frankie Goes to Hollywood's *Two Tribes* blasted out, air raid sirens and Patrick Allen getting excited. Two smooth young Asian guys. Mirror-shaded, like crime boys. Pover eased off on the sarnie chewing when he got a funny feeling.

Frankie kicked in as driver boy got out kitted in tracker gear. Ripping a velcro tit pouch, he pulled Marlboros, lit one, and paced down and up, sucking like his life depended on it. Moseying across to some fence, he watched a Pendolino haul past, doing central track to where Pover's North Welsh brethren hung out.

Guy footstomped to blaring music. Sunspots flared off his shades when he turned to give Pover some face.

Other guy got out far side of the RR, nursing a laptop. As he came into view, half boogying to the infectious music, Pover's sarnie chewing stopped.

Guy was dolled in padded black leather biker pants, going to town on trendy stitching and stretch spandex. Shiny embossed groin arch made it look like he'd got a big packet. Cop-style boots, Gothy-chunky, gave him height. His Cody combat waistcoat matched the pants. Seemed like he had a deformed mouth. But good strong arms made it look like he worked out.

Setting his laptop on the RR's bonnet, he got busy with stuff on screen. Pover saw video. Heard a tinny explosion through his open window. Sensed a nuke flash happen just before a guy swore for England.

Down went a gobful of masticated BLT.

Serious bad vibe time.

Too much Royal stuff at stake.

Pover needed to turn scarce.

He wondered if the guys knew he was there. When he poked the ignition they hardly noticed. He checked his rearview when he took off.

Through dust he sent up he saw sidekick reach in the RR for a Costa Ice. Next time he looked, the guy lifted the RR's back hatch to check something big, hidden under a sheet.

Randeep finished tweaking Hunter's effing and jeffing, shot at Wilmslow when North Dean went pop. Nahid banged down the RR's back hatch then noisily sucked dry his Costa Ice with a plastic straw.

After Wilmslow, they'd beaten a hasty retreat through the airport tunnels to the M56 and M6. Change of togs at Knutsford Services then a dash down to Crewe to see the Royal Train pass through a historically important railway station. Sense of things cranking before they let rip with a big gun. Frankie screamed, music hammered, proving quality Britpop was alive and well in the mid 80s till A&R killed it, according to Randeep's dad.

'We're cutting it fine,' Nahid told him, reaching in the RR to knock back the din.

'It's part of the buzz.'

'Train's less than an hour away.'

'We've plenty of time. I want to get this done so we can e-mail Hunter the link.'

Next up in *Hunter: the Movie,* a handover scene Nahid shot at Waterloo Station, when Hunter gave his kids back to the ex-wife after he'd had them for the weekend. Meaning the pretty little blonde who looked like the ex but seemed closer to Hunter than the dark one (who looked like him) was getting tearful. Nahid had zoomed nice and tight. Sound was loose. But when Randeep lost some bottom end, and notched Treble, dialogue became sufficiently audible. Blurry figures wiping frame added to a fly-on-the-wall feel.

Little blondie cried and sniffed in that plaintive way small kids do, refusing to go with sis and Sloaney mummy. 'I'm not going with them until you come home and be my real daddy again.'

Hunter knelt and cuddled her, stroking her long straight hair.

'I am your real daddy, sweetheart.'

'Then why don't you live with us and read us bed-time stories like you used to?'

Pert little voice was insistent.

Squashed between, seeming to demand an answer too, was a chunky handknitted Rupert Bear.

'Please Daddy,' little blondie pleaded.

'I'm so sorry, sweetheart.'

You could feel Hunter's heartbreak as he wrapped her in his big arms, trying to console her.

'Aww,' Nahid said. 'Dontcha wanna cry?'

'To be fair,' Randeep noted, 'the ex shat on him. He took a hike when he found out she was being poked.'

Cut to a short bald guy with a heavy gut, stood self-consciously with the ex, pretending to check his phone while they waited for little blondie to finish muling. Jump-cut to kids walking away with ex and the fat guy. Finish on shiny-eyed soppy daddy, kneeling at marble floor, looking like his world had ended.

'This is good stuff,' Randeep said. 'Like a decent mo-vie trailer it sells an emotional story. One more clip and it'll be ready.'

As if cued, e-mail pinged his Inbox.

'My God here it is.'

He popped it open and hit Download.

'How will he take it?'

'How would you react if your personal life and loved ones had been raped for a movie?'

'I'd be wondering about the blonde bombshell who was my latest cum bucket.'

'Succinctly put as usual.' Download finished. 'Speaking of our blonde bombshell, look at this.'

He imported the new footage. Slid it one way then a few frames back the other. Trimmed it at the head and added some video snow.

Hunter: the Movie was done.

Cruelly amused, he played it through.

Frankie faded in the RR. Last track on *80s Now,* meaning they heard loco stuff happening on the busy railway behind. It meant they also heard every word in the new clip all crisp and clear.

Sometimes Randeep was appalled at himself. At the evil men could do.

24

Cockney Roy "the Jackhammer" Ross.

Standing atop a railway cutting, near Sandbach.

Sun-a-scorching. High blue sky. Happy birds-a-tweeting. Jackhammer 'cause of his lethal left hook which had KO'd enough times with one swing to get him seen by Connors. Beady-eyeing West Coast main tracks, now Pover and Reynolds were doing their stuff.

Next to him, black ex-US football player Jason Thinnes. A brick shit-house, not quite on the scale of Connors but a serious contender. Over in Cool B for a cash-rich ride. His expertise: nothing specific. Instead he was a good all-rounder whose dry humour and solid reliability made him eminently likeable. He also understood bridges having blown up a fair few. Today he wouldn't pack Semtex under the skew arch brick rail bridge near where he stood with Ross, faffing with his X-treme tool belt. But bridge detail such as "chamfered acute quoins" and "stepped extrados" would have gone in.

New concrete steps complete with handrail ran down to tracks. Good news for Royal Train jackers. Health and Safety worried about rail maintenance gangs butt-slipping on wet grass, getting tempted by ambulance chasing 0800 ads talking No-Win, No-Fee.

'Sign of the bleeding times,' Ross despaired, uber Cockney, educating his tall American chum about how H&S made UK crime such a doddle.

He sounded like Michael Caine. So much so he once caused a laff saying Thinnes was only supposed to blow a bloody door off a Zurich bank job but got carried away and totalled half the street.

Down steps they bootclumped, laptop handed, togged as signalling guys, till they hit gravel packed under tracks. Holding them firm. Letting them breathe. Draining water so zillion-ton projectiles, flying past at 100+ mph several times an hour, plus lazy locals, didn't find a quagmire and sink into Mummy Earth.

Crunching gravel now.

Target: junction box two hundred metres away. Grey-yellow steel sci-fi thing oozing bio-mechanic cables and wires like some weird homage to HR Giger.

Pover should have set up at Crewe Gateway and got scarce. But Ross knew that as soon as they overrode the network, computers would go potty. They'd have thirty secs to KO the system before guys at starship consoles sussed gremlins in the works.

To complete the isolation, Ross needed to hook up with Pover at Sandbach to break the circuit. Meaning he had to access the junction box which is why Thinnes got down next to him, unzipping belt pouches. Out came a neat piece of kit he'd cooked from a phone. He rubber-sucked it to the junction box outer and switched on. Box was alarm-linked to Crewe Gateway.

Easy to KO, if you knew how.

Ex-phone beeped to say alarm override had boogied. Thinnes got to work with a cordless powerdrill, driving a titanium bit through steel outer in a jiff.

In with squidgy stuff and the guys crunched gravel back a short way. Thinnes nursed his laptop, checking they'd no audience from nearby bridge. Cheek-puffing at the hot day, he keypad typed. Junction box smoked and a little bang happened. Doors popped open, exposing a fibre-optics bag of knitting.

Ross was Blutoothed, ready for when Pover came on line. 'We're in, Glyn,' he said, joining Thinnes on bended knees back at the junction box. Both hooked up laptops fast. No reply from Pover. 'You there, boyo?' Still nothing. 'Shit. Come on you daft Welsh git.'

Thinnes checked his laptop.

'Six minutes fifty-eight,' he said all deep American, meaning how long till next train. Lines sang as faint vibrations fed along continuous welded rails. Long time since they were butt-joined with fish-plates. Clickety-clacks were no more.

'Jesus Pover,' Ross said. 'Come on.'

'Calm down dear,' Pover said back, mimicking Michael Winner's old TV ads.

'Where the hell are you?'

'Right now, I'm in Tesco's car park on this glorious hot day, eyeing pretty young girls all scantily clad. And I'm thinking that when God made this earth he made just two things. Women and the Welsh.' Ross sensed him reverse-park while he cranked the piss-take. 'That Ross, you southern English twat, is called a joke.'

'What you doing at Tesco's?'

Pover got serious and killed his motor.

'Two big time tossers gave me the creeps. I needed to be near folk and stuff happening.'

Connors came on line. They were doing open frequency, so they could chat all-ways.

'Hey Glyn. How goes it?'

'Good Craig. Everything's ready. Just telling Roy about two cool young Asian guys. Would like to have seen HRH go through but I can do my bit from here.'

'Did you say cool Asian guys?'

'Two of 'em.'

'Where?'

'By the railway, when I'd parked.'

'Jesus Glyn. What were they like?'

'Why?'

'Goddammit just tell me.'

'Good looking, in flash wheels. One togged like he was up for some gay clubbing. Odd for this time of day, now I think about it.'

'What were they driving?'

'Fancy exec white Range Rover.'

'Get back over there.'

'No point. They've gone. Saw 'em hitting Vernon Way in front of the supermarket, when I drove round looking for a space.'

'Shit. You mean they hauled?'

'Yeah.'

'Where did they go?'

'Dunno. Headed off north. What's it about Craig?' No reply. 'Craig?' He'd gone.

25

Connors was driving the Hummer away from Twemlow Station when he heard what Pover said. Kath sitting next to him. Nobody else aboard.

As he turned off station overbridge into the lane, he hit Freeman's number via buttons at the wheel. Freeman took time answering. Gave Connors time to take in the island platform as he trod gas. Guys were ready. Twelve tough-as-hell handpicked bastards. Swiping flies. Chewing gum. Looking very *Expendables,* big-gunned in designer shades.

Like Kath, everybody was dressed for Brit army desert combat. Only stuff Poulson could get hold of. In the excitement nobody would see desert troops. Freeman was gonna brainwash Royal Train Officer to expect a military escort 'cause of a "terrorist threat". Morning's two mystery mega bangs kinda helped.

Freeman was at an airbase, going by background noise. Sounded pissed. Like Connors bugged him when he needed to be some place else.

'Craig. I'm about to board a gunship.'

'Our two international playboys, Alex. One of my guys might justa seen 'em.'

'Where?'

'Crewe Station. Looking like they were ready to party. Get some aircops checking up here ASAP. White Range Rover. It's gonna shine against sun-scorched Cheshire green. Gotta be them. I'm telling ya, two bangs are gonna make three.'

'OK will do.' He covered his phone to mumble stuff off mike. Connors was pissed 'cause he couldn't talk to Freeman properly when he needed.

Again he looked at his Dirty Dozen on the platform, before they got blanked where the cutting got deep.

Hardware was for effect. Nobody seriously expected any muzzle flash. As jobs went they'd got little to worry about on the personal injury front. Guys on both sides would take extra special care in the presence of frail HRH. Big issue would be managing armed transport cops when they spilled off a Royal choo choo at a remote station stop.

Freeman came back.

'OK done that. I also took your advice and had the train checked at Leighton Buzzard. It was clean but I've sent a couple of gunships your way.'

'Where you at, Alex?'

'Flying over to Chequers to see the PM.'

'Jesus. If only the poor guy knew.'

He grinned at Kath.

Great girl.

She'd joined eleventh hour. Only group member at Twemlow from the Bill Martin hit. Connors had OK'd it for her to be in on the big one 'cause Reece had something going with her. She'd left HQ soon after Connors and Reece left that morning. Made sure she gave BM some time first. Called at her mom's on the way up. Connors knew she'd personal stuff going on. But he was easy, seeing as he was secretly fixing it with the guys for her kid to get his op.

As Connors thought about it Freeman came back saying, 'It's a dirty world, Craig. No point moaning.'

'Yeah,' he said, seeing Kath's dying kid.

'Good luck, Craig. I'm sure our Bermuda Triangle event will go well in your capable hands.'

'Yeah,' he said again.

Mute dash TV showed the Royal Train blast through Nuneaton.

Dramatic air shots whizzed in, out, up, away. Not live heli, since bogeyman Freeman made Royal airspace NG. Repeat ITV chopper shots pre-Milton Keynes action-movie-opening-style. Final one caught the train swinging round, hotspotting sun. Roof louvres heat shimmered as lead power car swept under camera.

'Tell your boys not to swear in front of Her Majesty,' the bogeyman said, doing dud Brit toff

'Done it, Alex.'

'Ciao,' he said, sounding awfully jolly.

'Yeah,' he said, final time.

Freeman broke call.

HRH is a very old lady, Connors had told the guys, a scuffed gunmetal and see-through-orange-bits Sheuze shotgun propped at his shoulder, while he marched down and up. *You'll be amazed how tiny she is. Five-two or -three. You'll treat her like your granny. Or as if you're helping an old dame cross a road. And you'll check your language if cops get spooked and go mouthing off.*

Mercenaries were like film crews.

Fed off director buzz.

Connors was directing arguably the biggest action movie of all time but suddenly his head was muggy. Despite Hummer aircon he needed real thing.

When glass right of his face lost itself, what blew in was hot-house hot.

Pissing him off.

116

Making him realize he'd gotten a crazy funny queasy goddamn feeling.

26

'Go from there,' Hunter said.

'Here?' said Gordon.

'Backwards from the bang.'

Everybody was sitting on a seat on the island platform, in hot shade. Gordon had the laptop on his knee, after uploading everything they'd shot.

For Hunter, a cool thing about modern filmmaking was how you could edit on set or on location. Big drawback of the old ways was realizing shots were missing when you had a rough cut and needing to go back to get "pick-ups". Even top Hollywood directors, doing storyboarded-to-death mega bucks movies, screwed coverage, realizing months later when actors and sets were history. Roughing out a film on the day on a laptop let you do off-the-wall stuff. Or grab extra shots if they flew into your head.

They were checking the bit when North Dean blew and Hunter spoke to camera. Something bugged him.

Something he could sense happened on the opposite platform when the oil terminal tanked. Subliminal impression. Itch at the back of his mind.

Gordon crept back the action then hit Play. When the bomb *vadoomed* Hunter talked to camera, hands going with enthusiasm as he went on about the Royal Train's bio fuel. Flash lit him and he swore, ducking from shot. Secs later Vanessa swung the camera round on Gordon's shoulder. Distant massive fireball came jerkily into view, rolling up. Debris flew to high summer sky, pipes twisting, boomeranging almost in slow-mo.

Hunter took the laptop off Gordon and crept the film in reverse for himself. Fireball sucked backwards, going from where it had come, behind trees. As the camera swung through one-eighty back to Hunter pre-bang, it wiped opposite platform.

He slowed everything right down, to see what happened across tracks.

The two young guys who'd been watching them were sitting there. Laptop guy, phone in hand, looked like he'd called somebody and was grinning. That was all. Amazingly he didn't seem to register mega bang-flash. Neither guy did which was odd.

Sarah's phone video next. Much lower res.

She'd been looser, swinging round to shoot Hunter from her beloved Dutch angle. She'd guessed framing from waist height, adding to a grungy, improvised feel. Similar to main camera stuff, but a few secs sooner, it also wiped the two guys opposite.

Laptop guy said something to his phone.

Looked like one word.

Hunter maxed his mouth tight. Sharpened it and let the laptop's fancy onboard software go to work. Image Scan meant video could be lip-read. Even blurry stuff with faces tiny. Laptop went through motions, scanning with a stop-motion swipe. *Gerdunged* and superimposed a word blink-fast-rapido on screen:

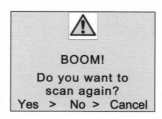

⚠️

BOOM!
Do you want to
scan again?
Yes > No > Cancel

Hunter fingered No.

Laptop guy says *boom* just before the station gets lit by a mini nuke, in blazing sunshine? In other words, he *knew* a bomb was gonna go off. His eyes were on where the flash happened but he had his phone at his ear when he said *boom*.

'Boom,' Hunter said amazed, baffled.

'Boom,' Vanessa repeated.

'He knew it was gonna blow,' Sarah added.

'How could he?' Vanessa wondered.

'Like he triggered it,' said Hunter.

'Never,' said Gordon, gobsmacked.

'Impossible,' Harry chipped in, from seat's end.

A student runner arrived with the carry cooler, loaded with new drinks. Not long now till the Royal Train. 'What's up, you guys?' he asked, setting down the cooler, *fdunking* open the lid.

119

They told him while he crouched, handing out ice-cold full bottles. 'Maybe he set if off with a phone call,' he offered, like it happened all the time. 'You do it in *Urban Spite*. It's crucial to Molotov's killing spree.' He was referring to an extremely violent video game.

'Jesus Christ,' Hunter said, turning cold as fresh fizzy water he'd popped. 'If he knew the bomb was gonna go, if somehow he set it off, then why the hell were he and his chum so interested in us?'

27

Reynolds powered through Stafford Station.

Typical West Coast mainline boxy stuff, a 1962 re-build, it had been part of the Modernisation Plan, pre-Beeching. Reynolds knew because he was interested. All Brutalist drab slab concrete dashed with pebbles, it looked better on period ads full of naïve optimism and nice-painted passengers, none of whom were fat.

His track was inside second left of four running dead straight, meaning he could stay fast. Flag wavers and photographers had gathered, as they had at stations all the way. Seeing flag patriots left him feeling embarrassed and guilty. Kids especially, cheering the Royal driver like he was as special as the Queen. At Nuneaton two kids had held up a feeble BM crayon scribble. It cut Reynolds up, knowing he'd denied BM seeing it on his last run. Drawback of being educated, intelligent, doing dirtiest work, was ending up victim of your own lousy conscience.

What he hadn't expected was the buzz he got from doing speed. He was enjoying himself so much he imagined a career move. Freeman's cool virtual reality sim had done its job. Reynolds recognized everything from West Coast drives he'd done for two months.

Clattering near soundlessly across Stafford's northern point maze he hit last lap. Upcoming crossovers did the weird high-speed thing where they zipped-unzipped as they fed under the loco. Opposite way trains flashed by as colour blurs.

When he hit 140mph, computer beeped to tell him max speed had happened.

Auto limiter. Pity. Royal Trains used to run slower, so regal passengers enjoyed a smooth ride. Modern tracks were so good they went fast as their subjects. Much rail upgrading to do meant 200mph was still a long way off. Not far now. Blutoothed, he was ready.

Time to catch up with the guys.

'Mike's the hero in this,' Connors told Kath.

On went their shades as the Hummer alarm-pipped behind them. They'd driven down to rural Twemlow Junction. Keeping back dense pines from the railroad was silver spiky fence which ran everywhere in a UK loopy on injury compensation. Disused tracks, rusty, overgrown, broke from the mainline and bent away through a cutting loaded with pink-magenta stuff Brits called willowherb but Connors knew as fireweed.

Reynolds had just called to say everything was good. Tramping ferns, Connors added, 'Not only has he pulled off a spooky Bill Martin impression. He taught himself to do scariest drive. Also, he's committed treason 'cause he's abducted HRH. Punishment in Cool Britannia for treason is supposed to be death.'

'Yeah I think you're right,' Kath said.

Because it was a rail junction, ground spread to give support vehicles access through electro locked double palisade gates.

Connors flicked open a keypad set in the frame and overrode its securicode using some nifty blackbox kit cooked up by Thinnes.

He poked chrome studs embossed with numbers and squeaked open a gate.

'No real need for us to be here.'

'Why are we?'

'Experience tells me never to assume anything will go to plan.' He nodded at junction points. 'Everything depends on those switching when Pover kills our section of track and hoodwinks Crewe Gateway.'

'What could go wrong?'

'Nothing in theory. Everything's automated. When Pover patches into the circuit he'll control the points. I'd just like to see it happen.'

Afternoon sun beat down.

Pines fended it.

Big sense of calm cut off from the outside world in a remote rural place next to a railroad. Bees and flies buzzed loaded stillness. Day sweltered. Oppressed. But sun was gonna lose it soon 'cause big clouds were piling ominously east.

Seeing them Connors got jittery, like when he'd talked to Freeman. Something was in the air.

'Calm before the biggest storm in British history,' he said, eyeing stacked clouds. He got back to what he was gonna ask Kath during the drive down, before Pover hit off about two mystery playboys. 'Hey I'm sorry,' he said. 'How's the little guy?'

'Poorly but stable,' she told him.

'What about the boy's dad?'

'Long gone.'

'Mom takes care of him?'

'While I'm on this gig. House in Hanley, Stoke-on-Trent. I don't think you have them so small in the States. Built for factory people. Pottery workers actually, where I grew up. My dad was a labourer. Died of a heart condition when I was four. We never had much money.'

'You had your mom,' Connors said, 'which is more than I had when I was a kid.'

They crunched gravel across to twin tracks. Concrete sleepered, dead straight, they did heat-hazy perspectives from each direction. Railroad tracks always seemed more imposing from the ground.

'Is there a Mrs Connors?'

'Used to be,' he said.

Crouching to the rails, he tapped nearmost with some fingers. Cody combat vested, smelling soapy clean but beginning to sweat, he was aware of his massive bulging arms embossed with veins.

'Also long gone. She took our new-born baby girl.'

Swiping flies, he got his head thinking back.

Memories which still hurt.

He liked how easy he felt about them next to Kath. As with most tough girls, noise she made in front of guys, fire tattoos burning her arms, were tribal human nature stuff to get her noticed. Hiding behind it was another insecure girl, desperate to find Mr Right.

'How old is your daughter?' she asked him, crouching with him.

Rails started singing vaguely.

'Eighteen.' Gazing at where tracks pointed to Crewe he picked up some gravel and chucked it. 'Never seen her,' he said. The gravel tinked something. 'Some years I have to try and remember how old she is.'

Pissed after all, he shook his head.

Rails sang louder.

'This is it,' he said, looking sharp. 'Singing starts miles off and HRH is still five or six away. But this is our Chattanooga.'

He stood up.

'If you wanna go back and chill with the guys, that's OK. I can tag a lift on the train.' He knew it was a mindless non-starter, soon as he said it.

'I'll stay.'

She stood up grinning but lifted her shades so Connors could see her smiley blue eyes. He gave it some high fives. Kath smacked hard.

28

Reece was Blutoothed, ready.

Guys stood about in muggy heat, waiting for a VIP train to call. Covered wooden steps connected the trashed overbridge building with the island platform. Rusty tracks split each end. Ran round, met again, and curved away under another overbridge. Track had been lifted from opposite platform. The station had been shut just a few years. Might have been shut forever, going by how fast nature had taken over.

Kath's red Cherokee cabriolet was parked in the overgrown station car park, next to a black double-decker Aztramonika USA tourer coach. Home to the guys for 48 hours till call-to-action. Soon after she got there, Kath went off with Connors in the Hummer.

Reece wondered if he might have something with her, if he wanted it. It had been a quick physical thing when they made the Transit rock at dawn. But they'd felt something afterwards, while they lay staring at the van ceiling like lovestruck teens. Last thing he'd expected when Connors hired him was getting soppy over girly stuff when he was second commanding the ultimate crime against UK's number one lady. Wanting Kath got him thinking about his role. Funny guilty feeling came on which he didn't like.

Young black Scouser, Webb, broke it.

'Why aren't we losing HRH on the mainline?'

'Another train might run into the back of hers. Plus getting a frail old woman down off a train is more hassle than walking her out onto a platform.'

'Do you feel bad about it being the Queen?'

'Bad's wrong word,' he said, standing near a bent sign naming an English country station lost to the mists of time. Sunshine faded as clouds rolled in from the east. Day was getting pre-storm close.

Along the platform guys chatted, eyes shade-blanked, posing for each other's phone pics. Nobody smoked. Place was a tinderbox with so much dry grass. Nobody had wisecracked about a tough girl being aboard. Said as much about Connors as the guys.

'None of us would be here if killing had been our brief,' Reece added. 'Freeman needs to lose her. Has his reasons. Not for us to ask why, or wonder why supposedly well-bred guys high up in this country are so corrupt. We do a job. We deliver. We get paid. We disappear. Most of us play dirty. But Craig doesn't go round killing old ladies. He chose us 'cause he knew we were sad bastards who felt the same.'

Knowing we're tough as shit but have kept hold of some humanity, his head told him.

'Craig seems like a smart guy,' Webb said.

Reece agreed, eyeing the gathering storm.

'Behind the bluster and biceps and the Stallone copycat look he's smarter than we think. Way smarter than toffs like Poulson and Freeman realize.'

Pover had his laptop on his knee.

It was crazy. No, insane.

Key dramatic moment and where was he at? In a van at Tesco's, shoppers trolley-pushing this way, thatta way. Bawling kids dangling from mummy arms 'cause it was the school summer hols. Prosperous Middle England enjoyed another boiling day. In their midst a Blu-toothed hairy Welsh cornflake twiddled a laptop, kicking off one of history's uber crimes.

On screen, HRH had recently left Crewe. Minutes till the hit. He watched a stylized virtual Royal Train pulse-ping along his track dio. Craig and Reynolds should be online. Ross and Thinnes had retreated to bush cover.

'You there, Mike?' Pover asked.

'Here,' Reynolds said. 'Just left Crewe and hit Manchester stretch. Reckon I'm invisible. Loving every sec of every minute. Sure will be sad when it's over. Might take up train driving.'

'Craig?'

'Yeah here Glyn. Standing near tracks to see it happen. I wanna remind you guys what a great job you've done. It's gone like a dream. You hearing, Reece?'

'Yup. Into final countdown hoping we miss the storm. Say "hi" to Kath for me.'

'Reece says "hey", Kath.'

'Hey,' she said off-mike near Connors, joined by some back bird twitter.

'OK girls, concentrate please,' Connors said. 'This is it. We're into closing moments. Plentya time for socializing at the after-gig bash.'

Pover got ready.

After months of work it boiled down to him and a finger. Three miles to go became two became one.

'Good luck guys,' he said. 'Finally we switch points.' He typed and whacked Enter. Crewe Gateway heedless. Phew, phew, triple phew. 'Wahoo,' he said, and puffed his cheeks.

29

Connors crunched gravel near the points. Far distant at Crewe end he saw the Royal Train come into view under a brick arch, still tiny. Silver nose winked at him after bridge shadow wiped it. Closing fast.

'OK Glyn,' he said.

'OK Craig.'

Connors didn't get Pover's drift.

'Switch the points.'

'Just did.'

'No you didn't.'

'Yeah, I did. Screen tells me they switched. Everything's A-OK my end.'

'And I'm telling ya they ain't switched.'

'Hell no,' Pover said, and swore big time.

'Shit,' Connors said. Told Kath, 'See what I said about stuff not going to plan? I musta jinxed it.'

Gathering clouds had timed to stuff going wrong. He lost his shades and got down next to the points, or turnout as he knew them back home.

Oily railroad track smell came up.

Kath asked him for the Hummer's key fob and dashed back. No time to ask why. Next to the points switchbit was a shiny steel circuitbox, maybe eighteen inches by ten. 'Try again,' Connors told Pover. Blutooth-free ear to steel, he saw a Royal choo choo getting bigger by the sec under hazy high-blue-grey.

Dull buzz in circuitbox.

'It's shorting Glyn.'

'Any gubbins near the points?'

'Got my ear to a box thing.'

'New looking?'

'Galvanised steel with aloominum gnurled bits. Looks like it's not been here long. Hey wait.' Same time he remembered seeing fresh tyre tracks when he arrived with Kath he saw a barcode sticker slapped on the box end under clear poly. 'I don't believe it,' he said, spotting a hand scrawled date. 'ATP anti-system override.'

'Automatic Train Protection?'

'Looks like it. Put in two days ago.'

Connors remembered something Poulson said ages ago. After some train accidents caused by dud points in remote places, Network Rail had been upgrading junction tracks. New fail-safe only let tracks switch via signals sent from signalboxes. Stopped track repair boys leaving them switched wrong ways when they walked from a job. Pover had overridden it. Except he'd switched points from a remote laptop, not by whacking keys at a Crewe Gateway console. System override had done its job. Connors recced junction points twice. He couldn't have predicted them being fluky list-latest two days before the hit.

'Sorry, Craig,' Pover said, sounding like he'd let down the side.

'Not your fault. Screwy stuff happens.'

Kath came back carrying a sledgehammer. Connors had heard her rooting in the Hummer while he had his ear to steel.

'Good thinking gal.' He stood up and took the hammer from her. 'Kath might justa saved the day. How 'bout we switch tracks manually?'

'You'll never force them, Craig,' Pover said.

'I mean what if I smash the goddamn box?'

'You won't do it. It'll be anti-vandal. Built to withstand close-range artillery fire.'

'Wanna bet? Can you isolate the box if it's alarmed?'

'Hang on.' Typing his end. 'Affirmative.'

Connors got down.

Put his forehead to the box and shut his eyes.

Rails sang louder.

Train gaining.

'What you doing?' Kath asked, amazed.

'Visualizing myself smashing this thing. Imagine doing something before you do it. It's how US basketball players get coached.' He stood up. 'Ever wonder how they get the ball in the net from so far every time? They see themselves doing it in their heads day in, day out. Believe me it works. See your little boy getting his life-saving op and he'll get it.' He winked an eye.

'Wow,' Kath said.

Reynolds wondered what to do as he bore down from a few hundred metres. 'Nearly there Craig. What if the points don't change?'

'Pray they do,' Connors told him.

Rails sang like crazee now.

Connors stood on the track, facing the train.

Took some secs to get in state, seeing the circuitbox in his mind's eye. Vital to see the choo choo nearing but not where the sledgehammer would hit. Success would come *imagining* where it was gonna happen. *That which smashes.* When he nanosec spun to unleash violence, like Thor smashing Mjolnir, his subconscious would channel his energy only when the move to obliterate his target was underway.

'For God's sake, Craig,' Reynolds said, panicking as he closed for the kill. 'I'm gonna run you over.'

Connors told Kath to stay back in case of shrapnel. Train was nearly there. He found time to tell Reynolds, 'Don't release windows, Mike. If cops peek out they're gonna see Kath and me.'

'Yeah don't worry, Craig.'

Reynolds controlled the train's central-locked electric doors and windows.

Then Connors went for it, letting loose his private thermo-blast. With a mad-as-hell yell he shut his eyes and spun-swung giving it everything he'd got. Saw the box zip up tight and smash to a million pieces, radiating from a cosmic flash of total annihilation.

When he opened his eyes most box outer had gone. Steel shattered like wax. Interior wires and circuit stuff feeding mechanics which worked the points had also been demolished.

Sparks happened then he *yeeowwed* at a minor lightning flash and raised an arm.

'Now Glyn,' he said, diving aside when train brakes hissed only a few metres behind him.

Pover did his stuff.

'May the Welsh force be with you.'

Fdunk as the points switched.

'Wahoo,' went Kath, fisting triumphantly.

Cheers over Blutooth, just as the sun went out.

Kath high-fived Connors before they dashed through the gate, so nobody saw them.

Connors turned to see Reynolds thumb-up from the cab window as he eased the Royal Train slowly across junction points onto disused tracks.

Incredible, feeling her so close after so much planning. Crushing fireweed, she did an ugly fingernails-scraping-a-blackboard train noise as she took the sweeping curve, wheel flanges binding metal-on-metal. Because of grassy tracks, Reynolds would do a steady 25mph to the station two miles away.

In the past hour guys had checked tracks were clear of crap. Connors and Kath had maybe six minutes max to get back, ahead of HRH.

30

Randeep and Nahid approached Twemlow village, on the A535. After Crewe they'd hightailed it back up the M6 a short way to Junction 18.

Sunshine had died since they left the motorway. Now fierce clouds massed ahead of a summer storm. Adding to an air of menace, two gunships appeared high overhead. Pummelling the gloomy day with mean Chinooky audio. Hazards partying. Nahid wondered if cops were keeping them company.

'Feels like they're shadowing us.'

'Unlikely, don't you think?'

As they reached twee Twemlow, shreds of sun found ancient cottages then winked out. Lead gunship peeled off, banking over the village. Other kept going to Manchester, over a disused railway north of Twemlow.

They'd cut it fine.

They'd seen the Royal Train approach Goostrey a few minutes ago, losing speed like it was stopping. Shame if they missed it and three million bucks spent on an Arnie gun went west, knocking some snazzy fireworks on the head. As if pre-empting this, as they drove out opposite end of the village, past its broad green, they hit a police roadblock. Parked cop 4x4 in the way. Traffic cones up front. Plods stood about, looking hot and bothered in leather and scuffed Kevlar. Biggest guy held out a hand and came across to meet the RR.

'This'll screw us,' Nahid said, sending down his window as he drew up.

'I think not,' Randeep said, feeling mean.

Fortyish fat cop had beetrooty cheeks and a tea stain 'tache under his nose. High blood pressure had crazed his face with broken veins. 'Road's closed sir,' he told Nahid, stooping to his open window, sniffing catarrh. 'I'm afraid you'll have to turn round.'

Randeep found the cop's eyeline. 'I say old chap. Is it to do with the Royal choo choo?'

'Yes,' he said, looking in the RR, weighing up Randeep, his lisping, his bust mouth, his OTT leathers. 'Area's restricted till the train's well past.'

'You'll have to let us through.'

'I beg your pardon?'

'You must let us through.'

'And why would we do that?'

'Because we have special clearance.'

Gobsmacked cop cosied to the window. Chucking his pals a knowing look, as if to say funtime lads, he said, 'Oh. You have clearance do ya?'

'No, old chap,' Randeep said, in his best upper-middle-class twang. 'We have *special* clearance.' Guffawing OTT, he gave the cop a quick once over. Encumbered in leathers creaking in godawful close pre-thunder heat the padded groin arch was especially eye catching. 'Gosh, this blamed hot weather's a fag isn't it?' Nudging up in his seat, he nodded at the guy's packet. 'Bet the old goolies are stewing, what?'

Oops. Red-rag-to-a-bull time.

Cop hadn't expected that.

Nahid, joining in the wind-up, overdid a pig-snorty laugh. 'Forgive my partner, officer. He lives dangerously in the company of a certain farm animal.'

Cop, doing a hard face, stood back from the RR. 'Out of the vehicle. Both of you.'

'Oh God Nahid,' Randeep said, cranking the Jeeves and Wooster thing. Big blobs of rain hit the windscreen. Spit. Spat. Spot. 'You've dazzled the obese bleeder with your spiffing white teeth.'

'Out of the vehicle,' cop said again. Other cops, sussing something was up, rushed over.

Gunship had got louder since Nahid stopped. Suddenly it came from nowhere, swooping low above the village, scarily of out place in a pic postcard scene. Randeep lost his seatbelt and chucked open his door. Nahid likewise. Rain hit the RR's roof like buckshot.

Randeep got out, holding his phone.

'I say, would you blighters mind if I made a call? Not to my lawyer, I assure you.' He pig-snorty laughed, like Nahid had.

Brewing storm had sent most villagers indoors. Din was incredible as the gunship angled round bum heavy to land. Churning the day, its hazards strobed against steel grey sky flung above ancient saggy roofs.

'Looks like we're buggered,' Nahid said, when the gunship finally dumped itself. Side door slid open, spilling aircops who tonned it across.

'You could be right, old friend,' Randeep said. 'Game up but not quite.' Still he right-handed his phone, his thumb over the button.

Vanessa was on the phone to Jane Kirby, the film student she'd booked to shoot some flypast stuff. Hunter had nipped to the loo. The guys were chilling, ahead of the train coming through.

Jane was a few miles north of Wilmslow, on top of Wellesley House, an old office block off Stockport town centre. She'd patched her baby HD cam live to Vanessa's Nexus. Vanessa watched her frame up like a rooftop sniper. Target from her rooftop POV: Stockport railway viaduct. Grade 2 listed. Twenty-seven tall arches marching across cluttered industrial yards, bodged inner ring roads, and six busy lanes of the M60 running under two brick spans.

The elevated position impressed Vanessa. Instead of setting up on Stockport Station, Jane would show the Royal Train in a historical geographical context. A pioneering railway engineering structure, the viaduct was one of Western Europe's best and one of UK's biggest. Vanessa didn't know if its eleven-million-brick total was achieved before or after it was widened in the 19th century. She knew it from Lowry's paintings.

It was as far as she thought before everything *whoomfed*. Via Jane's Nexus link she saw a container train cross the viaduct from Manchester end going away from camera. Picture white-out and Jane screamed after a mega flash happened too fast for the camera to cope. Vanessa heard a massive bang, tinny over her phone but dull-booming for real from not far off.

Like North Dean when it blew.

31

Connors was right.

Boom # 3 was most direct yet.

As he drove final half mile up the lane and rain came down hard, dash TV showed Stockport had taken another massive hit. Railroad viaduct, north of the station. West Coast mainline was finally a gonner.

'Jeez. This is crap crazy,' he said.

'Surreal,' Kath noted.

'What in hell's name is going on?'

While Connors wheelspun right onto the station over-bridge, trying to get a grip, Beeb big hair girl yakked on about twenty-seven arches and zillions of bricks, blah blah. Problem was, twenty-seven grand brick arches had been reduced to twenty-three.

Big gap at south end. Grey-yellow freight train hanging off like string pearls. Thank God it was the back end which splashed river thirty-four metres down.

TV said fatalities were flukily minimal if not zero. De-railed loco still on the viaduct, lopsided like a beached whale. A large dust cloud wafted across town.

Nearby traffic crawled freeway trying to nosy. When the view shifted to live office top, Connors saw far off dot folks holding up phones. Race would be on to get stuff on Youtube and Twitter.

As if this wasn't enough already, soon as he braked outside the station entrance thunder bang-flashed and Connors sensed trouble. Royal Train had beaten them back. But when he stood up from the Hummer to sling on his Brit army stuff and rain got soaking him, he saw a gunship flying in low. Twisting round it thudded over the station, looking like it meant business. Freeman had sent up two gunships to check out two Range Rover playboys. Connors wondered if he'd diverted this one, so he could lose HRH by air.

Plan was for nearmost bogus roadblock cops to whisk her away before her bodyguards-cum-transport cops knew what had happened. Up to Connors and his guys to deal with them. Surprise on their side, they'd drug them using tranquillizer guns, and leave them sleepy-timing aboard the train, before getting scarce in the Hummer and the crew's big black bus.

Connors saw the gunship come down in a field next to the station. He went in through the ticket office. Covered steps led down to the platform. Frosted glass both sides. Most smashed. From top of the steps, Royal Train filled platform right, its roof shiny with rain. Final two carriages and rear power car made it too long for the station. Front power car was under the overbridge behind him, nosing out other side.

Cops hurried from the gunship through a fireweed jungle which used to be a small freight yard. But it was who Connors saw getting down awkwardly from the gunship that stopped him dead.

'Sweet Jesus. What's he doing here?'

Kath had seen him too.

'I thought he was with the PM, Craig.'

A cop carried a pair of lightweight metal steps, presumably so Freeman could get up to the platform to greet HRH in person. Another cop held an umbrella over him while he swanned across in his flash suit.

'Stay up here,' Connors told Kath.

'What for?'

'Same instinct which sent me down to the junction.' Turning, he booted open the locked ticket office door.

'Hide in there. Freeman knows the guys are here, plus me. But he doesn't know you're here. Something tells me it's best it stays that way 'cause I'm getting a real bad feeling.' In she went shotgun in hand. Connors shut the door. 'Wedge it so they think it's locked.'

'Why would they check?'

'Just do it Kath. For your kid's sake.'

She OK'd and Connors went down steps, wondering what he was gonna find.

Rain had eased. Sky brightened.

Thunder rumbled further off as the day got fresher. Soon as he made platform, he knew something was wrong with the train.

Very wrong.

Sliding doors open all along it but no transport cops. No rail staff. No HRH. All he saw was his guys going in one door, coming out another, desert uniforms wet from rain. Shaking heads, sounding pissed, they appealed to Reece, who came up shaking his head. Water ran off his nose. By now aircops were climbing onto the platform. Reece spoke over the gunship which calmed in its field, turbines humming ominously.

'Train's empty, Craig.'

'You're kidding me.'

'Wish I was. Nobody's aboard.'

'It's a ghost train, boss,' Webb confirmed, stepping from nearmost door, big gun propped back. He clued in some cops but they chucked him deadpan mugs.

Driver Reynolds appeared from under the bridge, ripping off his BM make-up, shit angry when he sussed what was up. 'You mean I went through all that just to drive an empty bloody train?'

Cop down on the track rested metal steps against the platform. Cop with umbrella fussed over Freeman as he nancied up, like he wasn't used to getting more physical than climbing the odd stair.

Two police 4x4s had arrived on the bridge. Loads more cops, armed with machineguns, charged down to join the party.

It was only when Freeman stood up and Connors met his eye that he realized all cops looked like mean bastards, pointing guns. Funny crazy queasy goddamn feeling came back which he had last time he batted words with Freeman on the phone.

'Alex,' he said flatly.

'Craig,' came a knowing reply.

Amazing how two monosyllables could be loaded with so much meaning.

'Choo choo's empty I'm afraid.'

'Oh dear,' Freeman said, fastidiously smoothing his cuff. Seeds and bits of stuff, specking his pants from when he kicked wet grass, bugged him.

When he was sure every mercenary and their brick shit-house leader had two machineguns aimed at them he let some secs fatten, forcing Connors to go first.

Connors got the picture. 'You told me you were flying over to see the PM, Alex.'

'I must have lied.'

'What else have you lied about?'

'Most if it I'm sorry to say.'

141

Reece said, 'You mean we got stitched up?' Seething, he swung up his gun to pump it in Freeman's face, towering over him by a good six inches.

Freeman told Reece, 'There are two of us to one of you, you Irish buffoon. First one of you who steps out of line will be shot. Now, why don't you all do the decent thing and put down your weapons?'

'Screw you bastards,' Reynolds said.

Nearest cop smashed him in the face with his gun butt, knocking him out cold.

Connors had never seen anybody floored so brutally. And he'd seen some real pretty shit in his time. Reynolds landed flat on his back, where platform concrete edge slabs joined old blacktop and small yellow flowers squeezed from cracks. Blood came from his nose. Connors reckoned it was bust proper. Fake BM nose and much of BM's face were on the deck next to him.

High overhead, skylarks came back as the day hotted up again and sunshine steamed grass in nearby fields. Gunship's turbines had lost it so much they *phutted* intermittently, metronoming heavy tension.

'Now for the second time,' Freeman said, 'I shall ask you to down your weapons.'

Gum-chewing beefy Italian-Americano Derosa, bull neck messed by tattoos, pumped his gun. 'You're gonna have to kill me first, you creepy English asshole.'

Freeman said to nobody in particular, 'Americans have a marvellous facility with words.' To the cops he said, 'Aim at heads and hearts of everybody who is currently standing.'

Cops, creaking leather, covered guys two-to-one any-way but looked sharp and adjusted their aim. Red lasers found twin targets on every mercenary on the platform, including Connors.

Freeman said to Derosa, 'Forgive me, young man, but I didn't catch your name.'

'You can call me The Smasher, you piece of lousy god-damn two-faced crap.'

To the cops who'd lasered Derosa's heart and head Freeman said, 'The—uh-hum—"Smasher" gave us an ultimatum. He says we shall have to kill him. Would you oblige? No head damage please. I don't want any unnecessary visceral mess just yet.'

'Huh?' went Derosa, spooking back some steps. 'Huh?' he went louder.

Cop lasering Derosa's gut shot him. Silencered mach-inegun blew away much of his chest, killing him insta-ntly. Guys either side got spattered as they jumped and the big body ricocheted off them on its way to hitting deck. Everybody spread but not too fast, conscious of lasers hotspotting vital bits.

Time stretched a little. Freeman said, 'I shall ask you for a third and final time to down your weapons. Away from the platform, on the track, if you wouldn't mind. Switch off your phones also.'

Reluctantly everybody did as they were told, lobbing hardware first. Connors didn't.

'Craig?' Freeman sounded a tad pissed.

Connors held his shotgun vertical. Reckoned he stood seven, maybe eight inches over Freeman, who was in front of him and by Brit standards was lanky like plenty of his fancy-talking class.

His instincts had warned him.

Reece had a good instinct. It was why Connors had let him second command. A criticism he made of himself was that sometimes he didn't follow his gut till it was too goddamn late.

32

'Where the hell is it?' Hunter said again.

Something was up but everybody was trying to convince themselves the train would still show. It should have hit Wilmslow ten minutes ago. A weird sense of anticlimax hung over the quiet sunny station. Hard grey sky further south flashed every now and then. Storm driving it had stayed away.

Vanessa, holding the Nexus, stood next to Hunter. 'It must have been delayed after Crewe.'

They knew the train had got as far as Crewe because the guy they'd booked who shot it going through the station had phoned to say job done. Hunter phoned him back five minutes ago, when alarm bells started ringing.

Guy wondered if the train had hit duff red lights. Soon after it left Crewe a storm broke.

Hunter wasn't convinced.

Trains couldn't go past Stockport because the line had gone. Ironically, student Jane had shot the viaduct blowing. She was shocked but OK. Vanessa had patched her rooftop POV to the Beeb as an instant live exclusive. TV hadn't said much since.

With security tight on the ground, and airspace NG for media, as far as newsrooms were concerned the Royal Train was still headed north. Only nobody knew where it was. Stockport viaduct going pop said more than Sheffield and North Dean that somebody was out to top the Queen. TV's attempts to contact Alex Freeman's office also kept stonewalling.

'Freeman's probably keeping schtum so nobody can work out where the Queen is,' Hunter said, pacing his bit of platform, hands doing hips.

'Which is why it would make sense to stop the train and get her off it,' Vanessa added.

'Sounds reasonable,' Harry said.

Sarah was on Twitter.

'Guys Tweeting from trains headed south haven't seen the Royal Train,' she said. 'Before Crewe, folk going other ways passed it at regular intervals.'

'Can't be more than a few trains passing it between here and Crewe,' Hunter offered, dropping his shades to gaze hopefully at receding tracks.

A local train slid up to Platform 3 and disgorged passengers. Hunter, getting hemmed in, puffed at the heat and walked a few yards towards platform's south end, running parallel with the subway's glass roof. They'd been allowed to fence it off, so nobody got in shot.

'Surely *somebody* would see it,' Sarah added.

Train eased from the station.

Hunter paced back. Ticket office guy had come up onto Platform 1 across tracks. He looked worried.

'Where's the Royal Train?' Hunter shouted, lifting his shades back up.

'Dunno mate. Computer says it's gone through here. But obviously it hasn't.'

'Your computer must be on the blink.'

'Our feed's from Crewe Gateway. Their computer says the train should nearly be at Stockport. But as far as we're concerned it's done a Bermuda Triangle.'

'Oh my God,' Hunter said, the penny dropping. He'd been mulling such thoughts the more hemmed in he'd got but had avoided facing up to them because it meant admitting the unthinkable. 'If the train should have gone through here but hasn't,' he told the guy. 'If your computer says it's gone through but it hasn't,' he went on, 'it can mean only one thing.'

'What?' everybody asked, including the guy.

'It's somewhere else.'

A few press photographers and some rail enthusiasts had gathered on the platform. One of the trainspotters was around 30, big and tanned in fitted white shirt and stonewashed jeans. He didn't seem nerdy enough to say he was into trains. Hunter forgot this when the guy got all knowy showy and piped up.

'A disused line runs from Twemlow Junction to Knutsford,' he said. 'Tracks haven't been lifted and they still join the main line.'

Vanessa was on Google Earth. 'Here,' she said, showing Hunter the Nexus.

'How long for us to get there?'

She maxed AA Routefinder. 'Twenty-five minutes to the junction, if we pick up the A535.'

'OK let's go.'

He told the runners to stay and man the shop, shooting with their phones if the train showed. Gordon and Harry grabbed the gear.

As they dashed down the subway slope, Hunter glanced back. Bronze boy who clued them in about the shut line had distanced himself from his trainspotter chums to pull his phone. He had a vague limp.

33

Connors couldn't tell what the guy on the phone said but Freeman was happy.

'Excellent,' he said. 'It'll take them about twenty minutes to get here. Call Chelford. Tell them to keep roadblocks up till we're clear. When they're through, shut all roads behind them again within two miles of Twemlow Station, so they have the place to themselves.'

Before the call kicked off, Connors had reluctantly killed his phone and chucked his gun. Freeman indicated they were gonna wrap the scene and lose themselves anytime soon. Meaning upcoming minutes were gonna end in showtime.

Connors itched to know something.

'Where's the Queen, Alex?'

'Secretly removed from the train at Leighton Buzzard,' he said, sticking away his phone, 'along with her staff. Real reason for the stop and a seven minute delay. She was never going to land here.'

'Then why the hell did you have us spend months building up to all this?'

'Because we need to make it look like the Queen really has been kidnapped or killed.'

'You're gonna have to fill us in.'

Freeman paced a little behind beady-eying cops one-to-oneing the guys. 'Star of the show isn't you Craig, or your motley grunt crew, or even the Queen or the Royal Train. It's Hunter.'

'I still ain't getting a picture.'

'This elaborate set-up has been engineered so Hunter comes here with a TV crew and shoots what appears to be the aftermath of a daring Royal kidnap. It'll be his big moment, whipping up a frightening national hysteria. We needed you to help us stage it with absolute authenticity. We needed the world to see the Queen leave the

Palace and board the Royal Train at Euston. Once the journey was underway, we had to persuade the Royal household that something deadly was afoot and that Her Majesty had better vacate the train. Call I took just now was from our man at Wilmslow Station. Put there to put the right thought in Hunter's head at precisely the right moment.'

'So he shoots down here with his guys?'

Before Freeman acknowledged, everybody heard wheels arrive on the overbridge. Connors saw a white roof above rusted plate-iron. Assumed it was a cop 4x4 but realized it was a Range Rover.

A white Range Rover.

Freeman saw it too.

Not a happy bunny.

'I thought we'd sorted that little problem,' he told the goon who'd held the umbrella over him when he nancied across.

'They bunked off at Twemlow before the guys could get them aboard a chopper,' goon said. 'Took the piss out of our lads, big time.'

Connors saw the RR's back hatch go up.

Somebody got something big outta the back.

'Let me guess Alex,' Connors said, getting a picture for a second time. 'Our elusive flash playboys and you might just happen to know each other.'

'Ah yes,' Freeman said, enjoying warm sun, indulging in a satisfied smirk. 'The proverbial denouement. Possibly a bigger story catch than us crapping on you boys.'

'And Sheffield and Stockport?'

'Necessary to help persuade the Queen she'd better leave the train because some exceedingly nasty people really were out to get her. Words I used in poor unsuspecting Sir John Massey's ear were "international terrorists". Stockport viaduct was self-indulgence. Not part of the grand plan.' Sticking on his Oscar Goldman shades he looked at Connors from between fat cop heads. 'Like I told you Craig, there's a lunatic in the asylum who craves big excitement.'

Movement from the stairs coming down from the road. Into view came a monster Sheuze minigun. Young guy swinging it on a steadiframe was Arnie leathered like Pover had said. Guys gave it serious attention with *uh-oh* faces. Most had never seen the gun. Heavy silencered, selling points were its lightness and quietness. Chunky polymer barrels OTT'd with fat twin muzzles, like baked bean cans perfed with holes.

Time for Freeman to round off, now that Hunter would soon show.

Day had got back to summer, coaxing bees and butterflies. Wet platform was drying. Freeman nancied up and down it in front of the guys, like a manager rallying a baseball side before a crucial game.

'This is bigger than any of you can imagine. Bigger than making it seem to our nation and the world that somebody is out to kill the Queen.'

Before he could clue them in, he got irritated, turning his attention back to leather boy, who gun-played behind him like he was ready to have some nasty big gun fun. Freeman nodded discreetly at cop-with-brolly who

150

reached over and flicked something on the gun, pulling what coulda been a SIM.

Gun diodes died as it ka-putted.

'Good thing about analogue kit,' cop told the kid, 'is how it shoots till it jams. This fancy new stuff is all well and good till you lose the chip. Then you're screwed before you start.'

Furious kid stuffed a hand in the gun, trying to make it work. Cops snickered. Connors knew his guys were discreetly searching for strike time. Nobody risked it yet. Not after what happened to Derosa.

Connors could see how wealth had turned leather boy into a mean kinda guy used to getting his way. His pissed expression equivalent of stamping a foot, he unhooked the gun, snapped loose the harness, dumped the thing on the deck, and turned on his ass.

His sidekick came down with three bearded, brown skinned guys. Connors had seen their heads bobbing on the bridge. Togged in tracker gear, as scared as starving dogs, they huddled together, obviously wishing they were some place else. When they saw Derosa's bloody mess and cops displaying serious hardware they gave it some native tongue and turned to hightail.

Cops swore, shoving them other ways as leather boy and the sidekick beat it upstairs.

Freeman said, 'It's the end of the road, Craig. Or should I say "line"?' Amused he snapped some fingers at the cops, who looked sharp, pre-slaughter. 'No head shots please. When Hunter shoots this, we don't want the BBC censoring it for being too graphic.'

Before he gave the order to open fire, he nancied back down the ladder to the track. Connors reckoned it was so his suit didn't get messed.

'You posh scheming bastard,' Webb told him over a shoulder. Connors and the guys faced the train from the platform edge and would fall on empty track. 'Using HRH for your dirty rotten ends.'

'Yes,' Freeman replied, still chucking his weight but looking slightly ridiculous down on grassy track. 'Virtue of being a scheming bastard in the current situation, you Liverpudlian halfwit, is that I call shots.'

Amused by the irony of his words he turned but turned back. Into closing secs, Connors knew some fastidious detail was gonna get put right.

'And correct term for the Queen is "Her Majesty", not "Her Royal Highness" or HRH. That demarcation is reserved for those further down the Royal pecking order. HM definitely would not be amused.'

He never gave the order to fire.

Webb had baited him to distract him.

Moving like a Tasmanian sand devil, he led the guys in a flash dive.

Nobody stood a chance.

Silencered muzzle flash ripped into them. Connors saw Freeman make a run for it as red stuff flew. Nobody screamed. Just battle yells and plentya swearing. Connors took it hard in the chest. Felt like a truck ran him over as he got blasted back and hot red stuff splashed in a hamburger frenzy. Now his guys screamed like hell when their insides got minced.

Last things Connors saw shoot up fast as he twisted and fell were a rusty rail track and some poppies, bright red against dry grass. Brits linked red poppies to death. Seemed kinda apt.

But what hurt most in that final sec, showing how much it bugged him deep down, was never having seen his daughter. His head smashed incoming rail hard.

Death came swiftly.

34

Hunter was at the wheel.

As they got further south, roads wet from heavy rain were drying quickly in the sun.

Into rural Cheshire, he took back lanes fast. Only after they'd set off in a tizzy did they realize cops might scupper them. Roads were meant to be NG anywhere near the Royal Train. Weird thing was, except for a cop 4x4 getting small across fields near Chelford, they'd seen and saw no uniforms.

To find the disused line they left the A535 near Badgerbank. Took Bomish Lane over the West Coast mainline, past Jodrell Bank, and picked up the disused line near Blackden Heath. As they hit Blackden Lane they saw it running in a cutting.

Hunter stopped on a bridge. Jumped out and looked over. Double tracks overgrown and undisturbed. Birds tweeted from rusty overhead catenary poles. No trains had gone that way for a long time. Wondering if they were on a crazy wild goose chase, wondering why no cops, he got back in the car and took off.

Vanessa did GPS on the Nexus. 'Go south to Twemlow Junction and pick up the line at source.'

They never got there. As they tonned it down Twemlow Lane, and closed on Twemlow Station, disused line came into view again. Road ran parallel, up to a bridge over a cutting. Once upon a time it would have been the quintessential English country station scene.

Two things torpedoed such a romantic notion. First: the vandalized station building picked clean of anything with scrap value. Roof timbers silhouetted against clear summer sky. Amazing it had survived without being torched. Second, hitting like a shockwave: the Royal Train shiny-nosing like a giant silver bullet from under the station overbridge.

'Oh my God,' Vanessa said, when she saw it.

'Looks like we were right,' Hunter said, slowing and sensing bad, bad things.

'Shouldn't we stop and consider our next move?' Harry asked from the back, spooked. 'If skullduggery's afoot, our arrival might be inappropriate.'

Before Hunter could get his head round it, they arrived and he turned left onto the overbridge. Parked outside the station entrance was a black Hummer. Pulling up behind it, he killed the engine and popped his door. Place seemed dead. Eerie silence broken by a lone sky-lark going mad overhead.

'Bet that's the Hummer Bill saw last night,' he said, as stuff fell into place.

Out they got, wondering what the hell they were gonna find. Back to a beautiful hot summer day but Hunter's gut told him death was in the air. He was first to peek over the bridge.

Went OMG at what he saw.

Gut feel was doing its job.

Station was a slaughterhouse.

True horror hit them when they were down on the is-land platform. Gordon had the camera on his shoulder. Shooting wild in his own time, he panned onto the train then disappeared under the bridge.

'It's horrible,' Vanessa said, stepping round a big tan-ned guy with a tattooed neck and a mashed chest. Shud-dering, she linked Hunter's arm.

Hunter puffed his cheeks, trying to take it in.

Blood everywhere.

A serious Arnie gun. They'd stumbled onto some-thing big. He sensed it was gonna get bigger because of the film they were making.

He crouched at the platform edge, opposite the train. A dozen British soldiers lay dead on the track. Flies buz-zed them in searing stillness. Some guys wore shades. Staring eyes of those not shaded got to Hunter. They'd been massacred. Most had landed awkwardly, presumably after being lined up and shot on the platform. Some were more mangled than others. Biggest guy was at the end, covered in blood, padded uniform shredded. Neck likely broken because of how he'd hit a rail, twisting back his head.

Lying face down on the platform was a young guy in a rail uniform. He'd been shot in the back from so close his ribs were exposed. Lying close by were two bearded brown-skinned guys kitted in terrorist tracker gear. Both had been shot in the head.

Harry mopped his bald head with a hanky. 'Looks like soldiers were ambushed by terrorists, two of whom got killed in crossfire.'

'Three,' Gordon said from under the bridge. 'There's another over here.'

'Where's everybody gone off the train?' Hunter wondered, standing up, noting open sliding doors. 'If the area was cordoned off, surely the cops would have seen something. And why dead soldiers?'

'Assuming they're the real deal,' Vanessa said, linking arms with poor Sarah who was putting on a brave face but was clearly distressed by the gore.

Gordon stopped shooting.

'Looks like the train got hijacked and diverted here and everybody got taken off it. We must assume it included the Queen.'

Hunter weighed up the bearded terrorists.

Shotguns made it seem as if they'd blown away the other guys. But surely auto fire had done so much damage, suggesting the Arnie gun. He knew the gun from a TV doc they made about Sheuze. It would have obliterated them. Three guys with shotguns couldn't have taken on twelve.

'Terrorist-looking guys could be red herrings put here to hoodwink folk who hopefully aren't too detail conscious,' he said. Third guy had drip-trodden blood across to the loco but might have been carried. 'Those two have been shot in the head. Everybody lying on the track took it in the chest or belly.'

Crouching again, he spotted something in the blood next to the guy in rail gear.

Looked like a rubber nose.

'What the hell's this?' he said, bending closer.

He wondered if the guy's actual nose had got shot off. But it was still on his face, swollen. Hunter turned the nose over in blood. Cream coloured rubber insides had cinder toffee texture, like a Crunchie Bar. Bits of latex face and a grey wig were hidden under the guy.

'This is movie make-up,' he said, gobsmacked. 'It's a full-blown prosthetics job.'

'I'd lay bets he was made up to look like Bill Martin,' Harry said. 'He's wearing a Royal Train driver uniform. And the right tie.'

Wondering what they were getting into, Hunter stood up, swiping a buzzy fly.

They heard something but didn't know where it was at. Sounded like somebody scratching about in the entrance lobby up top.

Wrong. An acoustic trick.

It had come from the track.

'Goddammit, we got murdered by lousy cops,' croaked an angry voice, obviously hurting bad.

Vanessa was nearest and first to jump down. Kneeling to somebody, she called everybody over.

35

Connors couldn't believe he was alive. Saw sexy Vanessa. All chest like on Freeman's pics, in matching yellow blouse and tight pants. Smelling nice and girly scenty, she got big when she tipped bottle water to his mouth, chucked by the American kid.

He drank as best he could but his neck and spine were killing. 'Hurts,' he said, wincing. He also had a humdinger bruise on his forehead.

'Can you move your legs?' Vanessa asked him, touching them gently.

'Yeah,' he said, and proved it.

Hunter jumped down and got big, blocking sun. 'You've been shot,' he said in a *gulp* kinda way, like how the hell were they gonna handle it.

'Uh-uh.'

'What do you mean?'

Connors reached up and pulled his tunic. Slugs had ripped it. He felt and smelt fresh blood. Far as he could tell, none of it was his. He clawed at himself some more, showing them the ace up his sleeve.

'Gosh,' Vanessa said, realizing.

'Nice one,' Hunter said, getting the idea.

Somebody else thumped track gravel to make a trio of fussing, looming faces. Kath.

'Craig,' she said thanking God he was alive.

She pushed between Vanessa and Hunter, bending to him to be sure he was OK. She'd lost her army tunic and was in her Cody combat vest, all muscly arms and black hair strands dangling in his face. Her eyes were mascara messed. She'd obviously been crying.

'Where did she come from?' Hunter asked, standing up, appealing to the guys on the platform.

Connors didn't hear what old boy or the American kid said. 'I shouldn't be here,' he told them.

He was alive 'cause he was wearing a skintight bullet-proof vest. When he'd pulled his army stuff from the Hummer, when he arrived with Kath, first thing to go on was a Level 1 Kelov body vest. Variation on Dragon Skin anti-ballistic kit, and vastly more expensive at six dollar figures, it even resisted shells made from titanium. Guaranteed triple protection, so the tin said. If Freeman had shot heads, it woulda been bye byes. Luckily the bastard hadn't.

But when Connors took slugs so close he thought he'd died. Expected his arms to get shot but they hadn't 'cause they'd flown up in the excitement. He hurt like shit, though. OK the vest had stopped slugs dead. But he'd absorbed their energy and was gonna turn black and blue.

'Guess I'm a great big shit of a coward,' he said, shoving himself up to his elbows.

'Bollocks to that old chap,' old boy said from the platform, popping bottle water. American girl had plundered the carry cooler. It was still where guys had dumped it off the bus. 'Be thankful you're alive.'

Camera guy, maybe 45, big, heavy, was shooting stuff when it happened. Connors saw him pan onto him and crank in a slow zoom.

'Stop shooting, Gordon,' Vanessa said.

'This stuff is priceless. You guys are made.'

'I don't care. This man's hurt and is surrounded by his dead colleagues. We're not exploiting him for the sake of a TV programme.'

Connors grinned. 'He's doing his job,' he told her, but touched her arm gratefully and winked.

'What the hell happened here?' Hunter asked him.

Kath gave him her phone.

'I shot it from upstairs. If Craig hadn't got me to hide I'd be dead. I'm warning you it's not pleasant. But it's video evidence. It means we can nail that bastard Freeman. Kill sound. I don't wanna hear it ever again.'

Connors knew Kath was hurting 'cause of how she tried not to look at Reece. Horrors she'd seen were catching up. Hunter, wondering about the Freeman heads-up, leant against the platform.

Holding Kath's phone apprehensively, he hit Play Movie. Old boy, American kid, and camera guy crouched behind him to watch.

Ten minutes later they'd got Connors up on the platform. Feeling OK, he managed to stand.

He'd filled them in about everything.

'Freeman,' Hunter said, amazed.

He was equally put out from getting clued into the dead guys being mercenaries who'd been hired to abduct the Queen. OK they'd been murdered in ice cold blood. But it made them bad guys too.

'Let me get this right,' he said, pacing hands-on-hips, losing it. 'This happened because you lot were willing to kidnap the Queen, screwing consequences, letting Freeman pay you for the privilege. When we got here we thought we'd found a load of dead soldiers.' Sounded like he'd chucked Connors an ultimatum.

'I see where you're at,' he said, treading carefully. 'In my defence, I never killed anybody.'

'Pull the other one,' Hunter said, pissed as hell. 'Do you expect us to believe that? You might have walked out of an action movie. Your arms are nearly as thick at the top as Vanessa's waist.'

Kath joined the fray.

'It's not how you think.'

'How the hell is it then,' Hunter balked. 'These guys are dead because you two were involved in a crazy plot to kidnap or maybe even kill the Queen. If you hadn't been, nobody would be dead because it wouldn't have

161

happened. And what about bombs which blew away half of Sheffield and Stockport? You're saying two nutters we saw at Wilmslow caused them who're involved with Freeman and by default you. I repeat: if you'd not got going on this shit nobody would have been killed. Chew that on your lousy bloody consciences.'

Kath, hit hard, walked off shotgun in hand.

Hunter knew he'd struck a nerve.

Connors told him: 'She had something with a guy lying dead over there. Her little boy's also dying 'cause your free health service won't pick up the tab. Reason she got involved in this "shit" is 'cause it's the only way she could get the money together to send her kid to the States for a life-saving op.' Next bit he said quiet. 'The guys were gonna chip in to see it happened. She doesn't know, and it needs to stay that way.'

'Jesus Christ,' Hunter said. Pissed at himself, he angrily smacked nearmost metal station sign.

Connors could see Hunter's guys weren't used to seeing him get worked up.

'Take this or leave it pal, but my guys never killed an innocent. OK they made a living losing bad guys who deserve to get KO'd. But it's no different to soldiers killing enemies in line of duty. Even ass-tough mercenaries have a goofy moral code, or those I mix with do. Freeman would have hired somebody else if it hadn't been me. He's a double-faced murdering goddamn son of a bitch. But he assured me the Queen wasn't gonna get hurt. He mighta lied about that too. But hey it's why I'm standing here.' He paced a little, conscious of his bloody

MARPAT uniform. 'There's more to stuff than black-and-white, son. Lottsa greys overlap.'

'Yeah I know,' Hunter said, looking like he mighta realized something about his personal situation.

His phone hit off from his back pocket.

Against rural hot-sun silence, its old-style ringtone smashed in. Hunter pulled it, looking puke sick.

'Freeman,' he said, showing Connors the bogeyman's gawping mug pic.

'Don't say I'm alive,' Connors told him. 'Don't let him suss you know what happened here. If you do, you're dead. That's for sure.'

Still the phone did its thing, dynamite fizzing in Hunter's hand while he psyched himself to take the call. 'Mr Freeman,' he said finally, calm as he could.

36

Thinking *shit,* Hunter's mind raced when he heard Freeman's smooth upper-middle-class voice. Connors had said something about Freeman needing a TV crew to shoot the aftermath of the Royal Train hijack. Conversation hadn't got far enough for any detail.

'I assume you're at Twemlow Station,' Freeman added, after his smug hello. Bastard sounded like he was playing some cocky hide-and-go-seek thing.

'Yes,' Hunter said, steering clear of asking Freeman how he knew he was there. 'Something terrible's happened.' He struggled, mustering energy to play ball.

Freeman sensed it and got straight to the point. Much of it a rerun of what Connors had told them, without Freeman implicating himself. Hunter got the feeling he was seeing how far he needed to push him. Opening shot was him suggesting they should shoot stuff for TV, so the country and the world could get to grips with a daring Royal kidnap.

While Freeman rabitted on, Hunter saw Kath sidle back along the platform, avoiding his eye. Gauntish face prematurely lined, she looked like she'd had a hard life. Tattoo fire raked her muscly arms. God knew what she'd be like when she was a wrinkled OAP. Tattoo lovers didn't seem to think that far ahead. Tall as Vanessa, she seemed formidable. Putting down her gun, she got down on the track, and knelt next to a big dead guy, her shoulders hunched. First thing Connors had done when he was on his feet was go along the row of guys shutting their eyes.

Hunter saw Kath gaze off, taking her time, sobbing quietly. Under the big tough-girl show was a vulnerable working-class woman, needing somebody to be with. While Freeman blabbed in his ear, Kath bent over to kiss the dead guy's forehead, got up, and climbed back on the platform, backhanding her eyes. She'd pulled off her goodbye with dignity. Avoided being sucked into fashionable, self-absorbed telly blubbing.

Didn't matter what Hunter thought about the morality of an insane Royal Train mess. Two people had connected. One, a young mum, now had to cope with losing the other in a horrifically violent way, coupled to a living nightmare of her kid being terminally ill.

Temper flaring, he cut Freeman short.

'Listen, you clown. Why don't you stop bullshitting and get to the damned point.'

'I sense you need persuading just how precarious a situation the Queen is in,' Freeman said, getting nasty. 'Go to her saloon carriage fifth from front of the train, counting the power car. Go alone.'

Reluctantly, Hunter set off, waving for the others to stay put. Lone skylark still wittered for England high overhead. Day was going for it too on the sunny Celsius front. Phone at ear, he hit said carriage's nearmost door and went inside, grateful for cool aircon which emphasized a subtle perfumy reek.

Royal crested papers and stuff, spread on a glass slab table, looked like they'd been abandoned in a hurry. Fresh roses bouqueted from table middle. Scottish landscapes by one of the Queen's fave artists, Roy Penny, adorned walls. Carpet and leather furniture were plush Royal-blue. Grey blow-moulded everything else made the carriage feel like inside an aircraft.

'OK,' he told Freeman, noting how net curtains and tinted glass stopped guys outside from seeing in. 'I'm in the Queen's lounge by a big coffee table.'

'Excellent,' Freeman said. 'Sit on the sofa, left end facing you. Beneath you is a built-in storage drawer.'

'Yeah I see it,' Hunter said sitting, hunching over.

'Please open it.'

When he did, everything imploded.

Day had been going downhill since it began.

Bubbling under it were memories of last winter's violent nightmare. What he saw in the drawer proved he was caught up all over again. Royal Train commission going tits-up, death at Twemlow, discovering who was behind it, brought back a scary realization. Powerful elitist forces, bereft of any sense of public duty, grew ever more ruthless, trying to cling to power and privilege. Not even the Queen was safe.

Soon as the Beeb greenlit their Royal Train TV doc, Hunter knew his fate had been sealed. What stared up from the drawer was final cruel straw. He tried to tell himself *no* but everything blurred because his eyes filled up. Freeman knew where to hit him.

'You bastard,' Hunter told him, wishing to God he was mistaken. 'You lousy rotten bastard.'

Hayley's handknitted Rupert Bear.

Stuffed in the drawer, wrapped in his yellow check scarf. Last time Hunter saw him was at Waterloo two weeks ago after he'd had his kids for the weekend while Vicky was in Amsterdam with new boyfriend Roger.

Picking up the toy gently he felt his world crumble, sussing exactly where Freeman was at.

Flopping back on the sofa, he held Rupert close, smelling his sweet daughter on him. Favouritism was wrong for any parent with more than one kid but he'd a special bond with little Hayley. A year younger than Jenny she was the brighter, more articulate of the two. Ironically, she looked like Vicky but took after him in her nature. He felt burdened by it and blamed himself for it. His kids amounted to more than two successful acts of pro-creation with a woman he no longer really knew. They were a painful conjunction with his past which refused to let him go.

Bastard was at his ear again.

Bastard said, 'Do we understand each other?'

'Where is she?' he demanded.

'With your ex-wife and your other daughter Jennifer. In our safe care.'

Freeman taking his kids and Vicky was too much. They were supposed to be holidaying in France.

Now he knew why his e-mails to them that morning, sent on the way to the shoot before Sheffield blew, had gone unanswered. He felt physically sick, till blind rage overcame him.

'If you harm them, I swear to God I'll kill you.'

'No you won't kill me, you fool. You'll listen to what I'm about to tell you, and you'll do exactly what I say, when I say. This is deadly serious now. Breathe a word about what you know about me and I'll kill your child-ren and ex-wife. If I have to, I'll send bits of them to you first. Make sure everybody with you understands that.'

Hunter said nothing.

'Do I make myself clear?'

'Yes,' he said icily. 'Damned clear.'

'Good,' Freeman said. 'You're going to shoot the aftermath of the Royal Train hijack, so it can be shown quickly by the BBC. And you'll do it like this.'

37

Poulson was alone in the empty warehouse.

Mid-afternoon sun filled the open loading bay.

Except for the 8x8 wooden table and screens, which they were leaving behind, everybody and everything had gone. Head scanner and other high-value tackle had also been carted away. Two guys had rivet-gunned steel sheet back over doors and windows out front, and had just left. Poulson would be last off site.

With office doors and windows resealed, he'd exit via the loading bay rollershutter, letting it drop automatically behind him.

Only group members left were himself, Mark Hartman, and young Scot PA, Kerryann. A final check to make sure nothing of value had been forgotten then away by car to a private airfield near Bicester. Helicopter across to rural Southern Ireland, where they'd hole up for a few weeks till Royal kidnap dust settled.

He killed warehouse lights and headed through to the front office. Only other person on site was Bill Martin. Plan was to drop him off somewhere remote on the way to the airfield. But Poulson had decided it was too risky. He told Bill Martin this when he got up from his chair at the table under the window, blanked by sheet steel from the other side. 'We're leaving you here instead.'

Kerryann followed him in carrying a plastic tray piled with some M&S packed sandwiches, bottled spring water, an electric kettle, and some sliced lemon drizzle cake. She set the tray on the table and went out.

'Thank you Kerryann,' Poulson said. He told Bill Martin: 'As soon as we're out of the country somebody will call the police and tell them you're here. You'll be alone for a few hours. You have my word.'

'What if the police don't believe you?'

'We shall have to hope they do, Mr Martin. Outer doors will be locked or sealed but we'll leave this one unlocked, so you can use the toilet across the corridor. Sit tight and wait to be rescued.'

'I wonder why you don't just kill me.'

'Because we're not bad people, Mr Martin. Not how you think. We're old school. Contrary to what you think about me, I like my country and would have preferred to live out my days here. But we're corrupted beyond redemption. I believe in discipline and order but this is not the England I knew. Our future will be disorder and chaos, which is part of a general Western moral decline. History shows great civilizations fall when they can no longer govern themselves sensibly. The writing's on the wall, Mr Martin. You're retiring to Italy. I'm getting out too, while our currency is worth something.'

Having said his piece he turned, surprised at how much of himself he'd revealed, now that it was nearly time to bid farewell to his country.

'Have you killed the Queen?'

'No Mr Martin, we haven't. The Royal Train has been hijacked but the Queen is alive. She and her staff were removed safely from the train at a disused station called Twemlow, in Cheshire.'

'Sounds to me like you're as bent as folk you say got us into a mess. I'm not as clever as you. But I do know boomerangs have a habit of coming back and bopping heads.' Before Poulson could reply, Mark appeared in denim shirt and jeans. He offered a farewell hand to Bill, who balked saying, 'You're posh criminals but you're still criminals. I'd rather not get my hands dirty.'

'Suit yourself,' Mark said, unfussed. Something was on his mind. 'Can I have a word, Phil?'

Still thrown by how much of himself he'd revealed to Bill Martin, Poulson stepped into the corridor, snecking the door behind him.

'Freeman said everybody's final payment would land by lunchtime,' Mark said.

'That's right.'

'Mine hasn't. Carmen's hasn't and Kerryann's hasn't. Make-up guys are e-mailing saying theirs haven't. Did you check your bank account?'

'No. I hadn't thought about it because we were too busy sorting everything here.'

'Freeman gave assurances.' He held the metal door open for Poulson and followed him into the warehouse. 'Have you heard from Craig?'

'No I haven't.'

Door *thunked* shut behind them. Dust motes floated in mottled sunshine. Traffic swished from the nearby main road. Birds twittered from the sunny yard. Solemn after-the-event stillness worked the moment.

Feet scuffing shiny grey-painted concrete they crossed to stand in the open loading bay.

Mark said, 'Craig isn't online. His phone's switched off. Same with Reece.'

Poulson fished for his phone and found Craig's number. Sure enough, Netwerk Connex said his phone was switched off. Reece's too. 'Calling in from Twemlow would be the last thing on their mind,' he said. 'Besides, Alex e-mailed to say everything had gone to plan.'

'Wouldn't it have made sense for him to phone you with the good news?'

'Maybe he couldn't talk,' he said, flummoxed. 'He was flying over to Chequers to see the PM.'

'What about Mike Reynolds?'

'What about him?'

'Odd, don't you think? He's keen to impress you. He called as soon as he was aboard the train at Milton Keynes and again when he'd left Crewe. Surely he'd have rung from Twemlow. The Queen should be well away by now but not a peep from anybody.'

'Alex wouldn't mess us about,' he said. Going by Mark's expression he didn't share such optimism. Poulson's mixed feelings about leaving his homeland, and the prospect of his final payment being late, made him jittery. 'I'll call him,' he said, trying to brush it off. 'I'm sure it's nothing.' Not sure if he believed it, he stepped into the hot sun trap that was the factory yard and hit Freeman's number.

38

Pover was still in his van at Tesco's.

He'd switched back junction points, so trains following HRH could go through safely. Crewe Gateway's track dio would stay under his control till Craig rang to let him know the Queen had been bundled away.

No word yet and Pover was getting jumpy. Shouldn't have taken that long. Crewe was gonna get wise soon. On his laptop, TV news got uppity. A rail magazine bod sounded off about how deplorable it was that nobody knew where the Royal Train was. Nothing from Crewe Gateway, despite media gathering outside demanding answers. Nothing from Network Signal's London HQ. Everybody would be scared of sounding like dodos if they opened gobs and said wrong things.

Pover had tried calling Craig for a heads-up. Weirdly his phone was switched off.

Same with Reece.

He tried Ross.

'Yeah Glyn.'

'You heard from Craig?'

'Nothing. Everybody's phones seem to be switched off. Half an hour's way too long. Know any of the guys at the station?'

'Just Webbo. He's also switched off.'

Guys Connors had brought in to do Twemlow were unknown to Ross and Pover except for Scouse bagpuss Webb who Pover knew from way back. Way things had been set up was for each group to work independently with no communication. Alex Freeman's diktat, in case anybody got caught messing the bed.

'I heard Kath came up last minute,' Ross said.

'Don't know her number.'

'Should we be concerned if we can't contact our boss or his deputy?'

'Might be a phone blackspot.'

'Nah. Wasn't earlier. What about Poulson?'

'Rang him just now but he was on a call. I'll try again in a minute.'

When Vanessa saw Hunter step off the train, holding Hayley's Rupert, she knew the score.

Hurting bad, he shook his head at her, which said it all. His kids were his weak spot. All kids were his weak spot. Only time he'd broken down on camera was filming at a children's hospice, before Vanessa knew him. He'd written outspoken newspaper articles slamming the cynical commercial exploitation of kids, appealing for selfish, greedy, irresponsible adults to respect childhood innocence. He'd go beyond earth's end for his own kids, whom he adored.

'They've got the girls and Vicky,' he said, confirming what Vanessa sensed. Coping as best he could, he looked ready to kill somebody when he came across. Vicky too, she realized, giving him a reassuring hug. He got on better with Vicky than he'd ever done, which was good for his kids.

He was a maverick, a shit stirrer, but he was also a traditionalist who believed in total commitment to a woman. He walked out on Vicky when he found out she was having an affair. It kicked off an acrimonious divorce but Hunter's bitterness had eased since he hooked up with Vanessa. Finding his soul mate meant he'd found himself. Maybe it was why, deep down, he'd not settled with Vicky, making Vanessa wonder if he was the reason the marriage failed.

Hunter filled everybody in.

'Freeman wants us to shoot this bloodbath for *Panorama*, making it look like international terrorists are behind it. Whole thing's been staged for TV. Freeman knows the film will cause international outrage, pressurizing the Government to act fast when it gets handed a fat ransom demand.'

'Did he give a price tag?' Connors asked.

'Ten billion pounds.'

'Her Majesty can feel she's of value,' Harry noted dryly.

'Yeah,' agreed Hunter. 'Only we don't put that bit in the film. It's for a secret dialogue between Freeman's imaginary terrorists and ministers. He clued me in to make sure I play ball because of my kids.'

'Jeez,' Connors said. 'We were costing him only five million. Why does he want you to make a film?'

'Because of TV's power to control mass emotion and fuel mass hysteria. It will also make the markets jumpy. Telling the Government to act fast, or the Queen gets bumped off, is one thing. Seeing markets suffer and the country getting angry will make the Government do as Freeman says. He's got my kids and Vicky to make sure I shoot the film he needs to pull it off. I do as he says, or my loved ones die. I assume he's crapped on you guys because he's no guarantee the ransom will be paid. If it goes tits-up they'd be millions worse off. Sorry but you lot really were expendables from day one. Not my problem, though. My family is all that matters.'

'Freeman's a depraved bastard, dragging helpless little kids into this shit,' Connors said. 'How can you be sure he ain't bluffing?'

'He e-mailed this,' Hunter said, clicking something open on his phone but passing it to Vanessa.

She swapped it for her bottle water. Cradling Rupert under his free arm, Hunter took a long pull. He'd opened e-mail from Unknown Sender, embedded with a link. It was like landing on a Youtube page but was some kind of restricted FTP thing.

Hiding the phone from the sun with her hand, dreading what she'd see, she hit Play. Connors, Kath, and the guys stood with her.

Up came a title: *Hunter: the Movie.*

Edited highlights of their personal life kicked off since they'd been living together.

First up, both of them emerging from Giraffe, at Leftbank, off Deansgate in Manchester. She watched in a daze, seeing their passionate love exposed by some reject using jumpy handheld phone vid.

Next, Hunter and his kids at Legoland Windsor. A tearful public handover at Waterloo Station. Stuff lifted from ITV's BAFTA bash when they'd picked up an award for their celebrated cop series featuring the late David Kowalski. Film ran punchy like a movie trailer. When she saw them shooting at Wilmslow earlier that day, when North Dean blew, she sussed who the nasty rejects were and knew what they'd been up to.

Final bit was toughest to take.

Hayley sitting upright on a chair.

Impossible to tell where, because of tight framing. Room seemed echoey, so maybe a warehouse or kitchen. Sunshine slanted from a window across lime-green wall tiles behind her.

Nodding at somebody off camera, she'd obviously been told what to say.

'Daddy,' she said, seeming older than her years and surprisingly composed. 'Rupert's bringing you a special message. You must to do as he says.' Film jumped like it had stop-started, adding to its edgy feel. Back to Hayley, going through same thing. 'If you don't do what Rupert says, Daddy, we might never see you again.' Bottom lip trembling, she filled up.

Video jumped on.

Snow fizzed.

Done for effect, it cranked tension. Dark-haired Jenny was sitting with Hayley.

Crippled by distress the girls clung to each other, their pretty young faces red from crying. Hunter turned away when little Hayley, eyes streaming, bawled: 'I want my daddy! I want my daddy now!'

39

Hayley's anguish cut through Hunter like a knife, tinny on the phone behind him as he walked platform, angrily crushing the empty plastic water bottle in his hand.

Seeing his little girls ripped open by grief was the most godawful thing. Sarah hurried after him tearfully, linking his Rupert arm. He'd been drained by the video ordeal when he saw it on the train but had decided to channel his rage.

Make bastard Freeman pay.

When he arrived back with Sarah, Vicky was on the vid. Without make-up, looking strained, she said they were being looked after OK and being fed properly. But it was like she didn't believe it. She got cut off. Freeman would have done it like that to spook Hunter.

Vanessa hugged him again, keeping it together herself. Connors squeezed Hunter's shoulder, admitting he didn't know what the hell to say.

Hunter's mind raced. There must be a tiny audio detail in the video which could give a bearing on where his girls were being kept. Soon as he'd watched the vid first time he tried to copy it but found it was encrypted. Freeman said he'd give them long enough to watch it a few times, implying he'd kill the link.

Hunter asked Kath for her phone.

She wondered why.

'I need to e-mail somebody fast,' he said.

'Why not call them?' said Connors.

'Freeman will be scanning mine and Vanessa's and the crew's phones for e-mail and my AWV.'

If surveillance guys snooped they'd pick up his Audio Wave Form when he opened his mouth. But if he e-mailed from a phone they weren't scanning, they shouldn't be able to ID that. Last time he'd been in such a situation he'd been too scared to risk borrowing a phone to try it.

Connors took the phone off him.

Turned it over and slid open the back.

'See this?' SIM had been tampered with. 'It scrambles calls. Same on mine and everybody else's phones. Precaution taken by a guy called Poulson who set us up in business. Can't believe he's bent like Freeman but if he is this minor detail just backfired. They don't know I'm alive, like they don't know you're about to make a call on a phone which cannot be traced.'

Giving it back to Hunter he winked.

'Are you serious?'

'Trust me. It's 100% safe.'

Hunter thumbed a number.

'Who are you ringing, love?' Vanessa asked.

'Steve Hamer,' he said, praying he didn't get voice-mail. While the phone rang, he filled in Connors and Kath. Steve was a forensic scientist. Old uni friend working at Manchester's leading independent forensic lab, the IFI. Before he could give them the lowdown on how he helped expose bent cops behind last winter's shit, the man himself answered. 'Thank God, Steve,' Hunter told him.

'You're the only guy I know who just kicks off talking. What's up?'

'A video link's been encrypted. Can you unlock it and copy it fast?'

'Piece of the proverbial.'

'Will the encrypters get wise?'

'Not with our fancy kit. What's it about?'

'You'll realize. And don't worry about me when you see the content. I'm handling it OK. I'm about to e-mail you a web link. We might have a few minutes before it's killed.' Using Kath's phone he logged onto their production company account, forwarding the e-mail to Steve containing the embedded URL.

'Got it and am cloning now.' Hunter heard keys being whacked other end. 'Done.'

'Wow that's amazing,' he said, feeling the ball come back his way. 'I'll sort payment later. Don't phone or e-mail me. I'll contact you to discuss.'

'Serious is it?'

'Deadly.'

'Guess it means the phone you're using must be very safe. What am I looking for?'

'Background noise. Something too low for naked ears. Notch up bottom end. Pull as much from it as you can, no matter how thin it gets.'

'Kit's tied up on another job so it'll take a few hours. But consider it done.'

'Cheers Steve. You're a star.'

Poulson was still out in the factory yard.

He'd tried Freeman but got voicemail. He'd checked his bank account on his phone. Sure enough his final big payment hadn't landed. The unthinkable dawned. He felt like a character from an old British movie, *The*

League of Gentlemen. Half a dozen ex-officer types, who'd fallen on hard times, were blackmailed into committing a bank robbery but got their come uppance. Being ex-officer, Poulson felt like a similarly browbeaten well-to-do criminal who ought to have known better.

Realizing he might have been shafted, he wondered if his involvement in the Royal Train hijack was born of resentment. Bill Martin was right when he said boomerangs had a habit of coming back.

Poulson was angry that a once great country, which previous generations of his family had gone to war to defend, had gone to the dogs. The middle classes used to lead by setting a good example. Not any more. He blamed Royals for colluding in the atrophy. *What do they know of England, who only England know?* Frankly he was no better. Shrewd working-class Bill Martin got that right too.

Responsible good strategist in Poulson, which liked the company of people he'd managed, needed to know if they were OK. With Craig's and Reece's phones being inexplicably switched off he let Netwerk Connex do its thing. Thanked God when it scanned his address book, telling him Kath was still online plus Ross, Pover, Thinnes. Before he could try any of them, Mark waved him back over from the open loading bay.

'Look at this,' he said, stepping into hot sun to meet Poulson halfway.

Mark had his phone tuned to *BBC News.*

Stock shot of a gunship landing in Manchester at Central Police Headquarters (CPHQ). Aerial shot of four helipads stuck like giant clover leaves from top of the tower's forty-six storeys. Cut to Freeman dashing from the gunship, holding his necktie to stop it flapping in his face. Back to Indian studio girl with big hair saying, 'As concern grows for the Queen's whereabouts a statement is due from Head of National Security, Alex Freeman, live in Manchester.'

'I thought he was flying to Chequers,' Mark said.

'That's what he told me.'

'I don't remember a press call about the Royal situation being part of our strategy.'

'Neither do I.'

'Seems like he has his own agenda.'

'I can only apologize, Mark. I've honestly no idea what Alex is up to.'

'I believe you. I just feel sorry for the poor guys who did a great job here and haven't been paid. What I don't get is why Freeman would screw us.'

Before they could speculate Poulson's phone rang. He was stunned when he saw Freeman's face.

'It's Alex,' he told Mark, amazed. Not knowing what to expect, he took the call. 'Thank God Alex,' he said, sensing everything must be OK. 'Where've you been? We've been worried sick.'

'Sorry I've played hard to get, Phil. Things went badly wrong with the hijack. I had to fly to CPHQ in Manchester to face the music.'

'What's happened?'

'Can't explain right now. I'm on my way downstairs to a press call. Had to get clearance from the PM, to be

182

sure we say right things. It's been a total bloody night-mare but I wanted to catch up and say sorry.' Careful loaded pause. 'Are you chaps still at base?'

'We're ready to leave. I was beginning to think we'd end up being stranded.'

As he said this, he heard a car turn off the main road out front. Freeman had insisted on having them collected and driven to the airfield. Least he could do, he'd said, for his top two guys.

Inexplicably, Poulson got bad vibes. Former soldier's instinct, wondering about the convenient timing of Freeman's call.

'Car's here now,' he told him.

Needle-stab to belly when he saw a shiny black Merc, hotspotting sun.

'Good,' Freeman said. 'Let's catch up after the conference. Have a safe trip.'

'Nobody's been paid, Alex. What do I tell them?' He'd gone. Feeling sicker than ever, Poulson stuck his phone away as the Merc pulled up in the yard and its engine died. Pause before two stone-faced thugs got out, eyeing each other smirky-knowingly across some high shine roof. First thug beady-eyed Poulson before moseying across like an ape.

Mark sounded worried. 'If you think I'm off with those two, think again.'

He dashed into the loading bay.

Kerryann appeared in a dark trouser suit, suede ankle-boot heels clacking, make-up refreshed, carrying an overnight bag. First thug closed, feeling in his jacket under his arm. Second thug hung back to pull the Merc's boot. When Poulson saw what came out, his legs turned to jelly.

Bill was sitting at the office table, picking at a chicken sarnie. He'd heard a car pull up outside. Assumed some more of Poulson's crooked mob.

Still hard to believe what he was caught up in. He knew attempts had been made on the Queen's life over the years but there'd always been a media blackout. Often he imagined himself as a terrorist target. But nothing had happened to him or any loco driver he knew. He was amazed at lax security for guys who literally had Royal lives in their hands, ferrying them cross-country at killer speeds.

Shouting in the warehouse distracted him. He wasn't sure if it was laughter or arguing. Terrific mechanoid hammering killed it.

Muted through walls, it sounded like a pneumatic drill. He wondered if it was a revving supercharger Harley he'd seen parked in the yard. Realizing it was a machinegun letting rip, he knew in that terrifying moment it was over.

Scottish girl screamed.

Guy dying horribly groaned and swore.

Shotgun blasts shut him up.

In the corridor outside the office, the metal warehouse door flew open, pranging breezeblock.

Bill's heart flew to his mouth.

Footsteps, on a mission, closed fast.

Bill thought he heard a gruff voice say, 'Kill him,' from corridor's end.

Sounded like a bull elephant arrived at the office door trying the knob.

Door was locked. Bill heard a shotgun being pumped other side. Petrified, he stood up. Scenes from his life raced before him.

41

Conference suite was on CPHQ's 10th floor.

Ping went the lift, finally.

Doors split. Out Freeman went into a corridor rammed with frantic journalists. No matter how big a story, bastard media usually got there late.

Suzi, his skinny black dressed-in-black PA, was waiting Blutoothed, iPadded, looking the leggy, short-skirty biz. 'Five minutes,' she said, getting to it like they were doing a brisk steadicam walkthrough for *The West Wing*. 'Sky are gonna push you, Alex.'

'Let them,' he said, relishing a scrap.

He'd just sanctioned killing Poulson and Hartman but felt no remorse. It was a tough world. Guys said they'd keep the Scottish girl alive for a while, to have some fun. Freeman said it was up to them, as long as they tidied up. Bill Martin should be in an office out front and must also be killed.

'Seriously,' Suzi said, ducking a passing camera lens before it socked her in the eye. 'They'll ask you why that part of Cheshire's still conveniently no-fly.'

'Because I damned well say so,' he told her. 'What about the main line? Have they done as I asked?'

'Services between Crewe and Manchester have been cancelled. Local trains are running as far as Wilmslow from the north. Line between Sandbach and Crewe is effectively sealed off.'

'Good,' he said.

They arrived at the conference, wading through some scruffy delegates fouling the doorway with a fresh nicotine stink.

Suzi wasn't privy to the grand plan. Suspending rail services would make it look authentic and keep trains away from the area till Hunter had shot his film. After the event, questions would be asked about why it took so long for security to act. But dilly-dallying was in the order of things when it came to emergency services. Spectre of Health and Safety, driven by a compensation claim paranoia, clouded judgment. Freeman was using red tape boneheadedness to his advantage.

Point of the exercise was that the Queen had been kidnapped, but didn't know it. Bombs which had blown Sheffield and Stockport meant her advisors believed him when he said his office had learnt of a potentially fatal kidnap attempt. He'd "advised" hapless Sir John Massey that the Queen should disappear, till security got it sorted. It was why Massey agreed for everybody to leave the Royal Train at Leighton Buzzard.

Meanwhile, "terrorists" had told the Government they'd hijacked the train, taken the Queen, and were threatening to kill her if ministers went public. It was Freeman's way of keeping Massey in the dark, ensuring the Queen laid low while he screwed the country for ten billion. HM was quarantined in a remote hideyhole. No contact with the outside world being allowed. Not even with Westminster in case the Queen's whereabouts were squeaked to the press by the obligatory mole.

He took his position, front of conference.

Public lying at his level was a dangerous sport. He'd broker negotiations between terrorists and a very scared Government. Media would be fed same story as Massey. It would tell a worried public the Queen was in hiding. Sheffield and Stockport, Twemlow's staged massacre, Hunter's TV report, and a nervous Footsie, would make it plausible.

Meanwhile, Freeman would convince Massey he'd thwarted a kidnap. TV pics would prove it. Government would believe the Royal Train had been hijacked, and the Queen kidnapped. TV pics would prove it. Sworn to secrecy, neither side would know what the other had been told. Each believing national security chief when he insisted that, for the sake of the Queen's safety, nobody should utter a peep till the situation was resolved and she was freed.

As for Hunter, soon as he handed over his film he'd be dead. Same went for Vanessa and the film crew. Ex-wife and two kids were still alive. They'd remain so for a while, in case Hunter needed proof.

Suzi got everybody's attention.

Thanking her, Freeman put on a grave face and got his thoughts in order. He'd enough conscience to know he might once have made a half-decent human. But political power was like hard narcotics.

You needed big kicks.

You didn't know why.

'He's a good liar,' Nahid said.

'He's a pro,' Randeep told him. 'In our spotlit media age politicians are coached to lie with the right body language. Where they aim their eyes, when they spew crap, reveals what they're actually thinking.'

'I didn't know that.'

He put the tray on the table and slid a flat white over to Randeep.

They were sitting in Costa on CPHQ's ironically nam-ed Skydeck. Nothing to do with it being ten floors away from Stanley Street and New Bailey Street. It was media holding area for the conference room, journalists being prize coffee junkies.

Sky TV had sponsored the décor as a trade-off for the mezzanine coffee bar being named after it. Sky's logo and URL were on Costa's till receipts and serviettes. Central to the space was an OTT holographic telly. A big 3D slab of a thing slung in midair, it was tuned to Sky's broadcast from the press call Freeman had chaired next door.

'I can therefore reveal,' Freeman said, looking suitably worried, his lugubrious voice filling Costa, 'that we are investigating a serious incident on the West Coast main line, north of Crewe. All roads are sealed off in the area, which will remain no-fly till further notice.'

Questions erupted.

Freeman took them in his stride.

'He thinks ten billion's serious dosh,' Randeep noted. Back in fresh tracker gear, he slobbed on Costa's rustic leather sofa, Niked feet propped on a stool. 'Shows the level he's at, even for an ex casino banker.'

'It's a hell of a lot of money.'

'No it isn't,' he said through a yawn, gently patting his bust mouth while he watched Freeman bullshit.

BBC's tattooed girly black blonde asked him, 'Why does Crewe Gateway insist the Royal Train was nearly at Stockport when it was nowhere near?'

'I don't know,' Freeman lied.

Randeep wasn't listening. Pissed off with Freeman for humiliating him in front of cops, he was gonna show who was boss.

'What are we gonna do?' Nahid said.

'Freeman sticks people in at one end and craps them out the other when he's got what he wants. He made me look like a dickhead at Twemlow because he's an arrogant bastard. Worse, he's ignoring my calls.' Freeman's phone had gone to voicemail since Twemlow. 'How do we know he won't screw us on the deal?'

'You said you don't need the money but wanted to plan something big and blow stuff up. If it was all you got out of it, you said you'd get a buzz.'

'That's not the point. A deal's a deal.'

'Freeman's busy, smooth talking verbal diarrhoea to the world. He's got to manage the PR, now Hunter's shooting his TV report.'

'He needs Hunter's film for the PR to work, to prove what he's telling the Government and the world about the Queen. He's stringing everything out till Hunter's film's in the can, using his kids and ex-wife as leverage at *my* suggestion. Also my idea to stage the hijack, kill a bunch of mercenaries, and lure Hunter to Twemlow. Mugs Murphy here, handed shitten end of the stick, is the brains.' He yawned. 'Freeman's a tallyman.'

'So what are we gonna do?' Nahid said again, draining his cappuccino. Choc blobbed his nose end.

Randeep valued him, fagging since Oxford, obedient as a loyal pooch.

'Arnie gun was a toy. Sheffield and Stockport were damp squibs. We'll teach Freeman that you *don't* play with fire. Then claim what's rightfully ours.'

On TV, Freeman did as Randeep had scripted and pretended to take a phone call at just the right moment. Nodding, killing call, looking graver than ever, he turned to the media—to the world—and said: 'I've been told a TV journalist and his team are assisting our investigation. I'm awaiting further information but expect to make a formal announcement soon.'

42

Connors stood at the platform edge, gazing down at his dead guys who were now covered up.

Hunter had done some gory long shots before Vanessa hit on the smart idea of hiding the bodies under blankets. It drove home the horror of it all because, like a good movie, it left stuff to the imagination. One in the eye for Freeman. Seeing poor train driver Mike sprawled under cloth on the deck, hand stuck out, was saddest thing. Ironic to think blankets were from the Queen's bedroom aboard her train. Royal Crested. Soaked with blood. Tough moment for Connors, knowing he was gonna have to walk leaving his guys unburied.

Hunter and his guys were shooting in the loco cab under the bridge and had nearly done. Kath had gone to fetch some stuff from the bus. Vanessa was on the train, presumably searching for a bathroom.

She reappeared and came across to Connors, hands stuffed in yellow pants pockets, pink nail-varnished big toes peeping from yellow wedge heels. Strong girl, with stage presence, she was so blue-eye pretty it was kinda disconcerting. Feminine too she stood tall, assertive, like she took no shit. Connors liked that. He connected with smart women who acted like they could kick some butt.

'Mind if I join you?'

'Be my guest.'

Connors sensed everybody knew he'd needed space. Kath too. Made him feel like crap for exploiting the old Queen. Hunter and Vanessa being ready to give him time of day showed what great guys they were.

He looked at the twisted bodies, anonymous under bloody blankets. Booted feet stuck out along the line. When he spotted Webb's, all Bug Stomper cartoony, he had to turn away. Found it tough to meet Vanessa's eye when he turned back. After the fuss over Hunter's kids and ex, stuff had hit Connors hard.

'You mustn't blame yourself,' Vanessa told him.

'Yeah I know,' he said, rubbing his sweaty face and puffing, but not from heat. 'But I do. I say it as hard fact, not 'cause I'm doing self-pity 'cause I don't do self-pity. Thinking of the ripple effect hurts. They knew each job could be their last. It's why they were well paid. But it's wives and girls and kids never seeing 'em again which is my shit. No graves to go to. The guys will just be carted away to be incinerated.'

Freeman had given Hunter and his guys ninety minutes to shoot their stuff, and get the hell out, before he sent in meatwagons to clear up the mess. Connors felt a tsunami of despair. OK they were hard guys. But they'd lacked an essential mean streak which made bad men real nasty.

'I killed a guy last year,' Vanessa said outta the blue. Connors wasn't sure how to take it.

'We were hanging off a cliff,' she added. 'He was almost as big as you, holding onto my legs. I'd to keep booting his face till he dropped.'

'Jesus. Are you serious?'

'Yes,' she said. 'He was a ruthless killer. He murdered a policeman friend of ours. His punk got his arm blown off in front of me. I can still see his blood splattering snow and hear his screams when he fell to his death. I never knew that if you fall from a great height, and bounce off something hard on the way down, you disintegrate. They were going to use me for prostitution and eventually would have killed me. I wondered if I'd have nightmares trying to live with myself after taking a life. I didn't because I came to terms with it morally as soon as it happened. It was a fight to the death. Him or me. That doesn't make me a bad person.'

'It makes you a realistic person,' Connors said. He shook his head. 'Jeez lady, let me tell you a secret. I never killed anybody. I've bullshitted my way through tough-guy crap for twenty years. Some of these guys killed. Bad guys only but they still killed. I've come real close, when guys partying with me blew guys away. Somehow I always sidestepped the issue. I've broken limbs and bust plentya mouths. But I never took a life. When I told your guy he didn't believe me. Like I said, I'm a big shit of a coward.' Hands on hips, head clear 'cause of what this nice lady had brought out, he took some paces and scoffed at himself. 'I realized something else 'bout myself today. It hit me in a scary sec when I thought I'd died. What you just said will help me come to terms with it.'

He was about to fill her in but, job done, Hunter and his guys were on their way back over. Hunter gave old boy time to catch up. American kid pulled carry cooler lid and handed out fresh ice water. Taking a bottle from her, Hunter puffed from searing late-afternoon heat.

'OK,' he said. 'Finished.'

Vanessa held him to reassure him, sensing he was still hurting about his kids and ex. Connors could see their strong bond. Vanessa was older than Hunter. He seemed older, wiser, than he ought to for a guy starting his 30s so it kinda worked.

Connors knew chances of Freeman sticking to the deal were zero. 'He'll double cross you when you deliver your film,' he said. 'He's hardly gonna hand over hostages and let journalists walk when they know the truth about the Royal "kidnap".'

'Yeah I know,' Hunter said. 'But he needs the film. Till then time's on our side. I've no choice but to go with it and his unknown delivery arrangements. Hopefully he expects conditions. It's why I've got to believe my kids and Vicky are still alive, in case Freeman has to prove it. Meanwhile, we can even the score.'

Kath was coming back, still in her black vest, wading through fireweed, carrying an Adidas gym bag.

Hot sun had eased.

Even the noisy bird overhead had taken five. Kath chucked her bag on the platform and climbed up.

'Go on,' Connors told Hunter when Kath arrived.

'He threatens to kill my kids and Vicky, e-mailing me some video to prove it. Kath videoed him blowing away your guys, shooting off about how he's behind all this. Every word clear as a bell. When it's loaded on an Avid tonight, and tweaked, it'll be clearer. One mouse click and it's in every newsroom on the planet. I let Freeman know that and play him at his own game. E-mailing him a link to Kath's video will buy us time but we can't do it alone. There might just be enough room in the back of our car for Kath and an American brick shit-house to hide under some dust sheets behind the gear.' He stuck out his right hand. 'You helped get us into this mess. Please help get us out of it.'

Kath dumped her bag. 'I was gonna suggest we lent you guys a hand. It's why I fetched my stuff.' She shook Hunter's hand and crushed it.

'Jesus,' he said, and winced.

Everybody laughed. Old boy tittered.

Connors, grinning, shook Hunter's hand, telling Kath, 'He has a point, girl. We need a safe passage outta here. You up for it?'

'You bet,' she said. She'd pinned up her hair. Fixed her make-up. Stuck on wrapmirror shades. She looked tough. Sexy. Uber cool. Ready to kick butt.

Ready to avenge some deaths.

Connors picked up Kath's shotgun, saying to Hunter, 'Ever handled onea these?' When Hunter balked and said no Connors shoved it in his hands. 'Better get used to it, pal. Just point and shoot.'

195

'OK,' Hunter said, coolly propping back the gun, 'we're on the same page.' Eyeing his watch he said to everybody, 'Timecheck: 4.47pm. Let's get back to Manchester and hit bastard Alex Freeman hard.'

They all turned.

Hunter let them make some distance before he grabbed Connors by a shoulder.

'Thanks,' he said, meaning it.

He offered his bottle water.

Connors took it and popped it.

'I'm gonna get your little girls back for you,' he told him. He'd never said anything in his life and meant it so much. Eighteen years of canned rage were behind it but his head had never felt clearer.

He hung back to do some final goodbyes.

Part TWO

43

Sharron and Lisa were two sexy, highly with-it young road cops based at Milton Keynes. Heading away from town in a flash BM at 5.47pm, doing another bum shift. Much of it spent moaning about rank abolitions following private sector "consultations" (cuts), accelerated shift patterns (longer hours, frozen pay), and finally, as Lisa turned west off a busy A5, merits of wearing a short skirt on duty (woo-hoo) instead of pants.

Day's final heads-up had taken them in their cool, bullbarred, Battenberg plastered wheels to the A421, west of Bletchley.

Blonde, buxom, ballsy, on-the-button Lisa stuck on shades and stuck down a wedge platform-booted foot, rounding off skirt talk with: 'I don't care what some twat of a leftwing academic thinks. I love looking like a woman. If capitalist culture has conditioned me to enjoy wearing a mini skirt, long live capitalism.'

Brunette, also buxom, leggy, ballsier Sharron demolished a Cox's Pippin. She offered it to Lisa, who shook her head. 'Quangocrat Michael Mousers are unemployable in the real world.'

She went for last apple bite.

Unzipped her window.

Lobbed spent core.

Up came the window.

On went wrapshades. Down came hanky from sleeve to wipe sticky black nailvarnished fingers. '90% of them votes Labour. Driving their naughty socialist angst is a jealousy of good-looking folk. Worse than that, none of the blokes has a decent sized dick.'

'You crude, rude bitch you.'

'LOL. Makes two of us, hon.'

'You broke the law, losing that apple core.'

'I consciously fed a hedgehog.'

Call took them to a disused industrial estate, midway between Bletchley and Buckingham. Walkers thought they'd heard gunshots across fields. Machinegunfire, said walker # 1. No, shotgun, said walker # 2. Took two hours for them to hit the blower, after they were spooked by a Buckingham B&B owner who wondered if they might be deemed accessory if they'd heard something suspect but kept schtum.

They'd arrived.

Getting serious, Lisa said, 'OK here we go.'

She slowed to take an upcoming left, past a big TO LET sign into a dusty entrance slip, then left again behind some poplars into a weed infested factory yard set back from the main road. Nondescript 1970s grey brick. Shiny zinc plate, blanking doors and windows, winked sun. Steel palisade, topped by razorwire, spiked peripheral far gaps. Closer, a red Micra parked on its tod nosed a trashed outbuilding. Open rollershutter bay facing it from main warehouse suggested something smelly.

'Uh-oh, hon,' Sharron said, pulling her shotgun.

Slinging doors, out they got.

Bees and flies got to it.

Something spookily atmospheric about landing at an old abandoned factory, late on a hot afternoon.

They checked out the Micra. Lisa beady-eyed the open loading bay and got a funny feeling. Like maybe they were being watched. One-handing her shotgun, she unclipped her handset with her free hand and hit ANPR to scan the Micra's plate.

Handset pipped, doing its stuff:

LICENSEE>	WILLIAM (BILL) MARTIN
ADDRESS>	237 Thrupp Close Castlethorpe MK19 7PL

She knew the name from locker room guy-talk when she came on duty. Tweaking her headset she got Colin at Central Control. 'Hey Col?'

'Yes my love.'

'That TV guy who rang this morning was fretting about train driver Bill Martin, wasn't he?'

'Yes my love. Jules and The Spaz drove over to check out his bungalow but it was an NG.'

'He turned up for duty, didn't he?'

'Yes my love. He took over the Royal Train at Milton Keynes after lunch.'

Lisa was getting scared. You got a feeling which way a gig was gonna go, soon as you showed. She wanted to fast-forward to a cosy candlelit dinner with new guy Rob and shut out the big, mean, rotten, violent bloody world. Rob didn't waste time doing blokey stuff but let her be who she was. He'd brought out her squidgy feminine centre, surprising her more than him. 'Bill Martin's car's here,' she told Col. 'Parked in the yard.'

'What the hell's it doing there?'

'My thoughts. Especially when the Royal Train he took out of MK has by all accounts left the scene.'

'You sure on the ID?'

'Just scanned the plate. Assuming it's the real deal, we have a match.'

Creaking tight leather she made her way round. Peeked in and saw herself reflected in offside glass. Blonde hair stacked. Face done up to a bronzy tee. Dark stuff round big astute blue eyes.

Sharron was over at the open loading bay.

She whistled, looking sick. When Lisa arrived she saw why. 'OMG,' she said, fingerless leather gloved mitt going to mouth.

Gorging bluebottles exploded.

Possibly an older guy. Suited. Sprawled front down in a pool of blood. She meant *face down* but his head had gone, bits of it spread across shiny grey-painted floor. An eyeball stared at her. He'd taken machinegun in his chest. Back ripped open where slugs came out.

Lying nearby were a small black bra, an unopened pair of Sunkiss five denier knee highs, and a woman's brown suede ankle boot with a zipper back.

'Size 5,' Sharron said, one-kneeing down to check the shoe. 'Same as us.'

'Looks like a gangland killing,' Lisa said, 'with maybe a mol caught in crossfire.' She set her shoulder cam going, relaying live pics back to base. 'If it's a gang hit,' she added, 'why leave the shutter up?'

'Because of this,' Sharron said.

Door control panel on the wall had taken machinegun, probably from same spray which killed the dead guy. Sharron poked a Down button. No reaction. Just a dull buzz, like it had shorted.

Col said, 'For God's sake look sharp, you guys. I worry about you a hell of a lot.'

'That's 'cause you're a chivalrous old school plonker, Col,' Lisa told him, noticing an open metal door leading to a front office. 'Which is why we love ya to bits.' All the same, she was glad Col was with her. Thoughts got KO'd by stuff happening in the office.

They had company.

'Uh-oh, hon,' Sharron whispered.

Up came her shotgun to some pump-action. Sound of a glass, or a cup or something, hitting floor. Somebody scratching or crawling about. Vague moaning. Behind a big wood table they saw vic # 2, also minus head. Bits of head nearby, tufted with yellow blond hair.

They hit the corridor. On went Sharron's flashlight as she led the way. She set her shoulder cam going. 'Cover me hon,' she told Lisa. She told the office, 'Stay where you are and put your hands up now.'

Lisa, heart scaredy-banging, saw Shar silhouetting, torch waving. When she hit the office door and nudged it open, bright light hit her.

'OMG,' she said, amazed. Off went her torch. 'Come here, hon,' she said. Then more urgently, 'For God's sake, come here,' before she disappeared inside.

44

Hunter pulled over under a cavernous plate iron bridge on Great Bridgewater Street, just off Deansgate. Giving good cover because of its width, it used to carry massed tracks into Manchester Central. He found it gloomy and airless under there when he got out and moseyed behind the car to shoot the hatch.

Connors and Kath had been hidden under dust sheets all the way. They were glad to be back on their feet. Connors complained his bruised ribs were giving him jip. Before leaving Twemlow, he'd changed to a black scoop neck T-shirt and jeans. Kath had switched to a tan suede mini skirt, Red Indian waistcoat, and suede pixie boots which showed off her slender ankles. She was unrecognizable from the combat togged, shotgun wielding babe of an hour ago. Wolf-whistles flew from a passing open window when Hunter banged down the hatch and tailed her onto the pavement.

Vanessa got out. They'd dropped off Sarah, Harry, and Gordon at Wilmslow Station, where Harry had left his car parked all day.

Surge of enthusiasm from Connors about getting back the girls and Vicky had morphed to an unspoken *how the hell do we get outta this?* It had hung over the drive into town, culminating in the sombre moment when they stood awkwardly under the bridge.

Hunter and Vanessa had to get across to Sound and Pics on Quay Street to cut the film. Via the Nexus they'd picked up from *BBC News* that Freeman was in town and due to make a major announcement at 8.00pm. It would be when he'd tell the world how a TV crew had "stumbled" across the hijack and shot an exclusive report. They were going to hit him with Kath's video just ahead of his interview.

Everybody now had scrambled phones courtesy of dead mercenaries. Connors and Kath were gonna grab a bite to eat and catch up later, hence civvies.

Kath's bulging Adidas bag, slung by Connors over his broad shoulder, carried shotguns and Kath's leather cop gear. More weapons in the back of the Volvo. Hunter wondered cynically if they were doing final goodbyes. But there was a plan.

Back at Twemlow, Connors found his phone on the track and realized three of his guys, Ross, Thinnes, and Pover, were still alive. He'd got them to drive up from Cheshire, fast. Had an idea how they might get back Hayley, Jenny, and Vicky but wouldn't give detail and build hopes 'cause he wanted to sound out his guys.

'It's gonna be OK pal,' he said, shuftying his bag. 'I've gotta good feeling.'

'We don't know where Freeman's taken them,' Hunter said in desperation.

'Let's see what my guys think.'

'Yeah let's,' he said, not convinced.

'You're tired and hungry,' Kath told him, sensitive to his hurt. 'We all are.'

Irresistibly girly, pale-pink lipsticked, he'd assumed her husky voice was from smoking. But she'd told them she'd never touched a cigarette.

'Wouldn't you rather be with your little boy?'

'My mum's looking after him.'

Vanessa said, 'We appreciate you being here, love. You know we'll do everything we can to help you when this nightmare's over.'

Kath smiled and flushed under harsh halogen spots embedded in old brick railway wall. Hunter reckoned she was maybe 27 or 28.

When he was driving away with Vanessa, he told her, 'Part of me thinks we'll not see them again.'

'I know what you mean,' she said. 'But even if Connors decides to do a runner, which I don't think he will, Kath wouldn't let him. She'd take his balls off.'

'I like her. I found the tattoos offputting at first but she's genuine. Funny to say it about somebody who's in theory a criminal and puts on a tough show. But she's got no edge.'

When he turned right past the Museum of Science and Industry, he saw a white Range Rover in his rearview. Evil looking thing with slits for headlights. 'Didn't Connors say those two nutters from Wilmslow drove a flash white Range Rover?'

'Yeah he did.'

'Can you see who's behind us?'

She turned.

'Where?'

Hunter checked his rearview.

RR had gone.

'Bugger,' he said, and puffed his cheeks.

Dog tired, longest crappiest day had got to him. Connors had banged on about how he felt jittery ahead of the hijack going tits up and Freeman doing the dirty. It must have rubbed off. Hunter often noticed how, after ODing on adrenalin during a TV shoot, there was a fallout period of mega low spirits.

He kept seeing his terrified little girls. He was so desperate to be with them it hurt. And there was the rub. 'Why's it happening to us all over again?' he demanded, banging the wheel angrily.

'I don't know,' she said.

'I love you,' he told her, consumed by it. He did love her. So much it scared him. He couldn't imagine how he'd ever got through life without her.

'I love you too, darling,' she said, voice thickening. She touched his leg.

45

'That was lucky,' Nahid said.

'Life's all about good luck,' Randeep told him. 'Consider how you think about somebody and they suddenly e-mail or call you out of the blue. Storytellers depend on coincidence to propel plots. Balance of improbability isn't as daft as it sounds. Hence us ending up right behind Hunter and his fit good lady when we did.'

Randeep's teeth had been fixed.

He tapped them gently to be sure they were still there as Nahid turned into Atherton Street and down towards

Granada TV's former offices. 'Pull over,' he said, seeing a meter space on the left.

Nahid let the RR park-assist itself snugly and switched off. Where they were sitting, tucked away in a quiet corner near the old *Coronation Street* set, was secluded. Trees next to them acted like a sound barrier. Restaurants and bars a minute or two ago had heaved. Pavements outside loaded with fit young birds who needed shagging.

Seeing plenty of fresh leg meat had got Randeep feeling horny. God invented many beautiful things. Most important by a mile was the female form.

'What are you thinking?' Nahid asked him.

They spotted a traffic warden making his way up the street, a half-dozen or so parked cars away.

Meters used to give in at 6.00pm.

Now they exploited motorists 24-7.

'I'm wondering,' Randeep said, seeing the warden shoot a Smart Car pic and print a ticket, 'if I'd like to get to know Hunter's fit good lady.'

'You mean you fancy her?'

'I didn't say that.'

'You do fancy her, don't you?'

'OK what if I do then?'

'Hah,' Nahid said, and slapped the wheel. 'You've got a crush. Ever had an older woman?'

'No. But I hear they're not just as *tight*. I bet Vanessa screws the arse off Hunter. You can tell she runs the show, in the bedroom and out. I bet she opens her long legs so wide everything cracks.'

Warden slapped the ticket under the Smart Car's wiper. Seemingly unaware that he was being watched, he hawked, gobbed in a drain, and carried on doing his smug little Hitler thing.

Randeep added, 'I reckon women like Vanessa have more testosterone. They're feminine but when their girly psychology got done they imported some blokey bits. It's why they're ballsy and assertive and don't take shit. Vanessa looks amazing in a short skirt. Bet she looks better in a short skirt, holding a big gun.'

Traffic warden arrived.

He tapped Randeep's glass. Randeep frowned at him, as if he were a foul smell.

Glass lost itself, to a slick RR moan.

'Ticket sir?'

'No thank you old chap.'

'Have you got a ticket from the meter?'

'Golly gosh. It would appear not.'

Awkward few secs while the warden, an ugly little working-class Lancastrian shit, sweaty in red-and-black togs, weighed up two posh nobs gazing back from flash wheels. His blotchy pink face was like a bare botty. Bum fluff grew under fat hairy nostrils.

'Do you intend buying a ticket?'

'Afraid not old chap.' He yawned. 'But I might buy the outfit which employs gobshites like you and turn you into an unemployment statistic.'

Oops. Warden flushed.

Out came his camera. 'I saw you park up when I was further down the street. You've had plenty of time to buy a ticket or fetch some change if it was an issue. I'll ask you again. Do you intend buying a ticket?'

He indicated an armour plated thingy doing pavement close by. As if accused, it twanged internally while it counted cash or something.

Randeep said, 'Has anybody ever shot you if you've threatened to book them?' No reply. Just a hairy beetle brow, knitting above piggy eyes. 'Your bewildered expression suggests the answer is a resounding "no". In which case, do give me a moment.'

He opened the glovebox.

Warden, entranced, watched Randeep pull a shiny Sheuze pistol. Maybe he thought it was a toy. Or a joke. Randeep deftly screwed on a silencer and rested the gun on the window lip. Quick glance in wingmirror to check street behind was clear.

Then *phut*.

Weirdly, as the guy's head exploded and he flew back his camera somersaulted into the RR through the open window. Randeep grabbed it, switched it on, and took some pics of the headless mess. Centrepiece an impressive lumpy red splat.

'Jesus,' Nahid said, firing the RR so they could beat a hasty retreat. 'He was a guy doing his job.'

'He pissed me off.'

'You can't go round shooting folk who piss you off.'

'Oh yes you can. Everybody, once in their life, should do the world a favour and kill a traffic warden.'

46

Massey stood gazing from the window. Freeman was right when he said it was a remote enough spot to be last place terrorists would think of. The Queen's safety was paramount. Returning to Buckingham Palace or Windsor Castle was out of the question. Since Sheffield and Stockport blew, and a strike against the Royal Train was uncovered, eyes had been on the Queen's two main homes. Both surely key targets.

The Queen was sitting behind him in a red leather armchair, her stocking feet thrust out on a matching foot stool. She wasn't amused. She was of course gracious in her appreciation of everybody's concern for her welfare. But being ungraciously removed from the Royal Train at Leighton Buzzard six hours ago wasn't her idea of fun. She put her cup of tea on an occasional table next to the chair and reached for a custard cream. They were discussing Freeman being new to his job.

'What are your general thoughts, John?'

'Only in the murky world of British politics, ma'am, do people with zero experience in their job seem mysteriously best qualified to do it.' He gazed up at some fine clear sky. Early evening sunshine was strong. 'And we wonder why your country's in such a mess.'

'Has Freeman *no* intelligence background?'

Carole overheard this as she returned from the loo and slumped on the sofa, squeaking leather. 'He used to be a casino banker, ma'am.' Massey saw her reflected in the tall window. She reached for her cup of tea, holding it near her face. 'Applying the word "intelligence" depends on the nature of the question.'

Finally the Queen was amused.

She dunked her custard cream before she bit it.

Chris Hendry joined in. 'Story ran, ma'am, that when banks got bailed out by public money, it went into buying houses in exclusive parts of London, pushing prices to obscene levels. Alex Freeman was party to it and still colludes in such legalised crookery. Blood should run in gutters. Freeman's included, if you ask me.'

'Steady on Chris,' Massey said, turning.

'Sorry Sir John. Today's been stressful. My apologies for lowering the tone, ma'am.'

Massey knew he was worried about being away from his wife, who was expecting their first baby.

Freeman had forbidden them contacting anybody, including loved ones, in case it revealed their location. He'd insisted everybody left the Royal Train at Leighton Buzzard after intelligence sources discovered a hijack attempt was on the cards. He'd ordered the empty train to continue its journey, a decoy fooling would-be kidnappers, while the Queen and her staff got away.

Freeman chaired a press call in Manchester and phoned Massey after it confirming the hijack happened north of Crewe. Details were vague. TV folk who'd been due aboard the train tomorrow were filming fairly close, got worried, set off looking, and came across the hijack on a disused railway. Freeman wouldn't be pushed, other than to say the hijack scene was very bloody.

As yet, media knew nothing.

Massey intended to manage the situation so the elderly Queen would know nothing about the hijack for as long as possible, to avoid stressing her. It would prove difficult when TV got hold of it. But as there weren't any TVs where they were hiding, and as Freeman had confiscated everybody's phones and tablets, it was easy enough at present.

Chris Hendry was with them because the Queen liked to be surrounded by people she knew and liked. Everybody else from the train had been whisked to another secret location, for safe keeping till a potentially violent storm passed according to Freeman.

Earlier, the Queen thought she'd heard children crying. 'Listen,' she said, shushing everybody.

Massey heard it this time, remote and echoey, like it was travelling along old steam pipes. Plaintive wailing which seemed to come and go.

'I heard it ma'am,' Chris said.

'So did I ma'am,' Carole added.

They kept listening but it had stopped.

Chris loved kids. Folding his arms, looking glum, he frowned resolutely at a point in space.

'It's horrible,' the Queen said, clearly upset. 'They're crying for their father. Where are they, John?'

Massey crossed from the window and angrily grabbed a cordless internal phone from the coffee table.

'Hello,' said their Cockney police minder. Mouth full of grub, he chewed sloppily.

'We've heard those children crying.'

'You must have been mistaken, Sir John.'

'We're not mistaken.'

'I'll get it checked out.'

'You said that last time.'

Minder swallowed a gassy belch. 'Probably some of our lads watching a movie,' he added, slurping-hiccupping. 'I'll get them to turn it down.'

Massey put down the receiver and shook his head. 'It's a film we can hear, apparently.'

Chris caught his eye.

'Strange set up Freeman has here, in our "safe haven". Most cops I deal with on the ground are pretty decent chaps. This lot come across like a bunch of hired heavies doing fancy dress.'

'He has a point John,' the Queen said. 'How long do you think we'll be here?'

'Wish I knew, ma'am,' Massey said.

Before he could go back to the window, Carole shuftied along the sofa and patted it invitingly. 'For goodness sake come and sit down, John,' she said gushily. 'Stop fretting and have a nice cup of tea.'

She sounded so ridiculously jolly, so awfully middle class, it made plebs like Massey, who inhabited the real

world, want to shake their heads. It crystallized everything which was wrong and right with the country and
how it was run. But it was a welcome, unexpected show
of warmth from a woman he found physically attractive
whom he dismissed as being pretty hopeless upstairs.

'It's my job to fret,' he told her, doing as she asked,
despite himself. His eyes were on those long plaited legs
also in spite of himself.

She kicked off her shoes and buried her sheer stocking
feet in the deep sheepskin rug. It took up so much floor
it was more like sheepskin carpet.

47

Freeman entered a lift on CPHQ's 45th floor.

Shiny snazzy taxpayer suited for his imminent TV
appearance, he hit a button.

Steel doors *pinged* shut.

Lift got to it, gobbling floors.

Everything was going to plan. Just odd loose ends to
tie up. Poulson and Hartman were dead. But make-up
guys would see red when they realized they hadn't been
paid. With things looking so good on the ransom front,

he'd decided to pay the make-up guys, to shut them up, when his phone went off. He did a double-take when he saw who it was. Taking the call, he said flatly: 'I'm on my way to a TV studio. I expressly said I'd contact you about the handover.'

'We're still cutting the report,' Hunter said through a yawn, sounding sarky. 'There's a wee bit we can't make up our mind about. Thought I'd get the big tosser himself on the blower and ask for his input.'

'Now you listen to me Hunter—'

'No. You listen to me you murdering bastard. Check your Inbox. Then we'll talk about my girls and Vicky on *my* terms. I'll call you back when I'm ready.'

He hung up.

Freeman felt like he'd been smacked in the face. Hunter sounded nasty. Didn't tally with safety of his kids and ex being at stake. E-mail took ages to load because of hi-res junk.

34, 33, 32 went the panel, egging him on.

Lift was a glass bubble thing riding outside the building. Pipes and stuff kept criss-crossing, making evening sunlight flicker and flash.

Up came e-mail from Real Life Pictures.

Embedded link, like when they e-mailed Hunter Randeep's video. Freeman hit Play. Couldn't believe what he saw. Silencered machineguns sounded tinny on the phone. So did death cries. So much blood flew it looked digitally enhanced. Absurdly, he wondered if it was a CG trick done by SFX guys Hunter surely knew, being in the TV business.

Lift was nearly there.

Despite aircon it felt stifling. Manchester city centre got close then disappeared as the lift went down under, to CPHQ's basement car park.

3, 2, 1 went the panel, finally.

Awkward handheld moment, where he needed time to get a grip on the situation. Doors *pinged* and split in his face, jollying him along.

The Beeb had sent a car to ferry him across to Salford. It was why he'd got the lift, when the gate rang to tell him his wheels had arrived. Suzi had gone ahead to read the riot act to a young news producer while Freeman preened himself in his office. He intended to reveal all about the hijack attempt on live TV. Hunter's call had changed everything.

Waiting car was a Beeb VIP indulgence.

Silver Lexus Eco or a Merc or something. Tough to tell which because exec cars looked the same. Next thing he was sitting in the back and his driver shut his door.

His head was all over. How the hell had Hunter got the damned video? Looked like phone stuff shot from the station overbridge. He wondered if Randeep was behind it, peeved at being denied his big gun moment. But Freeman saw him drive off with Nahid just before Connors and his men were shot.

Car hit exit ramp top.

Zapata 'tached booth guy nodded and button poked, making the barrier shift.

Left onto New Bailey Street.

Driver was a tall young woman.

Leggy. Black leathered. Short skirt half up her back-side, she'd mumbled deferentially when she opened and shut his door. Wrapmirror shaded, tall as him in knee-length boots, she was more like a traffic cop than a TV chauffeur.

As they bumped rumble strips at the first crossing, he discreetly checked out her face in her rearview.

Stuff outside wiped her shades.

Tough looking.

Rough looking. Stacked black hair. Silver studs under pale-pink-lipsticky mouth. Such creatures insisted on defiling their stupid faces with jewellery. Equally pathetic fire tattoos, scrawling the back of her hands, disappeared up leather sleeves.

As they went under Salford Central Station bridge he looked at the Twemlow bloodbath freeze-frame parked on his phone in his sticky hand. One mouse click and it went newsroom global. Best thing was to go ahead with the TV grilling. Tackle Hunter after.

The woman slowed too soon as lights up ahead did green to amber. Most drivers would have jumped them. Freeman realized she was going the wrong way.

'Excuse me,' he said, bad vibing. 'We usually go along Deansgate and pick up Chester Road.'

48

'I go this way,' Kath told the bastard.

'Been driving long?' he asked nervously, discreetly fiddling with his door.

She'd locked them all.

'First day,' she said. 'In fact,' she added slyly, flexing her veined mitts doing ten-to-two at the chunky leather-skinned wheel, 'you're my first ass drive.'

Sense of power she had over this piece of shit who murdered Reece and the guys was awesome. Seemed like he was onto her. But he was so up himself he still talked down at her like she was scum fouling privileged air.

Just past Salford Central, she swerved left so fast Freeman nearly bumped his head. Big guy dashed from between the station's nearside tinted plate glass. Door opposite Freeman flew open and in jumped Craig, squeaking tan seat hide, rocking the car. Doing his signature lantern-jaw grin, he banged his door and rammed a Sheuze shotgun in Freeman's mug.

'Surprise surprise, Alex.'

Freeman's face was a picture in Kath's rearview. 'Good God no,' he said.

Gore Street was No Entry.

She'd three-point-turned flash quick.

Freeman implored behind her, 'I saw you get shot, Craig.' He waved his phone accusingly, like it had lied. Kath realized Hunter must have recently detonated her Twemlow phone-video bomb.

'Yeah. Only I'm indestructible see,' Craig told him. 'Or maybe I'm a ghost,' he added, sticking twin fat gun barrels up Freeman's nostrils. 'Come back to get sweet revenge on uber nasty Alex goddamn son-of-a-bitch Freeman.' He went 'Boo!' in his face, making him jump. Back on the main road, Kath took next left. Scene played in her rearview like a mini cinemascope movie. 'Hey I think you're scared, Alex,' Craig said, enjoying himself, pulling fresh gum.

'I'm sure we can work something out,' came a feeble toff reply. Rearview showed him do scaredy-cat head-shakes when Craig offered him a stick of gum.

'Wrong pal. You're gonna tell us where Hunter's little kids and lady are. HM too. Or I'm gonna take your head clean off.'

Brill idea of Craig's to snatch Freeman and trade him for Hunter's girls and ex, and maybe the Queen. When Hunter said Freeman was due to be interviewed by the BBC, Vanessa said a car would fetch him from CPHQ an hour before. Risky, taking him from under cop noses. But Kath agreed that kidnapping him tit-for-tat should swing the game their way. All she'd had to do when she arrived ahead of the Beeb's car was get out smiling and flash booth guy a bit of sheer black-stockinged—sheer black-tighted in such a short skirt—leg.

They hadn't told Hunter and Vanessa what they were up to. When Ross, Thinnes, and Pover arrived in Ross's Merc, which Kath was driving, they'd headed straight to CPHQ. Craig was a showman. He wanted to surprise Hunter with some ace news when they'd bagged bogeyman Freeman for def and were riding high.

49

Hunter and Vanessa had been cutting the film for over an hour. They hadn't used an in-house editor but were working on the Avid Symphony themselves to keep the thing under wraps as long as poss. Parked on screen was a gory long shot of dead guys.

Reception called to say Steve Hamer had arrived. Too dangerous for them to meet at the IFI. Instead Steve had brought the videoscan results over to Sound and Pics. When Hunter headed through to meet him, the idea of *Hunter: the Movie* giving audio clues to the whereabouts of Vicky and his girls seemed insane.

He'd filled Steve in on the vid's back story when he rang him to check on his ETA, using one of Connors's scrambled phones.

Going by Chelsea booted, six-foot-five Steve's face, when he offered a big hairy hand he sensed Hunter was having a hard time. 'Doesn't seem like five minutes,' he said, loping after him, laptop handed.

He meant since last winter.

Hunter had been to the IFI to get some DNA profile results. Soon after he nearly died. 'Time goes too quickly,' he told Steve when they arrived at the edit suite and he showed him in.

Steve hugged Vanessa, telling her how well she looked. Trepidation hung over the small airconned room. Responding to it, Steve popped his laptop.

'I pissed you off last time for leading you on,' he told Hunter apologetically, firing the kit.

He got a buzz taking clients through how he got a result. He liked showing rather than telling. Stringing it out last time meant somebody took an explosive direct hit meant for Hunter. Steve didn't play silly buggers this time but got to it. Hunter's hunch about the video holding tiny clues had been good. IFI kit had done top job. Steve knew where the girls and Vicky were.

Exactly where.

He told them straight.

'You're kidding me,' Hunter said, utterly gobsmacked. He hadn't expected a result. Wheeling over his chair, he sank down, trying to take it in.

'No jokes,' Steve said.

'Oh God Steve,' Vanessa said. She sat down, squeezing Hunter's hand reassuringly. 'Are you sure?'

'I wouldn't mess you guys about.'

'Shit,' Hunter said. 'Taking them there fits. 'And maybe the Queen too.' He wasn't sure how he felt. Angry. Scared. But just a tiny bit relieved.

'I thought it was a dead duck when you sent the link,' Steve said. He sat down. The laptop came to life. 'But when you get a hunch it's usually right.' He took them quickly through what he'd done, starting with Hayley's face thumbnail parked on screen. 'Key moment happens at the start,' he said. He set Hayley going where the vid jumped like it had stop-started, and she pretty much said the same thing twice.

Steve rewound, tweaking audio. In the background of the outgoing take they heard a distant whine. When he tweaked it some more it went so tinny it morphed to a high-pitch hiss. He pumped in some bottom end. Sound deepened to an approaching plane.

'Camera recorded sound,' Steve said. 'They stopped to let the plane go over, probably thinking it would clue you in to them being near an airport. Their dumb mistake was using their ears. They cut back the vid to get rid of the plane but didn't cut it back far enough. Audio picked it up over another sound. Only for a few secs but it was enough, before it gets blanked by this.'

Hunter had heard it but assumed it was some air conditioning thing. Low hum from which the distant plane emerged before it got cut.

'Extractor or something?'

'That's what I thought. It's actually an air recycling fan. Two buildings in the UK have it. It makes a unique sound, making my job easy. Ducts in top storeys channel fresh air so quietly you can barely hear it. Notching up the "plane" revealed it.'

'It isn't a plane?' Vanessa asked, wondering.

'Correct,' Steve said. 'Same people built it who built this.' He Google Imaged Glendale Tower on London's South Bank, then where the girls and Vicky were being held. 'Despite state-of-the-art soundproofing, somebody must have opened a window, letting that rogue sound seep in.' He zoomed up a laptop pic. 'I reckon Vicky and the girls are about here.' He pointed at the top. 'Where penthouse pads are. I know because I ran a directional audio scan. I won't bore you with tecchy bumph.'

There it was on screen, in all its glory.

Manchester's CPHQ.

'They heard a helijet,' Vanessa said.

'Flying into Piccadilly,' Steve added. 'If they've got the Queen there, it's perfect. Last place anybody would think of forty-odd storeys up. Bringing everybody in via a helipad on top meant nobody saw them.'

Hunter got up, crossed to the window, and shot the blind. CPHQ loomed close. Massive. Cutting clear early evening sky. Sun gilded it down a high-shine side.

Hayley.

Jenny.

Vicky.

The Queen.

So close yet so far.

'We know two gunships took off after the Royal Train at Kings Langley,' he said, as stuff fell into place. 'Our guys filming there saw them. Freeman told Connors he sent two gunships north. Must have been the same two. One with Vicky and the girls aboard. My God,' he said, shaking his head. 'They've been this close to the action all along. I bet Freeman put the Queen on the same gunship when the Royal Train stopped at Leighton Buzzard. One landed at Twemlow, carrying Freeman and his killer cops. Other must have kept going up here to CPHQ. My God,' he said again, amazed.

When Steve had gone, Hunter held Vanessa while they got it together.

At last he knew where his little girls and Vicky were. But gazing out at the sky-high, seemingly impregnable police fortress incarcerating them, the scary *Die Hard* scale of what they were up against hit him.

Lisa stood smoking with Sharron next to the Micra in the sunny factory yard. CSI was hard at it. Cameras flashed as the guys shot vics in the loading bay.

'I didn't know you smoked, Lisa,' black Carl said, standing away from the Micra's driver door to check his handset screen. He was dusting inside the car for prints. New to Thames Valley, built so solid he made the car squeak on its shocks when he ducked and dived in and out, he looked about 26. Amazingly he was 43.

'I smoke about three a year,' she told him, looking at the part-smoked ciggie with disgust before chucking it down and stamping on it. 'My partner hates it. He'd be mortified if he knew.'

She was playing it like she'd been upset by factory gore, to stop CSI boys taking the mick. How she felt went deeper than seeing two seriously wasted corpses, or the bizarre scene which met them in the office.

Lisa's personal life with new guy Rob was becoming an issue. Go back six months and she'd dived gung-ho into every Code 2 with Sharron. OK she was sensitive to danger and didn't do stupid. But a snap-judge fearlessness kept at bay on-the-job pussyfooting which could be fatal to a cop. She got paid to spend each day with her best mate. But behind the gobby banter doing North Bucks in a flash BM, the closer she got to her new guy at home, the more aware she was getting of her mortality at work. It had taken the edge off cop life.

And after all the scaredy build-up front office stuff, what did Sharron find?

Fox cubs.

Yeah, fox cubs.

Cute little bushy tail shysters, munching cakes and M&S sarnies. Moaning sound wasn't somebody dying but cubs play scrapping. Amazing how they'd bypassed fresh meat lying out front. Maybe mummy vixen, who took a hike with her yapping brood, soon as two leather-clad showgirls showed, was bringing up sweet veggie foxes.

Carl frowned at his handset. Lisa let go of a self-indulgent few mins. Doing some OTT American, she asked him, 'What's up in the crime lab, bro?'

'Bill Martin's pawprints are in the car,' he said. 'Three more sets on top. Most recent are this guy's, meaning he was last to drive it.'

He waved his handset.

Moon-face mugshot.

Bald young guy, age 25.

'Jack Stiller. TV and theatre make-up artist,' Carl added. 'IMDB credits back up his TV work. Underneath his prints are this guy's.'

Mugshot # 2.

Older.

Better looking.

'Mike Reynolds. An actor. Last screen credit a blink-and-you-miss-it part in *Eastenders* six months ago.'

'Maybe he's been doing theatre,' Sharron said.

'Yeah, maybe. Under his prints are this guy's.'

Handset flip number three.

Mugshot and bumph for an ugly young somebody-nobody of no fixed address.

'Three sets of prints on top of Bill Martin's. We know he drove to Milton Keynes Station in this car today because we saw it happen live on telly.'

'Right,' Lisa said. Touching her headset she got Central Control. 'Hey Col?'

'Yes my love?'

'Can you run a check on CCTV stuff from MK Station, when Bill Martin arrived this morning?'

'Better than that, my love, I can patch it through to your car so you can check it.'

Leather met leather as girls parked bums in scoop front seats. Up pinged CCTV stuff from Col's end, at the computer screen embedded in the dash. Carl crouched by Lisa's open door to watch.

She asked Col, 'When did Bill Martin land?'

'About half-twelve, my love.'

'OK,' she said, fingers pinch-wiping the screen. In went some timecodes.

Up came three high-angle thumbnail POVs of Station Square car park. She went for # 2's widest. Crept video forward. Nothing, so she crept back faster till they saw the Micra back out of a space and zip from shot because they were watching in reverse.

Playing everything forward in real time, zooming in, she brought the Micra back in shot. It parked then Bill Martin got out and surveyed the car park, like he was getting his bearings. He reached in the car and pulled a black attaché case, crossed to nearest pay station, paid, stuck the ticket in the car, then made for the station's jazzy airport-looking entrance.

'We know Bill Martin arrived in the Micra 'cause we just saw it,' Lisa said. 'Yet it ends up here at the factory. Let's see what happens in between.'

She stopped the video, typed timecodes six hours later, and hit fast-forward x32. Everything raced time-lapse fast. Cars and people zipped in and out of shot so crazy comic rapido it was tough to keep up.

Didn't matter. They were eyeing the Micra, parked solid as a rock.

Then it happened.

Somebody flashed up to the car, got in, and took it from shot so fast they missed it.

'Whoa,' went Sharron and Carl in stereo.

Lisa hit Pause and got the vid back to just before the car was driven off.

'Woo-hoo,' she said, zooming in, letting it play normal speed. There he was. TV make-up guy Stiller whose prints were on top of Mike Reynolds's. 'He fetches the car at 2.17pm. His prints are on top of Reynolds's, proving he's last person who drove the car. Yet the CCTV shows last person to drive it before him, whose prints are underneath, was Bill Martin.' She eyed Carl. 'You're saying Martin's prints are further down the pecking order, right?'

'Right,' he said.

'You sure about that?'

'Absolutely.'

'Get this then,' she said, realizing what she liked about cop life wasn't boy racing but doing clever deduction stuff where she got to use her smart mathematical brain. 'Stiller takes the car. Yet Bill Martin gets out of it before him when a fingerprint trail says it *should* be Mike Reynolds. He's an actor,' she said. 'Stiller does TV and theatre make-up. Soon after this innocent car park stuff happens, the Royal Train goes missing with the Queen aboard and Bill Martin driving.'

She got him back on screen.

Zoomed his face up nice and big.

'Are you guys thinking what I'm thinking?'

51

Connors and Kath had driven their prize Freeman booty away from town. Roads weren't busy, with it being a weekday evening. Merc's windows were smoked meaning no audience while bogeyman stared down a shotgun. Connors kept it low, outta sight.

They headed west past a big soccer stadium into some place called Trafford Park. Stacked ship containers and endless warehouses, old and new. Embedded railroad tracks bumped under, every once in a while.

Freeman kept stalling over Hunter's kids and ex. 'I'm telling you, Craig. We moved them about for security reasons,' he lied again. 'I don't know where they are.' Pro bullshitter, used to being top dog. Snapping nimble fingers to get his way.

'Nice try,' Connors told him, not buying.

Kath tut-tutted agreement, finding next roundabout. Crazy things roundabouts. States didn't have them. She twisted awkwardly out of her leather jacket, one-handing the wheel, revealing her cool arms.

Connors had seen her grow in recent weeks. It was kinda why he'd taken her under his wing. She was swell on the integrity front. When they'd driven into Manchester from Twemlow with Hunter and his guys, she said hardest thing she'd ever done was KO Bill Martin with a tranquillizer gun at the roadblock. She'd got showy for Reece and the guys because she wanted to save her little boy. But she'd hated doing it.

Connors could see himself under bedsheets with her. Knew it would be hot stuff. He killed the idea outta respect for Reece. Some guy-girl friendships needed to stay platonic. What they had going as buddies was way better than briefly fusing somewhere good.

They passed a big derelict brick place. Brewery, judging by ornate embossed stuff above a big entrance arch. Surrounded by steel fence and scaffold, whole place was coming down. Then Connors sussed scaffold had rusted. Crap and contractor stuff dumped everywhere said demolition guys had walked some time past. He told Kath to take next right. Freeman sat fright rigid, after double crossing them like he had. Connors kept hold of some manic eye. He wanted Freeman to think there was no telling what might happen next.

Road switched from blacktop to bumpy north country cobbles. Steel palisade kept them company then said hello to weed covered flat concrete where brewery out-buildings had been and gone. End opened out under a serious vaulted steel rail bridge. Connors had seen similar bridge stuff happening in Manchester, at Castlefield. Huge fat tubes, covered in rivets, zig-zagged by graffiti, supported a railroad. Buncha rusty burnt-out cars made the place feel creepy-uneasy, like Hell's Kitchen before big city clean-up.

Kath pulled up under the bridge, killed the engine, and slung her door. Water spit-spatted on the Merc's roof and windshield.

Otherwise dead quiet.

Connors let some time fatten like Freeman did when he showed at Twemlow with his killer cops.

'What will you do with me, Craig?'

'Reckon we'll gaffer tape you to a chair, douse you in gas, and cut off one of your ears.' Grinning, he tugged Freeman's nearest, making him jump. Naïve bastard hadn't first clue about pop culture. Connors's phone hit off, cracking open the moment. 'Stay right there, Alex,' he told him, eye-winking.

Kath knelt to cover Freeman with her shotgun over the back of her seat, showing pearly white teeth against her bronzy skin and sexy light-pink lips.

Connors kept a toothy grin going, goading Freeman while he felt for his phone.

Hunter's face.

'Yeah what's up, son?'

'We know where Freeman's taken them,' he said, surprising Connors, telling him straight.

'Jesus,' he said amazed, seriously impressed when Hunter quickly filled him in.

'Likewise our end.'

'Well, well,' Connors said, eyeing Freeman.

'Where are you?' asked Hunter.

'Few miles outta town in the back of a flash Merc with a real nice pretty lady, sitting next to one helluva scared Alex Freeman who's cosying with a shotgun.'

Almighty gobsmacked, *'What?'* from Hunter.

Connors got him up to speed.

'Why the hell didn't you say something?'

'No time to let you guys know by the time we hooked up with our guys and worked out what the hell we was gonna do. Plus, Uncle Craig does surprises. You still at Sound and Pics?'

'Yeah.'

'OK we'll bring him in.'

'You can't bring him here, Craig.'

'My guys can take him some place till we decide what to do next. See you soon.'

Hunter OK'd, sounding pissed at being kept outta the loop as he hung up.

'Clever,' Connors told Freeman as he stuck away his phone. 'Real clever.'

'How do you mean?'

'Sticking the Queen and Hunter's kids and ex at top of CPHQ. Last place anybody was gonna think of.'

Stunned silence from the toff.

Kath obliged, filling it with, 'Like wow. Is that where they are?'

'Seems so, sweet gal.'

Freeman asked coldly, 'How do you know?'

While Connors clued him in about the videoscan, Freeman watched Kath uncertainly. No sex in his eyes, which was kinda spooky. Dressed Royal-blue, he looked midways between a porn peddler and an ass riding ad exec. Connors revised his opinion, wondering if his Brit toff captive was just a tiny bit *street*.

'Game's on its way to being up, Alex,' he told him. He told Kath, 'Let's get back to town. Get Ross hands-off so I can talk to him without taking my eyes off our reluctant hot party guest.'

52

Kath OK'd and banged her door.

Before she could poke the ignition she heard approaching wheels. 'Uh-oh,' she said, eyeing her rearview. 'Looks like we got company.'

Serious company. And how.

Moment loaded with a monster black Audi 4x4 scene-stealing flash, bang, pulse pounding wallop. No window tint for this mean machine but *black* windows. Fat low-pro gripper tyres rode OTT black trims. Baked bean cans welded to noisy twin perf exhausts sounded off big time while the 4x4 skated cobbles, chucking crap.

Winking evening sun, it tonned towards the bridge like a missile homing for the kill. Kath knew they had trouble. Craig sussed it like a shot. Got out of the Merc, side furthest from 4x4, telling Kath to do likewise and stick her shotgun down the back of her skirt.

'Keep your back to the car and pray, girl,' he added and stuck his shotgun down the back of his jeans, walking round the Merc slowly, so he faced the 4x4 without it being obvious. He warned Freeman to stay put if he wanted to stay in one piece.

4x4 got there, finding sun-striped shadow under the bridge. Up went dust. Took some secs for it to waft, rounding off a noisy showstopper entrance.

Out got three swing dicks.

Tough-guy poser ensemble waving old-style shotguns. *Get Carter* stuff which went out with the Ark. Hardconked gangsta boys, up for some fun. Vin Diesel wannabes. Bald heads. Granite mugs. More tattoo than skin. Tight vests and pants, black to match the wheels. On went shades. Smirky pockmarked jaws gave it some heavy gumchew.

Flat-nose lead ape, craving attention to compensate for empty space between his ears, took steps to show he was *da man*. Voice echoing, he fired at Craig, 'Hey big boy. You ain't got no permit to be here.' Delinquent exhibitionism. Gorilla speak lifted from Hollywood blockheads who were his cardboard role models.

'We don't want no trouble,' Craig said, coolly gum-chewing like the ape, hands doing hips. Their voices thud-echoed it out, playing off each other.

'Looks like we got us some real Stateside muscle,' said ape # 2. Chin trendily goatee fluffed, he blew a bubble, popping it to show he could do *da man* too.

'Yeah, ain't we,' said ape # 3. Squeaky voiced balls-clamped-in-a-vice type. Giving it less basso macho on the echo front, his jaw gum-wagged twice as fast as his ugly bald bumchums.

Pigeons cooed from high in the bridge, poohing for England if the state of wavy cobbles was anything to go by. Odd birds fluttered among girders, spooked by the deadly scene playing under them.

Kath saw ape # 1 eyeballing her. Felt exposed in her short leather skirt. He told her, 'Off with your top, bitch. I wanna see your titties.'

'Ignore him Kath,' Craig told her.

'Don't worry,' she said.

She was scared. Bridge acoustics made her feel funny. Blood banged in her ears so loud she worried it might stop her hearing proper. Shotgun dug her back. Perched on wedge heels, she was afraid to move in case the gun fell out behind her.

Trying not to sound pissed Craig appealed to the apes again. 'We don't want no trouble, OK? If we walked some place we shouldn't we're real sorry. We'll get right back in our wheels and scene exit.'

Ape # 1 laughed. 'You ain't going no place outside a coffin boy,' he said, pumping his piece. 'After you've watched us hammer the bitch.' He told Kath, 'Lose the gear, babe. Everything.'

Other two apes joined in, pumping too.

Kath saw Freeman, cowering in the back of the Merc. Craig had relieved him of his phone and stuck it in the glovebox. Now was when he'd have secretly fingered it, calling cops. Current situ made bent cops a cosy option.

Craig, hands still doing hips, looked pissed as hell. 'I'm gonna say this one more time, guys. We don't want no trouble 'cause me and my nice lady here don't wanna to see *you* boys end up getting busted asses.'

Kath knew he was laying on US of A street jive, to try and wind up the tossers to distract them. She'd seen his hands creep round his hips. Knew why.

He added, 'Seeing you three assholes, waving pea-shooters, I'm thinking I don't wanna bust me any dumb Brit shit under this railroad bridge. You hearing me?'

53

Connors knew from experience that if you insulted guys like this in hot situations, a nanosec happened where they got so pissed they lost it and you got an opening you could use. Usually one ballbrain sounded off how he was gonna waste you as his temper rose. Pushing his dumbassedness till his reflexes went AWOL.

Ape # 1 was losing it. Upcoming nanosec where he gave other dipshits some eyeflash, before he shelled his piece, was about to happen.

Or it woulda done, had a feeble toff voice not piped up. 'Excuse me, gents. Surely we can come to an amicable arrangement.' As the bogeyman eased up from the Merc's back seat, Connors thought *shit no*. Freeman was too goddamn arrogant to know. 'Alex Freeman,' he added smoothly, introducing himself. 'These two kidnapped me. I carry senior jurisdiction. Help me escape and you'll be treated leniently.'

Oh Jeez, Connors thought. Bogeyman's thud echo was *uh-oh* portentous when it died.

Poor bastard wasn't a bit *street* after all.

Ape # 1, pulling a hard face, showing some serious white eye, appealed to # 2 and # 3.

'Is this posh pissbrain for real?'

Connors wanted to put his head in his hands but didn't. Sudden movement would have gotten him shot. As Freeman swanned over he felt in his jacket, presumably to flash some ID to prove he *was* real deal. Too late. Ape # 1's pissed expression, ushering that vital nanosec Connors had anticipated, got waylaid. Butting in on a high-anxiety moment, looking like you was gonna pull a gun, was gonna get you fried.

Soon as Freeman's hand went for his jacket up came ape shotguns. One. Two. Three.

Realizing what was gonna happen, bogeyman chucked up his hands to hide his face. Connors had gotten his nanosec. Not how he expected. But he got it.

Yanking his shotgun out from behind him he let rip. Kath took her cue and did same. In tandem they pumped away, wasting apes in a relentless gorefest. Sheuze shotguns were mean. Apes came apart at seams, arms flying. 4x4 behind them took it bad too. Shiny slug spats opened across it. Jumping on its fat tyres, glass popped while red stuff frenzied.

When it was over, the 4x4's alarm somehow got set off, *wee wee wee wee wee weeing* like crazy in all the excitement. Connors couldn't work it out. He went across, reached under the driver's dash, popped the hood, went round, lifted the hood, and one-hand-yanked wires like Arnie ripping a junction box before he wasted cops.

Wee wee wee wee wee weeing stopped.

'Oh God Craig,' Kath said, letting it come out, realizing what they'd done.

Her voice echo died while she dashed over and threw her arms round him.

'Hey it's OK,' he said, holding her.

'I never killed anybody.' She was shaken bad 'cause of how hard she held him.

'Me neither,' he told her, thinking back to his little talk with Vanessa at Twemlow. Thinking back to lottsa stuff. Big moment for them. Kinda appropriate they shared it. 'They would have wasted us,' he assured her, knowing it's how it woulda happened. He eased up her face with a hand. 'No two ways. Them or us.'

Wrapping her in his arms, he enjoyed an awesome protective feeling Nature meant guys to get from girls. Long time since he held a girl he liked. He struggled not to drop his hands to hold her by her ass. Now wasn't right time. But hell it was a tough few secs.

Stuff happening behind them got him turning. Last time he looked, Freeman kissed dirt. Shit scared but still in one piece.

On his feet, making a run for it, he nancy-boy skipped outta sight down a banking, far side of the bridge. By the time Connors and Kath made top of the banking, Freeman hit rusted rail tracks at the bottom. Choked in fireweed, tracks bent round, heading off to the trashed brewery over by the freeway.

Connors shouted, 'I don't know how the hell you got the nerve, Alex. Kath and me just saved your crappy life.' Freeman ignored him and kept going. Connors shimmied down the banking, Kath behind.

They hit a level area midway.

Connors held his shotgun out at arm's length, in one hand. Freeman kept on nancying, panting from the heat, his jacket tails flying.

Connors shot ground near him.

Freeman stopped, grabbing his head like he did when apes were gonna waste him. Puff of slug dust and fireweed bits wafted while thud echo did its thing. Getting the idea, Freeman turned and stuck up his hands. His pants and shoes were dusty. His shadow came from him rippling old grassy railroad sleepers.

Connors waited. 'I ain't hearing you, Alex.'

'He's a selfish pratt,' Kath noted.

'Yeah ain't he just.'

Being the kinda social smoothy who thought of no-body but himself, Freeman let some secs go by till he got Connors's drift. 'Thanks for saving my life Craig,' he shouted, pissed admitting it.

'Both of us,' Connors reminded him.

'Both of you,' Freeman tacked on.

'Now get your ass back up here.'

54

Randeep and Nahid had waited nearly two hours in the RR in Media City car park. Freeman never showed for his *BBC News* interview.

Beeb had made excuses but Randeep sensed something fishy. Because Freeman seemed to have crapped on them since Twemlow, they'd come to the BBC to kill him on live TV. UK's top security bod, showing to discuss the Queen's vanishing act and getting totalled live in studio would have made for incredible telly and Youtube hits to die for. Boy would it have spooked a watching worried world, giving Randeep his buzz.

Ever since they'd got involved with Freeman, some-thing kept telling Randeep the bastard wasn't for trust-ing. So he'd taken a precaution, early on, of preparing for such an awkward eventuality.

'Isn't it extreme, killing him?' Nahid said.

'Only thing left to do.'

Bored of Freeman talk, Randeep was ready to move on. They weren't staying in Manchester overnight. They were heading south to Milton Keynes, to make an early morning visit to pick up some very serious kit.

'What purpose does it serve?'

'Shows him who's boss.'

'Jesus Randeep. Get over it.'

'I'm doing it anyway,' he said. Pulling his phone, he found Freeman's special number. 'Chances are he'll still be at CPHQ, which would be kinda nice.'

'We should bide our time.'

Randeep was having none of it.

Time to draw a line under Freeman.

CPHQ punched distant evening sky going orange. City centre tower stuff, doing Manchester's skyline, was silhouetting. As country's security chief, Freeman had an office with attached apartment at CPHQ tip top, next to where Randeep suggested they imprison the Queen and Hunter's kids and ex. Not having spoken to Free-man since the Queen got taken off the train he'd no idea if she was there. He didn't care. He wanted Freeman's head. If, when he shot call, top of CPHQ blew, it would make for some cool CG-looky fireworks.

'Get ready my friend.'

They watched CPHQ up front.

Down went *the* button.

Boom, finally.

But not from CPHQ.

Not from Manchester city centre.

Looking round gobsmacked, Randeep went, 'Huh?' trying to work out where it was at.

'Behind us,' Nahid added, shuftying round awkwardly in his seat.

Baffled, they chucked doors and got out.

Mushroom fire nuke-rolled skyward a few miles west. Trafford Park maybe.

Or Port Salford.

'Why's he over there?' said Randeep, amazed.

Hadn't expected that.

Weeks ago, during a meeting about the hijack, Freeman left the room and left his phone on his desk. Randeep slipped in a piece of nasty Jap jelly, fixed to take *the* number in case he ever needed to put Freeman in his place. Way less of a boom from his phone than Sheffield and Stockport because it was a teensy-weensy bit of Jap stuff stuck under a SIM. But as it packed twenty times normal jelly power at least, it would still have obliterated everything within fifty or a hundred yards.

Including Freeman.

They set off towards the smoke before it stopped going up. Randeep got news channels on the dash. *Sky News* was soon on the case. Twitter. Getting excited about an explosion near a derelict brewery at Manchester's Trafford Park. Guys working at Port Salford, other side of the ship canal, said an isolated rail bridge, haunt of gangs and joyriders, had been destroyed. Teensy blob of Jap stuff not so teensy on the boom front after all.

55

Massey was back at the window. Sky high view was amazing. He could see across Manchester to the Cheshire Plain to Snowdonia's distant mountains.

Something nearer had recently caught his eye. Explosion at Trafford Park. He knew where he was looking because he could make out gigantic box warehouses at Port Salford, which the Queen had opened.

World class soundproofing to combat close gunship proximity meant he hadn't heard a boom. But whatever it was had been pretty big. Epicentre burned like a bonfire as sun went down.

Carole was sitting on the huge white leather sofa, legs tucked up next to her. She could see the distant blaze because of the floor-to-ceiling window wall.

'What is it, John?'

'Probably kids torching a car.'

'Looks rather more serious.'

Too right, Massey thought, especially after Sheffield and Stockport. News channels would be onto it like a shot. Ordinarily he'd have been checking them. Being cut off from the outside world wasn't such a bad thing. Although he wondered if they were being kept at top of CPHQ for ulterior reasons, the atmosphere was agreeably convivial. For six hours they'd indulged in the lost art of good conversation. Massey had really talked to Carole, liking her company. Coming to terms with how well they'd hit off troubled him nearly as much as his growing suspicion of Freeman's dodgy motives.

The Queen, wearing glasses, was working on some official papers she'd grabbed from the train. 'I wonder what's happened to Chris,' she said.

Massey agreed he'd been gone quite a while. Their penthouse apartment was self-contained. They'd been told that if they wanted to stretch their legs there were some public loos in the corridor. Cop minders were stationed behind sliding doors which led to the lifts and service area.

As if cued, Chris reappeared, looking flustered.

'Look what I've found,' he said, sounding mightily pleased with himself.

Massey couldn't believe what he saw.

Two cute, pretty little girls. One blonde. One brunette. Aged maybe 6 and 7. Hair nearly to waists. It explained crying children they'd heard. T-shirted, designer pink jeaned, huddled together, they wondered what they'd walked into.

'Oh good God,' Carole said, shocked.

'Hello there,' the Queen said smiling, putting down her pen, setting aside her papers.

Chris was great with kids.

Stooping slightly, he led the girls over, one each hand. 'This is Hayley,' he said, meaning the little blonde. 'This is Jenny. Come and say hello.'

'Hello Hayley. Hello Jenny,' the Queen said.

'Hello,' they said.

Either they didn't recognize Her Majesty because she was wearing glasses, or they were too young to know who she was.

Carole, smiling, dropped to her knees on the thick rug. 'Are you sisters?' she asked them.

Big vigorous nods.

'Where the heck were they, Chris?' Massey asked.

'I saw them peep at me from the Ladies when I came out of the Gents. Good job it was me who spotted them instead of a goon.'

'How did you get in there?' the Queen asked.

'From under the floor,' they said.

'Why were you under the floor? Carole asked.

'Our mummy found a way under the carpet.'

'Gosh,' Carole said. 'You were brave being in there all on your own. Wasn't it dark?'

Heads shook this time.

'It's quite bright inside,' Hayley said.

'It's a service duct,' Chris added. 'I've been in and had a look. There's no way out.'

Massey remembered seeing Hunter's face on the iPad, during the briefing aboard the train.

He said to Carole, 'Do you see what I see?'

'Not half,' she said, looking at dark-haired Jenny. 'The resemblance is striking.'

Massey said to the girls, 'Does your daddy introduce TV programmes?'

More nodding.

'What are you getting at, John?' Chris asked.

Massey said to Jenny, 'You look like your daddy don't you?' She nodded. He told Chris, 'Same daddy was due to come aboard the train to film us.'

'Seems like an odd coincidence,' Carole noted.

'Something's going on, John,' the Queen observed.

'I agree ma'am.' He took each girl by a small hand. 'Why are you here in this building?'

Hayley said, 'Bad man who took my Rupert made us come with our mummy.'

'Didn't you want to come?'

Heads shook.

'How did you get up here?'

Through the window a gunship approached Helipad 3, which jutted above the apartment. Its elliptical outer edge swept massively away. Mute because of sound-proofing, the gunship swooped in like an insect and dis-appeared overhead, hazards pinging. No sound. Only a vague judder sensed through the building.

'We came in one of those,' Hayley said.

'Why did the bad man take Rupert?'

Jenny said, in an exquisite sharing-a-big-secret way, 'He got a policeman to video us, so Rupert could take a special message to our daddy.'

'And what did they make you tell him?'

'That if he didn't do as Rupert said, we might never see him again.'

Filling up, they turned to hold each other as the memory shot back to haunt them. It was gut wrenching, watching them support each other shyly, trying to cover their eyes.

'Oh you poor sweet darlings,' Carole said, voice thickening as she knelt up and hugged them.

'My God,' Chris said. 'Freeman's a nasty piece of work. Doing that to children. Put me in a room with him and I'll teach him a thing or two. And this time, ma'am, I make no apology for lowering the tone.'

The Queen said, 'Find out what's going on, John.'

'Forgive me ma'am but we should think this through first. Freeman seems to have brought the girls and their mother here against their will. He's made them give Mr Hunter an ultimatum, suggesting he must do something to safeguard them. Meanwhile we're being kept all the way up here, ostensibly for your safety but with serious questionmarks, with no access to the outside world. I wonder what Alex Freeman doesn't want us to know. We need a volunteer to go with Hayley and Jenny back to their mother.'

'Guess that means muggins,' Chris said, loving the idea. 'Can you take me to your mummy?'

They nodded but were distracted by a plate of fresh egg sandwiches (white bread, no crusts) on the occasional table next to the Queen. A fawning fat cop brought them in, not long before Chris went to the loo.

'Would you like one before you go?' the Queen asked, reaching for the plate, holding it in front of the girls. Each chose a sandwich she liked the look of. Then they flopped to their knees to eat them.

56

Sharron and Lisa had left CSI to it and were on their way to Jack Stiller's place.

He shared a house with two guys in Stratford Road, across from Wolverton Rail Works. Interesting him living where he did when a certain Royal Train shedded there had disappeared.

Music thudded downstairs when they arrived. *I Predict a Riot* by Kaiser Chiefs. Terrace houses that part of the road were bay-windowed, red-brick, with patches of scrubby dry grass up front. Passing horn hit off when tosser-at-wheel spied leggy heat bumming a front door. Soon as Lisa chimed the bell, music stopped. Front door got pulled by a tall, dark, good-looking hunk, circa 25. Long scary-hairy legs in tight denim shorts. Bare footed, Stella handed, his eyes popped when they feasted on girly bumps and curves.

'Whoa,' he said, beaming. 'Today's my lucky day. It's a stereo coppergram, isn't it?'

Boyish slurp from can.

'Very funny,' Lisa said, finding it tough to stop her eyes wandering down, confronted by skinny-dip shorts. 'Can we come in please, sir?'

'As long as you promise never to leave.'

Front room was usual laminate floored young guy den, geared to lazy-time entertainment. Flat screen telly walled above fireplace doing mute Sky Sports. Gaming consoles. Stacked CDs and spent lager cans filled a low-flying Ikea table. Pair of two-seater red leather Klippan sofas squared off from two sides at ninety.

'What's up ladies?'

'Is Jack Stiller in?'

'Yeah he is.'

'Can you fetch him please?'

'Sure,' he said, and left the room. He shouted upstairs. 'Hey up Jack. Two policebirds want you to seduce them with your irresistible charm.' He sounded to run on the spot in the hall then came back, grinning, rubbing hands in anticipation. 'I'm Jack. I hear you'd like to talk to *moi*. Who's first up for a spot of charming?'

'Bugger,' Lisa said.

'Guess I'm not your man,' he said, turning dead serious. 'What am I supposed to have done?'

Lisa unhooked her handset.

'Recognize him? Apparently you're him.' Stiller wagged his head. 'You wouldn't be winding us up, would you sir?'

'Come on,' he said. 'You must get a feel for folk. I've a big gob and love the female species. But I wouldn't take the piss over stuff like this.'

Sharron said, 'You into film or TV make-up?'

'Yeah, now that's an odd one,' he said, slumping on the couch facing the fireplace, nodding for girls to park bums on the other. Seemed like an old wound had been re-opened. 'It's a tough business. Long hours soon got to me.' He swigged from his can. 'I teach kids with special needs now. Glorified art classes, really. But I do regular time and pay's not bad.'

Back went the can again, his blue eyes on Sharron's, Lisa noted.

She sensed a light go on next to her.

'Meaning I get time for some social,' he added.

They chatted to him for an hour. He was an OK guy. No clues as to how his ID got thefted. Seemed liked he'd been picked at random. Him living across from the rail depot, and the movie make-up thing, seemed like co-incidence but got Lisa thinking.

Hollywood could make people into clones. Real Stiller confirmed it by showing them some amazing website stuff on the TV. It's why they were with him so long, picking his brain about movie prosthetics. Crazy stuff, even if CGI had nearly killed it.

'Seems like a nice guy,' Lisa said, clunk-clicking when they were back in the BM.

'Yeah,' Sharron agreed.

'His eyes were all over you.'

'Were they?'

'Yours were all over him.'

'Excuse me?'

'I can tell when you're falling in love 'cause you stop calling me "hon".'

'Sure I do hon.'

Lisa had bogus Jack Stiller on her handset.

No explanation for his prints being on top of Mike Reynolds's when CCTV showed Bill Martin getting out of the Micra.

They'd taken real Stiller's fingerprints inside.

No match. ID of two headless vics at the factory said "antiques dealers". As if. Prints lifted from the pack of knee-highs threw up a black girl, Kerryann Foster, who ran a cake decorating service.

Bigger as if.

Phone rang before Lisa pulled out.

Carl.

Still at the factory.

'Yeah Carl?'

'We've done the office. Real Bill Martin's pawprints are all over. He was here for def.'

'Plot deepens,' Lisa said. 'Cheers Carl.' She lost him. 'I wonder if we should call this TV guy, Hunter, first thing in the morning.'

'What for, hon?'

'He was due to interview Bill Martin and might be able to shed some light.'

She checked her wingmirror.

'In other news,' she added, pulling out, looking for- ward to getting home to her guy and letting him explore every bit of her. 'What does a lovestruck cop do when she fancies a fit guy helping with enquiries?'

'Go on, hon,' she said. 'Enlighten me.'

'Knocks on his door when she's off duty?'

57

'What the hell happened, guys?'

'We nearly bought it,' Connors told Hunter from the back. He stuck his shotgun under Vanessa's seat.

Kath jumped in next to him and stuck her shotgun under Hunter's seat. 'Three close calls in one day's enough,' she said, feeling for her seatbelt.

Hunter headed back up the lane to the main road. They'd found them hidden among trees at the end of Chapel Place, at Barton Road Swing Bridge.

Their SOS came as Hunter and Vanessa, at Sound and Pics, picked up news of an explosion at Trafford Park. By the time they got there Ross, Pover, and Thinnes had been and gone. They'd taken Freeman to Ross's place north of Manchester. With Freeman hostage, pressure on delivering the film was off. Plan was to go to Sarah's boyfriend's place in town and work out a plan. Ross and his guys were gonna make Freeman phone in, gun at head, warning his people to hang fire and wait to hear.

Hunter let a bus go by then turned right onto the swing bridge. Joining Trafford with Salford Borough it was pivoted from a narrow island in Manchester Ship Canal. When ships needed to pass, the bridge—controlled by a tall brick valve house—swung through ninety degrees. With Atlantic Gateway a reality, and Port Salford booming, the bridge and adjacent historic aqueduct were swinging more than they'd ever done.

Vanessa was front passenger. She handed out bottled ice water from a red PVC coolbag.

'We saved Freeman's life,' Connors said, taking a bottle from her, popping it. 'Bastard made sure we knew he'd inadvertently saved ours.'

'How'd he manage that?' Hunter asked.

'After we tangled with those crazees,' Connors said, 'Freeman took a hike. We went after him.' He pulled water and backhanded his mouth. 'As we climbed back up to the Merc, it blew before we went over the top. Rail bridge took it bad. Secs later and we'd have been buzzard meat. My ears are still zinging.'

'Mine too,' Kath said. In his rearview Hunter saw her ruffle her black hair with a horsy head kick.

'I figured cops and firefighters would soon show. So we took off with Freeman, at gun point, along an overgrown railroad and ended up by the ship canal. Called you guys and kept going till you found us.'

'What do you reckon caused it?' Vanessa asked him. 'The bang?'

'Yes.'

'Freeman's phone musta been booby-trapped. Can't see how it was anything else.'

'Why would it be rigged?' said Hunter.

'Good question.' He took more water. 'What I'd like to know is why it went off when it did.'

'Maybe he primed it before he ran off,' Vanessa offered.

'Don't see how. We stuck it in the glovebox, in case he tried to call his guys without us seeing. But that was ages before we got to the railroad bridge. No way could he have primed it, anticipating he'd be able to make a run for it.'

Hunter had skirted Eccles back round to Centenary Way and back over the ship canal to Trafford Park to get to the city. As they passed a trashed brewery, Connors said it was where they'd turned off with Freeman. Sun was going but sky was bright enough for them to see bomb smoke billowing between passing silos.

Hunter wasn't taking it in.

He'd seen something coming straight at them across next roundabout. Braking hard, he skidded sharp right into a crappy cobbled sidestreet straight across from the brewery.

'Jeez,' Connors said, lurching.

'What's up love,' Vanessa said, steadying herself.

Saying nothing, he pulled up past a loaded rubble skip and dived from the car. 'Stay here,' he told them, grabbing his phone.

'What's wrong, pal?'

Street faced the old brewery offices. Flagstone pavements had been looted. Rusty rail lines, embedded in cobbles, ran dead centre but disappeared where they got chopped by the main road. Hunter ran to the end and got down behind a torched car. Got his phone camera going and hit zoom. Shooting through the car's smelly burnt-out shell, he panned with an approaching white Range Rover as it growled up and past. When it had gone he ran over to opposite corner and peeped round. Indicators flashing, the RR turned into the road Connors said they took to get to the rail bridge.

When he got back to the car, Connors was standing next to it, draining his bottle water. Hunter set the video going and gave him the phone.

'Another bomb goes off,' he said. 'Blip compared to Sheffield and Stockport but look which two nutters happen to be cruising the area.'

'You were quick on the draw there son,' Connors said, watching the vid. On the phone, mirrorshaded playboys gooned like flash tossers from the RR. 'Wish I knew what the hell goes on. Weird those two being here if it *was* the bogeyman's phone which blew.'

Soon as he mentioned phone Kath's kicked off in the car. 'Whoa Craig. Look who it is.' Shuftying across the seat she passed him the phone.

'Who is it?' Hunter asked, trying to see.

'Poulson,' Connors said, spooked. 'I'd kinda forgotten he existed. What do you reckon, Kath?'

'Our phones are scrambled. Phil set them up. If we answer, and it's a trap, he can't trace us.'

Connors weighed stuff up while the phone kept going. 'I had screwy feelings 'bout Freeman. But Poulson seemed like a swell guy.'

'Who is he? Vanessa asked.

'Guy who pulled everything together and managed the make-up crew. Bill Martin clone stunt was his idea 'cause he has family who work in movies.'

Kath said, 'Why's he calling me if he knew we were due to be killed at Twemlow?'

'Does he know?' Vanessa wondered.

'Guess I'm assuming he's bent like Freeman,' Connors admitted. 'Being his right-hand guy.'

'Yeah but what if he isn't?' Kath said.

Still the phone did its thing, counting down to voice-mail flip.

When it flipped Hunter said they ought to lose themselves, in case the RR came back other ways.

58

As Craig and Hunter banged shut their doors Kath said, 'This is gonna sound off the wall guys. Bear with me.' Idea came soon as Poulson rang. He seemed OK to her.

Posh. Easy to wind up 'cause he wasn't street. But good at mucking in, for a toff, which was cool. 'Phil organized an awesome Bill Martin movie make-up job, right?'

'He sure did,' Craig told her.

Buzzing, she went for it.

'Get this then. What if he's on our side?'

'Holy shit,' Craig said, getting Kath's drift.

Hunter got it too. Looked to be thinking OMG when he shuftied round in his seat to listen to her.

'If he did it once,' she said, 'surely he can do it again, *if* he's on our side.'

'What are you getting at?' Vanessa asked.

'We've got Freeman,' she said. 'What if we created a Freeman dupe and sent him into CPHQ, to get your guys out?'

'Who'd be dumb enough to be up for that?' Hunter said, blundering in.

All eyes were on him.

'Oh for God's sake *come on*,' Hunter said, getting hemmed in. He knelt up defensively in his seat. 'You cannot be serious.' He appealed to Vanessa. 'Help me out here.'

Craig asked him, 'How tall are you?'

'Three foot six,' he said, pissed off.

Craig held a flat hand near his face, weighing up Freeman's height. 'I'm just over six-five. I reckon Freeman's six foot, like you. Skinnier, but the nancy loose suits he does are gonna hide that. We got the right flash threads 'cause he's wearing 'em.'

'No,' Hunter said, firmly wagging his head from side to side. 'Absolutely not.'

'This could be your big chance to rescue your little girls,' Craig said, flashing him some knowy eye. 'Maybe show some allegiance to your fine old Queen.'

Hunter buried his face in his hands and swore.

Vanessa told him, 'It's not fair to expect Craig and Kath and their guys to get Vicky and the girls out.'

'I didn't mean it like that,' Hunter said. 'I'll be first into CPHQ waving a shotgun if I have to. But posing as Freeman? They'd suss it right off.'

'Our guy pulled off Bill Martin in full view of world media,' Craig said. 'You saw it on TV, in killer clear HD close-up. He fooled you guys.'

Kath touched Hunter's arm. 'I saw them make up Mike. It's spooky. Those guys are so talented. As long as you're roughly same height and build, you cannot tell. Freeman says make-up doubles sometimes stand in for world leaders at risky public do's.'

Hunter, looking sick, reached over to high-five playfully with Kath.

She interlocked their fingers but gave his hand a reassuring squeeze. He was a kind of guy she'd once have described as "serious". Codespeak among girls she grew up with in the backstreets of Stoke-on-Trent for "sensitive". Highly fanciable, he was out of her league and strictly NG because he was deep in love with Vanessa, who was quite posh like Poulson.

'I knew you'd be trouble,' he told her.

Craig told her, 'We could do with going back to K-Tech and getting Simon Kane to knock up a CPHQ sim, so we can check the place out.'

'Why do you say that?' Hunter said, stunned.

'K-Tech's where we rehearsed the hijack on a crazy lab simulator.'

'At Milton Keynes,' Kath added.

'Jesus Christ you guys,' Hunter told them, despairing, looking more hemmed in than ever. 'Six or eight hours after we hook up and you casually mention K-Tech's involvement.'

'Conversation didn't get there yet, pal.'

Vanessa said, 'K-Tech is developing new generation cop uniforms. They're also into virtual reality kit and advanced cyber systems. Last we heard, they were developing some highly top secret thing.'

'Mighta been the lab sim,' Craig said. 'Train driver Mike trained on it. Welsh guy Pover rehearsed on it, before he hit Crewe Gateway.'

'Are you saying Simon Kane's involved in the Royal hijack?' Hunter said, looking like he might have got up from a road having just been run over.

'He was involved 'cause K-Tech does government stuff and by default works through Freeman's office. I met him a few times and saw him cosying with Freeman. I got the impression it only went as far as the sim. I wouldn't have said they were bed buddies.'

Vanessa said, 'There's more to that insinuation than you might think.'

'I don't wanna know,' Craig told her.

She Googled Simon Kane pics on the Nexus. Similar creepy-looking smoothy to Freeman but less weedy and sporting the craziest Javier Bardem mullet.

Kath's phone pinged in Craig's hand, forcing them to get back to where they'd been at. 'Looks like Poulson's left a lengthy message.' He gave Hunter the phone. 'Put it through the speakers, pal, and let's cross fingers.'

59

Randeep and Nahid couldn't get near the rail bridge. Cops blocked the long cobbled road. 'Area's restricted,' plump girl piggy told them through Nahid's open window when they pulled up.

Randeep got her false eyelashed eyeline and did innocent sightseer. 'I say, what's happened, officer?'

'There's been an explosion.'

'Anybody dead?'

'We don't know.'

Randeep could see the blazing bridge outlined against gathering dusk. Emergency vehicles were spread under it like dominoes. Strobing lightbars found steel girders bent by the blast. Radio static spat and fizzed. Fire engines had put out a car and were hard at work. Junked cars, probably joyrider kills, were chucked about. Remains of a 4x4 smoked. Not much else left. No mistaking, even at that distance, which twisted lump of scrap was Freeman's phone bomb epicentre.

Two more emergency vehicles arrived, bumping cobbles. Girl cop waved them through, telling the RR: 'Can you gents get scarce. You're blocking the road.'

As Nahid three-point-turned he asked Randeep, 'Why would Freeman be down here?'

'Wish I knew my friend.'

On dash TV, Sky speculated about latest bomb. Starved of live news feed, aerial shots ran showing a crowd building outside Buckingham Palace as concern grew for the Queen's safety, now she'd been "forced into hiding". Like Randeep predicted, markets were nervous. International outrage was growing.

Dissolve to a sombre candlelit vigil at Westminster Abbey. Slow pan across sobbing kids while VO droned about temporary school closures. Cut to slimy private sector psychotherapy MD, angling for some lucrative public funded counselling.

Randeep saw something on *BBC News*. Killing Sky, he maxed Beeb full-screen when Freeman's mug pic flashed up, cueing next story.

Studio black guy said, 'Joining us, live, is our North of England correspondent, Lynn Sewell.' He turned to face a 3D telly which had unzipped behind him to some CG fuss while he shot his intro. 'Lynn, I gather there's been a shocking development pertaining to why Alex Freeman missed his TV interview with us this evening.'

'Yes Andrew, there has,' said an older brunette whose bloated face was pumped full of so much botox only her bottom lip went up and down, like a Supermarionation puppet. 'In the past few minutes, Alex Freeman's office released a statement saying he was abducted tonight before he reached the BBC.'

Randeep was gobsmacked.

'Abducted?'

'Shit no,' Nahid added as RR headlights auto flicked on full, pooling upcoming cobbles.

Botox girl added, 'Seems he was daringly picked up from CPHQ in a car driven by a young woman posing as a BBC driver.'

'How close is he to today's events?'

'Very close, Andrew.'

'Do you think his abduction could be linked to the Royal Train going missing?'

Somebody handed her a note from off camera. Studio black guy's toothy busty sidekick waffled about Freeman's political clout, giving botox girl time to scan the note. Back she came.

'Andrew. A statement has been issued saying Alex Freeman has just phoned in. In a short sharp message, he apologized for missing his TV interview but said "something urgent" came up. He's being treated well and will be in touch soon.'

Codespeak for kidnapped.

Not much else studio black guy could say. Touching his earpiece he thanked botox girl and said they'd go back soon for an update.

'Jesus. It's a fix,' Randeep said, fuming. 'Why the live TV drama like that? It's a set-up.'

'What if they're fibbing about when he rang in?'

'Why would they?'

'If he just called, it means he's still alive, man.'

They were nearly back at the main road.

Huge brewery came up left, looming smashed-windowed like something from an old horror movie as sun went down.

'What the hell's he up to?' Randeep said, trying to work it out. 'Hang on a minute,' he added, suddenly getting it. 'I bet the Government's pussyfooting over the ransom. The country thinks the Queen's in hiding. Freeman's told the Government she's been kidnapped. Bastard faked his own kidnap to spook them into coughing up the dough.'

'But why did his phone blow at the bridge?'

'How the hell do I know?'

He hated being in the lurch.

'What are we gonna do?' Nahid said, indicating right as they reached end of the road. Cars and trucks swished this way and that, headlights flaring.

'We go south as planned,' Randeep said, feeling better already. 'If Freeman *is* still alive and we get another shot at killing him, next time I blow his head clean off. Same time we blow Royalty right out of the water. And I take my rightful place in the history books.'

Nahid pulled out but saw something in his rearview as he straightened. 'Hey, I'm sure Hunter's Volvo just pulled out across from that derelict place.'

Randeep half turned to look but couldn't be fussed. 'I doubt it,' he said.

'We should go back and check. You're always going on about Six Degrees of Separation.'

'We've too much to do if we're to get back up north before morning. Let's get going. I'm starving. We can stop at Keele Services for something to eat.'

Nahid OK'd and took off.

Simon Kane had just landed at CPHQ. Fretting all the way, he'd flown up as soon as they told him Alex had gone AWOL ahead of his TV interview.

Because of K-Tech's involvement with the MOD Kane had been able to hitch a lift on a gunship. After seeing *BBC News* on his phone, he wondered if Alex had staged his own kidnap to jolly the Government along on the ransom front. Kane couldn't risk checking with Alex's PA, Suzi. She didn't know what was going on *viz a viz* the Queen.

He'd arranged to meet Dave Bishop for a coffee on Skydeck. Dave had been Alex's trainspotter plant at Wilmslow Station. Put there to egg Hunter and his crew into heading to Twemlow.

Dave looked leaner than when Kane last saw him. T-shirted, tanned lustrous bronze by relentless sun, he smelt of clean linen shot with carbolic soap. Because of it, Kane felt heady as they carried coffees up to a mezzanine and found a quiet corner. 'What do you reckon?' he asked as they sat down.

'I wonder if Hunter's being clever.'

'Surely he wouldn't risk it, with his children and ex-wife being at stake?'

'Who knows?'

Kane fished for his Hermesetas dispenser and discreetly thumbed it twice over his coffee. Table had recently been wiped. Three crumbs had been missed, annoying him. 'Did they shoot the TV stuff?' he asked, before blowing the crumbs away.

Dave nodded. 'Alex sealed off the area after Hunter's Volvo went in but was more concerned about keeping the public away, so nobody saw the Royal Train. Volvo came out with the TV crew and went back to Wilmslow Station. Hunter dropped off the Godfrey and other crew members then came into town with Vanessa.'

'Didn't Alex track them?'

Dave emptied brown sugar over his coffee. It sat on top of milky froth. 'Only as far as Wilmslow Station. He seemed to think Hunter wouldn't risk playing silly buggers because of his kids.'

'What do you think?'

'I'd think of taking Alex hostage.'

An attractive middle-class blonde, pushing 50, sat down opposite. Dave's eyes were on her long shiny legs soon as they crossed. If her mini dress had ridden any higher she'd have shown all she'd got.

Kane said, 'Hunter's still editing his film?'

Dave nodded. Dave yawned. Seemed like he'd rather be some place else. A walking gym ad, he'd been invalided out of the army at 27. Kane knew Dave didn't like him. Kane knew Dave joked about his hair. Dave said, 'He told Alex it would take all night to cut and dub. I reckon Hunter could have delivered it offline with minimal tweaking. Low-res phone vid is transmitted on TV all the time. Alex says Hunter got technical, saying the Beeb's tech review is tougher than Sky's.'

'Alex fell for it?'

Dave nodded.

Dave sank back.

The woman sank back, mirroring Dave's body language. Slipping off lilac peep-toe canvas wedges, she revealed smooth bare feet with matching painted toenails. Kane found the gesture strangely erotic. Kane felt something suppressed stir deep inside him.

'Did you fall for it?'

'For what?'

'The tech spec stuff.'

'Not entirely.'

'Didn't you flag it up to Alex?'

'Of course I did.'

'And?'

'Alex knows best,' Dave said bitterly. Bunching his fists defensively like rocks at the table, his class consciousness got the better of him. 'I'm a lowly ex-soldier who went to a crappy State comprehensive. I'm only amazed Alex gives me the time of day.'

'What's the name of the edit facility?'

'Sound and Pics.'

Kane Googled the number. No need to stop his number showing before he squeezed the green button. He'd got one of Poulson's special phones.

Call answered before first ring.

'Sound and Pics,' said a bubbly, strangely asexual husky young creature. Kane couldn't tell if it was male or female. It rather excited him.

'I gather Real Life Pictures are working with you tonight on an urgent TV job.'

'Yes they are.'

'Can you put me through?'

'They're in session.'

'It's important.'

'I'm sorry. They can't be disturbed.' On the offensive, no doubt seeing UNKNOWN NUMBER doing its thing. 'Who's calling, please?'

'I'll call again tomorrow.' Kane killed call. 'Hunter isn't there,' Kane told Dave, temper rising.

'You should have said you were the cops.'

'Better they think we think they're still there.' Putting down his phone he made sure it was square with the table's nearest edges, equidistant from both. 'Did Alex leave anybody behind at Twemlow to make sure Hunter shot the film?'

'No.'

'How many bodies?'

'Connors and his crew?'

Kane nodded.

'Exact number.'

Dave shook his head.

'Dunno. Ten. Twelve.'

'Find out. Let me know.'

Kane hadn't touched his coffee. Kane sat forward in his seat. Back straight. Legs crossed.

Uncrossing his legs, Kane held his knees together. He noticed his phone, square on the table, and felt anxious gazing at it.

'What about Poulson?'

'Dead.'

'Are you sure?'

'Not my job to know, Simon.'

Dave seemed intense and aggrieved. When he suffixed a name it meant he was angry.

'Alex isn't detail conscious,' Kane told him, also feeling intense and aggrieved because he regarded Dave as a good looking young man, going to waste. Dave wanted to mate with the crude blonde bitch opposite. Kane's anger rose. 'Alex thinks everything takes care of itself. Get over to Sound and Pics. Kick the bloody doors in if you have to. Find out where Hunter and Vanessa are.'

61

Freeman was in the back of another flash saloon, staring at another shotgun. It poked from under a leather bomber jacket. Black trigger happy American hunk sitting next to him, munching gum, had a solemn look of disgust on his hard, brick-like face.

Two guys in front were familiar to Freeman from hijack briefings. Electronics wizards who'd fixed Crewe Gateway and Twemlow Junction. Ross, a witty Cockney who talked like Michael Caine, was driving. Hairy Welshman Pover, who fancied himself as a stand-up comic, slobbed back next to him, big booted feet up at the dash. His phone kicked off as Ross took next left into a backstreet dystopia, where lit streetlamps receded to a misty orange murk, now that day had conceded to night.

'Craig boyo,' Pover told his phone. Pause while he took a question. 'Dunno. Where we at, Roy?'

'Nearly at Bury.'

'Turn round and go back to town.' Ross wondered why but Pover waved for him to shut it while he took instructions from Connors.

Freeman couldn't tell what was being said. It sounded serious. He didn't expect them to harm him, especially now Connors was helming. After they'd rendezvoused with Hunter and Vanessa at Barton Bridge, they made him call in and tell his people they'd better not lay a finger on Hunter's kids and ex.

Or the Queen.

Pover was careful to speak in such a way that Freeman couldn't get the call's gist. When it ended his phone pinged with e-mail. 'Change of plan,' he said, flipping up the e-mail to show Ross an address. 'We meet here, in thirty minutes.'

'Mark Follon Studios,' Ross read. 'Don't say we're gonna take some poxy bloody photos of him?'

Distracted, he hit an upcoming road hump too fast but used it as a place to three-point turn. Odd ghostlike figures scurried past the car, jeering vaguely.

How the other half lived, Freeman decided.

Street after street of shabby brick terraces bisected his back window POV. Most downstairs doors and windows wrought-iron barred. As Ross reversed, Freeman saw graffiti zig-zag an adjacent gable, ominously declaring: NO LAW ZONE.

Something landed heavily, soggily, on the roof, making him jump.

Ross swore, going forward into second turn.

'Druggie bastards,' Pover told his window.

'Don't open it,' Ross warned him.

'Yeah I know,' he said through a noisy yawn, before deep-burping like a vulgar Welsh pig.

Freeman knew the drugs thing was allowed to carry on as unofficial policy. Better for an underclass, now superfluous to economic requirements, to be distracted by drugs addiction, and live in fear of gangs, instead of marching streets demanding jobs. Drugs could be eradicated, if the political will was there. It wasn't there because drugs and drugs crime helped police the underclass by forcing it to fight among itself.

As Ross took off back the way they'd come, Freeman was horrified to see a pig's bloody head roll from the roof, down the rear window, into the road behind.

Pover said, 'Studio's a place to work. Guy who owns it's some photographer Hunter and Vanessa know. He's coming into town to open up.'

'What are we doing?'

'Dunno. Poulson's driving up an' all.'

'I thought he was bent, like twatto in the back.'

'Me too,' Pover said, not letting on.

Freeman knew there had to be a mistake. Prayed for it. 'Poulson is dead,' he told them defiantly.

'Freeman says Poulson is dead,' Pover told Ross sarkily, as if they were alone in the car. 'From what Craig says,' he added, turning to evil eye Freeman when they clunked next road bump, 'Phil and Mark *should* be dead 'cause poncy Alex bloody Freeman made it so.'

'A regular serial killer, eh?' Ross noted, eyeing Freeman accusingly in his rearview.

'Yeah,' agreed the black, obviously feeling left out.

They were back on wide main road.

Ross eased on the brakes for some red lights.

Pover looked down behind Ross's seat, effecting to peep at Freeman's feet. Cranking his Welsh accent, he told Freeman sarkily, 'That a neat pile of bricks I see emerging from your posh botty?'

62

Bill popped the lid from a styrofoam tub of watery mango chutney and poured some over his lamb korma. Now that he was alone with Hartman at the big, pine kitchen table, enough Indian takeaway stuff between them to feed a small army, he told him straight. 'The only reason I'm sitting at the same table as you is because you saved my life. I don't condone what you did.'

He felt justified sounding like a broken record after the longest, scariest day. Hartman, to his credit, took it on the chin because he wasn't a bad bloke. Bill had dismissed him as a posh nob. Turned out he was a working-class lad and former Green Beret who lost his Brummie accent when he left the army and got a late education. It was because he was a former soldier that he'd had the guts to think quick, grab a gun, and act how he did back at the factory.

When Bill heard somebody arrive outside the office, and thought it was time to die, it was worked-up Hartman, telling Poulson to finish off the blond ox-like hood who'd stubbornly refused to die.

Nearby village church chimed second of ten. Hartman snapped a poppadum, using it to scoop daal.

'You don't condone us for hijacking the Royal Train,' he said. 'What are your thoughts about the two thugs? Do you approve of me killing them so you could live?' He sounded sarky. Bill knew he didn't mean to.

Before he could say anything, Kerryann came back to the kitchen. Downstairs loo cistern hissed shrilly from passage's end when she opened and shut the door. Realizing Poulson was still in the garden on his phone she slipped his curry in the oven, to keep it warm, and sat back at the table next to Bill.

The house was in an idyllic spot, off the A41 east of Bicester, and so pic postcard twee it was unreal. Six hundred years young. Pink outside walled. Thatched so heavily it hung like thick snow where it met eaves. It belonged to Carmen, the Latin-looking woman Bill met that morning, finishing off his spooky double. They'd driven straight over to the house from the factory in the dead thugs' black Merc.

Carmen creaked floorboards above them while she aired beds. Village church had got to chime seven when the back door opened and Poulson appeared, swiping moths. He'd been on the phone outside for ages after enthusiastically taking a call from a guy called Craig. Bill knew a big discussion had been going on.

'Have you a minute, Mark?'

'Sure,' he said, getting up.

'Find Carmen, will you?'

Hartman thumbed the stairfoot door's Suffolk latch and shouted up.

'Phil wants a word.'

Tenth and final church chime bonged sombrely.

Carmen OK'd and came down.

When she'd followed Hartman outside and snecked the door behind her, Bill told Kerryann, 'You're too nice a girl to be mixed up with this lot.'

'I didn't really want to get involved,' she said, slicing a samosa with her fork. Bill couldn't decide if her intense eyes were blue or sea green. 'I knew it was wrong. They assured me the Queen wouldn't be harmed. I wanted to put a deposit on a house. If you rent, you usually pay off somebody else's mortgage.'

Her soothing Scottish accent made her seem older than 26. No wonder people responded best to Scots call centre folk. Bill felt protective of her. Back at the factory, he'd managed to get her out to the Merc without seeing the headless dead men.

'They're not bad people,' she said, meaning Poulson and Hartman. 'But I never trusted Alex Freeman. I was scared of saying anything to Phil.'

'He probably fell for his rotten charms because they're from the same background.'

Poulson and Hartman came back in, stooping under the low beamed ceiling. Carmen was on the phone in the back garden lost against deep twilight. Old country kitchen was muggy from the humid night, thick with curry smell when everybody was at the table.

Bill felt obliged to remain standoffish but was coming round to the awkward realization that he owed these men his life and it was futile to resist. Didn't matter if their outrageous kidnap plot had turned his life upside down and put it in danger to begin with.

Hartman resumed wolfing his food.

Poulson's plate stayed empty.

'What's the matter?' Bill asked him, sensing he needed to say something.

'This young TV chap Hunter, who was interviewing you. Alex Freeman has kidnapped his ex-wife and two daughters. You might have heard an American chap at the facility this morning. He's kidnapped Freeman, in retaliation, in Manchester.'

'Why did Freeman kidnap Hunter's family?'

'It's a long story. Freeman not only double-crossed Mark and me, and sent those hoods to kill us all. He's murdered nearly everybody else.'

'Everybody?' Kerryann said, shocked.

'Except for Craig and Kath, everybody at Twemlow has been killed, including train driver Mike. Thankfully Glyn, Roy, and Jason are still alive. At the root of this affair is none other than Mr Simon Kane, who heads a company called K-Tech based at Milton Keynes.'

'I thought he was involved anyway,' Kerryann said.

'He loaned the advanced CG simulator which Mike and Glyn trained on. Craig thinks he's behind the whole thing with Freeman and a gang of corrupt MPs.'

'Doesn't Kane fund the Tories?' Bill asked.

'He did,' Poulson noted. 'He funds whoever bribes him with next fat, lucrative public sector contract. Mark and I didn't know how involved he was. Freeman planned to kill us all along, including you, Mr Martin. If it's any consolation, none of us has been paid. Meanwhile Freeman's been holding the Queen to ransom and is endeavouring to take the country for a cool ten billion. It wouldn't surprise me if he's intended to kill Her Majesty all along as well.'

'God almighty,' Bill said, and puffed his cheeks.

'I know you disapprove of us, Mr Martin. I've apologized for dragging you into this mess. But we're going to get Mr Hunter's family and the Queen out. To do it we're making a Freeman double, like we made a double of you. Carmen is calling the technicians you saw today, to see who'll help. We're heading north soon.' He meant Hartman, Carmen, himself. 'You two are welcome to stay here. You should be safe.'

'Why the change of heart?' Bill asked him.

'It's something I need to do.'

Overhead spots found his moist grey eyes. Troubled by something, he sat back, dismayed.

'I can't understand why powerful very rich men want yet more money and will slaughter other men wholesale to get it. I can only say how deeply humbled I am that those caught up with me are willing to give me their continued support.'

'I want to come too, Phil,' Kerryann said. 'There must be something I can do.'

Hartman scraped back his chair and stood up. Bill wondered if he'd caught Kerryann's eye. She found her handbag and the two of them went upstairs.

Poulson waited till boards creaked overhead, before leaning forward steepling his hands on the table in front of him. 'You've no obligation to us,' he told Bill. 'For what it's worth, when this is over I intend to hand myself in. I've waged a pointless battle for a very long time. I should add that I'm not hoping to rescue the Queen I helped kidnap in the hope she'll be good enough to pardon me.'

'I wasn't thinking that,' Bill said.

'I know you weren't, Mr Martin,' Poulson said. He had a knowing twinkle in his eye. For the first time, Bill saw a wry smile crack his tired red face. 'It's why you're a better man than me.'

Bill didn't know what to say.

'You're free to go home,' Poulson told him. He stood up. Found an oven glove and got his curry out of the cooker. 'We can ring for a taxi.' He bumped the cooker door shut with his free hand. 'All I ask is that you don't contact anybody till we've attempted a rescue. Because of Freeman's influence on the police, I wouldn't advise you contact the authorities yet. You'll know from TV if we're successful in Manchester.'

'Pauline's in Italy,' Bill said. He'd called her from the car on the way to the cottage, using one of Poulson's scrambled phones. 'I'm hardly going home and dashing straight back out for a plane. Daft as it sounds, with all these bent MPs and coppers running about, I feel safer with you. And will you stop calling me "Mr Martin". It's Bill.'

Poulson emptied a bright red curry on his plate and sat down heavily. He seemed weary, defeated, and was clearly put out by such vivid coloured junk food.

'This has been an insightful journey for somebody who spent most of his life taking far too much for granted, who thought he knew it all,' he said. He held his knife and fork ready but seemed to lack the courage to tackle the gunk loading his plate.

Bill had chosen the curries.

He knew Poulson was disconcerted by the Danzak but didn't want to give offence by declining. Bill opened the uneaten chicken Kashmir. 'The bright red stuff puts me off too,' he said. 'I heard they use cochineal. I'm sure it's some nasty food colouring. Try this. It's mild and creamy.' He got up to put it in the microwave to reheat it for him. He set it going.

Poulson thanked him, waiting till the microwave had nearly finished. 'I want you to know how truly sorry I am for what we've done to you.'

'I know you are,' Bill told him over the microwave *bweee wee wee*. Church clock acknowledged the quarter hour as he tipped food on Poulson's plate and sat across from him. 'It's why I'm coming with you.'

63

'I'm here to see Real Life Pictures.'

'Are they expecting you?'

'Good answer.'

'I'm sorry but they can't be disturbed.'

'It's a police matter.' Dave flashed fake plainclothes ID at husky voice black bird lording the desk.

It had taken longer than it should for him to get over to Sound and Pics. As far as he was concerned, Hunter and Vanessa had surely blagged Freeman and done a runner. After Kane buggered off from Costa Dave hooked up with the blonde sitting across.

Sound and Pics was on 10th floor of Sunlight House at the corner of Quay Street and Little Quay Street, just off Deansgate. Scheduling sex had been Dave's priority. He'd bullshit to Simon OCD bloody Kane about how his gammy leg had played up while he walked the half-mile from CPHQ.

Girl on Reception did her level best to stall him. She had dyed short white hair, loud pink lipstick, and did that funny black girly make-up thing where she powdered herself pale matt to look honky but resembled a bog-eyed zombie. Under the face nonsense was a gorgeous black girl with ace bone structure.

Dave said to her, 'Why don't you ring and tell them I'm here?' He leant on the hammered steel desk. 'Let me guess. They aren't here and you're stalling, like you did when we rang earlier.'

He reached over for the log sheet to find out which suite Hunter and Vanessa had booked.

'I'll call Security,' she threatened, sounding like a wooden actress doing a walk-on one liner.

'Go ahead darling,' Dave said. 'And I'll charge you for obstructing police work.'

He checked the log.

Edit 23.

He'd done a virtual tour on the Sound and Pics website before he came. Edit 23 was on the floor below.

He took off down a spiral staircase hole-punching Reception's floor. Treadplate steps bonged hollowly under him. Sound and Pics ran 24-7. Hummed like NASA's Mission Control with gibbering voices and overlapping telly sounds.

He called Kane on the way.

'They're not here,' he told him.

'It's taken you till now to find out?'

'Apparently so, Simon.' Loaded silence other end. 'Like I said, if I were them I'd be taking a hostage.'

'What do you suggest?'

'That guys like you and Alex pin back your lugholes and listen to guys like me when you come up with your birdbrain ideas. I said from day one you'd be dealing with guys way smarter than you. But Alex knows best. You'd better hope he doesn't squeal about where you've hidden H's kids and one serious VIP.'

He got to Edit 23.

Door was ajar.

He barged in.

'Shit,' he said.

'What's wrong?'

'I'll ring you back.'

He dropped his phone after he killed call. Because of his gammy leg it was tough bending over, as he liked to joke with Kane, winding him up.

Vanessa obliged and got up from the edit console. 'Small world,' she said, picking up Dave's phone for him, recognizing him from Wilmslow Station.

'Yeah right,' Dave said.

She was alone. Tall and eye-poppingly fit, she came over like a classy ex-public school girl who no doubt pronounced her aitches when she orgasmed.

He weighed up the edit suite scene.

Twemlow TV doc thumbnails studding Avid Symphony. Gruesome shot of dead mercenaries parked on playback monitor.

Half empty bottle water.

Two spent banana skins, turning black.

Everything Hunky D.

Hunter came in, like he'd been for a tiddle.

'Small world,' he said, shutting the door. He regarded Dave like he was a hole in the air but said sarkily to

Vanessa, 'I wondered if they'd send over one of their creeps to check we're doing as we've been told.'

Feeling relieved, Vanessa high-fived Hunter when the guy had gone. A few minutes later they saw him from the window, under a streetlamp down in Quay Street, on his phone. 'Good job we came back,' she said. 'What if he'd taken a pop at you?'

'I'd probably have killed him. When Freeman rang me at Twemlow and said he'd got Vicky and the girls, I told him I'd kill him if he harmed them. It scares me because I reckon I could kill him, if it came to it.'

The guy hadn't hung around. Hunter had got in his face, sounding convincing when he said they'd picked up from TV about Freeman going AWOL.

They'd dropped off Connors and Kath at Mark Follon's studio in George Leigh Street behind the old Daily Express building. Ross and the guys were on their way back into town with Freeman. Poulson was driving up from Bicester with his guys. They expected to land at Mark's in the early hours. They'd crack on with Freeman and wanted Hunter there for 5.00am, to start his side of the make-up.

Vanessa and Hunter had decided to spend the night at Sound and Pics, just in case. If they hadn't got Freeman, they'd have burnt midnight oil anyway, cutting and dubbing the film. It was safest place to be, scuppering Freeman's mob from getting funny ideas about who might have snatched him.

Good job.

When they'd got back, Amy on Reception said a posh guy had phoned asking for them while they were out.

Across from Edit 23 was a tiny apartment where they could get some sleep. They could be out of bed and back editing in a flash, if goons got clever and came back to check they were still there.

Hunter reached for Vanessa.

Long day was nearly over but she'd sensed this coming. He kissed her, cupping her big boobs through her blouse. She was amused to think her chest had trended on Twitter when she was news with Hunter last Christmas. She felt guilty for wanting sex when his loved ones were in danger.

'Are you sure you want this?'

'I know I shouldn't,' he said, nuzzling her. 'I'm worried about my kids. But when we get shoved in a shitty corner we work in crazy ways.'

He slipped off her blouse and bra and pulled his T-shirt over his head.

'This is all I've been able to think about for hours. Alternative is that I'll have to scream. Something's gonna have to give.'

64

Connors knocked back a Coke. Ad photographer Mark Follon was a nice guy. In his 50s, fair and lean, he seemed younger 'cause he looked like he took good care of himself. Similar guy to Hunter. No airs. No graces. Easy to be near. He finished telling them where everything was then headed off home.

Studio was a rollershuttered one-level lock-up behind tatty storefronts across from an OTT pagoda'd Chinese cash-and-carry called Wing Yip.

Mark was on location tomorrow. They had his place to themselves. Lights, space, tables, and a 1950s dentist's chair left over from a magazine shoot, and so shit heavy they had a hard time lugging it, made it a good place to get a Freeman dupe ready.

Freeman was gaffer taped to an upright pine chair in the kitchen, back of studio. Ceiling spots over him turned his bony face sinister. He hadn't said much since Ross and the guys brought him in.

Connors finished his Coke and stuck the can in a recycler. 'I still don't get how you could crap on us, Alex.'

'I do,' Pover said. He munched on a bag of beef potato chips. 'Only I won't go on about bodily waste in front of a lady.'

Kath, arms folded, back in her Red Indian gear, leant by the sink, seeming all long bare legs.

Poulson and Hartman were due in a few hours. In the studio next door guys were setting up the head scanner. They lived south of Manchester and had come straight up, not having unloaded the scanner from the van since they'd taken it from the abandoned factory in the afternoon. Poulson said that without the scanner they'd have had a tough time doing prosthetics fast, lacking enough raw materials to make face moulds instead.

Freeman met nobody's eye.

His pants had ridden up his skinny ankles. His blue silk socks looked to be quality. His pale legs, going by bits showing, looked hairless.

'Say something Alex,' Connors said. Freeman eyed the floor till he noticed Kath's legs which also were hairless. 'You could make it easy. Let us trade you for Hunter's folks and the Queen and call it quits.'

'I'd rather die,' Freeman piped up.

'Happy to oblige, boyo,' Pover said.

He held his empty chip bag on his palm and clapped. Bag popped.

Freeman jumped.

Pover was amused.

'Why would you rather die?' Kath asked Freeman.

'You wouldn't understand.'

'Why?'

'You're a woman.' He eyed her like she was crap. 'Or it's what they tell me you pass for.'

Pover swore and moved at him.

Connors held him back.

'Easy Glyn. Kath ain't fussed.'

'You're right,' she said. 'I'm not fussed.' Her suede mini had fringed side pockets. She stuck her hands in them and stood, legs defiantly spread, in front of Freeman. 'You're a murdering bastard. You sum up everything that's wrong with this country. But do you know what? I feel sorry for you. I wish I didn't but I'm glad I do 'cause it means I'm better than you. All the guys here are way better than you.'

One of the scanner guys stuck his head round the cyclorama dividing kitchen from studio.

'OK we're ready.'

Connors took a tranquillizer gun from the kitchen table, checked the cartridge had liquid, and set the thing to Stun. Everybody looked sharp. Freeman struggled on his chair, making it creak.

Kath took the gun from Connors.

'Let me do it.'

'You sure?'

'Yeah I'm sure.'

'What are you going to do to me?' Freeman asked, getting hemmed in.

Pover scoffed at him.

'You don't get it, do you boyo? You double cross us. You kill most of us. You screw us on pay. And you've the nerve to sit there and ask what the bloody hell we're gonna do to you. Anybody with real feelings in their 'ead would think oh deary me. I'm a cold-blooded killer. If these guys knobble me, it's my own stupid bloody fault. But what does poncy Alex bloody Freeman say?' He did a namby pamby Welsh toff voice. 'I say, you foul smelling plebs. But dash it, just what *are* you going to do to moi?'

Kath stood behind Freeman's chair. He let her push his head forward and stick the gun to his neck. Loaded silence hung over the kitchen while Kath eye checked everybody, like she was drawing a line.

Before she pulled the trigger, Connors saw Freeman look at him. His eyes shone. Connors knew bogeyman had heard everything Kath said.

TUESday

65

Sharron and Lisa were at K-Tech for 8.05am.

Another hot day already, shoving sun in faces.

Colworth Park, north of Milton Keynes, was an ever expanding Silicone Valley adjunct. Boulevards and avenues instead of humble roads. On went wrapshades as Lisa pulled up past K-Tech's security gate, threw her door, and stood up from the BM. Lonely sparrow tweets made quiet early morning seem melancholy.

CSI was in the security booth, popping flashes. Lisa saw blood and bits of gunk splashing windows. Banging her door she eyed a nest of razorwired CCTVs stuck high on a pole where K-Tech's entrance broke.

Carl met them at the booth door, coffee in hand. 'Morning ladies,' he said cheerily. 'Sorry to dump another headless on you this early.'

'Security guy?' Sharron asked.

'Yep.'

'Mindless fun killing, or a good old-fashioned British crime of passion?'

'My gut feel is both.'

They followed him inside.

Latex gloved CSI boy, and two black girls, knelt over a plump body, heaped far side of a bloody desk. Papers and stuff everywhere. Live CCTV pics were all black because cameras outside had been aerosol sprayed.

Minus head, only clue to vic being a silver surfer were sausage finger hands, specked with liver spots.

Left hand held a red Nokia. Wedding ring on same hand made Lisa's heart take a dive and got her thinking back to relationship girly stuff she'd thought last night at the factory. With the poor guy's head being all over the floor they'd to be careful where they put their wedge booty feet.

Carl said, 'Killers cut the fence and went round the back to avoid cameras.' He nodded at the open back door letting in sad back bird twitter. 'Shot him through here. He probably had it open 'cause it was hot. Cool operators. After they killed him, they shimmied up the pole out front and KO'd the CCTVs. Before they cut the fence they shot the camera spying at Kane Boulevard.'

'Who found him?'

'UPS new boy arriving early at wrong place across the way.' He waved at corrugated ship containers stacked behind shiny steel palisade. A forklift fussed behind it, hazards flicking at fence gaps. 'Colworth Park's "zones" screwed him. K-Tech doesn't usually do nights but has security on 24-7. UPS boy got lost and came over to get directions.'

'What time was this?' Sharron asked.

'6.50am.'

'TOD on the vic?'

'Around 2.00am. Looks like our headbangers were suited up and in stretchy shoe covers, so no shit got left to get us sniffing. Too many TV cop shows teaching bad guys how to avoid dropping DNA poop.' He cocked a thumb at the back door. 'There's this though.'

They followed him out into hot sun behind the booth. Lisa got dazzled in shades. Day would soon scorch. Carl stopped and turned to nod at booth back wall.

Sharron and Lisa turned. No windows back of booth. Brick halfway up, till white embossed uPVC took over, running across. Big black spray graffiti said:

THE QUEEN IS DEAD

'Jesus,' Lisa said, feeling the spine chill thing folk went on about.

'Seems spooky,' Carl added, rubbing his neck. 'After the Royal Train driver stuff yesterday.'

'Maybe they've a sick sense of humour,' Sharron suggested, because of what was happening nationally now the Queen was in hiding.

'Or maybe they're trying to tell us something the world doesn't know,' Lisa offered.

'Might be the work of latter day Smiths fans,' Carl risked, drolly. 'We assume same spray did the CCTVs. We haven't been up the pole yet to check.'

They didn't go back in the booth but clicked a turnstile at the side to get round by the barrier. Carl nodded at K-Tech HQ across sunbaked grass.

'Looks like they wanted something from over there,' he said and drained his coffee.

Place looked like some groovy top secret Government lab from 1970s US TV sci-fi. *Six Million Dollar Man,* Lisa decided. Slab concrete topped by curvy balconies doing rooftop gardens with palm trees. Smoked glass angled back in places. Forwards in others.

Only a few cars parked up front hotspotted morning sun, with it being early.

'Vibe we got this morning is K-Tech would prefer us not to have found this mess,' Carl added. 'Only reason we did is 'cause UPS boy dialled 999. When management turned up and saw us they showed us long faces. And not 'cause they've a security vacancy to fill to keep insurers happy.'

Somebody called him into the booth.

He said he'd catch the girls later.

Lisa knocked up her shades, top-of-head, and did hands on hips, gazing across straw-patchy grass at K-Tech with its giant chrome logo stuck out front.

Sharron was with her, shades going up too.

'Women's intuition, hon?'

'Yeah.'

'Me too.'

'Something big's happening. We're getting sucked in. I'm scared, Shar. The Queen's supposedly in hiding. Her train does a bunk. Weird Bill Martin car fingerprint stuff last night. Now this. Everything's linked.'

'What do you reckon?'

'K-Tech works on top secret Government stuff. Somebody came here middle of the night to get something and wanted it badly enough to kill.'

Down came her shades.

'I wanna know what it was.'

Simon Kane and Dave were in Kane's 87th floor flash, minimalist, delightfully kitsch, Modernist Revival, New Piccadilly Plaza penthouse pad.

Entire south wall was non-reflective twelve inch thick, frameless, barless, argon filled self-clean glass. Only window of its type in the world. Cost £1m in an apartment setting Kane back a cool £11m.

Some clever polarizing effect made it seem like glass wasn't there. Kane stood nose to it, only thing between him and midair a half mile in Manchester sky. UK's highest living space by far. Nearest rivals were Beetham Tower and CPHQ. Both nearly fifty storeys high. Both forty storeys way on down.

Dave had just come in.

Dave said, 'Guys say K-Tech got hit last night and Stan's dead. Is it true?'

'Yes it's true.'

'Jesus,' Dave said, shaking his head. 'He was such a nice guy. It'll finish his poor wife.'

Kane couldn't care less.

Both prototypes had gone from the lab. Whoever went in knew what they were after. Only people up on development were Kane, his right-hand man and K-Tech CEO George Wymark. Plus lab boys and girls. All trustworthy. Others in the know were Alex, the PM, and a few senior Ministers.

Dave went on about the dead gateman's cancer-stricken wife. Kane wasn't listening. Typical Dave fussed over a replaceable security guy getting bumped off. Kane's concern was that somebody had clobbered K-Tech who surely had insider knowledge.

Dave sensed Kane's attitude.

'Did you know Stan?' Dave demanded.

'I noticed him on occasion,' Kane said, baiting Dave. 'If my driver stopped at the gate.'

'Is that all you can say?'

Kane sensed things unravelling. Kane was used to being in control. K-Tech's overnight hit was bad enough. But with Alex gone their Royal hostage project had hit buffers. Everybody was waiting to see what demands Alex's captors made.

'A security man losing his life is unfortunate,' Kane said. 'What's gone, costing millions in R&D funding, is vastly more important.'

Cocky Dave, hands on hips, crossed to stand by the sofa. A huge, modern, white leathered thing going off in several directions, with built-in spots and gadgets, it looked like it should be in an airport lounge. Like much in Kane's life it was a pointless extravagance.

'Do you know what pisses me off about guys like you and Alex?' Dave said. 'Your disregard for human life. You're supposedly cultured. Educated. Rich. Powerful. You always get what you damned well want. But deep down you're nastier than the toughest gangsters. They at least have some weird sense of honour.' He turned to leave. 'I don't care why you dragged me up here, Simon. I'm not cut out for this shit.'

'I don't think you're cut out for it either,' Kane told him. Soon as Dave was criticized he bit back, no matter how slight the inference.

Cylinders firing, Dave said, 'And what's that supposed to mean?'

'Did you go back to Sound and Pics?'

'No. Why?'

Before Kane could answer, the intercom buzzed. They were dotted round the apartment.

Crossing to the nearest, Kane held down a button. A young foreign female said, 'Your items have arrived, Mr Kane sir.'

'Send them straight up.'

'Certainly Mr Kane sir.'

Kane crossed back to command the room from some priceless white tigerskin.

'Why didn't you go back?'

'There wasn't any need. They were editing when I got there. They must have done what Alex said. I assumed they'd blagged him.'

'Have you checked if Hunter and Vanessa are there this morning and how far they've got with the film?'

'No I bloody well haven't.'

'It was your job to go back and check.'

'What the hell is it with you? They were working on the film all along.'

'How do you know?'

'They were in the edit suite. The film was on the computer and TV monitors. Vanessa was sitting at the console when I walked in.'

'You were supposed to go back and check.'

'I must have forgotten.'

'You mean you were screwing that whore from Costa. You were on assignment. Satiating your sexual needs, emptying yourself into a female who's nearly old enough to be your mother, took priority.'

'OK so I laid a fit older bird. I'm telling you. Hunter and Vanessa are working on the TV doc.' Dave let Kane have some hard eye. His way of letting Kane know he believed he was telling the truth.

'What about Randeep?'

'What about him?'

'Where is he?'

'How do I know?'

'He's disappeared.'

'So I gather.'

'Don't you think you should know where he is?'

'Why should it be my responsibility? Alex probably pissed him off.'

'You dealt with Randeep.'

'I didn't.'

'Alex said you did.'

'Alex lied to you.'

'Alex would never lie to me.'

Dave knew he'd struck a nerve.

Dave stepped forward, vilely amused.

Dave scoffed.

'Alex is Randeep's slave.' Goading Kane, he laughed at him. 'How do you know they haven't a bit of something going, eh?'

'How dare you.'

Dave told Kane, 'Randeep's driven this whole damned Royal kidnap action adventure. He's a clever good-looking guy who knows how to work a pair of gullible middle-aged old women with grand ideas who're actually thick as two short planks.'

Kane kept it together.

Kane implored: 'Alex is in control.'

'Not when he isn't here,' Dave chucked back. 'Or when he *is* here, for that matter.'

Fuming, Kane turned to face clear glass. Far distant, an incoming Virgin helijet winked sun.

9.30am shuttle from Manchester Airport. Kane's flat was on New Piccadilly Plaza's penultimate floor. 88th housed heliport lifts and loos. Lounge and barriers were at a busy transport interchange on the ground. Heliport was on the roof.

Kane's apartment sprawled between east and west towers and was completely soundproofed. Helijet arrivals and departures happened mute.

67

Dave had seen the approaching helijet.

Through his feet he sensed a faint judder as four huge deflectors on the roof lumbered up, ready to receive the flight.

Dave sensed Kane had brought him upstairs to make a point. Kane turned back.

Kane, losing it, said, 'Let me show you something.'
He found the TV dibber.

Filling wall left-angling the big window was a mural.
Photo of what looked like desert dunes. Actually it was
a close-up abstract of a huge bare bottom. Dave knew
from seeing a piece about the apartment in a design mag
that it was a girl's bum. Architect's wife. Kane had no
idea. Interesting as a concept because of how highly he
rated it, boasting about it being a reason he bought the
place. Dave had never had the heart to spoil it for him.

Bum bullseye was a 72 inch telly.

Kane had patched his laptop wirelessly.

Waving the TV dibber, he hit Play.

High wide-angle CCTV view of Sound and Pics Reception. Dave came in and swanned up to the desk.
Kane said, 'That's you arriving last night.'

'You don't say.'

'10.37pm, when you eventually landed.'

Kane hit fast forward x16 then fast forward x32. Video
raced on. He must have marked it but wanted to make a
point by making Dave watch.

Video slowed.

'4.37am,' Kane added.

Hunter walked into shot, coming up the spiral staircase embedded in the floor. Mouth hidden by the ob-
lique overhead angle, he mumbled something to the
black girl at the desk then left by main exit.

Dave got wondering.

Realized that Kane might have hauled him up to set
him up.

Kane said, 'We checked the CCTV video, which we assumed *you* had done. Hunter didn't come back.'

Kane nodded at the TV again.

Next pre-mark.

New CCTV showed Hunter getting in a Volvo in an underground car park.

'4.42am,' Kane noted as the car fired. Lights came on. It slid from its space and left shot. 'Hunter knew what he was doing and where to go to avoid CCTVs. They lost him within minutes.'

Next pre-mark.

'8.47am,' Kane added, eyeing his Rolex with some bluster to make the point. 'Forty minutes ago.'

Dave was getting it now.

Vanessa came up the spiral staircase at Sound and Pics and left by main exit.

'We checked CCTVs but they lost her too,' Kane added. 'I sent some of our guys over to Sound and Pics just now to check the Twemlow files. You're right in your assertion that Hunter and Vanessa started the film. But it's far from finished. It was saved at 8.07pm last night. Last time *any* work was done to it. When you saw Vanessa working on the film no edits had been made for several hours. She and Hunter fooled you. If you think I exaggerate,' he added, mullet bobbing now, 'take a look at this.'

Next pre-mark.

'This is from earlier last evening.'

CCTV from Sound and Pics Reception showed Hunter and Vanessa leave at 8.28pm and return at 9.47pm.

'While they were away I phoned to speak to them, when you and I were sitting in Costa on Skydeck. I was told they were in session.'

'Maybe they went out for something to eat,' Dave said. Plausible as an excuse. But he knew he'd blown it. Kane was obsessively detail conscious. He was always ahead of the game.

Door buzzed.

Kane went over to open it while Dave digested what he'd seen. Kane complained to some coveralled dark-skinned lackey about stuff being late then fished in his trouser pocket for a tip.

Kane caused the door to shut.

Kane turned.

The guy had brought up two brand-new garden implements from a hardware store on Piccadilly Station approach. Full length garden fork and spade set. Hammered carbon steel. Stylish yellow-grey plastic handles, embossed with non-slip silicone. Kane would use the tools once and throw them away.

Same fetish with socks. Kane wore silk socks once and chucked them. Kane spent £10,000 a year on silk socks. Sometimes Kane got through three pairs of socks a day, depending where Kane was at.

Helijet banked into its final descent over New Piccadilly Plaza. Kane couldn't see it because it was right overhead. Kane sensed it break sunshine as it passed through it.

Tool in each hand, Kane crossed the room.

Dave gazed at the TV.

Dave said, 'I'm sorry I screwed up.'

'So am I,' Kane told him.

'I thought they were working on the film.' Dave watched Kane rest the garden tools against near wall. 'What do you want with those up here?'

Kane picked up the garden fork to show Dave. Kane felt spasms of hate and drove the fork into Dave's chest. Felt prongs scratch bone.

Dave yelled.

Dave fell crying, waving, fork stuck in him as he went down on the sofa. Dave called Kane a bastard. Retching blood, spitting it, Dave called Kane nastier stuff. Kane kept pulling out the fork, driving it back in. Shoving the handle forward. Wrenching it back. Feeling ribs snap. Feeling ribs crack.

Seventh strike Kane hit Dave's breastbone.

Fork prongs skimmed off.

Kane nearly stabbed his own foot. Jumped aside in time then sent the fork back in and lifted it with both hands. Dead Dave impaled he dumped him down. Kane found a roll of silver duct tape. Got it going on Dave's face and wrapped it round his head, turning him into an Egyptian mummy send-up. Kane had killed handsome beefy six-pack Dave. There was much blood. Kane's hair was messed. Kane panted.

Kane pulled his phone. Kane hit a number. 'Some of you get over here. Bring an industrial carpet cleaner and some carry boxes. Make sure they're opaque. Make sure they're plastic. Cardboard is absorbent.'

'Yes Mr Kane.'

Kane rolled out some clear PVC sheet across the carpet. Kane unspiked Dave and dragged him onto it. Kane lifted the spade. Kane angled the blade flat and whacked Dave's skull once, hard, splitting it.

Just to be sure.

Kane stripped down to his socks and Y-fronts so he didn't mess his suit. Kane lost his socks so his feet didn't slip on the plastic. Kane decided he looked absurd in nothing but underpants. Kane took them off, feeling in his element now that he was a fully fledged, fully exposed, hard naked killer. Kane fetched the spade and angled it side-on, to chop. Kane raised it high in both hands over Dave's neck.

Kane got to work.

Randeep was on the 9.30am Virgin helijet service landing at New Piccadilly Plaza. Nahid had dropped him off at Manchester Airport on the way back from K-Tech. He was incognito, butt-parked among butt-parked suits. Most were glumly reading Kindles and tablets.

Flight had taken five mins, some of it used by the helijet to bank round and find the Plaza, punching Manc's hazy summer sky. Like a gigantic glass hand sticking two fingers up at London, it symbolized the north's renaissance. It was UK's tallest building.

Last night had gone like a dream.

They'd got what they went for. Leaving a tantalizing spray clue would get cops and Freeman's crowd scratching heads. *The Queen is dead*. She would be by lunchtime, if everything went to plan.

She was at top of CPHQ. Randeep and Nahid needed to get to her. Hijacking a police gunship and going in from the top was risky. They might have to wait days for an opportunity. Best way in was from the bottom. Kit they'd blagged last night meant they could take the place apart.

But first they needed to rid CPHQ of as many potentially troublesome piggies as possible. Best way to do that was by making a large puff of fire and smoke happen nearby.

PA system dinged on.

'Good morning ladies and gentlemen,' young Irish girly flight womanager said. 'We're landing in Manchester. Please ensure you take all your belongings with you and have your travel tickets ready.'

Helijet dropped fast.

Through his port, Randeep saw the docking arm's black rubber concertina thingy stretching out to a Moonbase Alpha landing pad, stamped with a big exhaust-fume blacked yellow "H".

Four massive steel deflectors were angled at forty-five, ready to receive the helijet, enclosing it like a Venus flytrap. Idea was, if a landing went tits-up last sec and a helijet crashed, deflectors would contain it and stop the wreckage dropping on dot multitudes teeming far below. Randeep felt nasty.

Slabs of metal so big were gonna sound like church bells bonging down Heaven's distant stairs when they fell off and smashed busy city streets.

Hunter was nearly ready. He was lying on an old dentist's chair at Mark's studio. They kept wanting to show him how he was coming along by waving mirrors but he kept saying no. He'd avoided looking in a mirror in the loo when he went for a pee.

First they'd scanned him. Two guys who owned and worked the scanner skullcapped him, fussing, asking him to keep still while the laser worked its way slowly round. When it was done, Hunter saw his 3D head revolving slowly on a PC. Perfectly detailed down to skin texture, which was exaggerated.

They'd scanned Freeman before Hunter got there, drugging him unconscious so they could keep him still because he wouldn't have co-operated. They'd done the same with Bill Martin last night. In the digital domain, the computer combined Hunter's and Freeman's scans. Because Hunter was the host, his scan was male output. A 3D laser-printer cut his scan in solid grey acrylic.

Result: perfect 3D Hunter head, minus hair.

When it came to Freeman, the computer got clever. Assessing Hunter's and Freeman's head volumes, it allowed for differences in head mass, contour, and bone structure. It flipped Freeman's scan, making it a female image, debossing every tiny detail.

Flipped scan was split to make front and back head halves. They also were output in 3D and lasered in solid grey acrylic. Result: slightly bigger Freeman front and back head halves which fitted snugly over solid Hunter head. Thin cavity between was filled with liquid movie make-up rubber. When the mould was cracked open, a skintight Freeman mask had formed over acrylic Hunter's head. It went over real Hunter's head like a rubber glove. It needed artworking and very carefully blending round the eyes which a woman called Carmen had been doing for two hours. Time had gone fast because they'd talked shop.

Hair had been trickiest when time was short but was spot-on. Poulson's hair girl was technician most reluctant to join the gig after Freeman crapped on her payday. Job done, make-up guys and girls, knackered after doing two days and nights on the trot, had taken five.

Hunter had shaken all their hands. Finding time to say thanks, meaning it, was part of his DNA.

Bill Martin was in the kitchen frying up some breakfast for everybody while having a friendly argument about Dr Beeching with Poulson and Hartman.

Freeman was lying asleep under a blanket on a sofa in a small reception area front of studio. Pover and Ross were sitting with him, chatting in low voices. Poulson reckoned it could be another hour before Freeman came round. How somebody reacted to the tranquillizer depended on their metabolism.

Vanessa finished ironing Freeman's jacket and passed it across. 'Never thought I'd not want to kiss you,' she said. 'Seeing you is creepiest thing.'

'Hope we can pull this off.'

He wasn't sure if they could. Sense of things building as he stood up, done, and his big moment neared.

Connors appeared from behind the cyclorama dividing studio from kitchen. Bacon butty in hand, he said through a full mouth, 'You'll do fine, pal.'

Kath was behind him, a loaded shotgun in each hand. Stacked hair showed her sunburnt neck.

Hunter put on the jacket. Freeman's clothes fitted OK. Bit tight round bum and shoulders. But tailored loose cut and pleated pants top helped.

Main issue was shoes.

Hunter was size 11. Freeman was a dinky size 8, despite being a gnat's twitch under six foot. Soon as shops opened, somebody had been into town to buy some new black brogues as much like Freeman's as made no difference. Amazing how small details being off centre didn't matter.

Thinnes's Audi was parked in the loading bay. Connors did final run-through, ahead of the drive down to CPHQ. Kath swung up her shotguns.

On went shades all round.

Thinnes got over to the loading bay door and hit a button. Rollershutter juddered up.

Nerves set in for Hunter.

Psyching himself, he let Vanessa link his arm. In came the hum of traffic from nearby Oldham Road. In poured another boiling day's brilliant sun.

70

Sharron and Lisa were fed up of waiting.

K-Tech CEO, a smooth jowly geezer calling himself Dr George Wymark, had naffed them off.

'Come on, Shar,' Lisa said. She took off across Reception towards labs round the back.

Reception desk headgirl stood up doing reception girly threats, stilettos clacking her patch of marble floor. Reception hall was a cavernous place of 70s brute concrete loaded with chrome and steel. Vibes Lisa had been getting got worse. One-handing shotguns they shoved doors, covering shiny floor fast.

They hit dark main lab, where lights were off and blinds shut. Wymark was in conference with cronies under hotspots. All of them had swanned in and out of Reception for an hour, bullshitting, keeping two young girl cops hanging round. Arrogant posh nobs who took cops to be not-so-bright working-class divs, there to have the mick taken.

Everybody looked up as uniforms gatecrashed. Wymark was shiny silk suited, grey hair swept back. Mouth plumb loaded, caught on the hop, he showed authority by telling Lisa rather plebbily, 'Now see here.'

'No. You see here,' she said, swinging up her shotgun so it didn't point at anybody. 'A security guy was killed here last night, yet none of you seems bothered. You've made excuses, stalling talking to us when we're supposed to be conducting a police investigation. Our forensic guys are convinced you wouldn't even have reported the crime if UPS hadn't.'

Wymark nodded at his cronies, who got scarce. When rubber doors had blinged shut, he said, 'This is a top secret Government facility.'

'No it isn't,' Sharron said, correcting him. 'It's a private sector outfit which works for the Government. It has links with the MOD via Alex Freeman's office.'

'Don't you think you should tread warily?'

'Not when a man has died.'

'Not when the Queen's in hiding,' Lisa added.

'I beg your pardon?' asked Wymark.

Lisa wondered why she'd said it.

Wondering why police back-up still hadn't shown she crossed to the door and hit switches, taking in lab situ as main lights flicked on.

Wide high space.

Balcony up top, leading to outside roof garden.

Fat bendy girders doing holes.

Running across the back was a steel pressure chamber, raised on hydraulic feet. Glass across it at least a foot thick. Made her think of lab stuff from a 1970s TV show. *Incredible Hulk.* Chunky bunkered thing, which Dr Banner smashed out of first time he went green. Reason she thought it was 'cause Rob was into retro TV sci-fi. Hulk. Bionic man. Bionic woman. Not Lisa's scene. But it was why she'd decided K-Tech looked very *Six Million Dollar Man* from outside, after she saw Rob watching ep after ep the other night.

'What's it for?' she said, meaning the bunker.

'Testing,' Wymark said vaguely.

'Testing what?'

'Endurance capabilities.'

'What about this?' Lisa added, turning to a windowless car-sized silver thing, jacked up on hydraulic rams. Blue Expamet steps tangoed with yellow handrails up to an open sliding door.

'Nothing of any significance,' Wymark said.

'Something that big, obviously costing serious dosh, and it's of no significance?'

'It's a simulator.'

'What does it simulate?'

'Nothing important, I assure you.'

'I'm interested,' Lisa said, looking up metal steps. 'Show me what it simulates.'

'No need, hon,' Sharron said. 'Check this out.'

She was next to main starship console.

Wymark got nervous.

Sharron turned, weighing up the sim, sensing which embedded PC screen, whizzing with a helixy screen-saver, linked. She pinch-wiped.

Wymark said, 'Please don't touch that.'

Lisa stood with Shar at the console. Screensaver lost itself. Computer screen had thumbnails parked. Each seemed to be a sim file. One, ID'd "Grossglockner Pass", looked like a cliff road in Swiss Alps. Another thumbnail hooked Lisa and Sharron's IQs same time.

'Yeah I see it,' Lisa noted.

Tile ID'd itself, "West Coast mainline principal run". Parked frame grab. Loco cab POV.

Lisa poked it.

Behind them the sim came to life, giving off cool servo noise via chunky rams. Door hissed shut. It primed itself with a neat motion-control jig.

Same time virtual train journey thumbnail vid kicked off on screen.

Lisa maxed it.

Euston Station platforms passed either side.

'Dr Wymark,' she said, looking hard at him. 'The Royal Train used the West Coast mainline yesterday and is missing. Graffiti sprayed across your security lodge says the Queen is dead. This thing simulates the rail route she took north. You'd better explain.'

71

Randeep entered far cubicle in New Piccadilly Plaza's 88th floor Gents loos.

Virgin had won the helijet franchise. Like any airline it worried about plane security in the sky. Safeguarding heliports got much less attention.

Two piggy-looking loo security guards shifty-eyed him as he shut the cubicle door. Peeping through the gap he lifted his eyebrows smuttily. Guys frowned and looked away. Randeep shot the latch, grinning as he turned to consider the bog.

Nasty Jap jelly was harmless as plasticene. Only when excited by a phone signal passing through an embedded microchip did it turn nasty. You could roll it paper thin. Knead it like dough. In a bloke's loo, if you had a crucial British sense of toilet humour, you could have some fun shaping it. Make it plop.

Heliport toilets ran on a separate sewage system. Loos fed waste into silage tanks underneath. Freeman's uber-creepy partner-in-crime, Simon OCD Kane, owned a penthouse right under the loos.

Jokes Randeep had cracked in front of sense-of-humourless bad boy Freeman indicated Kane had no idea he shelled out £11m for a flat which had a human cesspool stored on top.

Randeep unzipped his pants.

SecuriScan hadn't picked up his concealed Jap jelly as he left the helijet. No matter how security potty the modern world, it was easy to hoodwink. Jelly was warm as he rolled it into a ball, kneading it.

Fishing in his pocket for the chip he embedded it and made a decent-sized stool. Held it over the toilet bowl, little finger crooked, and let it go, making a convincing plop. Rattled the loo roll holder. Finally he poked Flush, grateful it sensed his finger before it touched.

Away the turd went.

He doubted if Simon Kane was in town, chilling in his tacky bachelor pad underneath. But the idea of his giant bum mural taking tons of exploding shit, when silage tanks blew, amused Randeep no end.

Toilet guards avoided his eye as he washed his hands then let Dyson's jet-powered hand dryer G-force them.

'Time you guys working till?'

'Lunchtime,' said porker # 1.

'Started at two this morning,' said zit-face porker # 2.

Just when I blew off a security guy's head, thought Randeep, pulling the door.

'Jesus. Ten hours, doing bogs?'

'Yeah,' they said, pissed at being outed.

At least he'd be putting them out of their misery. Bog door bumped shut behind him.

He made for a lift.

72

Massey and Chris were in the corridor.

Last night, Chris crawled with the girls through ducting back to their mother Victoria who was actually Hunter's ex. She said they'd been holidaying in Lille. Cops came, middle of the night, taking them by car and chopper to an airbase, south of London. A gunship brought them north. Travel cabin was split, windows blanked, like the gunship which had brought the Queen, Carole, Chris, and Massey. Vicky said that when they landed at CPHQ they weren't taken off right away. Chris reckoned it was because goons had got the Royal party off first. Massey bet everybody had been brought up on the same flight, sitting either side of cabin split.

As an ex-cop, he knew a coterie of political crooks ran the country. It was his job to try and insulate the Royal Family from their influence. Downside was him tending to give duff superiors benefit of doubt because he was a decent chap who couldn't believe everybody was bent. Codespeak for wishfully thinking Alex Freeman surely wasn't crook enough to have taken the Queen and her counsel for being dicks and pulled a fast one.

Massey now believed they were caught up in a daring Royal kidnap. As Royal security chief, he'd decided it was time to demand an explanation. He wanted Chris's input, to be sure he was doing right thing.

Weighing up options, they stood near smoked glass, gazing across Manchester's gridlocked, map-like, inner-urban mess. 'Don't see how we've a choice,' Chris said, sounding ready for action. 'Freeman doing what he did to Hunter's kids says it all.'

'Goons might turn nasty,' Massey noted.

'We can't go on sitting around up here like noodles. It's the Queen we're talking about, John.'

'OK. Let's go for it.'

As they looked sharp, a big flash happened outside, high overhead. Massey half-thought it was thunder but it was a cloudless summer day. Despite CPHQ gunship soundproofing they heard a dull thud.

Looking up amazed, horrified, they saw Piccadilly Plaza heliport, forty-odd storeys away from their 45th, become a fireball. It coiled on itself, spreading. 10.00am shuttle flight to Manchester Airport had just taken off but was far enough away not to be caught by the blast. Lurching forward like a model hanging on wires, the explosion chased it while pilot hit full throttle.

Massey was transfixed. From so far, everything seemed slow-mo against clear sky. Glass across Plaza's 87th floor blew out, fragmentizing. He thought he saw a tiny naked, kicking figure before fire engulfed it. Heliport deflectors slid and fell as top storey supporting them crumbled. Chunky hydraulic support rams went too, chrome pinging sun, finding shadow, pinging sun again as the giant steel plates twisted over.

Seeing mute carnage happen on such a scale made it seem scary surreal. Nearest deflector smashed between Plaza towers. Underslung Z-girders peeled off. Massey knew surrounding smaller office blocks would get hit. Seconds had passed. Felt like an eternity.

Hideously logically, he wondered how long it would take the deflectors to hit the ground from half a mile, crushing traffic, trams. People. How far could panicking Manchester folk flee from death's vast looming shadow?

Massey prayed for them.

73

Hunter was alone driving Thinnes's Audi.

Seeing Freeman gaze back from his rearview, albeit mirrorshaded, was spooky. Crazier was New Piccadilly Plaza going pop. At first he couldn't believe it, seeing fire and smoke balloon over foreground rooftop clutter, while trying to eye the road. Staying focused while Manchester burned was tough. Hunter hated thinking it should help divert attention from what he and the guys were doing.

Vanessa was right behind in the Volvo.

Connors and Kath were with her, hidden under dust sheets. They'd gone via the MEN Arena, picking up the ring road to get down to CPHQ. Lucky they'd not gone via busy Piccadilly which usually was clogged with traffic. Hunter was linked to Vanessa and Connors via Blutooth. Hidden from the Plaza by the MEN, it took them a minute to realize a bomb had gone off. Connors sensed two bad boys were in town.

If so, why blow the Plaza?

They'd *ummed* and *ahhed* about best way into CPHQ. They decided Hunter should just walk in and make out Freeman had escaped.

Tailed by Vanessa, he'd drive into CPHQ's underground car park. As a regular press conference delegate, Hunter knew CPHQ was easy to access, despite piffle about high security. Connors, Kath, Vanessa and himself would take the Chief Commissioner's lift to the 45th floor. Cops would probably be on guard up top. Bogus Freeman would order them to take the Queen, Vicky, and the girls down to the basement using same private lift. Connors and Kath would drug the cops and drive everybody out. If cops didn't play ball, big guns Kath and Connors were cosying in the Volvo should do the trick. Hunter's big worry was sounding like Freeman.

Connors insisted that as long as he talked like him as best he could, going on about a froggy throat after kidnap trauma, nobody should suss.

He was right.

When Hunter pulled up at the barrier, it seemed like booth guy didn't know Freeman was missing. He'd probably not spoken to chauffeur-driven Freeman, a toady who didn't easily engage with the lower orders. Hunter small talked about the Plaza going up as being a reason for driving himself. Booth guy knew Vanessa from press calls. Her arriving behind Freeman wasn't suspect. All around, cops took off on foot and in squad cars from nearby cop exit chute. So much excitement helped cover Hunter and the guys arriving.

He drove down the ramp and found a space. Letting Vanessa park, he sent down his window. Thinnes had given him a neat piece of kit to knock out a CCTV watching the lifts. Laser hotspot helped his aim. Kit froze the cam on an empty frame-grab but caused motion grain, so it didn't look suspect to security boys desk-jamming upstairs. Hunter did his stuff.

They waited till the coast was clear then piled out of cars and made it to the CC's private lift. Since Driscoll's disgrace, no new Chief Commissioner had been appointed for Manchester. Hunter reckoned it was why Freeman's job had been dreamt up.

Lift ran up outside of CPHQ. Only way in was with an ID swipe card. They'd gambled that with Freeman being national security chief, and a CPHQ regular, his would be one of a select few cards which worked.

Hunter swiped.

Ping.

Bingo. Doors split.

Soon as they were in, Connors stuck out a hand and hit Thinnes's nifty piece of kit in reverse making sentry CCTV resume real time.

Lift got going.

Hunter, feeling it now and worrying about Vanessa, told her, 'You should have stayed at Mark's.'

'Where you go, I go,' she said, shotgun in each hand. She was in Kath's cop leathers, in case they needed a pretend lady cop to charm goons. She was barelegged because she hated wearing black tights, even sheer ones. She'd pinned up her hair so it didn't get in her face.

Kath was in her combat vest and camouflage pants, hair stacked so it didn't get in her face. Like Vanessa she held a shotgun upright in each hand. Three rolls of duct tape bangled each arm.

Sun pinged as the lift escaped from underground and city rooftops fell away. Tiny emergency vehicles blue-flash wailed down in city streets.

They looked round for the Plaza.

Lift went up CPHQ's south face.

From their POV, Piccadilly was hidden.

'Thanks, you guys,' Hunter told them, shuddering at the enormity of their undertaking.

'Easy pal,' Connors said, squeezing Hunter's shoulder. 'We're rooting for ya.' Baseball capped, he had a big Arnie gun, clipped to a chest steadiframe, held vertical like a sawn-off bazooka.

If it could be so easy, Hunter wondered why they'd bothered with a Freeman dupe. Connors quite rightly said they needed him because they didn't know what to expect when they got up top.

74

Wymark had continued to bullshit. Lisa was losing it. She knew Shar also wondered where back-up had got to. Both girls kept schtum, in case Wymark got funny ideas. Lisa set her shoulder cam going and headed over to the pressure chamber for a better look.

'Hey Col,' she said.

'Yes my love?'

'You getting this?'

'Just a sec,' he said on a full mouth. 'Just having me toast an' a brew.'

Lisa made the chamber.

'Got it,' Col said.

Something happening furthest from where she'd been at got her attention. Sharron was with her. They padded along front of the thing, seeing high-shine reflections. Lisa turned to hard-eye Wymark, letting him know he'd better stay put. Turning back, she couldn't believe what the hell she saw when she got to bunker's end.

Soon as her cam took it, full-mouth Col went, 'Whoa my love. What in crap's name is that?'

'OMG,' she said.

'Shit hon.'

Hanging off chamber end: a thick, round steel door. Bank vault thing big enough to climb through, leaning to sci-fi with embossed-debossed panels. Nested among oily conduit one side was a fat, recessed plasticote handle. Like those which pull down with a cool decompression hiss to herald spaceship self-destruct.

Running down opposite side were three big knuckle hinges. All heavy weld lines and thick steel folded over six-inch titanium bolts. Door had been smashed open from inside, blowing top two hinges. Top door corner, opposite where it hinged, was bent out showing it to be around eight inches thick. Lisa got closer. Somebody or *something* in the chamber had knocked seven bells out of the door to escape. She clumped up treadplate steps and stood in the opening.

Col had gone quiet.

Over her earpiece, Lisa heard amazed control room guys next to Col swear as live pics got piped. She could see where a fist had trashed the door. Numerous pummel indentations. Whatever caused them hit like an express train.

Sharron came up the steps and held a gloved fist in a corresponding punchmark.

'You seeing, hon?'

'Yeah I'm seeing. Hey Col?'

Col sounded strained, like he was about to crap on his fave girl but hated doing it.

'I've got the CC for you,' he told her flatly.

Chief Commissioner Culver came on, doing his usual la-dee-bloody-dah condescending self in Lisa's ear.

'Hello Lisa.'

'Hello sir.'

No mincing, he got to it.

'You're at K-Tech.'

Statement of fact.

Not a question.

'Yes sir, we are.'

'You're out of there.'

'Sorry sir?'

'Leave immediately.'

'But sir.'

'No buts Lisa. You and Sharron get out of there. Or I have your badges, as our friends say across the pond.'

She looked at Wymark who stood, arms defensively folded, by lab console. He watched her but didn't know what was going on in her earpiece. Lisa knew why back-up hadn't shown. Why K-Tech management had gotten away with keeping cops hanging around.

From his office, Culver could access any Thames Valley cop's live shoulder cam, if he needed.

Lidding anger, Lisa stepped in the chamber to keep out of Wymark's eyeline. She asked Culver, 'Are you seeing my pictures, sir?'

'Which pictures are those?'

Lisa unclipped her handset to check what her shoulder cam could see. Video snow. She commlock-flipped her handset to access the cam file she'd uploaded back at base, via Col. Access denied.

Sharron looked at her, sensing rotten stuff. Winking, she pulled her phone and hit video cam.

'Oh dear. Sorry sir,' Lisa said. 'Seems to be a gremlin in the works at my end. Funny how nasty horrible conniving gremlins screw up works at inappropriate times. Wouldn't you agree sir?'

Sounded like he was agitated. His Christian name was Dennis. Lisa's goofy art school younger sister Kaye told her never to trust guys called Dennis with two N's 'cause their name spelt backwards was Sinned.

'Are you out of there?' Five words able to snuff twin cop careers in a jiff.

'Yes sir,' she said cheerily.

'Good girl,' sexist pig said. 'You and Sharron come up to see me, soon as you get back.'

'Certainly *sir*. Looking forward to it *sir*.'

Screw you said a voice in her head.

Randeep was in Waterstones on Deansgate when first deflector hit. Soundsmash tremor was incredible. His analogy with church bells crashing through Heaven a good one. Chain explosions had followed.

He'd set off the bomb from the bookstore's upstairs coffee bar but hadn't seen New Piccadilly Plaza blow. Youtube and Twitter would soon be loaded with stuff he could enjoy at his leisure.

Meanwhile, war scale pandemonium. Hard to believe so many emergency sirens could scream in so short a time. Hard to believe so many scared folk could scream. Sun had gone out, sky hosting it blotted by a giant dust cloud. It had got as far as St Anne's Square, billowing from sidestreets onto Deansgate. Comparisons with 9-11 would be inevitable.

Nahid met him across from Waterstones, in King Street West. They decided to park bums on a piazza seat and sup Cokes, till the furore died down.

Cops everywhere.

Mass cop exodus, as predicted.

Squad Cars. Uniforms.

Headed for the meteorite hit that was Manchester's Ground Zero.

75

Poulson, Mark Hartman, and make-up guys not sleeping were standing in the sunny studio car park. They'd rushed outside, soon as they heard the bang. Burning New Piccadilly Plaza fingered high summer sky. Poulson reckoned top three or four storeys had gone.

Plaza was like a giant chrome tuning fork, skinned with ribbed red and grey plastic laminate. A heliport used to run across the top, joining twin towers. If not for exposed support girders housing lifts, holding everything together in the middle, he imagined both towers would sag outwards and collapse.

Steel bits kept falling off each, remotely crash-clanging down. Water spray gushed from bust mains. A huge heliport deflector hung precariously off shattered east tower. Black smoke boiled, flicking buzzsaw sparks. Manchester was alive with sirens. A media chopper circled like a vulture. Chinooky thudding, it would be offering live aerial feed to news channel high bidder.

'What do you reckon, Phil?' Mark said.

'I wonder if those two hoodlums did it who Craig says Alex has had blowing up the country.'

'Why New Piccadilly Plaza?'

'Why indeed.'

'Why don't we find out?'

When they went back inside, Alex was sitting on a Reception sofa, looking like death warmed up. Because he hadn't much strength, Ross baby-fed him bottle water. Poulson wasn't enamoured with Alex after what he'd done to them but he'd no wish to see him dead. He worried he was dehydrating. Water dribbled on his dressing gown as Ross tipped the bottle. Aproned Bill Martin came through with a plate of buttered toast and set it on a low-flying granite coffee table in front of Alex.

Pover would be happy to see Alex snuff it and wanted everybody to know. He sat opposite him, booted feet thrust out on the table, a shotgun's fat double muzzle aimed casually between Alex's pale skinny legs.

As Poulson and Mark crossed over, Pover told Alex, 'We need to keep your head in one piece, boyo, in case it needs to fill us in on crucial information. Your knackers we can afford to lose, if I slip accidentally on purpose and this thing goes off.'

'That's enough, Glyn,' Poulson said.

He thanked Bill for bringing Alex toast.

Bill went back to the kitchen.

Alex croaked, 'What was that explosion, Phil?'

'The Plaza's been blown up.'

'All of it?'

'Just the top.'

Alex looked poorly but he also looked worried digesting what Poulson said. Didn't seem like he knew the Plaza had been due to go up in smoke, going by his expression. Something bothered him all the same.

Poulson knew Simon Kane had a place between Plaza forks, under 88th storey. It had gone. 'Simon Kane had an apartment at the top, didn't he?'

Alex nodded. Missing past tense he chewed his toast with some effort.

'Is he involved in this?'

'How do you mean?'

'Oh stop playing bloody silly games, Alex. Craig told us about these two young chaps you've had blowing everywhere up.'

Kerryann came through with her iPad. 'You should see this, Phil.'

BBC News was going to town on Manchester's blast with main news studio being at Salford Quays. VO went on about the attack's audacity, setting the scene for viewers tuning in. Cut to a local black blonde reporter in the thick of it. Warning viewers they might find pictures distressing, she turned as the camera widened to reveal large chunks of smashed masonry. Emergency uniforms wiped this way and that.

Camera panned across smoking rubble which might once have been a sand dunes photo mural. Blood splattered it, along with what looked like thick brown paint.

Black girl, covering her nose as if she'd smelt something unpleasant, said, 'Remains of a large mural you can see behind me were part of a penthouse apartment at the top of New Piccadilly Plaza, owned by leading international businessman Simon Kane.'

Poulson saw Alex jump.

On the iPad, black girl spoke as a fireman emerged from smoke carrying a blue plastic tote. Frowning, he dumped it near the camera and popped the lid.

Black girl cued a young French girl. Stuffing her lollipop mike in her face, she told camera, 'Gimet works at the Plaza. She thinks Simon Kane was in his apartment when the bomb exploded.'

Alex moaned in horror when he overheard black girl speculating that Kane was dead.

On the iPad, before black girl could let young French girl confirm, the fireman shot the tote lid behind her. He dived away from it swearing, appealing to Jesus Christ at what was inside.

Alex's moan became a hideous traumatized cry of anguish. Retching heavily, he threw up, spraying the coffee table. Pover jumped in his seat, swearing when his dumped projected legs took loads of frothy sick. In the kerfuffle his shotgun went off.

76

'We're here to kill the Queen,' Randeep said.

Shock horror from guy on the desk.

Beefy, in his 50s, probably an ex-cop put out to pasture, he looked ridiculous doing a woman's job. Bent round his tough face was a clear plastic rod hooked over a Blutooth thing glued to his ear. Nipple-mike end was nearer his fat hairy nostrils than his mouth.

'I beg your pardon?'

'We'd like to report a very daring crime. Somebody's blown up New Piccadilly Plaza, dash it.'

'You said you were here to kill the Queen.'

'No I didn't.'

'Yes you did.'

Randeep turned to Nahid. 'Did I say we were here to kill the Queen, my friend?'

'I think you did actually.'

'Awfully sorry, old chap,' Randeep told desk guy. 'This Royal stuff going on, old girl doing a bunk, plus these naughty bangs, must have caused a slip of the old tongue. Real reason we're here is to case the joint before we take it apart and have some fun upstairs.'

It was the truth.

They needed to get up top but weren't sure if they should use public lifts or try to access the CC's private lift from basement car park.

CPHQ's OTT rusty-metal reception desk had been designed by a Turner prizewinning arty fartist. Much of the world's population lived in mud huts. Yet taxpayers had underwritten such agonizing self-indulgence. Not all that long ago, Randeep decided, when there was no such thing as a bloated public sector, desk guy would have been a humble *Evening all* desk sergeant dumbbell, stuck behind a bit of polished wood.

'Why don't you bugger off?' this dumbbell said.

'Are you implying we're gay?' Randeep looked up at a nearby CCTV blimp, diodes flashing. Knowing its HD capture could be scanned and lipread, he told it, 'This public sector employee, replete with hairy conk, is suggesting I'm a homosexual.'

'I shall call security,' desk guy said. He shouted across at somebody where the desk went off at a blowtorched tangent. 'Get these nutters escorted out, Jo.'

Randeep addressed the CCTVs again.

'Furthermore, this public sector employee is making prejudicial remarks pertaining to me being mentally deficient, when in fact I gained a First at Oxford. Video evidence pointing to a fat compensation claim, wouldn't you bastards agree?'

Two Kevlar'd, spandexy-packeted goons arrived.

Stocky Zapata 'tached piggies.

Only things missing were sombreros. Gothy boots of mustachio # 1 squeaked when he trod on them.

'You should oil those, old chap,' Randeep told him.

'Out,' said mustachio # 2.

Randeep, turning nasty, asked desk guy, 'How clued up are you on iconic popular culture?'

'Try me,' desk guy said, sounding bored.

'There's an old saying, old chap. You and your colleagues should note' —he indicated Nahid. Gave mustachios a quick once over. Coolly hooked on shades. Doing heavy Scandinavian, he added—'*We'll be back.*'

'Out,' said mustachio # 2 again.

Headcases trying to get into cop stations was a modern fact of life, hence mustachios on CPHQ's revolving door. Randeep and Nahid had got through the net because they were good-looking guys.

77

Wymark had faked feeling sick.

Lisa sussed it right off. Driving it was a naïve belief that somebody in a corner could pique a good girl cop's good nature. Lisa wasn't having it. Chief Commissioner Culver had chucked serious cards on the table. But she was gonna find out what had gone on in the lab.

'Review your situation, Dr Wymark. A man has been murdered. Evidence here shows a link between K-Tech and the missing Royal Train. Your willingness to assist might have favourable consequences.' Pausing, she laid it on, uttering tosh. 'Charges against you as a K-Tech employee could be transferred to K-Tech.'

Wymark got her drift and relented.

Wheeling across a chair, he sat down. 'Your uniforms were developed here,' he told them, nodding at their quasi-superheroine blue-black body armour. 'Or rather, yarn they're made from was.'

'Go on,' Lisa said.

'Your stab vests are covered in what is really sophisticated medieval chainmail. Made from high tensile biweave Kevlar, it's bulletproof. Next stage up for us as product developers was to use new generation police uniforms as a basis for advanced army combat armour. Armour which could not only protect infantrymen but enhance battlefield performance.'

'Exoskeletons?' Sharron said.

'Not exactly. Exoskeletons have been used by industry for a good few years.'

'Powerchargers?' Lisa added, remembering.

'Yes. Germans devised them for heavy industrial use. But they're cumbersome and restrictive. They're really a glorified JCB "worn" by an operator.' He pinch-wiped a screen. 'All governments dream of super-soldiers. Early in the 2000s, the US military flirted with Future Combat Systems. The more advanced we become as a society the more science fiction becomes science fact. Nowadays, "science fiction" really means aliens and interstellar or time travel. Anything else is technological advancement, which happens sooner or later.'

'How does that link to a steel door hanging off over there?' Lisa said, nodding at it.

Shar said, 'Think I'm getting a picture, hon.'

Wymark brought up a CG thing on screen.

'Two sets of prototype battlefield armour like this, developed for the army, have been stolen.'

'Powersuits?' said Sharron.

'Sort of,' Wymark agreed. 'They incorporate bionic technology, instead of crude power-assist stuff which drives exoskeletons.'

'Looks like the original Robocop,' Lisa noted.

'First one we built looked like a *Star Wars* stormtrooper uniform. Modern artificial limbs—bionics to you and me—work by responding to nerve impulses. As computers become more advanced, replacement limbs get more versatile and life-like. If somebody loses part of a leg or arm, the stump tries to work as if the rest of the limb is still there. A sophisticated mechanical replacement has numerous tiny sensors which interpret nerve impulses in the stump.'

'Steve Austin,' Lisa said, thinking back to Rob watching his DVDs the other night.

'We took the same principle to develop our power-armour. Main difference is sensors feed off whole body movement by encasing it. It's the inevitable progression of bionic technology which has given war veteran amputees new arms and legs for many years.'

'So we *are* talking exoskeletons,' Sharron said.

'No,' Wymark said. 'An exoskeleton is an exterior mechanical skeleton which resembles and mimics a human endoskeleton beneath. Our powerarmour greatly enhances body movement. Punch a brick wall, hard, and you hurt your hand. But what if you punch a brick wall, hard as you can, wearing armour which protects your hand, changing it to reverse kinetic energy? Magnified many times, your punch goes off like a bomb.'

He poked the screen.

Video came on of the pressure chamber door. Something was hitting it like hell from inside. Camera zoomed in slowly. Lisa imagined somebody lacing into the door with a sledgehammer would sound similar.

They watched for maybe half a minute.

Relentless *wunching-verdunching*.

Eventually the door gave. Top hinge popped, *clunk-clinging* to the lab floor, tinny on screen.

Second hinge blew.

'Oh God,' said Lisa.

Piledriver sound carried on as the chamber door had the shit beaten from it. Laid under was a sonic whiplash morphing to a loaded ricochet, like the sledgehammer in Lisa's head was hitting an anvil.

Change in momentum.

Slower whacking-smashing.

Wymark said, 'He's using his feet.'

'Jesus,' said Sharron.

Door gave. Started buckling.

'It's all about micro servo-actuators and electroactive polymers,' Wymark said. 'But the tecchy stuff doesn't matter. Suffice to say that as microprocessors get smaller achieving massively increased strength is easy. Micro-sensors interpret and amplify velocity, converting it to lethal kinetic energy. Karate does the same thing with flexion forces. It's why human hands can smash bricks or breeze block without being damaged.'

'How strong are we talking?' asked Lisa.

'The armour has limitations,' Wymark said. 'Wearing it you can't lift a car or chuck it. But you can roll it over and rip a door off. You can easily throw a chap across a room, through a wall.'

They watched the screen carry on *wunching-verdunching*. Chamber door finally got booted open.

Powerarmoured figure filled chamber entrance, causing interior shaftlight zing.

Sort of looked like Robocop, Lisa decided, because of MOHAWK full-head helmet with fancy add-ons. Grey MARPAT camouflage gave it grungy soldier kit appeal. Heavy-duty gauntlets and chunky Gothy gripper boots nodded at modern cop togs.

Doing cool servo sounding *hiss-thunks* with each step, it clunked down metal chamber steps, triumphantly thumbing-up. Small round of applause off camera. Powerarmour guy popped his helmet and horsy headkicked curly, long blonde hair.

Powerarmour guy was a girl.

'Oh wow,' said Lisa.

Girl's head looked dinky due to armour bulkiness. Two guys came into shot to help her de-kit. Video ended before she got anything off.

While Sharron and Lisa got their heads round what the hell they'd seen, Wymark hit a console button. 'Sort some breakfast will you, Chan?'

'Yes Dr Wymark,' said an oriental sounding girl.

Lisa's mind raced.

She was scared.

Wymark folded his arms. 'Whoever came for the armour must have known it was here,' he said gravely. 'We should assume they want it for a reason.'

78

Massey and Chris were still in the corridor.

Seeing the Plaza go up had knocked them for six.

45th floor vantage gave a bird's eye of Market Street and the Arndale when deflectors hit Piccadilly and explosions chased across it like buzzbombs.

Piccadilly Gardens used to be a pleasant green oasis and award-winning sculpture park. It had become a smoking volcanic hole. Buildings all around had gone. Burst water mains fought fire engine hose sprays, making it tough to tell them apart.

Only time Massey had seen destruction on such an epic scale was when the World Trade Center fell. Everywhere was hazy with dust. Another mute explosion chucked up some cars, spinning like they did in movies. Probably a gas main.

Carole emerged from the apartment and saw latest fireball erupt through the window. 'Oh please God. Not another,' she said. 'This poor city. I can't bear to look.' Filling up, she pulled a hanky from her sleeve.

'How's Her Majesty?' Chris asked her.

'Coping. Cynics are cruel. They think grief's an emotion Royals don't deserve to have.'

'I worry about her,' Massey said.

'She's tougher than you think, John. She's a lot tougher than us. She wants to be alone for a while, to pray for the dead and wounded.'

Carole dabbed her crow's feeted eyes.

Massey wanted to comfort her. He knew from how she discreetly watched him, smudging her mascara, that they must put aside any personal needs. Whatever Alex Freeman might be up to, Massey had decided that to safeguard the Queen they should stay put while Manchester burned. Earlier he'd revealed to Carole and the Queen what he thought might be going on.

'If it's as you think,' Carole said, picking up where she'd left off, pushing her hanky back up her sleeve, 'it must go higher than Freeman.'

'Agreed,' Chris said. 'Somebody senior has an agenda, marooning the Queen all the way up here.'

Doors to their minders slid open, surprising them.

Three goons were on duty in Reception.

Flatscreen TV yattered from a wall.

Porky Pig was nearest, chomping gum. 'I was coming to see what you guys want for lunch.'

'Have you seen what's happened,' Massey told him, indicating outside.

'We could hardly miss it, Sir John.'

'What's your assessment?'

Slobbed at the desk was a fat shaven-headed Scouse artist, full of cold. His chair creaked under its load when

341

he said nasally, 'The lads and me don't know what big words like "assessment" mean.'

'Where's Alex Freeman?'

'Up a pig's arse in America,' said goon # 3.

'You revolting creature,' Carole snapped. 'Have you no sensitivity? Manchester has been partially wiped out this morning. All you can do is sit there like an odious slob, making filthy jokes.'

Goon grinned but didn't bite back. Instead, he chucked up a peanut, catching it open mouthed.

'How long will we be kept here?' asked Massey.

'It's up to Mr Freeman,' said Porky Pig.

'Can we see him?'

'He's been unavoidably detained.'

'When will he be available?'

Before the goon answered, matching sliding doors, opposite side of Reception, slid open.

Goons turned casually and jumped. Massey was stunned to see Freeman steadying himself against the jamb, looking poorly.

'Mr Freeman sir,' said gobsmacked Scouser, getting up, sniffing catarrh. He came out from behind the glass desk. Nearest other goon joined him.

'For God's sake help me,' Freeman croaked. Goons were glued to the floor. 'I managed to escape.'

Alarm bells set off in Massey's head.

Something wasn't right.

Chris joined him and Carole by the door. 'What's he mean he escaped,' Chris whispered.

Freeman looked like he was ready to pass out.

342

Desk goons rushed over to catch him before he fell. Soon as they got there four Sheuze shotguns found their heads. Two each from either side of the door.

Guys froze.

Freeman was suddenly OK and got out of the way. Two women appeared, waving the guns.

First—tattooed, combat vested, army panted—looked tough. Massey knew the second. Classy older blonde in short-skirt black leathers. Before he could wonder what Hunter's partner Vanessa was up to, a Rambo lookalike joined them. Swinging a double-barrel machinegun with twin, fat perf muzzles, he got Porky Pig in his laser-sights, dazzling Massey.

79

'Raise 'em, pal,' Connors told the cop, getting the hot-spot to his forehead. He told Massey and those with him, 'You guys might wanna quit my firing line.'

Getting the message they got scarce each side of door frame. Cop doing open doorway sent up hands when laser hotspot joined, letting Connors guide him across to the curvy smoked-glass desk.

'Take it nice and easy, pal.'

Kath and Vanessa, holding shotguns at arm's length, ushered the other two cops round to the desk.

Guys knew the pack drill. Spreading hands across the desktop, they let Vanessa kick apart their legs before she pulled their guns. She stuck two down her skirt but chucked third over to Hunter.

Kath asked fat funny voice bald cop, 'How many of you guys are up here?'

'Just us three.' She rammed a shotgun up his asshole. *Yeeowwing* he jumped up tiptoe. 'Jesus Christ, love. It's the bloody truth.'

Other cops backed him up.

Massey reappeared with the young guy and the nice PA looking woman. Connors recognized Massey from hijack briefings with Poulson.

'What's going on?' he demanded

'Easy pal,' Connors told him.

Massey ignored him. 'What the bloody hell are you up to, Freeman?'

'Shut it,' Connors told him. 'It's in your interests as well as ours that we KO the uniforms.'

Kath let Connors and Vanessa cover her while she got busy with duct tape. Yanking funny voice fat cop's arms behind him she did up his wrists.

Hunter anxiously asked the cops, 'Where are the little girls and their mother?'

Cops did *Huh?* expressions over shoulders, wondering where bogeyman was at. Obviously Freeman should know where prisoners were being kept.

'Where are they?' Hunter repeated angrily, sticking his gun to nearest cop's head.

Fat funny voice cop, end of line, nodded past Massey. 'Far end behind the sliding door sir. Where you had us put them.'

Kath did cop # 2's wrists.

Massey, watching her rip-wrap tape, said, 'Is this some kind of a sick joke?'

'Shut it pal,' Connors told him again.

Connors knew Hunter was desperate to find his kids. He took off past Massey, the woman, and young guy, who parted to let him through. Grey laminate-walled corridor did far perspective. Halogen spotlit, it fell to acoustically muted shagpile darkness like in a big city hotel. Far end, a stainless steel door caught light.

'Vicky,' Hunter shouted.

Massey told him, 'They won't hear you. Like the policeman said, they're at the far end, behind that door.' Easing nearer to Hunter, he checked out his face. Like maybe he was adding two to two.

'Vicky,' Hunter shouted again. Door near him opened. Tensed as hell, he spun, pointing his gun. 'Shit,' he said, lowering his gun fast, realizing what he'd done. Movie make-up meant his expression didn't show too good. But Connors sensed from his voice that his face woulda been a picture.

The Queen came into the corridor. Connors was amazed how small and frail she was.

'I'm sorry I swore, Your Majesty,' Hunter said humbly, towering over her by about a foot.

The Queen ignored him. 'What's happening, John? Why are these people here with guns?'

'I'm sorry, ma'am,' Massey said, going to her. 'But we don't know.' He stood away from the Queen. Connors remembered hearing nobody was meant to touch her.

The Queen came forward.

She might be tiny and very old. But she sure carried herself like a regal mini powerhouse.

'Who are you people?'

'We've come to rescue you, Your Majesty,' Connors said, feeling weirdly humbled.

Seemed like she got his drift. Connors sensed from her expression that she probably knew she'd become a pawn in some crazy political game.

'Are you the SAS?'

'Not quite, ma'am,' Connors said, hearing himself do *ma'am* how they did it across the pond.

'You're an American.'

'I guess so,' he said grinning.

Kath had taped third cop's arms.

Massey said to everybody, 'I think you'd better explain yourselves.'

Connors told him, 'We're here to get you guys out. Alex Freeman had you brought up here for safe keeping while he makes it look to the world like the Royal Train was hijacked and the Queen kidnapped.'

'If he's done that,' the nice PA lady said, stepping forward, hands at hips, 'why is he here with you?'

Near Hunter and the Queen was a John door embossed with a stylized bronze girl. It inched open, revealing

346

two cute, staring wide-eye faces. When he saw them, Hunter moaned and fell to his knees. Thanking God he stuck his gun down his pants and reached out. 'Come to daddy,' he said, trying to contain himself.

Seeing Vanessa, the girls crept out warily.

Dark one seemed feisty. She told Hunter, 'You're *not* my daddy. You're the horrid bad man.' Lunging at him, she waved her fists but backed off and chased her sister who called for Aunty Vanessa when she saw her coming through to greet them.

'Hey you guys,' she said, kneeling to hug them, creaking leather. Like jumping jacks they attached themselves to her, hugging her tight.

Hunter turned on his knees.

Connors saw his eyes shining.

Knew what the hell was coming.

Losing it, Hunter chucked up his hands and in a mad frenzy ripped off Freeman's face to reveal himself. Puffing, he wiped make-up stuff from round his eyes with his fingers and jacket cuffs.

'I guessed as much,' said Massey when Hunter lobbed the rubber Freeman mask and ruffled his hair.

'Bloody hell fire,' train officer added.

'Jesus lads,' said fat funny voice cop.

The Queen was amused, for the right reasons.

Realizing what had happened, the girls detached themselves from Vanessa.

Shouting, 'Daddy! Daddy!' they ran across to him and bowled him over, long hair flying. Hunter picked himself up so he could hug them. Overjoyed, overwhelmed, the girls started crying. Dark one smothered her daddy in kisses and told him she loved him.

Hunter nearly lost it. It didn't matter.

Connors thought he might lose it too.

Seeing Hunter reunited with his kids got him thinking 'bout stuff that was in his head when it hit a rusty railroad track and he thought he'd died.

'Give it a rest Glyn,' Poulson said.

The Welshman was all mouth.

Everybody was in the kitchen. Hair expert Charlotte had been into town to get something vegan to eat. Pover filled her in on what happened. Spooked by Alex's vomit, he'd slipped off his seat. His backside hitting floor had made his shotgun go off when he ended up wedged down between the coffee table and sofa.

Alex, looking miserable, sat on an upright pine chair across the kitchen. He hadn't said much since TV had confirmed Simon Kane's death.

Bill Martin had kindly cleaned up Alex's mess, using a mop and bucket. Two make-up guys were patching a hole which Pover had blasted in the studio's front outside wall. His army pants were in the wash. Wearing baggy shorts, he sported shockingly hairy legs. Being a frustrated stand-up comic he thrived on attention, rubbing his back to embellish his story.

'I told the bugger my finger might slip,' he told Charlotte, playing up his Welshness. 'Swung up my gun in the nick of time.' He liked the idea Alex was suffering. 'Shame I didn't put him out of his bloody misery like his boyfriend with the crazy hair.'

'I said leave it Glyn,' Poulson said, hard enough for him to get the message. It wasn't in Poulson's nature to kick folk when they were down.

Kerryann was next to him, pinch-wiping news channels on her iPad. 'Look Phil,' she said.

BBC News scrolled BREAKING NEWS.

Something happening at K-Tech.

Earlier they'd picked up that gateman Stan had been murdered. Media had gathered in blazing sunshine at K-Tech's gate but since the earlier report everybody had moved behind the security lodge. Poulson assumed the new report was to do with some revelation about poor Stan's death. It wasn't.

Cut to two young policewomen, holding an impromptu live news call. Blonde one, heavily made-up, hair stacked, shotgun held up, said, 'The Queen's in hiding. Because of terrorist bombs which blew across the country yesterday and today, and after what happened here last night, we believe a deadly strike against a key Royal target is imminent.'

As she said this, camera panned across graffiti spray-ed on the lodge wall. Media hadn't been allowed near it first time round. Poulson knew because Indian studio big hair girl had noted the lodge was off limits.

'Good God,' he said, seeing the graffiti.

'Hell's bells,' Mark Hartman said, joining him, mug-ged coffee in hand.

Voices blabbed off camera.

A question got through.

'And you're saying advanced weaponry developed at K-Tech could be used in the attack?'

Poulson saw Alex buck up.

Brunette policewoman, black nail varnish flashing as she kept her shotgun upright, said, 'K-Tech has devel-oped military battle armour which increases strength and is impervious to bullets. This state-of-the-art kit has been stolen. We've seen a video demo and evidence in K-Tech's lab of what it can do.'

New camera POV.

Limo. Bulldozing media support crews in front of the security lodge. When it pulled up a back door flew open and a uniformed skinny senior cop got out.

Police heavies jumped from a squad car behind as it finished screech-stopping. Poulson recognized senior cop. Thames Valley CC. Followed by the two heavies he dashed in the lodge.

Camera round the back picked him up as he came out the back door. Beeb studio big hair VO'd the remarkable unfolding drama happening live. Confirmed the senior cop was Chief Commissioner Culver.

Getting in front of the policewomen, he held up his hands and told the jostled camera, 'Sorry ladies and gentlemen. This news conference is over.'

Cop heavies tried to drive the policewomen away but they fought back. Feisty brunette floored first cop heavy with a fireman's throw. Blonde's stacked long hair unclipped as she scuffled with second heavy.

She yelled, 'No it isn't over *sir*.'

Shoving beefy cop # 2 away, she swung up her shotgun and stood in the lodge doorway to fire at the sky. Everybody looked sharp.

Clawing messed hair from her face, she added, 'We believe our Queen's in terrible mortal danger, wherever she is. I'm also convinced this twat of a Chief Commissioner, Dennis Culver—that's Dennis with two N's—is implicated.'

Camera picked up Culver as he composed himself, looking pissed off. His phone went off in his pocket, playing a feeble pingy ringtone which somehow made him seem an even bigger twit.

Poulson crossed to stand in front of Alex. 'Did you know about this stuff K-Tech has developed?'

'Of course I did.'

'Who else knew?'

'K-Tech staff. The PM. Senior ministers.'

'Anybody else?'

He said nothing.

'Come on Alex.'

'I might have let it slip to the guys who blew up Sheffield and Stockport.' He looked feeble. No, Poulson decided. Totally bloody pathetic. 'They're confident good looking lads, Phil.' Looking up at Poulson like a broken man he held his knobbly knees together, pigeon footing effeminate feet. 'I don't know if they blew up the Plaza.'

'Do they know the Queen's at CPHQ?'

'It was Randeep's idea.'

'Bloody hell fire.'

Poulson checked his watch.

Eight hours since stuff got nicked from K-Tech. Bags of time for two thieves to get back to Manchester. If they planned on hitting CPHQ, best thing would be to clear it of cops first. Best way of doing that would be to blow up the city's biggest landmark.

He pulled his phone.

Mark said, 'What are you doing?'

'Calling Craig.'

81

Randeep and Nahid were nearly ready.

They'd got hold of an old brown UPS mailvan. Boxy height meant they could stand up properly in the back to get changed.

They'd parked on a meter in Stanley Street, which broke from New Bailey Street and had been realigned to become CPHQ's dead end. Mad cop panic had dwindled. Area was quiet.

As they suited up Randeep heard background choppers buzzing Piccadilly's blitzkrieg. Van walk-in back door was dark windowed. Dust fogged day. Nahid pig-snorted when he put on his helmet and a rogue cop 4x4 shot from CPHQ's underground ramp. *Weeooo weeooo weeoooing* past in a tizzy, it rocked the van.

'Like lemmings, eh?' Randeep said, feeling nasty as he sensed the 4x4 hit street end before screeching right up to Deansgate.

They pressurized their suits.

'All because of us, man,' Nahid said, getting off as their big moment neared.

Now they were togged up, comparisons after the event with Robocop would be inevitable. Randeep felt more like a battle armoured supersoldier from the Halo movies and video games, given a makeover by a comic book artist doing cyberpunk on speed.

It was like wearing a bulldozer.

Chunky body plates formed an interlocking shell over a skintight black Kevlar undersuit. Armour was like an exoskeleton. Dynamic contour lines did grungy machine stuff at arm and leg pivot points. Hefty chest and shoulderplates housed an onboard computer, powerpack, and two hours of oxygen. Slick visored helmets were Blutooth linked. Both suits finished in army desert grey MARPAT camouflage. If they'd had more prep time they'd have sprayed them sexy colours. Batman matt black. Or Royal blue.

On the way back from K-Tech overnight they'd stopped off somewhere to check out the kit. Two weeks ago they'd got Freeman sozzled on a bottle of his fave plonk. Got him showing laptop stuff about how the armour worked.

'Let's do it, my friend.'

'Yeah let's.'

'Are you up for making the ultimate sacrifice, to take your rightful place in history?'

'If you want me to.'

Poor fawning sod Randeep thought, knocking Brownie points off his street cred. Randeep was up for some fun. But he'd run a mile if he thought he'd get hurt.

For the hell of it, he booted off the back door.

Pranging parked cars behind, it flew up the street as if yanked on wires. Wearing the armour was weird. Exert just a teensy bit harder and your strength massively increased.

They'd parked on north side of Stanley Street. River Irwell ran in a deep dip, other side of some tacky stainless steel fence doing GMP's Star of David.

As they shut visors and got down from the van, another cop 4x4 bumped up from under CPHQ. Lightbars hit off when they made foggy day.

Gripper tyres squidge-turned.

'Ah-ha,' Randeep said, voice enclosed in his helmet. He *hiss-thunked* into the road to meet the 4x4. 'Piggies emerge from their sty.'

4x4 came at them, strobing lightbars muted through Randeep's tinted antiglare visor. He held up a hand like he was stopping traffic.

Down came 4x4 driver window.

Out popped squashed-up piggy mug.

'Bugger off, Captain Kirk.'

'Nutters,' said other cop, opening his door.

'He thinks we're sci-fi fancy dress nerds,' Randeep said. 'In which case, let's party.'

Before second cop got out, Randeep smashed the 4x4's bonnet, hard as he could with twinned fists. Power kick was awesome. 4x4 crumpled like cardboard. Front wheels blew off, tyres popping. Road blacktop cracked, he'd hit so hard.

'Woo-hoo,' went Nahid over helmet headset.

Front end trashed, the 4x4 flipped up bum first. Its windscreen blew, spraying glass pebbles.

Somersaulting horizontally through one-eighty, it *wunched* upside down shaking the ground. Wide-eyed cops dived out and took off. Randeep and Nahid rolled the 4x4 over to the fence and smashed it through. Pause before stylish pyrotechnics, heavy on the boom front, and pedestrianized riverbank got totalled. As the fire-ball rolled Randeep looked up at CPHQ towering massively. Plaza dust cloud diffused tip top and high summer sky. Four helipads clover leafed. The Queen was up there. All they had to do was get to her.

4x4 cops who'd got scarce took pot shots from behind the parked UPS van. Randeep lobbed a 4x4 wheel at them. Tonking a parked car, it set off its alarm.

'Come on,' he said, *hiss-thunking* over to the car park's entrance slip. 'We need to get down to the CC's lift before any cops left in there get to us.'

82

Vanessa had seen the 4x4 get trashed down in the street. CPHQ gate guy's grey plastic booth flew into the road, cracking open like a glass-fibre egg when it smashed a parked truck. Gate guy fell out, got up, and ran for it.

'They're coming, Craig,' she said.

Poulson had rung and told them what Freeman's pair of bomber nutcases must be up to with K-Tech armour. Introductions had been made to the Queen and her guys and the scene set. They'd found Vicky and stuck three tied-up cops away, down at the far end.

Now everybody dashed through to the CC's lift at the opposite end. Royal party brought up the rear, giving the elderly Queen more time.

Vanessa, creaking leather, got there first and smacked the button. Too late. Lift had been called and was nearly at basement car park. Vague thudding fed up the lift shaft. Only senior cop swipe cards could access it. Anybody could summon it. The nutters had probably called it and trashed the steel doors to get in.

'Back to the main lifts,' Connors said, swinging his big gun upright on its steadiframe.

Everybody rushed back through.

Only two of CPHQ's lifts fed tip top.

It was like being stuck high in a busy hotel at breakfast time. Both lifts kept coming then stop-started way off before going back down.

Kath, shotguns in hand, ran back to check where the CC's lift, and the nutters, were at.

'They're halfway, Craig.'

'This is hopeless,' Hunter said frustratedly. Stooping, he held Hayley and Jenny by a hand each.

'Couldn't we use the stairs?' Vicky suggested.

She was wearing tartan tights, gold pixie shoes, pleated black mini skirt, and a baggy lacy top. Vanessa often heard Hunter despair at how bad his Sloaney ex-wife was dressing since they'd split. Understandably strained by her abduction ordeal, she wasn't made-up and was also having a bad hair day. Vanessa knew from her eyes that she regretted dumping her ex-husband.

'No,' Massey said. 'Her Majesty can't exert herself down so many steps.'

'I'll be OK, John,' the Queen said.

'No ma'am,' Carole said. 'It's too dangerous.'

'She's right,' Hunter said. 'Pinky and Perky would be on top of us in no time.'

Connors looked up. 'We go to the roof.' He weighed up the petite Queen, whose face was a foot-and-a-half below his. 'Which means I'll have to touch ya, ma'am.' Unhooking his big gun, he leant it against the wall then scooped up Her Majesty in his bulging arms.

'Couldn't you carry her downstairs?' Chris asked.

'Too risky. I might trip and fall. And if those bozos get to us going down the stairwell, we've had it. Come on,' he told everybody, turning.

Massey asked, 'Why the roof?'

'I'll fly us out.'

'Can you fly a gunship?'

'Sure I can, pal.'

'They're nearly here,' Kath shouted from the CC's lift. Slinging a shotgun over a shoulder, she stood back from shut doors to pump the other.

'Get back here, Kath,' Connors shouted.

'Please come back,' shouted Hayley and Jenny, copying Connors, hopping each end of Hunter's arms in that excited little-girl way.

Kath rushed back. 'Give me your gun harness, Craig. I'll stay and man the fort.'

'Hell no. You gotta come with us.'

Vanessa knew she had to stay too. 'She's right. We need a diversion so you guys have time to get Her Majesty aboard a gunship and take off.'

'No,' Hunter said, realizing Vanessa was angling to stay and fight. She knew he was torn between staying with her and being with his kids. Getting tearful, they reached for her, begging for her to go with them.

Connors put down the Queen, unsnapped his gun harness, and gave it to Kath. She hooked it on and they got to it clipping plastic buckles. Connors hoisted up the gun and fitted it back on its stabilizing mount. It looked shit heavy. Harness supporting it made swing-aim easy. Kath waved it this way and that and flicked on the laser. Shiny twin fat muzzle-ends silenced it.

'Gosh, young lady,' said Carole. 'You look jolly formidable, I must say.'

Connors scooped up the Queen again, telling Carole, 'Hey lady, I should be the hero here.'

'We understand young man,' the Queen said. 'You must stay if you wish.'

'Take the Queen, Craig,' Kath said. 'Save her.'

Vanessa agreed. 'You can carry Her Majesty fast enough and only you can fly a gunship.'

The Queen looked old and frail in Connors's muscly, vein embossed arms. Because of a $200m train's inaugural run, a working-class girl from the Potteries and a TV producer from Yorkshire were about to do their duty and potentially blow part of CPHQ to kingdom come, defending the head of the Realm.

The Queen said, 'I shan't forget this.'

'Neither shall we,' said Massey and Carole.

Craig told Kath, 'See you later gal.' First time Vanessa had seen him look scared. 'Stay safe.'

Winking at her, he booted open the staircase door and headed up carrying the Queen, everybody in tow. Vanessa saw the Queen, cradled in Connors's huge sinewy arms, watch her and Kath before the door blinged shut.

Lift pinged far end, in the CC's lobby.

'This is it,' Vanessa said.

She went over to the reception desk console and slid shut the doors they'd come through when bogus Hunter-Freeman felt sick. Kath hid side of open facing doorway, diagonally opposite the desk. Vanessa hid across from her, diagonally opposite the lifts.

Kath, psyching herself, swung her gun up straight on its mount and backed up to her bit of wall.

'You OK?' she asked Vanessa.

Back to wall, she nodded and pumped a shotgun.

83

No way was Hunter leaving Vanessa.

Soon as he got Hayley, Jenny, and Vicky safely aboard, and had belted them in, he headed through to the cockpit. When he got there, feeling guilty but knowing he was doing right thing, he got Connors to shut fuselage ports so he could get off the gunship without being seen. As Connors fired her up, three white-helmeted aircops burst out onto the helipad from a crew lift.

Pulling guns, they charged the gunship. Connors kept on pulling levers and stuff and studding buttons on the scary 747 display.

Outside VTOL turbines hotted. Up wafted crap which had settled on the helipad. Fallout dust from the Plaza. Hunter swore when he saw cops. Slid open his door and jumped down as they arrived.

Gobsmacked Air Sergeant's laser found him. 'What the bloody hell are you doing?'

'Rescuing the Queen.'

'Get out of the aircraft,' second cop shouted to Connors, assuming the two-handed gun-pointy pose they did in TV cop shows.

Third black cop told his helmet, 'Urgent back-up to helipad 3, Jill. Guys stealing a gunship.'

'We're rescuing the Queen,' Hunter said again.

'Sure you are,' lead cop said, joining the TV cop show posing. 'On the deck,' he told him, guiding him away from the cockpit. 'Arms spread.'

Hunter felt a hotspot on his chest but ignored it. Time was running out for Vanessa and Kath. 'I'm telling you. We've got the Queen aboard.'

'He ain't bluffing,' Connors said, jumping down behind Hunter. He smacked a fat red button next to the gunship's fuselage door.

It slid open revealing the Queen and everybody strapped in their seats gazing out. Royal party faced forward. Vicky and the girls sat across, backs-to-front. Sweet little ones waved at daddy, cutting him up. Wry smiling, the Queen waved deftly at the cops, like she waved at folk from horsy carriages on the run.

'Whoa,' went the cops, spooking back. Third black cop moved off quickly to say something to Central Control. Funny how uniforms softened up, soon as they saw HM was real deal.

Massey told lead cop, 'I'm Sir John Massey, in charge of Royal security. This, as you can see, is our gracious Queen. These brave men came to rescue us because Alex Freeman kidnapped us and held us up here without any of you chaps knowing.'

Lead cop, riding high on career driven form filling, asked Hunter, 'Why didn't you report this to Reception down on the ground?'

Hunter balked at him.

'Are you bloody serious?'

Connors, sounding pissed when he sussed time running away, said, 'Hey look pal. We had to assume Freeman had all *you* guys kow-towing.'

Lead cop said he'd fly the gunship out. Nodding at his number two they climbed aboard, crouching in front of the Queen while Massey filled them in on what was gonna hit CPHQ's 45th floor.

Connors asked black cop, 'Where's the Arnie gun?'

Cop climbed in.

Typed a keypad at cockpit side of the door. Digi stuff flashed on his visor. He pulled open a kind of upright steel gunpod, taller than him. Slid it over to the door on a metal track sunk in the floor. Popped something. Pulled again. Gunpod retracted from where it came, exposing the monster Sheuze gimballed ready for action when the gunship was skyborne.

Cop swung it horizontal. Connors jumped up, twisted stuff underneath to release it, and unhooked it. Dumped it and got back down on the deck to reach in. Hoisting the gun, he pulled a silicone-embossed chainsaw hand-grip at the back.

'I assume from her weight she's loaded?'

'Yeah,' cop said, meaning the ammunition drum carousels hanging underneath. 'But she'll not last a minute tops, if you buck her on the run.'

Hunter knew the gun from a TV doc they'd made. He'd seen one dumped on Twemlow station platform yesterday. Big problem handholding old-style Gatling guns like a Vulcan M61 was heavy weight, combined with limited shell capacity away from a loaded, fixed mount feed. Sheuze's ironically named "minigun" was made from lightweight polymer.

Duration was still an issue. Six rotating barrels emptied shell drums in no time, even if fed from a full ammo backpack. Sheuze's USP was its minigun shells being tipped with nasty Jap XTC jelly.

Handheld, it might shoot for only thirty or forty secs before it ran dry.

But when a round let rip, it was like hundreds of tiny grenades exploding at once.

84

Randeep checked the CC's office to make sure nobody was hiding.

Lording over it was an OTT glass slab desk, fizzing with tinted liquid. Gobs of waxy stuff bobbed lazily inside it, like in a lava lamp. Randeep had met Freeman there a few times. When he took over national security, and decided a 45th floor office suited his ballooning ego, he had disgraced Chief Commissioner Driscoll's outrageous desk brought up from ten floors down.

Moulded in its console was a PC showing live CCTV thumbnails from around CPHQ. Randeep flipped open his visor to see better. Heavy armoured gauntlets were hardly keypad friendly. But the PC's touch screen made it easy to poke a menu.

Nahid *hiss-thunked* in from the corridor.

'What you doing?'

'Wondering why it's quiet up here.'

'Surely everybody's up at Piccadilly.'

'Maybe. But I want to have a secret nosey before we crash the party.'

He maxed 45th floor Reception CCTV just along from the office, behind *Star Trek* sliding doors they'd seen shutting when they came out of the lift.

Wide-angle of empty lift lobby.

Camera POV from high on window wall, behind the desk, faced lifts and a stairs door. Curvy glass desk in foreground. No cops on guard. Highly suspect, with Royal booty being kept up there. Pack of spilled peanuts and screwed hankies on console made it look like somebody left in a hurry.

Randeep was ready to try another CCTV when something caught his eye. Behind the door jamb. Queen's apartment side of screen. He zoomed tight but didn't risk turning camera, just in case.

'Look my friend.'

Nahid popped open his visor.

Tattooed girly arm, ultra clear in HD, hidden behind the door frame. She moved slightly, revealing a double-barrel machinegun stuck straight up, pivoted on a combat harness like an *Aliens* smartgun.

'Looks like our Queen has her very own private girly sentry,' Randeep noted sarkily.

Office was fantastically soundproofed. Instinctively they sensed something happening on the roof. Randeep knew helipad 3 was right overhead.

He picked up its CCTV, revealing a gunship gearing for take-off, fuselage door wide open.

What he saw shifted everything.

Rarely did he get angry. Limitless wealth pretty much killed passion. Having everything you wanted in the material sense, lacking financial boundaries, needing to strive for nothing, meant emotionally you partly died, if indeed you ever lived. Hence Randeep needing bigger, crazier buzz fixes.

But when he saw the Queen and her folk and everybody being rescued, he felt a deeply satisfying rage-lust. Driving it was seeing baseball capped, wrapmirrorshaded Craig Connors dashing to the staircase door, monster gun slung in hand, phone at ear in the other. Presumably he'd helped the Queen escape.

Hunter was behind him, waving a shotgun. In high background, the Plaza surreally burned. Sky around smudged with dark smoke.

Nahid got spooked.

'Hey what goes on, man? We're screwed now. She's getting away. And how come Hunter and Connors are a twosome bouncing the bed?'

'I don't get it,' Randeep said, shit angry as he tried to work it out. 'Connors should have been shoving daisies since Twemlow.'

Gunship lifted off. Secs later it got small through the office's massive widescreen window.

He got back Reception CCTV just as stairs door nudged open. Unaware he was on candid camera Connors appeared, checking coast was clear. Despite helming the Queen's kidnap he seemed to have mysteriously de-kidnapped her. Randeep had come to CPHQ to kill her. It would have incensed the world if he'd done it. But he bore her no malice. Same went for hundreds killed and maimed by his bombs. They were statistics.

New situation was different. Closest he'd got to feeling how he felt was going to Media City to kill Freeman live on TV. Goalposts had shifted.

The Queen had left two tantalizingly close surrogate targets. Randeep and Nahid were indestructible. Killing Connors for denying Randeep his Royal kill thrill meant at last he'd have a *motive.*

Giving him biggest buzz of all.

85

Connors had just phoned Poulson to let him know the Queen was safe. Pleased to see Kath, he sure was glad party fireworks hadn't started.

Vanessa held Hunter, thanking him for coming back. Connors was touched, hearing 'em go all soft. Dumping the gun he lost his shades, hooking them over his T-shirt scoop neck. 'You guys go while there's still time. Kath and me can handle this shit.'

'We stay,' Hunter told him straight.

Vanessa, creaking black leather, agreed. 'We're with you and Kath.' Her loaded chest pressed against Hunter who looked scared, holding her by her ass.

Connors reassured them. 'K-Tech armour we're about to face is slugproof. But I have a theory.'

One-hand lifting the Arnie gun by its carry handle, he took hold of the chainsaw grip with his other hand and swung her, showing her off.

'This baby can blow satellites outta orbit. But chances are that when K-Tech did their fancy lab tests they stuck to peashooters.' He waved the gun, his big veined arms bulging. 'Uncle Craig's gonna show you how nothing is bulletproof when it meets one of these mothers. Sheer velocity of shit she churns is gonna drive our bad boys back.'

'She'll not last long away from a fixed shell feed,' Hunter warned him. 'We saw a demo for a film.'

'Yeah but she'll still kick some serious butt. Speaking of assholes, where the hell are they?'

Everybody watched shut steel doors opposite. Connors dumped the gun and crossed to the desk.

'What're you doing?' Kath asked him anxiously. She covered him, standing in the doorway, swinging her kit side-on, lasering shut doors.

'Checking the CCTV by the lift,' Connors said, poking console buttons. 'Shit,' he added, realizing. 'It's fried from when we KO'd it.'

When they arrived in the lift, before they could come out, they'd used Thinnes's piecea kit to KO a CCTV spying on the lift lobby, outside disgraced cop's office.

Desk accessed three CCTVs on 45th floor.

1 was by the CC's private lift. Screen frozen since they'd KO'd it, so desk cops didn't see them.

2 did Reception.

3 did far end, where Hunter's kids and ex had been kept prisoner.

Connors brought up # 2 on the wall behind. Saw himself at the desk and turned to weigh up spycam.

'What's wrong?' Vanessa asked him.

'Just wondering who might access that camera.'

Hunter said, 'Judging by the avalanche of cops since we got here, only that desk.'

Connors wasn't convinced, with the Chief Commissioner's hangout being so close. In the States, chief cops could access everything and everybody. He found some peanuts on the desk and went back over to Kath, flipping his baseball cap round wrongways.

Hunter seemed to be feeling it. 'Why are we still here, Craig? We came back for Kath and Vanessa. Let's make a run for it down the stairs.'

'Hell yeah pal, you're right,' he said, knocking back peanuts. They weren't obliged to defend CPHQ. They'd come back to get their girls but got hooked on potential party time. They needed to turn scarce. Thinking how cool Kath looked, he looked forward to getting to know her, now they were through with this shit. 'Come on sweet gal. Let's haul.'

Before she A-OK'd, life as he knew it ended.

When it did he saw Kath watching him.

Her blue eyes had something, as they had since Connors and her tangled with crazees at the railroad bridge and ended up getting closer because of it.

Floor erupted under him.

369

Insane freeze-frame moment when Kath's eyes met his a final time and he sensed something special, which mighta happened, was gonna get snuffed by violence. Seemed like a truck had crashed up through the floor. He didn't know what in hell's name it was. Some big industrial steel-yellow bullnose thing.

As deck opened under him in a debris explosion, he fell through. Arms going like crazy, he tried to stop himself. Same time he tailspun down, he saw wall left of the shut doors blow, showering Reception with smashed cinder block. They'd expected the jerks to hit the doors. Bastards had lost wall next to them, taking out the floor instead. Next to the doors some camouflaged mechanoid military looking thing appeared, punching out the wall, *hiss-thunking* Manga awkwardly.

As Connors fell through the floor, some more MAR-PAT flashed, hitting him like an express train coming from nowhere. Grabbing him, it threw him diagonally back from where he'd come. As he human cannonballed up, his bust face sprayed blood and he knew bones had snapped. When he smashed into Reception's suspended ceiling, stuff hit him hard. Not just roof stuff, which trashed him.

Personal stuff.

Daughter stuff.

Seeing Hunter reunited with his kids had got to Connors. For eighteen years he'd been running from himself. Sure he was big. Tough as old hell. A walking brick shit-house. But losing his precious baby daughter pissed off his young self so much he got lost in a crazy mercenary life, trying to neutralize his rage. He'd made good money. But macho ballyhoo had been a self-sabotaging dumbass show. Eighteen years ago he was a proud Arizona Joe, starting a family with a girl he really loved. She'd duped him, getting him to father her kid before she walked. He thought he was over it. Some stuff stayed for life. Deep down it bugged him like hell, not having seen his little girl grow.

This shit came back as ceiling hit him, caving in, and he raggy-dolled down, dragging shiny twirly duct pipes and cable tangles. Shit came back at him 'cause he was gonna meet his Maker. Finally he could face himself, now his inner guard had dropped.

He hit reception desk hard. Bent all wrong, he bounced off spitting red and bits of stuff that mighta been lantern jaw teeth. Hurting like hell, blacking, he slammed deck between desk and floor hole.

Vanessa thought a bomb had gone off, blowing up Connors. Before Robo 1 trashed the wall she heard vague *hiss-thunks*. Soon as she realized shit had hit the fan she grabbed Connors's monster gun and swung it round. In her haste she hit the trigger early.

Muzzle flash strobed.

Shell spray wiped shut doors opposite, obliterating them like tin foil. When she found her Robo target, he vanished in an incredible hale of mini explosions. The gun let loose awesome destruction, thudding basso deep sexy in such a tight space.

Robo 1 flew back through pulverized breeze block. Vanessa kept pumping, losing the dividing wall by the doorway, chewing everything but everything to bits. Connors's high velocity slug theory was good. Lost among exploding concrete, sparking from slug hits, Robo 1 got bowled along the corridor leading to the CC's lift like a rioter blasted back by water cannon.

Hunter was behind her, pumping his shotgun at Robo 2 as he came up through the floor, climbing what Vanessa realized was some steel industrial conveyor he'd rammed through it. To surprise them, he'd trashed the floor, attacking from below, while the other guy hit solid wall by the desk. Hunter was right about the Sheuze's short lifespan on the run. Before Vanessa could aim at Robo 2 the gun ran dry. Kath was with her, letting him have it full blast. Slugs just bounced off.

She stopped firing in case stuff flew back and hit anybody. Battle-cry lunging, Vanessa swung up her spent gun and *clunked* Robo 2, hard as she could. She knocked him sideways but he ignored her.

He wanted Connors, who was in a bad way, heaped by the desk covered in rubble.

Smashed ceiling coffers fell off him when he tried to get up. Face and head bleeding bad, showing teeth, he was hurting.

As Robo 2 *hiss-thunked* across to him, Vanessa decided the armour was clunkier than she'd expected. Robo 2 did a heavy stilted walk, like original movie Robocop. Connors grabbed a steel pipe to defend himself, hitting Robo 2 with a feeble metallic *whunk*.

He stood no chance.

Clunky or not Robo 2 grabbed him by one hand and lobbed him straight through the ruptured doorway Vanessa had blasted. Partition wall other side, running along the corridor facing tinted outside windows, was the CC's office. Framed photos of CC's over the years ran its length. Connors smashed through it just past the doorway. Lucky it was a stud wall. But he cried out and blew a plasterboard hole crashing into heavy metal stuff other side.

Robo 1 rolled about in the corridor, struggling to get up. Robo 2 *hiss-thunked* after Connors, walking through the wall like it wasn't there.

Ceiling and steel duct crashed down. Brave Kath dived in, pipes and stuff clanging around her. Swinging her gun side-on, she let Robo 2 have it. Muzzle flash strobed to deep-thud reverb. Slugs hammered armour like buckshot hitting steel.

Kath scream-swore when her gun also ran empty. Unclipping it, she threw it at Robo 2.

Vanessa and Hunter got over to Robo 1, blasting him point-blank with shotguns.

Horrified, Vanessa saw Connors fly full length of the office from the corner of her eye.

87

Sharron and Lisa dashed back to K-Tech's lab.

Some posh guy called Poulson had got through to Lisa saying he was with Alex Freeman. Last night Carl pulled Poulson's prints from the factory. ID suspect, like everybody else's. Now wasn't time for Lisa to wonder why, shoving open lab rubber doors, Shar behind.

Poulson had begged Lisa for help. Sounded on the level when he told her the Queen was safe. Guys who helped rescue her were in extreme danger. He needed to know if they could kill the powerarmour.

'Dr Wymark should know how,' he told her over her headset as she hit the console, panting.

'You know him?'

'I've met him at K-Tech.'

'What else do you know Mr Poulson?'

'Not now Lisa, please. You have my word the Queen is safe. Get your colleague to phone Aircrew 3 at CPHQ in Manchester. They'll confirm.'

Col was patched three-ways.

'Hey Col. Can you check that?'

'No need, my love. BBC's onto it. Mr Poulson's telling the truth. Somebody's given media a nod. The Queen just landed in said gunship at Media City.'

CG thingy was still on screen from when Wymark briefed them about the kit. He disappeared after Culver showed with two bruisers who weren't Thames Valley cops Sharron and Lisa knew. According to Thai girl Chan, Wymark's phone was switched off. Lab guys and girls were at an Olympia show. Chan was out in the corridor on her phone, trying to get through to somebody to find out how to kill the armour.

'I don't know what to look for,' Lisa said.

'There must be something,' said panicky Poulson.

Poking the screen ineffectually she managed to open the matrix. It stacked over the armoured figure.

'Check the other screens, Shar.'

'Sure thing hon.'

Lisa tried to check stuff on her screen but it was gobbledegook. She couldn't take anything in.

Lab doors burst open. In swept Wymark with Chan, who explained the situation. Ecstatic, Lisa told Poulson, 'Dr Wymark's come back.'

'Oh thank God,' Poulson said.

'What's happening?' Wymark asked.

He nursed a hand. Lisa got the feeling it had recently hit somebody hard. She told him, 'Guys who stole the armour are trashing CPHQ in Manchester. Guys facing it need to know if it can be shut down.'

'My God,' he said. 'As if Manchester hasn't suffered enough today.' He coolly zoomed up the CG figure on screen and poked it, pinch-wiping to enlarge powerarmour detail photo-realistically. 'They'll be able to shut it down if they can hit this,' he said, zooming in for Lisa to see. 'It works like an On-Off. But if men are engaged hand-to-hand with it, I wouldn't risk getting close enough to try.'

88

Soon as Lisa had told him what to do, Poulson rang Craig. Worrying, he paced from kitchen to studio and back while call rang out.

He got through to Kath. She was in a hell of a state. Sounded like a war zone over the phone.

'Craig's being killed,' she sobbed.

'Where are Hunter and Vanessa?'

'Fighting the other bastard in the corridor.'

Sensing the worst, Poulson kept it together. Calmly he told Kath how to knock out the armour.

'Couldn't Freeman have told you that?' she sobbed over tinny background gunshots.

Poulson realized she had a point. Ending call, he breathed deeply to steady his nerve. Wymark's info was probably too late. Shutting his eyes, he prayed for Craig. When he opened them Alex came out of the shower in his dressing gown, shifty-eyeing everybody as the door bumped shut. Being a photo studio, it had a dressing room and shower where fashion models prepped. Alex had said he wanted to freshen up.

Angry as hell, Poulson confronted him.

'Did you know about this?'

'About what?'

'How to shut down the bloody armour. You heard us panicking over what to do.'

Alex knew all right.

He hadn't said anything because he hoped Craig and the others would be killed. He'd gone in the shower to keep out of the way. Furious, Poulson punched him in the face so hard he hurt his hand.

'Nasty to the end, eh?' he said, massaging his fist. Alex rolled about on the kitchen floor, checking his bust mouth. Knocked for six, he exposed himself when his dressing gown accidentally unfastened. His penis was so small and shrivelled Poulson looked twice.

Pover too. 'Oh deary me,' he said, maliciously enough not to undermine CPHQ situation's deadly seriousness, which had put a dampener on everything. 'My three-year-old has a bigger willy than that.'

Randeep knew Connors was dead. Umpteenth time he threw him at the far wall, where he left bloody skidmarks as he fell down behind the smashed glass desk. Randeep bulldozed it first time Connors landed close. Congealing wax gunk covered the carpet.

He *hiss-thunked* over and picked up the battered muscly body. Connors's T-shirt was so badly ripped most of it had gone. Lacerations on his neck and head oozed dark blood, which had splattered the office.

Randeep could have killed him quickly, crushing his head with armoured hands. But he wanted the hysterical tattooed girl to suffer. She'd just taken a phone call but got offline fast before potshotting at his breastplate. Seemed like she'd been clued into the On-Off depressurize button, hidden behind a flip panel.

Randeep *hiss-thunked* over and chucked dead Connors defiantly down in front of her. Crouched among rubble, she backed off warily, pointing her shotgun, desperate to go to Connors but too scared.

Although he'd killed the American lummox, Randeep felt unfulfilled. Story of his rich, increasingly pointless life. Nahid had been floored by Vanessa's opening Gatling gun assault. But he quickly got it together, chucking her and Hunter about the corridor. While Randeep had smashed Connors, he kept seeing bloody-faced Hunter fly past outside, through the hole in the wall.

Everything was portentously still.

Then Nahid smashed through a solid part of the wall, making Randeep and tattoo girl jump. She scrambled over stuff, eyes mascara smudged from crying. That end of CPHQ's 45th floor had been demolished. Everywhere cables and pipes hung from trashed ceilings.

Randeep had heard Nahid grunting over his headset while he'd scrapped with Hunter and Vanessa.

'Are you OK my friend?'

Nahid couldn't nod in the bulky armour. Black visor tint hid his face. Twizzling some fingers, he pointed at his helmet, like his headset had packed in.

Randeep understood. He decided it would be symbolic to finish by throwing Connors through the window. Then they could get the hell out and seek next big adventure. 'Give me a sec,' he told Nahid.

Nahid thumbed-up and turned purposefully back to the corridor. Randeep reached for Connors. Heard cool *hiss-thunks* over digi-sounding microservo whines, giving the armour sexy internal audio.

Vanessa, shotgun in hand, looking highly screwable in a short black leather skirt, came in through the trashed wall, coughing at the dusty air.

She joined tattoo girl, linking her arm with big sis reassurance, whispering something in her ear. Drawback of wearing powerarmour was crap hearing due to it being pressurized. Helmet mikes piped tinny outside like it was heard over a phone.

Chunky *hiss-thunk* gripper boots raised Randeep six inches over the bitches.

They knew it was over.

Knew they'd lost.

Not a damned thing they could do.

Randeep enjoyed his sense of triumph. Remembered feeling the same before Slim caught him off guard and slapped him in Sheffield yesterday.

Realized he felt like that again 'cause he'd just been caught off guard again.

Before he could bend over to retrieve Connors's broken body, Randeep saw Nahid spin back.

Then a battering ram hit him.

One sec he saw dead-as-a-doornail Connors lying face down among rubble, coming closer.

Next sec Connors got small after something hit Randeep's chest so hard ribs might have cracked. He flew across the room and smashed through the end wall dividing office from staircase. Wondering what had happened, he remembered seeing a small detail nano-flash through his peripheral vision when he turned from Nahid to grab Connors. Hunter's discarded black Gringos lying in the corridor. Sometimes called Terminator boots because Schwarzenegger wore similar in the second movie after he nicked a greasy biker's leathers. Hunter had lost his boots so he could wear something else.

As Randeep slammed into the stairwell he realized what the hell that something else was.

Armour was smashproof. Nobody said it could resist an attack from identical kit. Randeep hurt *bad*. Another detail registered while he shattered breeze block. Tattoo girl fisting air triumphantly when she realized Randeep had been floored.

Hunter's voice came loud and clear over his headset. Saying he was gonna kill him.

89

Riding adrenalin, riding high, Hunter *hiss-thunked* over to the wall and walked through it.

While main guy had trashed Connors and the office, they managed to get the sidekick's armour off. He might have been kitted in tecchy battle gear but he fought like he hadn't first clue. Helmet had taken a hit from Vanessa's Gatling gun, blowing its locking studs. Knocking it off, they knocked him out cold. Got the kit off him and after some faffing got it onto Hunter. They hadn't bothered with the Kevlar undersuit.

Sidekick had yelled for "Randeep" just before they KO'd him. Meaning Hunter knew his opponent's name. He'd dropkicked him, surprising him when he bent to pick up a very dead looking Connors. Cool armour did what the tin said. *Verdunk* from chunky boot and Randeep was office history.

While Vanessa and Kath took care of Connors, Hunter went after Randeep who'd taken a serious gut hit. Some of his dented armour had blown off. Sprawled on the staircase landing, buried under rubble, he tantrum-swore over his headset. Hunter was more confident in the armour but lost his footing after he'd bulldozed what remained of the wall. *Hiss-thunking* on so much smashed breeze block, he fell sideways onto down-coming steps leading to the roof.

Randeep was first up but was all over the place due to Hunter's lethal opening kick. Lying back on the stairs, Hunter swung up his legs, booting Randeep straight through Reception's door, blowing it off its frame, de-molishing the dividing wall.

Up he went at an angle, straight through suspended ceiling. Air conditioning gubbins, hidden behind, crash-ed down with him as he dropped back hard, landing next to the hole he made in the floor when he'd first hit Connors. Sprinklers hadn't kicked in because there was no fire. On they came to latest ceiling smash, instantly soaking everything, losing plaster dust fogging every-where and everything.

Hunter knew Randeep was damaged but let him have it. Possessed, he laced into him, smashing him up in a frenzy of wholesale demolition.

Driving his rage was Connors's unnecessary death and mass murder this trash he was trashing had caused. Connors reckoned Randeep was a spoilt rich English-man seeking crazy thrills. Hunter knew he was symp-tomatic of a smug, super rich, thoroughly bent Metropo-litan elite driving modern UK plc's politics and media. Freeman was of the same ruthless, amoral breed which had infiltrated Westminster and was slowly destroying the country from the inside out.

As he used Randeep to lose party wall, he remember-ed something. User friendly, the armour had gone to-gether easily enough. Vanessa found an On-Off behind a sliding breastplate panel when she helped suit him up. Triggering electroactive polymers, it fed current through the kit, firing it.

Hunter lost the same panel on Randeep's breastplate. Punched him so hard, slab floor shattered under him, ripping carpet, exposing steel toughening rods. Same time, lock actuators blew across Randeep's armour at arm and leg pivot points.

Killing it dead.

Still no cops which was odd but typical of modern UK plc's well shagged, NIMBY feel. Hunter had heard Van-essa and Kath coughing tinnily over his helmet before sprinklers came on. They emerged soaking wet from the bombsite that was the CC's office, awkwardly carrying Connors on a makeshift duct stretcher. Staircase was ex-posed, now that most of Reception wall had gone. Van-essa watched Hunter gravely. Discreetly shook her head while she and a tearful Kath carefully trod rubble, stret-cher slung between them.

They disappeared up the steps, through a metal door at the top, onto the sunny roof.

Randeep was out if it. Armour so badly dented he looked like a trashed beer can. Bits of it had come off re-vealing his Kevlar undersuit. It formed a second layer against bullet hits. Headset link had gone.

Hunter felt like shit and wanted rid of the armour so he could get to the roof. Hitting the chestplate panel he depressurized. He could still walk but the kit felt heavy, like he walked it rather than it walked him. Releasing helmet locking ring he lifted off the helmet, dumping it.

Next, gauntlets and arms.

Next chest- and backplates, hooked over his shoulders, held together clever-magnetically. Releasing them exposed a stud which worked the legs.

Flank and calf panels *fdunked* open with cool electro-lock precision. Hunter had to step down from the legs because of chunky *hiss-thunk* six-inch power boots, like deep sea diver boots souped-up by a sci-fi geek. Puffing, he left both legs standing behind him and fetched his Gringos from near the slumbering sidekick.

Earlier, before he put on the armour, he'd taken off his T-shirt, not knowing the kit was thermo cooled. Stripped to the waist, face bleeding from sidekick bops, he wore only chinos and boots.

He went up to the roof where he found Vanessa and Kath with Connors by the aircrew lift. Some aircops had shown. One of them knelt over Connors, hitting his chest, trying to resuscitate him.

Plaza burned in high background.

Remote sirens and thudding choppers worked a red-hot smoky summer day.

Hunter felt like he was in some post-apocalyptic hell. It sickened him seeing Connors's lifeless bloody body. He'd enjoyed his company during the short time he'd known him. Tough to believe somebody his size could have been chucked about like that.

Nobody could survive such a beating.

Not even a guy as big as Connors.

As Hunter arrived, wet-hair Vanessa came to him and let it come out when he wrapped her in his arms.

Cop kneeling over Connors reluctantly got up looking fed up and shook his head. 'I'm sorry,' he told Hunter. 'He had a faint pulse when we got here. There was nothing we could do. He probably lasted as long as he did because he was so strongly built.'

Poor Kath was distraught, kneeling to Connors, holding him, begging for him to come back. Tanked on adrenalin after seeing him get pulped, seeing guys massacred yesterday, fretting over her little boy, she was worn out. Watching her lift the lifeless hulk, his limp muscly arms splayed, Hunter felt for her.

He'd just knocked seven bells out of a bad guy. When he thought of hundreds killed and maimed, billions in environmental damage, the trashed bloody mess which was Connors, he felt no shame.

Something had shifted.

Past twenty-four hours had hardened him.

It was an ugly feeling.

Three
MONTHS
Later

90

Hunter stands before the Queen, on eye level with her because she's raised on a dais.

She fastens the medal on his jacket, her deep blue eyes attentive. A pin has been put there to reduce potential faffing and keep the investiture running smoothly. As the Queen fusses over him, checking the medal is straight, he feels like when he was a kid and his mum would wipe his mouth clean with her hanky.

It's the first time he's seen Her Majesty since he helped rescue her from CPHQ.

He feels guilty, standing in the Ballroom at Buckingham Palace receiving the George Cross. It happens to pro heroes, not TV impostors. His shame is rooted in knowing his kids and Vicky had been his *modus operandi* when he went into CPHQ doubling as Alex Freeman. Vanessa feels the same. She received her medal first and has rejoined the other hundred-and-twenty guests behind him, also there to receive honours. Some of them firemen, cops, and ambulance guys and girls, who were properly brave when northern cities burned.

As far as Hunter is concerned, his medal belongs to Connors and Kath. When the Palace wrote to let them know the Queen wanted to honour them for saving her life, "the American" and Kath were included in correspondence. Hunter explained the situation and that was the end of it. But he knows from the Queen's eyes that Connors and Kath are in her thoughts now. Same for his kids and Vicky. They're in a nearby holding area, watching him being presented on an OTT flatscreen telly, which seems way out-of-place among so much gilt and red carpet opulence.

Knowing the moment would mean something to the Queen is another reason Hunter has gone along with the medal. As she stands in front of him, small and very old, he has a surreal shot in his mind of Connors carrying her across to a gunship. When he thinks about Connors, lying dead on a CPHQ helipad, strong emotion comes back. He feels inadequate. Depressed.

'Thank you ma'am,' he says anyway, getting it together, knowing "the American" would have approved.

'Thank *you*, young man,' she says, smiling.

'You're looking well.'

'You too. Have you any plans?'

'A much needed holiday with Vanessa.'

They've been working flat out.

Soon as the Royal kidnap was exposed their world went crazy. Hunter and Vanessa realized the Twemlow massacre footage Freeman had them shoot was a goldmine. For the past three months they've been cutting a two-hour documentary which is getting a global cinema release before TV.

Hunter had a decent influx of money from last year's book deal. His agent reckons that with the anticipated success of *Royal Kidnap* and Academy Award nominations his earnings will go stratospheric. Talk of a Hollywood action movie is in the air, bringing more guilt to the equation. His life and loved ones were threatened. But he's cashing in on the fallout. He intends paying for Kath's little boy to have his op.

'Where are you holidaying?' the Queen asks, sounding genuinely interested.

'Scotland ma'am.'

'Near Aberdeenshire?'

'Actually yes ma'am. I think so.'

He isn't sure of the geography. Vanessa has booked a National Trust crofter's cottage.

'When are you going?'

'Week after next ma'am.'

'You must call at Balmoral to see us.'

Hunter is gobsmacked. 'Er yes ma'am.'

'I hear you're partial to a good toasted currant tea-cake.' Her eyes are on his. Equerry behind her moves in, wanting to move things along. The Queen raises a hand to keep him back.

Hunter says, 'I'm meant to be an edgy current affairs TV journalist ma'am. Secretly, my idea of indulgence is sitting in a cosy café on a wet afternoon, eating a toasted currant teacake smothered in salted butter and proper homemade jam, watching the world go by.'

'Then I shall look forward to seeing you,' the Queen adds, having settled what is clearly an important matter. Lines on her face deepen when she smiles and shakes Hunter's hand, saying goodbye.

Touched, he bows and steps back slowly to Vanessa, remembering to keep his eye on Her Majesty like the Lord Chamberlain said.

91

Later they have official photos taken in the Inner Court-yard and do some TV interviews. Happy to be fussed over they pose with the medals, individually and as a couple. Hunter poses with Hayley, Jenny, and Vicky. Throughout he feels like a fraud.

He tells Sky, 'Vanessa and I are proud. But these medals belong to two guys who were with us that day called Craig and Kath.' Questions erupt. Hunter raises a hand. 'With a film release pending I'll say only this. I'm not religious but our thoughts and prayers are with Craig and Kath because it seems appropriate.'

When they get to the car, he needs to hold Vanessa for a while before they get in, thanking her for being part of his life. He's as proud of her as he is of his little girls, seeing them all dolled up.

Vanessa wears a shiny silver two-piece. The skirt is a more sedate length than usual. She also wears a dinky blue silk hat cocked at an angle on her head, making her look girly-vulnerable. He loves that.

Weather is fresher. Sky a richer blue as days shorten and autumn gears. Hunter is looking forward to lazing in front of an open fire and doing some Scottish hill walking. Remembering scare stories about savage Highland midges, he unlocks the Volvo. Two words go off nearby like a bomb blowing in his head.

'Hey pal.'

Looking round, he tries to work out where they were at. Car doors open. Two familiar faces show. Either side of a black Ford Shelby parked near the Volvo.

Three months ago a miracle happened, raising scary questions about whether consciousness remains after a body dies. Connors came back from the dead. His heart had stopped. It started again, just like Bolton footballer Fabrice Muamba's did at White Hart Lane in 2012. Cops didn't know the hell how. Connors reckons it was Kath, sobbing in his ear, begging him to come back to her and pleading with cops to apply CPR when ambulance aircrew arrived. Connors died for nine minutes. Nowhere near Fabrice Muamba's whopping seventy-eight.

But still a miracle.

With fuss over George Crosses, and the Palace wanting to award Connors and Kath for their bravery as well as Hunter and Vanessa, Connors decided they should lie low till dust settled and his broken bones had healed. OK he helped rescue the Queen, as did Kath. But they hijacked her train and were party to her kidnap. Doesn't matter if Freeman shafted them and got the Queen off the train before mercenaries got near and they blagged it empty. Connors still helmed a Royal hijack. He couldn't accept a bravery award. Not that she'd have given it if she knew. It's a difficult aspect of the film which still has to be resolved.

Connors looks different. He's still a good six-five if not six. But his poundage has dropped. He's built more like an ordinary guy. The amazing arms have deflated. He looks older and a bit gaunt like somebody who's lost a ton of weight too fast.

Glad to see Hunter, he takes his hand. 'Kath and me saw what you guys said about us on TV.'

'It's how it is,' Hunter tells him, meaning it. He stuffs his leather-cased medal in Connors's hand. 'You and Kath have this. I can share Vanessa's.'

Hunter knows Connors isn't fussed. He takes the gift because he knows how much it means to the guy giving it. Connors tells Vanessa, 'I never imagined a girl could look as beautiful as you.'

'Oh Craig. That's so sweet.' Lost for words, flushing, she links Kath's arm.

A breeze picks up, lifting both women's skirts, forcing Vanessa to hold onto her hat.

Hunter reaches for Kath and hugs her tight. Tattoos have gone. She's all girly feminine and scenty.

'What happened to the arms?'

'Soon as I hooked up with Craig I wanted rid.'

'Did it hurt?'

'Yeah.'

'How's your little boy?'

'Had his op.'

'How?'

'We don't know.'

'Mysterious benefactor,' Connors adds. 'I woulda paid. Doing what I did for eighteen years has its compensations. Somebody got there first.'

Toby had a rare liver condition. The NHS wouldn't pay for an op with a small chance of success. Hunter told Sir John Massey and his *confidante,* Carole Kelly, early on. Hard to believe what everybody is thinking can be true. They leave it at that.

When they're ready to leave and the women have got in the cars Connors shakes Hunter's hand again. 'I owe you my life, pal. Bastard in the armour woulda finished me off good and proper.'

'Kath saved your life Craig.'

'You gave her a head start.' He winks an eye. 'Where you two headed?'

'Back up north.'

'Kath and me too. We're renting a place in the hills near Kath's mom. Nice scenery. You and Vanessa are welcome to drive up and stay a few days.'

'We'd like that.'

'Kath'll e-mail you the address and zip code.'

Hunter opens driver door.

Before he gets in, he tells Connors, 'I keep seeing you carrying the Queen up to a gunship. Wish we'd videoed it on a phone for the film.'

'Yeah pal. Been meaning to talk to you about that. I sure was glad those aircops showed.'

'Why?'

'I never flew a gunship.'

Hunter swears at him.

'What the hell would you have done?'

'Hoped I pulled right levers?'

'Jesus. Did you hear that?' he says to Vanessa through his open door. She's heard.

Grinning, shaking his head, looking forward to the next few days, Hunter's gloomy feelings, lingering since the investiture, disappear. Getting in the Volvo he presses the ignition. To his amazement, *It's My Life* by Talk Talk kicks off on the radio.

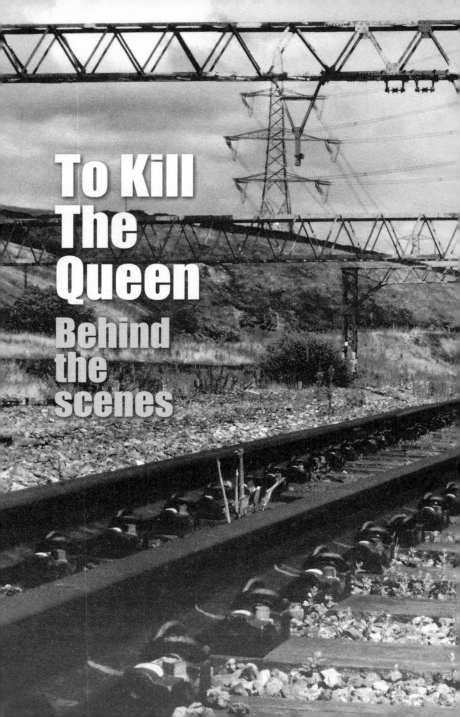

To Kill
The
Queen

Behind
the
scenes

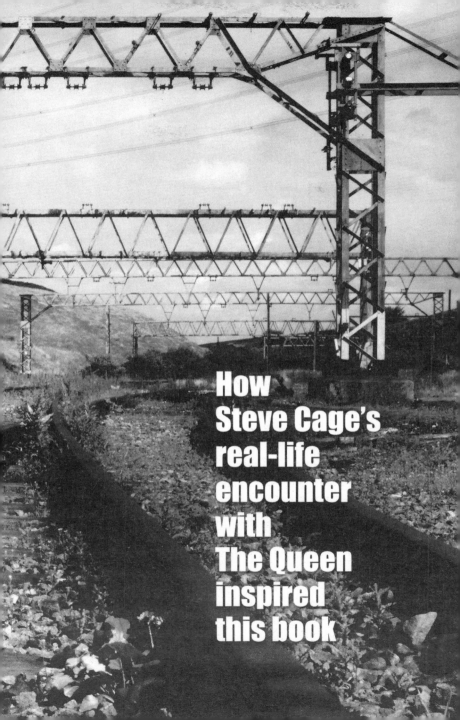

How
Steve Cage's
real-life
encounter
with
The Queen
inspired
this book

Origins of To Kill The Queen

[CONTAINS SPOILERS]

(1)

The idea for this book goes back thirty years.

From late 1982, and for most of 1983, I lived at Windsor in Berkshire. I was a young special effects modelmaker working for Gerry Anderson on a puppet TV show called *Terrahawks*. It was a dream job that happened so quickly I arrived on my first day at Bray Studios (home of Hammer horror) with nowhere to live.

Soon missing my fiancée, who was at uni in Hull, most weekends I blew a fair chunk of my wage catching a train north to be with her. This meant I'd to live frugally during the week, near Windsor town centre, in a grotty unheated bedsit which had bed bugs when I moved in. Sometimes my fiancée came down south to stay with me. One Sunday morning, one such weekend, we went for a stroll in Windsor Great Park.

To get there, we walked to the end of my street, crossed a busy road, and within minutes were on The Long Walk, which runs from the gates of Windsor Castle. I can't remember the time of year but it was very cold. As I'd moved to Windsor just before Christmas, and left by next September, it must have been during the early months of 1983.

I was used to seeing a flag flying at the castle if the Queen was at home. It was flying that morning. As we approached the statue of George III, about a mile from the castle, we heard a car tootle up behind us. We were holding hands but parted each side of the path, my fiancée to the right (driver's side), me to the left. The car was an old chrome-bumpered black Rover P5, which slowed to let us get out of the way.

As it slid past, I saw the Queen gaze up at me from the front passenger seat, a few feet from where I'd stepped onto grass. I can see her now, in crisp sunshine, like it was yesterday. She wore an overcoat and a headscarf and looked as unassuming as anybody's granny. It's the only time I've been near the Queen and it's closer than most of us will ever get. An overcoated bodyguard was at the wheel.

Amazed how exposed she seemed, I wondered if the car was bulletproof. It got me thinking. It kept me thinking in a high concept, action adventure, James Bond sort of way for decades to come.

(2)

Twenty-five years later I met Granada TV's then Head of Drama, Kieran Roberts, in Manchester.

My wife and I were independent film producers. On the back of our latest cinema release we'd decided to pitch some drama ideas to ITV. I'd met ITV Network's

Head of Drama, Nick Elliot, in London a few years earlier. We'd got on OK. He asked to see some stuff (including our second movie script before we filmed it) but
it went nowhere. Being Manchester based, I figured a
way round the Londoncentric nature of TV would be to
hook up with an ITV regional studio, develop something with them, and let them pitch it to the network on
our behalf. Before ITV semi-imploded, soon after we got
in bed with them, Granada was strong on drama and
just down the road from us.

I wanted to resurrect the British action adventure TV
show (think *The Avengers, Man in a Suitcase, The Champ-
ions, Department S*), giving it the jazzy modern energy of
America's *CSI* franchise. Our meeting went well. Up-
shot was that we started developing a fast-action series.
News at Ten had been brought back after being off air for
a few years. Instead of 90 minute or two-hour dramas,
Granada wanted three- or five-part 60 minute post-wat-
ershed mini series, which could be screened over cons-
ecutive nights between 9.00-10.00pm. I saw an opportunity to do energetic stuff, ending on a cliffhanger each
time. They assigned an enthusiastic young script editor
to the project and off we went.

I'd steered clear of TV police procedurals. Equally
toxic for me was hospital-set drama. In TV drama circles
they bandy the term "cops n' docs" to describe much TV
drama output. If I tell you the leads in my series were a
pair of Manchester based current affairs TV producers
called Hunter and Vanessa, you'll get where it was coming from. Granada liked the concept's originality and

their script editor loved my series title *Hunter*. We started developing *Hunter* with ITV before a BBC cop drama appeared with the same name. We got as far as casting ideas. James Murray was mooted as Hunter. At the time he was a lead in ITV's hit fantasy *Primeval*. I considered Fay Ripley (best known for *Cold Feet*) as Vanessa after I saw a photo of her with long blonde hair.

We had two *Hunter* stories. One was developed and had been floating around for years as a hi-octane movie script called *Dark Millennium*. I'd first discussed it as a big screen project with long defunct British Screen Finance in London in 1998. Working against it in the grubby, subsidy-dependent world of British cinema was my straight commercial attitude. Later I pitched the script to ITV Network when I met Nick Elliot in 2001. Based on a novel I'd written years earlier, revamped and much expanded and improved, it eventually became first Hunter thriller, *Now The Killing Starts*.

Story two which we pitched to Granada was much less developed. It was about a plot to kill the Queen and it had ITV written all over it. When I'd first explored the idea it was more police procedural in scope. Influenced by my encounter with the Queen back in 1983, it started with an assassin holing up in Windsor in my grotty bedsit, planning a Royal hit in the Great Park.

A parallel storyline had the guy's elderly mother being found dead in a grim northern town. Underpinning it was a screwy Oedipus complex which partly resurfaced as Driscoll's mother complex at the end of *Now The Killing Starts*. Typically dismally psychologically British, it was slow and small scale, atmospheric and grey skied. Sombre detective stories have the same effect on me as TV's "cops n' docs" and crime fiction's never ending serial killer stuff.

Fast action, rip-roaring, spectacular, populist entertainment is where I'm at, so I thought big and embraced a Hollywood sense of scale, kickstarting my Queen story with a Royal Train hijack. Being a producer, I thought about practicalities of shooting. Near to us was the East Lancashire Railway. I'd filmed movie scenes there and knew it well. Unusually for a preserved railway the ELR had diesel locos and modern passenger stock. Crucially it had some Mark 3 coaches which make up the current Royal Train. It would be easy to paint them in Royal colours. Knowing I could make a Royal Train hijack happen convincingly for the screen sparked the high concept which eventually became this book.

(3)

Before you develop an idea with a potential TV backer they usually want a story overview.

Most writers I know hate having to think out a story up front. The idea that you can come up with a story scaffold to order and just fill in detail as you go along is how everybody thinks writers do it.

I read an interview with Lee Child, who's regarded as a very good storyteller. He said he starts with a blank page and sees where a story takes him. The interviewer pooh-poohed the idea. Nobody can write a novel without planning it first, ran the argument. Oh yes they can. It's how I do it and it's the only way I can work. Planning a story is a hindrance. Having a rough idea in my head of where I'm going is enough.

With *To Kill The Queen*, Granada insisted on seeing a full story overview before they committed to full-blown development. I'd no choice but to write it. I sat crosslegged on my living room floor, scribbling balloons and arrows on big sheets of paper, trying to devise a plot. I gave up and offered to write Part 1 of the script to give a better idea of how the thing would play.

Story flows when I write for real. Reason it flows is because writing is driven by the subconscious. Most fictional stories, whether uber-commercial like the Hunter thrillers or literary novels, are driven by a sequence of interlocking emotional impulses. By trying to predict them you force them with the conscious will, or with the "front part of the brain" as John Braine said. It's like trying to picture everywhere you'll pass through before you set off on a mystery tour. I'm constantly surprised and amazed how a story reveals itself while I write it and where it decides to take me. Many writers who go through what is often a frustrating creative process say a story seems to write itself. It's like it's already written in the subconscious. As storytellers we persevere, exposing it bit by bit.

Story dynamics for screen and novel are different and endlessly fascinating. I wrote Part 1 of the *TKTQ* TV series as a single finished draft, in three days, straight onto my PC. It ended with the Royal Train being diverted onto the branch line by Connors and the guys. Hunter and the TV crew arrived to find a bloodbath like they do in the book.

Cliffhanger was Ross and Thinnes not switching back junction points as a Virgin express approached at killer speed. Breaking the story there worked for a nightly TV show but became redundant in the novel. Till then, the story resembled the first quarter of the book. The novel has more texture, more characters (and is bigger, ballsier), but the basic plot is the same.

Main difference between TV and book was Connors. For the book he became a lead character who started the story. That he wanted to start it was something I'd no control over. He was in the TV series but he wasn't American. He was a secondary character, like Reece in the book. In the book, Reece is exactly how Connors was on TV. First time we saw him on TV was when he arrived at the hijack site with his guys and they got to work fixing points to divert the Royal Train.

Kath didn't exist for TV. She was based on a customer I saw when I did a booksigning at Waterstones in the Trafford Centre. An attractive young woman came in pushing a toddler in a buggy. Tall, lean, like she worked out, she wore a vest and had an elborate tattoo filling an arm from top to bottom. I remember her jet black hair and strong face, her gentle manner and her polite older son. That brief bookshop encounter created Kath. Indirectly Waterstones helped bring her to life. She developed so Connors had somebody to spar from. But she's crucial to his journey of self-discovery. She comes from

Stoke-on-Trent because it's where my wife is from. Kath's dad died when she was 4 because my dad died when I was 4.

Although episode one of the TV series resembled the early part of the book, hardly any of the story overview ended up in it. Hunter's kids being snatched by the bad guys did. I knew it would be a key aspect of the plot before I wrote it. Steve Hamer deducing where Vicky and the girls are being kept (in a "low budget" stately home for TV) also migrated across.

When the Everyman edition of *Now The Killing Starts* was published we included first three *TKTQ* chapters as a teaser. I wrote them without really knowing where the story would go. All I had when I started the novel proper were Part 1 of a TV script and a sketchy 14 page synopsis which I'd eventually provided for Granada.

A *TKTQ* promo page at the back of *Now The Killing Starts* referred to ex-Soviet missile launchers. My website mentioned a crazy car chase. Both were lifted from the TV synopsis and included in preview stuff we put out because *consciously* I thought TV series and novel would go there.

My subconscious knew different.

(4)

Granada didn't put *Hunter* into full development. As so often happens, it was about bad timing.

ITV had hit serious problems. They shut down Yorkshire TV and soon knocked most of Granada's extensive drama output on the head. Literally overnight, most of northern England's drama production—which previously had driven ITV's drama schedule: think *Cracker, A Touch of Frost, Heartbeat,* etc—was torpedoed.

Later, my wife and I trooped up and down to BBC TV Centre in London for meetings with their drama folk. But I knew before we got on the first train that *Hunter* was too commercial for the Beeb. I remained philosophical because it had gradually dawned on me, while developing *TKTQ* for Granada, that *Hunter* was too ambitious for TV. I knew big, Bond-scale stories were trying to get out. Driven by writing about strong characters, I sensed Hunter and Vanessa first needed to live in an internationally successful book series.

Books have greater longevity. They let us get to know characters in a way screen stories never can and never will. Having written stories for books, and written and filmed them for the screen, I'm convinced those which are first explored as novels are fundamentally sounder and somehow less throwaway.

Ironically, books also seemed to suit my racy, cinematic American style. When it comes to popular culture the Americans do it so much better than us. As a writer and filmmaker, America is really my spiritual home. To see what I mean, look at the Amtrak train on the front of this book. Promo cover designs were e-mailed to me before *Now The Killing Starts* was published in 2011, before I'd written *To Kill The Queen.* Actual Royal Train would have looked deadly-dull on a thriller cover. Too square and too boxy, it just isn't sexy enough.

I dismissed cover roughs because the train lacked energy. It drove the action. It needed to look slick and exciting. I wrote an Amtrak train into the story to suit its stylistic American punch. It's plausible that corporate Amtrak might provide a Royal Train. The idea was in my head, sitting in meetings at Granada. It was a non-starter, being too expensive to stage for TV. But with my visual effects background, I knew it would be a doddle using miniatures and CGI, if given a big screen budget.

And there's the rub.

If *TKTQ* had been made as a British TV series it would have been done on a TV scale. We couldn't have used new generation inter-city locos but would have made do with yesterday's trains to tell our modern story. We'd have faked mainline shots on a single track steam railway. An audience knows.

By developing *Hunter* for TV, I'd compromised. To suit the type of ambitiously energetic stories I was writing, the Royal Train needed to be a big flashy American thing. If filmed, *TKTQ* needed a $150m action movie budget, not the £750,000 per TV episode we'd been discussing. With that realization I walked away from TV, removing *Hunter* from the table.

ITV's problems were the best thing that could have happened to Hunter and Vanessa. I'd turn their stories into an explosive series of books instead, giving them the big scale they deserved.

Derelict Twemlow Station (looking south) as it might be in To Kill The Queen

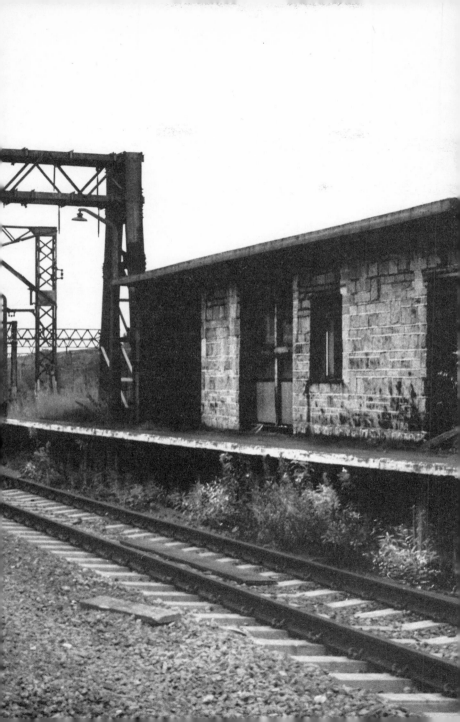

Hunter's World

(1)

Guns. Hardware. Exoskeletons.

The *Aliens* marines-feel to Kath and Connors at the end of *TKTQ* crept in because I worked on the *Aliens* movie, on most SFX miniature sets. With the interview following are some photos. Much atmosphere processor entrance detailing (opposite) was mine.

Although they are set in the present, the Hunter thrillers have a futuristic tecchy twang because I worked for Gerry Anderson. I still think *UFO,* with its mix of heavy hardware and English country cottages, was pretty convincing. The Century 21 thing worked because it didn't overstate the case. Likewise, Bond stories have ambitious set pieces and plenty of cool techno-kit. It's the sort of world Hunter and Vanessa inhabit.

Powerarmour in *To Kill The Queen* is based on science fact. Future Combat Systems, which Dr Wymark refers to, was the real deal. The US military has been developing exoskeletons for donkey's years. Main drawback seems to be sustaining onboard power. They developed an exoskeleton as far back as 1965. A hefty thing called the Hardiman, it was so much like the powerloader Sigourney Weaver used in *Aliens* I assume it inspired James Cameron.

While devising my powerarmour, what tipped it for me was seeing a Channel 4 TV doc about building a bionic man. A scientist who lost his legs from the knee down due to frostbite has devised bionic legs so lifelike it looks as if the *Six Million Dollar Man* is happening. In fact his artificial legs, with perfect ankle joints and simulated tendons, were more like chrome *Terminator* skeletons. When I was at school, not that long ago, computers filled rooms. Equivalent kit now fits in an area the size of a fingernail. Seems reasonable to assume that in Hunter's world they'll problem solve reliable onboard power cells for exoskeletons.

Robocop and Halo bodyarmour description is a form of literary short-hand. In commercial crime fiction like the Hunter thrillers, forward story momentum is key. Rather than getting bogged down in description (which readers of books like this don't want) it's easier to refer to existing pop culture to keep a story moving. Most of us know what Robocop looks like. Plenty of younger readers are familiar with Halo computer games. Referencing both, adding some brushstrokes of my own, is enough. Folk of all ages have an instant picture in their minds and are into next paragraph.

Powerarmour developed because I needed Randeep and Nahid to spectacularly hit where the Queen was hiding. Originally I thought they might shoot their way in with big guns. I had in mind *The Terminator*, where

Schwarzenegger blasts a cop station to bits. This posed a moral problem, as well as being potentially derivative. *We'll be back* seemed OK as an in-joke. But I was uncomfortable with wholesale cop slaughter.

I know there's violence in *TKTQ*. Randeep killing a traffic warden is deplorable casual violence. I used it to show the type of ruthless guy Randeep is. He's educated English upper-middle-class, from a wealthy background. Inspired by folk like him I've dealt with over the years, he's deeply cruel and insensitive to the human condition. This nasty, thuggish aspect of supposedly cultured people has always scared me. It proliferates in the media and entertainment industries. It's why in *Now The Killing Starts* Addison compares a minority at the top of society to those at the bottom. In *TKTQ* Connors tells Reece how Freeman lacks "an essential streak of humanitarian DNA". It's a left hook at hard-nosed, well-bred bastards like Freeman.

Some thriller writers portray terrorists as clichéd Western hating scruffbags. I turned it on its head. As well as being the anithesis of gay Kareem (one of the cleverest guys on the planet) in *Now The Killing Starts*, Randeep provides dark grim humour, which for me is essential in a thriller.

Besides Randeep's casual killings, there's mass death and destruction in Sheffield and Manchester. But it's indirect. Having Randeep and Nahid slaughtering cops would have required detailed description of cop killing. All I could think about was their wives and families. I was uneasy because I've a conscience, some cop readers,

Derelict Twemlow Station (looking north) as it might be in To Kill The Queen

and a retired Chief Inspector in our family. I also once signed a book for a former Royal bodyguard.

While writing this book, I knew the Queen must be kept away from violence. It's why I removed her from the Royal Train ahead of the bloodbath. Having her at Twemlow when the mercenaries are slaughtered didn't sit comfortably. Luckily it increased entertainment value by adding an unexpected story twist.

The book's explosive finale not only facilitated the Sharron and Lisa subplot for Part Two. It enabled me to write big action scenes which hopefully delivered but kept Her Majesty at arm's length from bloodshed, in as much as a story like this allows.

(2)

Central to *TKTQ* is a disused railway which doesn't exist but nearly did. Writing commercial fiction means artistic license often is necessary to help tell a story. I needed a disused railway. With most of the book being factually accurate I wanted to stay realistic.

The railway which the Royal Train is diverted onto runs from Twemlow Junction to Knutsford, joining two main lines. The London and North Western Railway was granted Parliamentary approval for such a railway in 1865 but never built it. I found out that some railway modellers had built parts of it, to show what the railway-which-never-was might have looked like. In *To Kill The Queen* the railway was built. I moved its junction with the mainline just south of Chelford, and put rural

Twemlow Station a couple of miles north of my imaginary Twemlow, bearing in mind stations are sometimes a fair distance from places they serve.

Twemlow Green exists, as does Goostrey. Back lanes Hunter and the film crew drive through to reach derelict Twemlow Station—Bomish Lane, Badgerbank, Blackden Lane—are real and Street Viewable. I reimagined geography near Jodrell Bank by squeezing in the disused railway and inventing Twemlow Lane.

I took the disused railway photos in this book, and the photo of Windsor Castle. It doesn't matter where the disused railway was. The photos are to help you imagine my disused line and derelict Twemlow Station in the middle of a hot British summer. It was a modern electrified railway, like the line in *TKTQ*. Perfect for our marketing needs.

Will there be a Hunter book 3?

Yes, and books 4, 5, 6 upwards. I'm working on book 3 as I write this but don't want to say anything about the story because it's early days. It's untitled but watch for same cover style as the first two books. Or keep updated via my website.

Steve Cage interview Part 2

Cosgrove-Hall to Aliens

Photos by John Lee

Steve Cage
interview

Part 2

Part 1 of this interview is in the extras section at the back of previous Hunter thriller, Now The Killing Starts.

Before writing full time, Steve worked for many years in film, TV, and advertising visual effects, and latterly as an independent movie producer.

This second part of an in-depth interview continues discussing his work with Gerry Anderson, TV commercials, and being headhunted to work on the Aliens *feature film.*

Q: You've explained how you and your colleague John Lee got into special effects in 1982, fulfilling a teenage ambition to work for Gerry Anderson. Did you work on every Terrahawks **episode?**

A: No we didn't. 39 episodes were made but John and I left halfway through. Money on the series wasn't brilliant and eventually took its toll.

I'd been engaged to be married since I was 19. My fiancée was at uni in Hull but might as well have been at the other side of the world. Wanting to be with her, I caught a train north most weekends. Getting home late on Friday nights, having to travel back south on Sunday to do *Terrahawks* on Monday, meant we only managed a day-and-a-bit together.

During the week I rented a tiny bedsit, first in Maidenhead then in Windsor. Cost of this in conjunction with intercity train fares, which in those days were higher in relative terms, plus day-to-day living, meant I couldn't save up to get married.

Bray Studios was also difficult to get to unless you had a car, which I couldn't afford. Each morning, when I lived in Windsor, I walked down to a busy main road and stood by a lamppost, sometimes in pouring rain, hoping somebody I worked with would drive past and give me a lift to the studio. Often it was Gerry Anderson in his brand-new Rolls Royce, which now seems surreal. Every day there was this awkward pressure, in case I couldn't get to work.

John and I met some effects guys who freelanced on TV commercials in London. They were earning £300 a week—twice what we earned on *Terrahawks*. Thirty-odd years ago £300 was good money in your early 20s and too good an opportunity to miss.

Q: Did you regret moving on? Do you wonder how things might have been if you hadn't left *Terrahawks*?

A: I've no regrets but sometimes I wonder how things might have turned out if we'd stayed.

I never bothered with *Terrahawks* when it was released on VHS, not even when my son was growing up. But recently I bought the DVD boxset and finally watched all 39 episodes, most of which I'd never seen.

Although John and I did sixteen or eighteen shows I was surprised how much of a presence we had in the rest of the series. Our models got re-used and chopped about. We made the Overlander, which everybody remembers. John made the front drive unit and I made the trailers. It featured several times. After we left, not many new "guest models" appeared. Scriptwriting got better. Some of the adult humour in later episodes is agreeably non-PC.

After quitting the series I took a few weeks off, went back up north to recharge my batteries, then joined John at Clearwater Films in Battersea.

Q: Working on TV commercials?

A: Yes. Clearwater had two divisions. Two guys started the company who like us had worked for Gerry Anderson back in the 1960s but moved on.

Part of the studio made the *Thomas the Tank Engine* TV series, which had just entered production, with Ringo Starr narrating. The other part made high-end TV commercials and it's where John and I worked as freelance modelmakers. Before CGI wiped out an entire SFX sub-industry, most things were filmed live in studio as practical effects. We worked on ambitious TV ads for Panasonic, Woolworth's, etc.

The Panasonic ad was for a new desktop micro colour TV, the CT-3311A, which had a three-inch screen. Along with a couple of other guys, we made a massive close-up section of the bit where the real thing pivoted on its "boomerang" base. (Previous photo.) This let the camera swoop in, making the TV set look as big as a skyscraper. John made the giant whistle-shaped section. I made the curved base and barrel unit which it sat on. Between us we made the vertical side and horizontal base panels, as well as some stylized big-scale stuff for an interior circuitboard. Nowadays they'd CG render the whole thing, twisting it round in that motion-control way. Modelmaking wouldn't come into it.

Clearwater work wasn't always taxing. I was standby props guy on a Cadbury's ad. My job was to wipe saliva off a square of resin chocolate after a girl had popped it in her mouth for each take. Remember those close-ups of liquid milk and chocolate pouring in old Cadbury's TV ads? We did it with emulsion paint. Now they do it with computers in the digital domain.

I'd left *Terrahawks* in September 1983. While working at Clearwater in the run-up to Christmas I was offered a full-time job back at Cosgrove-Hall in Manchester, starting first week of January 1984. I jumped at it. At last I could live at home in the north, not out of a suitcase down south. I'd be closer to my girl and back doing top quality work on a decent TV show. I took a drop in pay but wasn't fussed because it corresponded to how much I threw away on London train fares and renting digs during the week.

If I'd stayed on *Terrahawks*, and Cosgrove-Hall's offer had come up, I'm sure I'd have taken it.

Q: What did you work on?

A: *Wind in the Willows* again but this time on the weekly TV series. I did some of my best work, including a cobbled quayside (overleaf) and a barge. There wasn't the mad rush of doing *Terrahawks* episodes every ten days. Stop-frame animation meant each *Willows* took a leisurely six weeks.

The barge was for episode one, The Further Adventures of Toad. It was boatbuilding in miniature and a very satisfying thing to do. I handpainted all the period writing on it and did little paintings of castles and stuff on two doors at the front. At the time my fiancée and I went horse riding on Saturdays at Brighouse. Horses we rode were called William and Pride. I referenced this on the barge sides when devising tradesman's names. I also called it Catherine after my fiancée and dated it 21: 2: 84 (the day I finished it). It's what modelmakers do, or did. On *Terrahawks*, John and I wrote our initials and dates of birth on our stuff in Letraset because, insanely, the modelmakers didn't get a screen credit.

For the first time at Cosgrove-Hall I also did some intricate metalworking and made fully-functional props for the puppets. I made a replica Dursley-Pedersen bike for Toad, spoking the wheels like the real thing, using special hi-tensile dental wire, which didn't kink. Tyres were rubber vacuum-cleaner rings, frozen solid before being turned on a lathe. I also made a tiny pair of scissors which cut a ribbon for real on film at a fete. It was like watchmaking or jewellery work and a different discipline to making arty illustrative Edwardian sets.

Q: Didn't guys work at Cosgrove-Hall who were at the forefront of Manchester's music scene?

A: Yes. Bernard Sumner, who founded Joy Division and was in New Order, worked there.

John Squire, guitarist and founder of The Stone Roses, was a modelmaker when I was there in 1984. He'd lend me Stone Roses demo tapes to listen to on my Walkman on the train. He also got me into The Sex Pistols when he lent me the *Bollocks* album. If you look at the knackered wooden door on the quayside set I made for *Wind in the Willows*, you can just make out Bodies 1977, written in heavily-weathered Letraset. It's a nod to my favourite track on the *Bollocks* LP, and a secret in-joke between Squire and me. He was a good modelmaker, with the arty eye John and I had. In a spare room at his flat in Chorlton he built me a big 1/8th scale model set for a TV series I was planning. Tecchy aspects of the show crept into *Now The Killing Starts*.

Writing was my other passion. Enthusiastic and keen to prove myself, I'd submitted some unsolicited story outlines for *Terrahawks* when I was on the show but was promptly put in my place. (One of my reworked scripts will become a Hunter thriller.) Cosgrove-Hall was amenable and open to ideas from studio employees. They

put out a memo asking everybody to submit script outlines for *Wind in the Willows* and quite a few people did.
Mine were the only two accepted. Another episode called *The Piano*, written by a group of us but driven by my
title and story idea, was third one accepted.

Unfortunately, while I was at Cosgrove-Hall my en-
gagement broke off in the summer. With my northern
ties gone I wanted to escape. It was inevitable, emerging
from a long, committed relationship.

Q: You headed back down south?

A: Yes. I was at Cosgrove-Hall for much of 1984 then
went back to TV commercials in London, living out of a
suitcase for a year. First I went back to Clearwater then
to an offshoot called PPL and a similar outfit in Wands-
worth called Asylum Models, which is still going strong.
I was at Asylum quite a while, working on high-end TV
ads for Nissan, Michelin, etc. We did some subcontra-
cted Disney film work. Another time I marbled a large
wooden sarcophagus for a movie called *Billy the Kid vs
The Green Baize Vampire*.

In a mid 80s TV ad a model lorry drove out of the sea
onto a Devon beach. I can't remember what the ad was
for, or the lorry's scale. It might have been 3rd scale but it
was a big heavy thing we made at Asylum. These days
they'd add it digitally. Like the Panasonic TV ad we did,
it makes you realize how things have changed.

Another that comes back is a Swan National ad which
we did at Shepperton Studios. A full-size Mini Metro

crashed through a wall into a car hire office. My not-very-taxing job was sticking plastic leaves into chunks of polystyrene to make an artificial privet hedge. Gary Numan had a recording studio there. Rock City Studios. Each morning we walked past his white Corvette, parked outside.

Q: Were you happy in your work? Did you see yourself settling down to a life in special effects?

A: I never saw myself settling down to a life in SFX, doing the same thing forever. I intended to do creative designer-modelmaking for a while because I wanted to learn the business.

I wanted to direct SFX. In fact John and I had been competent fledgling SFX directors shooting our 16mm stuff in Huddersfield before we went professional. But I soon realized that special effects in those days tended to be only as good as the modelmakers, who never got the credit they deserved. Certainly it was like that with sci-fi. It put me off SFX directing because there weren't enough guys around with true sci-fi creative flair. John and I were easily capable of directing SFX on *Terrahawks*. We couldn't have made the models as well.

I know guys who've worked in SFX ever since I started in 1982. We meet up from time to time and have a laugh. They're happy still doing the same work and I'm pleased for them. I'm not interested. Doing what I did thirty years ago isn't where I'm at. I always wanted to be an ideas generator, using my intellect. If that meant doing things not connected with film and TV, such as writing books, so be it.

John and I planned our own Andersonesque puppet TV show when we worked for the man himself. Called *Starforce* it was how everybody imagined a new Anderson puppet TV series should have been.

Q: In other words you wanted to become a film and TV producer?

A: Yes. By the mid 80s I was making good money and was able to take time off to develop films and TV shows. I'd also been mortgage-free since I was 20 after my mum passed away suddenly while I was at college. Inheriting a house gave me a certain amount of financial freedom because I didn't have the spectre of a mortgage hanging over me. Ironically, I left Gerry Anderson because most of my pay funded train fares and living out of a suitcase. There were other reasons but money's a great mitigator when you're young.

Driving my frustration was being stuck in a grubby southern bedsit while owning an empty house 200 miles away. Selling up and moving south for good wasn't an option. My house in Huddersfield was worth £8,500. Equivalent in Maidenhead was £32,500. I wouldn't have got a mortgage. I looked round when I started on *Terrahawks*. My house would have bought me an eight-grand mobile home near Bray. Crazy.

After working at Asylum I took six months off, developing and pitching my first sci-fi TV series to Chan-

nel Four. Inspired by a Gary Numan LP title, it was called *Berserker*. It was an insanely energetic steampunky mix of *The Terminator* (leather clad cyborg lead character called Berserker), Gerry Anderson (explosive SFX), British kitchen sink dramas (gritty northern industrial setting), Marvel Comics (I've collected them since I was a kid), and *Spitting Image*.

Yes, *Spitting Image* which at the time was all the rage. Supervillains in the series would have been part-puppet, part-human like Luck and Flaw did it. My TV show was also bizarrely Pythonesque. I have to see the funny side of life, which is why there's humour in the Hunter thrillers. *Berserker* moved around in time like *Dr Who*. An episode set in 1963 sent-up Beeching shutting down much of British Railways. I had this gigantic robot called The Beeching Monster romping round on SFX sets, ripping up railways and eating them. It was my homage to man-in-suit monsters from the old Japanese Godzilla films, which had amazing energy in their day. The robot had a false cartoon moustache, which makes me laugh if I look at the drawings now.

Q: Channel Four didn't pick up the series?

A: Correct, although my production company pitched it to them again nearly twenty years later using the same presentation. It hadn't dated at all, which is another way of saying it was ahead of its time in the 80s.

Around the time I first developed it in 1985, Gerry Anderson similarly combined puppets and live actors in a TV pilot called *Space Police*, which eventually morphed into *Space Precinct*. One day the phone rang and it was Mark Harris, with whom I'd worked on *Terrahawks*. He said James Cameron was over from Hollywood to make a sequel to *Alien* and did I want to work on it? As I've said, the original *Alien* fired me to shoot my own stuff. Cameron had also just made *The Terminator*, which had blown me away.

I'd fulfilled one ambition, working for Gerry Anderson. Just a few years earlier, my 6th form art teacher had told me I couldn't make model spaceships for a living. Yet I'd done exactly that. When I went back to see her, and told her never to tell students they couldn't fulfil a dream, she took it on the chin. Being asked to work on the sequel to a movie which had played a crucial part in making me shoot my own SFX and get into the industry brought everything nicely full circle.

Q: You took up the offer to work on *Aliens*?

A: Yes. Mark Harris basically headhunted John and me, bigging us up. Like us, Cameron started out as a model-maker working for Roger Corman, who was a sort of American Gerry Anderson. I'm sure he knew they needed guys with a sci-fi tecchy eye.

Mark phoned me, I think, on a Thursday and I started at Pinewood Studios early the following week. It was interesting that key personnel and Heads of Department on *Aliens* were American. In *To Kill The Queen*, Connors thinks at one point about roundabouts. This came from one of the *Aliens* guys telling me, decades earlier, how scary he thought British roundabouts were because they didn't have them in the States.

Same guy asked if I wanted to go over to Hollywood to work. He thought I'd find it easier to get ahead on the production side in the States as opposed to cliquey UK. Aged just 24, with an elderly grandma my last remaining family member who looked forward to my regular visits, I didn't want to up sticks.

Q: What exactly did you do on *Aliens*?

A: I worked on most of the model sets and the dropship that crashes. (Previous photo.)

Sets were big, made to Action Man scale. On *Terrahawks* John and I made models completely from start to finish, usually designing them. Models on *Aliens* were much too big to do it like that. Teams of us dressed and detailed everything.

Q: Which sets did you work on?

A: Loads of stuff. Hope Base set was first as I recall. You see it when the marines land on the planet in the rain. A shot looks down a muddy street (next two pages) while a door on a foreground building bangs open and shut in the wind. John was inside, doing the honours.

Some of the big buildings on the right of the set were discarded shipping containers from Heathrow Airport. Made from lightweight aluminium, they'd got dented at

one side. We turned damaged bits away, dressing good sides to camera with rubber pipes and stuff.

I also worked on the atmosphere processor. (Double-page interview start.) It's the huge structure on the alien planet, shaped like an Apollo lunar module. John and I did the dressing, fat pipes, and detailing in the "maw", which the camera tracks in through at one point. We used plastic construction kit bits and EMA architectural modelling parts.

Sometimes I'd quickly knock up units on my work-bench (opposite) which got used on bigger sets. Another monster model set I worked on was of inside the atmosphere processor. You see it at the end of the film when the dropship swoops in to rescue Sigourney Weaver and the place starts blowing.

There's another scene where Sigourney is in a lift, on her way to the alien Queen showdown. Through a window behind her, you see gubbins passing as the lift descends. I did that myself, hot-gluing loads of plastic TV and video recorder bits and bobs to a vertical wooden flat. We didn't even paint it.

To shoot it, they ran a camera past on a dolly, looking through two foreground girder sections to create shifting perspective. It's rear projected behind Sigourney in the lift. Not the height of creativity. But whenever I see it I know it's mine.

Part 3 of this interview continues in the extras section of next Hunter thriller.

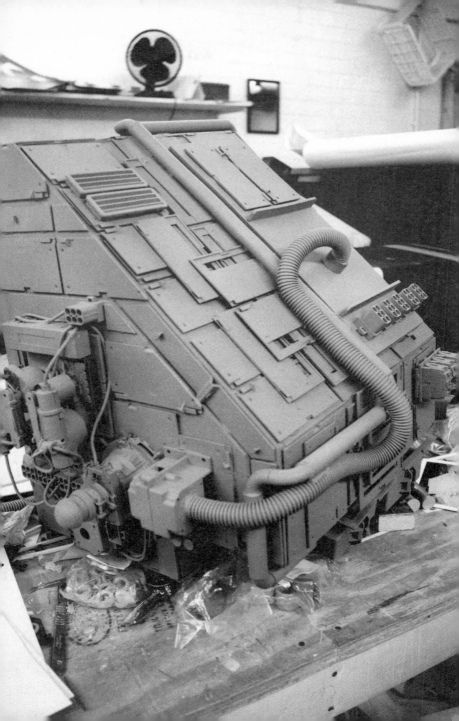

Most review quotes in this book are from real readers like you.

"Over the past few years I've done hundreds of bookshop signings and spoken to 10,000 customers one-to-one.

"We gave out thousands of leaflets loaded with emailed reader review quotes. For every two leaflets taken, one person bought a book - a stunning 50% conversion rate. You also trust bookseller advice - hence Waterstones quotes across my books.

"I've insisted my books have a more democratic feel by including quotes from real readers like you.

"Please email us, or Tweet or Facebook me your comments, on the understanding that we can quote you and where you live.

"Anybody who's quoted will get a signed free copy of that book. You might see yourself on a future Hunter book cover, or inside. Thank you."

Steve Cage